OXFORD WORLD'S CLASSICS

THE END OF THE TETHER AND OTHER STORIES

JOSEPH CONRAD was born Józef Teodor Konrad Korzeniowski in the Russian part of Poland in 1857. His parents were punished by the Russians for their Polish nationalist activities and both died while Conrad was still a child. In 1874 he left Poland for France and in 1878 began a career with the British merchant navy. He spent nearly twenty years as a sailor before becoming a full-time novelist, writing in English though it was not his first language. He became a British citizen in 1886 and settled permanently in England after his marriage to Jessie George in 1896.

Conrad is a writer of terrifying power and great subtlety; works such as 'Heart of Darkness', *Lord Jim*, and *Nostromo* display technical complexities which have established him as one of the first English 'Modernists'. He is also noted for the vividness with which he communicates a dark and disturbing view of human life, personal and social, in such works as *The Secret Agent*, *Under Western Eyes*, and *Victory*. Despite the immediate critical recognition that they received in his lifetime, Conrad's major novels did not sell well, and he lived in relative poverty until the commercial success of *Chance* (1914) secured for him a wider public and an assured income. Since his death in 1924 his reputation has steadily grown, and he is now seen as a writer who revolutionized the English novel, became a major writer of short stories and novellas, and was one of the most important literary innovators of the twentieth century.

PHILIP DAVIS, Emeritus Professor of Literature and Psychology, was Director of the Centre for Research in Reading, Literature and Society, University of Liverpool. His books include biographies of George Eliot and Bernard Malamud, and works on Shakespeare, Samuel Johnson, William Wordsworth, and the Victorians. His most recent publications include *Reading and the Reader*, *Reading for Life*, and, with Fiona Magee, *Arts for Health: Reading*. He is an editor of two OUP series, *The Literary Agenda* and *My Reading*, and *Studies in Bibliotherapy* for Anthem. He has edited Margaret Oliphant's *Hester* (World Classics), selections of John Ruskin (Everyman) and Elizabeth Barrett Browning (21st century Oxford Authors), the works of Bernard Malamud (Library of America), and poems of Stanley Middleton (Shoestring Press).

OXFORD WORLD'S CLASSICS

*For over 100 years Oxford World's Classics have brought
readers closer to the world's great literature. Now with over 700
titles—from the 4,000-year-old myths of Mesopotamia to the
twentieth century's greatest novels—the series makes available
lesser-known as well as celebrated writing.*

*The pocket-sized hardbacks of the early years contained
introductions by Virginia Woolf, T. S. Eliot, Graham Greene,
and other literary figures which enriched the experience of reading.
Today the series is recognized for its fine scholarship and
reliability in texts that span world literature, drama and poetry,
religion, philosophy, and politics. Each edition includes perceptive
commentary and essential background information to meet the
changing needs of readers.*

OXFORD WORLD'S CLASSICS

JOSEPH CONRAD

The End of the Tether
and other Stories

Edited with an Introduction and Notes by
PHILIP DAVIS

OXFORD
UNIVERSITY PRESS

OXFORD
UNIVERSITY PRESS

Great Clarendon Street, Oxford, OX2 6DP,
United Kingdom

Oxford University Press is a department of the University of Oxford.
It furthers the University's objective of excellence in research, scholarship,
and education by publishing worldwide. Oxford is a registered trade mark of
Oxford University Press in the UK and in certain other countries

First published as an Oxford World's Classics paperback 2022

Impression: 1

Published in the United States of America by Oxford University Press
198 Madison Avenue, New York, NY 10016, United States of America

British Library Cataloguing in Publication Data

Data available

Library of Congress Control Number: 2022935989

ISBN 978-0-19-289682-7

Printed and bound in the UK by
Clays Ltd, Elcograf S.p.A.

CONTENTS

Introduction   vii

Note on the Text   xxx

Select Bibliography   xxxi

A Chronology of Joseph Conrad   xxxvii

THE END OF THE TETHER   I

AMY FOSTER   121

THE RETURN   148

THE DUEL   197

Explanatory Notes   271

INTRODUCTION

THERE is a moment in 'The Return' when an affluent, conventional-minded husband asks his vain trophy-wife why she has returned home. He has only just read the letter that she had left on her dressing table, telling him she has gone off with another man, a pseudo-literary type. But there suddenly, weirdly, she is, back within no time, not having gone through with it after all. It is almost as if nothing had happened. But he must still ask her, 'Is this letter the worst of it?', hardly daring to give the scale of infidelity a name. No, she replies strangely, 'The worst is my coming back.'

If you look at the manuscript of 'The Return', lodged in the Berg Collection, New York Public Library, you can see that the husband then asks a further question in response to 'The worst is my coming back'. But though the question-mark is clear enough, Conrad heavily scored through what the question actually was. Even so you may just about make out through the dried ink the erased and hidden text: ' "What made you?" he said.'

What made you come back? Before Conrad decided to cut it, there follows the woman's reply, which Conrad then even more heavily inked out, but is clearly just one word, some short word, now hardly legible. It is like an image of all that is missing in Conrad's world—explanation, comfort, clear meaning; anything that might stand securely in place of a black hole. Instead the manuscript, and later the printed text, goes on past the deletions: 'There followed a period of dead silence during which they exchanged searching glances.' Silence often has to be the alternative in Conrad.

But although Conrad blotted out the single-word reply to the husband, if you photograph the manuscript page and increase the brightness-contrast, then the word from the wife seems to re-emerge. It looks like 'Fear'.

Part of Conrad always wanted a key word, the one word that as the narrating language-teacher puts it in *Under Western Eyes* (1911)

could stand at the back of all the words covering the pages; a word which, if not truth itself, may perchance hold truth enough to help the moral discovery that should be the object of every tale. (Chapter 3)

It is the word that Kurtz, the dying white imperialist, managed in a whispered cry at the end of Conrad's most famous tale, 'Heart of Darkness': 'The horror! The horror!' 'I myself have wrestled with death', says Marlow, the tale's narrator, in sombre contrast: 'I was within a hair's breadth of the last opportunity for pronouncement' but 'found with humiliation that probably I would have nothing to say'. That is the other side of Conrad, this divided man, who felt there was no one summarizing word and feared that instead there was simply nothing—no words, not really, because no meaning.

This fear of there being 'nothing' was related to the writer's block from which he habitually suffered. As he wrote to his mentor and friend, the literary critic Edward Garnett, 29 March 1898, 'You know how bad it is when one *feels* one's liver, or lungs. Well I feel my brain. I am distinctly conscious of the contents of my head. My story is there in a fluid—in an evading shape. I can't get hold of it . . . no more than you can grasp a handful of water.'[1] Writing—Conrad's second career—was not like action on board ship, his first occupation. On the page, with its dubious reality, even more doubts crept in. The agony of writing 'The Return' was related to, and indeed confusedly identified with, the physical and psychological pains so minutely described within it: 'The work is vile—or else good. I don't know. I can't know', he wrote to Edward Garnett, 'But I swear to you I won't alter a line—a word—not a comma—for you. There! And this is because I have a physical horror of that story. I simply won't look at it any more. It has embittered five months of my life. I hate it' (CCL vol. 1, 386). Everything might be there in Conrad's mind: 'descriptions, dialogue, reflexion—everything—everything but the belief, the conviction, the only thing needed to make me put pen to paper . . . All this is here, but I am not as the workmen who can take up and lay down their tools. I am, so to speak, only the agent of an unreliable master.' He was not, in the words of W. E. Henley's poem 'Invictus', the master of his fate, the captain of his soul. All the effort he exerted should have been sufficient, he said, 'to give birth to masterpieces as big as mountains', but it brought forth only 'a ridiculous mouse now and then' (CCL vol. 2, 191). This selection of shorter works claims more than that. On a better day he wrote that the extreme

---

[1] *Collected Letters of Joseph Conrad*, ed. F. R. Karl and L. Davies, vol. 2 (Cambridge University Press, 1986), 50 (hereafter cited as CCL).

experiments available in the short form may most starkly reveal 'the master's hand' (CCL vol. 1, 124).

That hand, often writing in fear and trembling, is revealed in this selection, beginning, like Conrad himself, with the sea and the sailor in 'The End of the Tether' (1902), and ending with the soldier in 'The Duel' (1908), but in between showing the horror in the lives of both the bourgeois London businessman in 'The Return' (1897) and the poor foreigner of 'Amy Foster' (1901) washed ashore in a village in Kent. Sailor, Soldier, Rich Man, Immigrant: four outstanding stories, written across ten years of the richest stage in Conrad's career, yet each too often neglected or underrated, are brought together here for the first time. 'The End of the Tether' was the most neglected of the volume of tales in which it first appeared, alongside 'Youth' and 'Heart of Darkness', but no less than Henry James himself judged it superior to the other two.[2] Along with 'Amy Foster', said the literary editor of the *Boston Evening Transcript* in 1904, it represented 'Joseph Conrad at his best', for direct heart-breaking power.[3] And the four together show what Edward Garnett called the 'wonderful chameleon-like quality' of Conrad's writings (CCL vol. 1, 59), in different encounters with fear and trial.

One of Conrad's great readers, the philosopher Bertrand Russell, described in fine detail his own encounter with the writer, in reading and in person. He met Conrad for the first time in September 1913. He had just turned forty, the novelist was in his later fifties, and Russell for all his own intellectual accomplishment was nervous. They went for a short walk together and 'I plucked up courage to tell him what I find in his work—the boring down into things to get to the very bottom below the apparent facts', as though sinking through

---

[2] Henry James is reported as preferring 'The End of the Tether' to 'Heart of Darkness' precisely because there was no Marlow, no narrator-intermediary to get in the way of the narrative more directly working itself out (see Thomas C. Moser, 'From Olive Garnett's Diary: Impressions of Ford Madox Ford and His Friends, 1890–1906', *Texas Studies in Literature and Language*, 16 (1974), 525; *The Diaries & Letters of Olive Garnett: An English Girl in Old Russia 1896–1897, & in England 1897–1958*, ed. B. Johnson (Tab House, 2019), 5 January 1903).

[3] *Joseph Conrad: Contemporary Reviews*, ed. A. H. Simmons, J. G. Peters, and J. H. Stape, 4 vols (Cambridge University Press, 2012) vol. 1, 230 (hereafter cited as 'JCCR').

layer after layer after layer.[4] Conrad 'seemed to feel I had understood him', he went on, and 'we just looked into each other's eyes for some time'. Then Conrad broke their silence by saying 'he had grown to wish he could live on the surface and write differently, that he had grown frightened. His eyes at the moment expressed the inward pain & terror that one feels him always fighting.'

'Always fighting', fighting 'the inward': this was still the same impression when, more than forty years later, Bertrand Russell recalled that first meeting of his with Conrad in a memoir, *Portraits from Memory*, especially with this sentence—perhaps the finest ever written about him:

He thought of civilised and morally tolerable human life as a dangerous walk on a thin crust of barely cooled lava which at any moment might break and let the unwary sink into fiery depths.[5]

And that, even when—especially when—one felt most safe, as on the much-travelled route or within the well-established home.

This selection of four tales is about such radical insecurity as Russell described, lone human beings involuntarily forced into confrontation with a terrifying universe in which they can never be wholly at home; exposed to a geographically wider and experientially deeper world than normal. 'If at the bottom of our hearts, below our network of defences', wrote the novelist John Galsworthy of Conrad, 'we did not feel uncertainty, we should expire—suffocated in the swaddling bands of safety' (*Critical Heritage*, 204). The uncertainty was vital, and some primal element in Conrad almost secretly wanted the test, needed the challenge, to bring itself out into existence, for all the countervailing fear of hubris and disaster. Yet another side of Conrad also wanted to keep clinging to the surface, if only he could. But he could not: H. P. Lovecraft, the American science fiction and

---

[4] Bertrand Russell to Lady Ottoline Morrell, quoted in Owen Knowles, 'Joseph Conrad and Bertrand Russell: New Light on Their Relationship', *Journal of Modern Literature*, 17.1 (Summer 1990), 139–53; 142.

[5] *Portraits from Memory* (Allen and Unwin, 1956), 82. So also in 1908 John Galsworthy had written of Conrad and the cosmic spirit: 'a power of taking the reader down below the surface to the earth's heart, to watch the process that, in its slow inexorable course, has formed a crust, to which are clinging all our little different living shapes'. *Conrad: The Critical Heritage*, ed. Norman Sherry (Routledge and Kegan Paul, 1973), 203 (hereafter cited as *Critical Heritage*).

horror writer, called Conrad the master of the 'terror element' in modern literature.[6]

He came out of a traumatic early life. He was born Józef Teodor Konrad Korzeniowski in 1857, in the Polish Ukraine under Russian rule. His father Apollo Korzeniowski, Romantic poet and Polish nationalist, was arrested and imprisoned by the authorities in 1861 and, convicted of political conspiracy, was sent with his wife and young son into exile in Russia. The mother, Ewa, died there in 1865. The father, released from exile in 1868, died in Cracow in 1869. There the boy was raised by his maternal grandmother under the fatherly guardianship of his maternal uncle Tadeusz Bobrowski. Tadeusz had never approved of Apollo's extreme politics and offered instead a disciplined practical alternative to what he took to be the poet's dreamy Romanticism. It was one the first of many such splits in the boy's make-up.[7] In 1874 the young Józef took himself off into what was this time voluntary exile, escaping the land-locked world by going to sea, aged only sixteen.

He did not become a writer until 1889 and did not publish his first novel, *Almayer's Folly*, until he was thirty-eight. It was written in English but English was not even his second language, French being his alternative from childhood. His late father had been a translator of Shakespeare and Dickens into Polish, but the son did not actually speak English until he landed in England aged twenty-one and joined the merchant navy. Not only did he have to turn from Polish to another language, but then he also turned to another world in a different way, from seamanship to writing, albeit writing initially about the sea, to try to bridge the cracks, using what he had gained. No wonder he was to call himself a '*homo duplex*', a double man, a man of dual and conflicted nature, which 'has in my case more than one meaning' across a whole series of self-divisions (CCL vol. 3, 69).

As he recalled in a belated prefatory note to his second novel, *An Outcast of the Islands* (1896), Conrad had still not given up the sea

---

[6] H. P. Lovecraft (1890–1937) in an essay 'Supernatural Horror in Literature' (1927).

[7] Edward Garnett considered the difference between father and uncle as responsible for two fundamentally temperamental moods in Conrad: see *Joseph Conrad: Interviews and Recollections*, ed. Martin Ray (Macmillan, 1990), 80 (hereafter cited as *JC Interviews and Recollections*).

after the publication of *Almayer's Folly*, not knowing whether he would dare write again. I was still clinging to the sea, he remembered:

all the more desperately because, against my will, I could not help feeling that there was something changed in my relation to it. 'Almayer's Folly' had been finished and done with. The mood itself was gone. But it had left the memory of an experience that, both in thought and emotion, was unconnected with the sea, and I suppose the part of my moral being that was rooted in consistency was badly shaken.

This is the paradoxical Conrad, the man trapped within and divided by his own dialectical opposites—here, in the desire for the consistent and the experience of the unconnected. What is more, these opposites ironically co-operated, the insecure need for a tough and practical consistency only making whatever felt inconsistent all the more neurotically disturbing and needy. At the time of completing *Almayer's Folly*, those contrary stresses had only served to produce a state of immobility. It was then that his mentor Edward Garnett almost casually said to him of his novel-writing, 'You have the style, you have the temperament; why not write another?' Garnett was desperately keen for Conrad to continue but it was the careful way he phrased it, said Conrad in the *Outcast* Preface, that made the difference:

Had he said, 'Why not go on writing?', it is very probable he would have scared me away from pen and ink for ever; but there was nothing either to frighten one or to arouse one's antagonism in the mere suggestion to 'write another' . . . The word 'another' did it.

'Another' did it—in the tone of 'why not?'—as the imperative 'go *on*' would not have.

That is why instead of the terrible on and on and on, Conrad in his chronic uncertainty preferred to begin to write in short and separate forms—tales that only if they then grew longer under the pen became long short stories, novellas, or novels, the boundaries between the different forms of tale and story never quite clear even in terms of length. Conrad had thought, for example, that *Lord Jim* would be the third story in a collection containing 'Youth' and 'Heart of Darkness', each narrated by the sailor Marlow, but it grew under his hand to become a novel. Consequently, to fill the gap, Conrad composed instead a story finally of novella length, over 50,000 words, about the end of life, 'The End of the Tether'. The lead story in this selection, it was originally designed to match 'Youth' at the beginning of *Youth: A Narrative and Two Other Stories* with 'Heart of Darkness' in the middle, to form 'the three ages of man'.[8]

But whatever their final length, the tales were mainly short in inception because in that way they might be manageable, without Conrad's having to plan too much in advance. And they were short also because, for all the effort at continuity, Conrad kept finding experience existing in sudden, eruptive, discontinuous events, rather than the flowing narrative of a connected life. From Poland to England; from sea to shore; from physical action and routine to the mental work of pen on paper in a mixture of memory and imagination. This is why the shortest tale in this selection of shorter works, 'Amy Foster', is so vital to this volume, as the equivalent story of what it is to feel oneself a stranger, a foreign immigrant washed up in England, speechless and treated by the English villagers as a beast.[9] 'He remembered the pain of his wretchedness and misery', but then worse, even more vulnerably, 'his heartbroken astonishment that it was neither seen nor understood . . .' It was the reflections, the feelings of lack, that most hurt him.

Looking back in 1922, Conrad said that it had been his 'set artistic purpose' to leave these factual and biographical sources 'indefinite, suggestive, in the penumbra of initial inspiration' (CCL, vol. 7, 456–7). But that is true not just of his sources from the past but for his impressionistic style as a whole: to Conrad the over-clarity of simple, literal explanation, however much yearned for, is untrue to the surrounding shock and haze intrinsic to powerfully immediate experience. So, for example, a reviewer of 'The Return' in *The Literary Gazette* in 1898 described Conrad as giving not only the husband's

---

[8] 'I knew very well what I was doing when I wrote "The End of the Tether" to be the last of that trio': G. J. Jean-Aubry, *Joseph Conrad, Life and Letters*, 2 vols (Heinemann, 1927), vol. 2, 338.

[9] This is the only text in this selection that has an explicit narrator in Dr Kennedy, framing the story, bridging the gap between the villagers and Yanko, and translating Yanko's experience for his listener. Gail Fraser in 'Conrad's Revisions to "Amy Foster"', *Conradiana*, 20.2 (Autumn 1988), 181–93, shows how revisions in the manuscript held by the Beinecke Library, Yale University, frequently worked to get inside Yanko's own tone and impressions, defamiliarizing the English village as seen from his outsider's amazed and vulnerable perspective. See the Explanatory Notes to 'Amy Foster' for specific examples

words and 'the thoughts born and fully present in his consciousness', but also in the midst of crisis—

those dim masses of thought, imagination and emotion, which at times of spiritual shock and stress throng upon the threshold of consciousness, and crowd the mind with the rapidly changing phantasmagoria, suggestions and terrors of dream. (JCCR vol. 1, 249)

It is this surrounding 'penumbra' that makes the reading of Conrad a slow immersive encounter, even in these shorter writings.

'No one has known', Henry James wrote to Conrad in 1906, 'the things you know'—beyond or beneath the little worlds of domestic realism.[10] From the earliest reviews Conrad was always spoken of as 'elemental', and that was not just to do with the sea but what the sea stood for to Conrad. As he insisted in a letter of 1916, 'I am something else, and perhaps something more, than a writer of the sea—or even of the tropics' (CCL vol. 3, 589). That 'something' was to do with primary experience, felt as if for the first time again when the secondary social veneers were all taken away; when a single individual is left exposed as though the first or the last human being on earth. Suddenly in 'The Return' the conventional bourgeois chauvinist 'was a simple human being removed from the delightful world of crescents and squares': 'He stood alone, naked and afraid, like the first man on the first day of evil.' Or in 'The Duel' the duellist lies awake, awaiting dawn, 'in the agitated watches of the night, which might have been his last on earth'. 'Man infinitely small, and the universe infinitely large.'[11] This is why, for example, in 1971, in her retrospective introduction to her feminist novel *The Golden Notebook* (1962), Doris Lessing singled out Conrad as one of the crucial influences in taking English fiction beyond its parochialism into those areas of both personal and global breakdown that most interested her in her own journey from her parents' colonial Rhodesia back to England.[12]

---

[10] *Twenty Letters to Joseph Conrad*, ed. G. Jean-Aubry (First Edition Club, 1926), 1211
[11] From a review of 'The Point of Honor', the American title for 'The Return' in JCCR vol. 2, 51912
[12] See for example her short story of sea-water rite de passage, 'Through the Tunnel' (1955), and her novels *The Four-Gated City* (1989), *Briefing for a Descent into Hell* (1971), *Memoirs of a Survivor* (1974), *Shikasta* (1979), *The Sirian Experiment* (1980), and *The Making of the Representative for Planet 8* (1982); also *The Good Terrorist* (1985, in relation to Conrad's *Secret Agent*).

This volume exists to remind readers that Conrad is not just the teller of sea stories and tales of imperialist action, not only the author of the ubiquitous 'Heart of Darkness', and not merely a writer for men. It shows the radical insecurity within Sailor, Soldier, Rich Man, Immigrant, each in different ways vulnerably displaced from their nominal role and normal function, in extremities of crisis on land as well as sea. That is what it is like when a figure such as Feraud, the Napoleonic warrior-soldier in 'The Duel', finds his occupation and his orientation gone with the fall of Napoleon himself:

No longer in the army! He felt suddenly strange to the earth, like a disembodied spirit. It was impossible to exist. But at first he reacted from sheer incredulity. This could not be. He waited for thunder, earthquakes, natural cataclysms; but nothing happened.

Crises come in many different forms, none of them expected. But here still in this anticlimax are the Conradian words: 'strange', 'impossible', 'incredulity', 'could not be', and above all 'nothing' again. You can hear that last resounding in the silence that follows. 'Every paragraph he writes', said T. E. Lawrence, Lawrence of Arabia, 'goes on sounding in waves, like the note of a tenor bell, after it stops. . . . and as he never says what it is he wants to say, all his things end in a kind of hunger, a suggestion of what he can't say or do or think.'[13] 'This could not be. He waited . . . but nothing happened.'

Such tales are not the simple boyhood adventures of Captain Marryat or James Fennimore Cooper, for all their influence on the youthful Conrad, but neither are they the symbolic work of Melville's *Moby Dick*, which Conrad thought to be written by someone who knew nothing of the sea (*JC Interviews and Recollections*, 133, 171, 176–7). The stories here are none of them quite what they at first seem to be: a different reality, or sense of terrible unreality, breaks through the surface and explodes upon the reader, almost like a form of madness. Exposing a world of crisis and trauma and conflict— a world perhaps newly and recently awakened to us now when even global

---

[13] *The Letters of T. E. Lawrence*, ed. David Garnett (Jonathan Cape, 1938), 301–2. Edward Said quotes the letter from March 1920 in *Joseph Conrad and the Fiction of Autobiography* (Harvard University Press, 1966) where he also says, 'Often he will bring the ceaseless activity of his mind to a kind of brief nervous stop, in much the same way that a man presenting a detailed argument stops because he needs to reflect, to take stock of what he has said. Then the movement of his thought resumes' (8).

safeguards fail—the vulnerable effect of these tales is like that which Conrad himself experienced in reading Stephen Crane's American Civil War novel, *The Red Badge of Courage* (1895). Crane's novel, said Conrad, detonated upon 'our literary sensibilities with the impact and force of a twelve-inch shell charged with a very high explosive'. It was not that the subject matter was some brutal masculine delight in war. It was rather that the depiction of the inner predicament of the young soldier itself carried out a form of psychological warfare, a second metaphorical war, upon the civilized world's unthinking securities by creating 'an incomparable insight into primitive emotions': 'He dreads not danger, but fear itself. He stands before the unknown.'[14] The practical, old nineteenth-century, ship-shape part of Conrad just wanted the world to stay solid, to deny psychology an overwhelming reality. Captain MacWhirr in 'Typhoon' (1902) is saved from losing his mind by invasion from the raging storm, through simply finding a small box of matches still in the orderly place it should be on a shelf near his cabin table[15] But even there the triumph of what Garnett called the practical Bobrowski influence over the romantic Korzeniowski element was itself a desperately near thing, in writing that was still Korzeniowski-inspired.

In her essay on Conrad in *The Common Reader* (1925), Virginia Woolf wrote of such stolid captains as Whalley in 'The End of the Tether' and MacWhirr in 'Typhoon' that writer and reader 'must be able to live on equal terms' with those men 'and yet hide from their suspicious eyes the very qualities which enable one to understand them'. It requires a 'double vision' to value such men, she said: 'To praise their silence one must possess a voice. To appreciate their endurance one must be sensitive to fatigue.' The simply practical, stubbornly unflinching 'qualities' of the stoic seamen were understood, that was to say, through their very opposites: the power of imagination, the sense of terrifying and unspeakable complexity, the liability to disbelief and doubt. It is a strange asymmetry, not unlike that between the two duellists in 'The Duel' where D'Hubert knows more than Feraud and yet is still tied to the obsession in Feraud that

[14] Joseph Conrad, 'His War Book: A Preface to Stephen Crane's "The Red Badge of Courage"', *Last Essays* (J. M. Dent, 1926), 180–1.

[15] On the relation of this grasped solidity to 'The Return', see William Bonney, 'Contextualizing and Comprehending Joseph Conrad's "The Return"', *Studies in Short Fiction*, 33.1 (Winter 1996), 77–90.

he cannot shake off from himself. Conrad in particular, Woolf concluded, 'was able to live that double life': '*homo duplex*', the nineteenth-century Realist and the twentieth-century Modernist, the Romantic and the Sceptic, the writer who found reality alternately in the mundane and orderly and solid, and then perhaps just once or twice in a lifetime, at the extreme, in the terrible reality of the chaotic and indefinable.

In Graham Swift's novel *Mothering Sunday* (2016), it is the volume *Youth and Two Other Stories*—'Youth', 'Heart of Darkness', and 'The End of the Tether'—that an uneducated but inquisitive young woman, working as a maid, begins reading one Sunday in March 1924 in her employer's country-house library. 'Oh Conrad—he was the one', she would tell an interviewer years later when she was an accomplished novelist herself, and pointing to her influences:

'I used to love all that seafaring stuff.'

'But a man's author, don't you think?'

'And your point is . . . ?' (*Mothering Sunday*, Scribner 2016, 126)

Her point is that, under cover of boys' books and adventure stories, she has long since begun to think of Conrad as a sort of secret agent, 'slipping between worlds' (128).[16] In her own way she too, from a lowly class, had had to find a language almost as much as Polish-born Conrad did, in order to become a writer. When Conrad died in August 1924, a few months after her first acquaintance with him, she thought of him intimately: 'The gravity, the beard, the expression in his eyes as if he were seeing something far off that was also deep inside' (130), something else, something more, than a writer of the sea. That August, at the time of his death, was when Virginia Woolf wrote her seminal essay on Conrad.

'As if he were seeing something far off that was also deep inside.' Conrad always worked in those two dimensions, physically out there

---

[16] In Graham Swift's earlier novel *Waterland* (Picador, 1983), the teacher-narrator offers two theories, two versions of reality close to Conrad's dual vision. One is of everyday flatness and uneventfulness, when as usual, ninety-nine times out of a hundred, nothing much happens. But the other is what, mercifully, visits human beings only on rare one-off occasions, moments shocking and disruptive in their surprise attacks and unexpected test. 'How many times, children, do we enter the Here and Now?' the teacher muses, mainly to himself, 'How many times does the Here and Now pay us a visit?' (52).

and psychologically in here, at once. In *A Personal Record* (1912) Conrad suggested that had he been a religious man in ancient days, he might have described the strain of writing as like Jacob wrestling with the Lord for his creation. But as he was not a believer, he could best think of his work only through 'a material parallel' from the other side of his life: the struggle to complete the westward winter passage round Cape Horn. 'For that, too, is the wrestling of men with the might of their Creator, in a great isolation from the world, without the amenities and consolations of life, a lonely struggle under a sense of overmatched littleness, for no reward that could be adequate, but for the mere winning of a longitude.' To some people, even that might seem an almost absurd and spurious act of heroism. And yet at the least

a certain longitude, once won, cannot be disputed . . . whereas a handful of pages, no matter how much you have made them your own, are at best but an obscure and questionable spoil. (Chapter 5)

That was the crucial difference: the pages could never be so real, *if* 'real' meant definite, physical, something that could be pointed to in the world—the sort of thing that in *Lord Jim* led Jim to go back to the place where he had shamefully jumped ship to try to see outside his own mind some trace of it still. 'Even writing to a friend', wrote Conrad to his own friend Garnett, 16 September 1899, 'to a person one has heard, touched, drank with, quarrelled with—does not give me a sense of reality. All is illusion—the words written, the minds at which they are aimed, the truth they are intended to express, the hands that will hold the paper, the eyes that will glance at the lines' (CCL vol. 2, 198). Conrad was never sure writing was real, as compared to sea-faring—unless or until it suddenly became overwhelmingly and almost maddeningly so, and something devastatingly terrible came out. What the handful of pages that make up volumes like this one had to try to do was to work inside and out: to make as imaginatively material as they could crises that were essentially immaterial and metaphysical, modern, existential, and psychological in their meaning. Or in their lack or loss of meaning. That means that even the sea stories are not just sea stories, though the sea remains literal and material enough and not merely symbolic.

So the castaway Yanko in 'Amy Foster' offers a material parallel to a less material sense of never being at home in the world. Or in 'The

End of the Tether' Captain Whalley's growing blindness, without ever ceasing to be so physically and painfully itself, at the same time becomes a literal metaphor for 'the light ebbing out of the world', for the darkening of old-world beliefs. When the old sailor trusts his habitual route, what he cannot see is not just the shoreline and the rocks but also the betrayal by his co-owner that sends him fatally off-course. Even as his ship loses its bearings, the author's own inner compass can almost measure by it the degree of deflection through which, at a less material level, Whalley is no longer going straight.

'The Duel' is even more complex in its movements across levels of meaning. At the literal level, the series of personal sword and pistol fights, conducted over fifteen years between two cavalry officers serving on the very same side, absurdly interrupts the Napoleonic Wars. As an early reviewer in the *Dallas Morning News* acutely noted, the duels went on until bizarrely the war itself had become for the two duellists 'simply an armed truce' (JCCR vol. 2, 538). That duelling then takes on a life of its own, in which Conrad cannot help but be interested in the way that courage required for a duel is subtly different from the courage that is needed on the battlefield. And as the feud goes on and on, it increasingly assumes its own strange psychological mutations. The code of honour requires that the duellists can only be of equal military rank, lieutenant versus lieutenant in the first encounter. But then, when one becomes captain, so must the other; when one is promoted to general, then again the other follows—not just because of the rules any more but because of a strange symbiosis that must not be broken. It is as if to continue the duel had become the main motive and mechanism of one '*homo duplex*' made up of two opposing parts: Feraud the hot-blooded believer of the south, D'Hubert the cooler rationalist from the north. As Edward Garnett said, the two men were yet another clue to Conrad's own self-divisions, their relationship two sides of the same man (*JC Interviews and Recollections*, 79). Indeed D'Hubert can only in the end overcome Feraud by overcoming his own survival instinct, laying down and leaving behind his pistols in order to out-think rather than out-fight his rival. And yet at another level still, their long duel also symbolizes, in miniature, what it exists in the intervals of: the seemingly endless continuation of those bloodily romantic wars and the vocations dedicated to them, in the absurd pursuit of purpose on earth. Napoleon's world wars, says Conrad, turning the whole tale inside-out from the very first, 'had the quality of a duel against the whole of Europe', though Napoleon himself 'disliked duelling amongst the officers of his army'. In adding duels to wars, Feraud and D'Hubert were, says Conrad, like 'insane artists' trying to put more gild on already refined gold. By the end, as the two split and D'Hubert turns to more of a life beyond the military, Feraud has himself become like a minor Napoleon in exile, as well as a loyal victim of his failure: 'No longer in the army! He felt suddenly strange to the earth . . .' It is that little word 'to', for example, existing in the cracks instead of merely 'on', that alerts the reader to something metaphysical within the physical.

In 'The Return' nothing materially has 'happened' after all, the wife has come back without committing herself, and to all social appearances the marriage might resume, papering the cracks, as if nothing had been untoward. And all the more so, if she had only got back before the letter was found and read. But her words, and the husband's echoing response to them out loud, are there still, indelibly, in the midst of shock: 'Gone', 'Why?' 'It was terrible—not the fact but the words.' And at the very point of the attempted return to normal, the husband knows as if for the first time that there are *imm*aterial realities he has never really believed in before this. As the dark comes into the house like an overwhelming sea, why doesn't the house fall down? It's an early tale but it hints at the future in the way that Virginia Woolf recognized in her essay in *The Common Reader*: 'though the last word might have been said about Captain Whalley and his relation to the universe, there remained on shore a number of men and women whose relationships might be worth looking into'. It was as if, she said, the susceptible Conradian narrator, such as Marlow in 'Heart of Darkness' or Dr Kennedy in 'Amy Foster', had given the seaman in Conrad a volume of Henry James to read on board.

'There were two natures interwoven in Conrad', Edward Garnett concluded, 'the one feminine, affective, responsive, clear-eyed, the other masculine, formidably critical, fiercely ironical, dominating, intransigent' (*JC Interviews and Recollections*, 79). Or as a *New York Times* reviewer of 1915 was to say of Conrad's work, 'it presents that curious and vital mingling of strong crude action and of delicate psychology' (JCCR vol. 3, 448). That mix is what the contemporary novelist Salley Vickers, following Woolf and Garnett, identifies as a tense blend in Conrad of what we have previously or traditionally called masculine and feminine elements, which actually are found 'in different quotients' within different people and different works. 'Conrad is deemed such a male writer', she says, 'and yet I feel he has a greatly underestimated feminine sensibility, the now perhaps passé notion of what was called feminine insight into character. I applaud this rounding combination in his writing, and the day a reader says one of my novels reminds her of Conrad, that's the day I'll be really thrilled.'[17]

These tales not only explode upon a reader, they implode upon themselves, as in a fission of what cannot be held together for much longer. What they do is related to what another of Conrad's admirers, H. P. Lovecraft, describes at the beginning of his own novella, 'The Call of Cthulhu' (1928), as if in the very voice and language of Conrad:

The most merciful thing in the world, I think, is the inability of the human mind to correlate all its contents. We live on a placid island of ignorance in the midst of black seas of infinity, and it was not meant that we should voyage far.

But, Lovecraft went on, there may come some unmerciful day when the little illusory island we live on will no longer suffice us, and then—

the piecing together of dissociated knowledge will open up such terrifying vistas of reality, and of our frightful position therein, that we shall either go mad from the revelation or flee from the light into the peace and safety of a new dark age.

Our habitually supposed reality, writes an admirer of both Conrad and Lovecraft, is primed to ignore 'the strangeness of our being'— holding it back 'as a dam holds back water, only allowing such flow as will power those practical systems that get us through the day'. But if the dam ever broke, 'we should drown in the vast chaotic roar of a flood that would sweep away our limited-reality consensus like

---

[17] See my *Reading for Life* (Oxford University Press, 2020 Chapter 11, from which these comments at interview are a previously unpublished part, and Salley Vickers's own Introduction to Conrad's 'A Smile of Fortune' (Hesperus Press, 2007): 'The captain's desire cannot survive the scrutiny of a comprehending third presence, which lifts what has been fiercely secret into the cool, accounting gaze of the objective world. Conrad's insight is positively Freudian' (page x). On the fluid use and usefulness of stereotypical masculine and feminine terms within the dynamic of psychoanalysis, and in the context of Conrad's own dictum 'in the destructive element immerse', see Marion Milner, *A Life of One's Own* (1934), indebted to Virginia Woolf's 'A Room of One's Own' (1929), and *An Experiment in Leisure* (1937).

a chicken coop'. 'The real thing is what comes through the cracks when you fall apart.'[18]

And so it proves in 'The End of the Tether', where the weary young sceptic, Van Wyk, gives warning to old Captain Whalley, so naively trusting and faithful, against the treacherousness of the world. And yet it is the young man who is most undone by the old man's final defeat. It is Van Wyk, as though displaced from the safer perspective of narrator, who can hardly bear to witness the sight of the old man's secret blindness; Van Wyk who, even in the very fulfilment of his own prophecy, is himself well-nigh destroyed by the old man's destruction. This is the way these stories turn round upon themselves from within, each half destroying the other, in the implosion of an almost unbearable and unliveable knowledge. There is no guaranteed protection even back on shore, at home; no secure position in distanced foreknowledge or attempted precaution; no safety still yet in truth itself. Conrad might try to be less human, viewing from outside with black humour, the historical absurdity of 'The Duel' for example; but he kept being dragged back to the view from within. As it is written bitterly of the husband in 'The Return', 'he knew instinctively that truth would be of no use to him'. Even so, instead of pretence, the man and the woman in that house have to face it, however partially and intermittently. Lovecraft wrote that Conrad had 'the sense of ultimate nothingness and the evanescence of illusions.'[19] And yet what is both paradoxical and vital in Conrad is that this sense of nothingness and of meaninglessness cannot itself mean nothing to him.

So it is in all these tales. Bertrand Russell was among the first to see how Yanko's experience in 'Amy Foster' was a key to the psychology of Conrad himself, the stranger writing in English as a foreign language. But the symbiosis goes even deeper. In his fever, Yanko cries out incomprehensibly in his native tongue to ask his wife for help, thinking he is speaking in English, not understanding why she who was the first to pity him many years before now turns and runs away. That too had been Conrad, in feverish delirium and unthinking

---

[18] Russell Hoban, *The Moment Under the Moment* (Jonathan Cape, 1992), 180; *Fremder* (Jonathan Cape, 1996), 8.

[19] H. P. Lovecraft, *Letters, Volume 2: Letters from New York*, ed. S. T. Joshi and D. E. Schultz (Night Shade, 2005), 127 (25 May 1925).

reversion into the mother tongue on his honeymoon in 1896, as his wife Jessie described years later:

For a whole week long, the fever ran high and for most of the time J.C. was delirious. To see him lying in the white canopied bed, dark-faced, with gleaming teeth and shining eyes, was sufficiently impressive, but to hear him muttering to himself in a strange tongue (he thinks he must have been speaking Polish), to be unable to penetrate the clouded mind or catch one intelligible word, was for a young inexperienced girl truly awful . . .[20]

What is more, Jessie Conrad also writes of a recurrence in 1910, years after the publication of 'Amy Foster', following the exhausting completion of his novel *Under Western Eyes*:

He spoke all the time in Polish, but for a few fierce sentences against [his agent] poor J. B. Pinker. That day seemed endless. I could get no one to help me but the old maid. I scarcely left his side for he was constantly calling upon me to sit on the side of the bed to make a rest for his back. Hour after hour I sat in that cramped position. Day and Night I watched over him, fearful that if I turned my back he would escape from the room. I slept what little I could on the couch drawn across the only door. More than once I opened my eyes to find him tottering towards me in search of something he had dreamed of.[21]

And this small tale gets bigger and bigger in its rippling impact. For what, above all, this vision of living between dual languages imaginatively emphasized to Conrad was how, really, *all* language was foreign, in its very self, paradoxically estranged from whatever it described, expressed, or tried to reach. And, worse, the final implosion of the tale, its turning rounding upon the previous kindness of Amy, meant that being securely at home in life, loved and settled and fully understood, was *never* finally assured. It wasn't just Yanko's literal foreignness or Conrad's, however much this experience of exile of itself has resonated with later writers such as Doris Lessing or Edward Said (in *Reflections on Exile*, 2000) or W. G. Sebald (in *The Rings of Saturn*, 1995); but take away the secondary supports and habits, and anyone could find themselves just so hopelessly alone on earth. Speaking of its resonant extension 'to any puzzled suffering soul cast up upon the

---

[20] Jessie Conrad, *Personal Recollections of Joseph Conrad* (privately printed, 1924), 25–6.

[21] Jessie Conrad, *Joseph Conrad and his Circle* (Jarrolds, 1935), 143–4.

shores of life', an early American reviewer of 'Amy Foster' wrote, 'The reader must read this into the story for himself'—Conrad will never overtly 'give the realism of his work a touch of allegory' (JCCR vol. 2, 132). Rather, the symbolic extension of Conrad's autobiography—from his own estrangement to estrangement in general—is part of the very method of these tales in a way that is frighteningly subtler than simply expanding the 'autobiographical' into some 'universal' theme. For these are Conrad's simultaneous double meanings of '*homo duplex*', the literal and the symbolic inseparably fused into each other until the meaning bursts forth.

It is a dangerous process. It was around the time that Conrad was writing 'Amy Foster', while also collaborating with Ford Madox Ford, that Ford reports what happened one day—when suddenly, deep in writing at a table in the middle of their shared study, Conrad felt a presence come across the pages from a window facing him. At that moment, Ford said, Conrad unaccountably screamed out in agony and terror, 'Good God!'—only afterwards admitting, when the harmless tradesman had gone away, that he had thought it was the bailiff.[22]

Why the bailiff?

Conrad was beset by severe financial debts and tensions at that time, even though the house was Ford's not his, and he was a welcome guest. By 1900 he was earning about £300 per annum, where the average national income was under £100. But the pressures of his own extravagance, in the foreigner's anxious wish to retain his position among the wealthier English classes, was wearing down Conrad's nerves, and this is where the writing of short stories seemed to offer some relief. The market for shorter fiction and serialization was booming through the growth of large-circulation magazines, and in his early career Conrad could earn for a short story up to three times as much per thousand words as he earned for his novels. A novel could take two years in the writing and earn him no more than £400. Conrad was a poor manager of money anyway, and being a slow writer customarily managing no more than 2000 words a week and sometimes blocked for weeks, he hated the pressure of target lengths and deadlines. In the midst of writing 'The End of the Tether', Conrad lost

[22] Ford Madox Ford, *Joseph Conrad, A Personal Remembrance* (Little, Brown, 1924), 154.

much of the manuscript for the second instalment when one night on 23 June 1902 an oil lamp exploded on his desk. He may have somewhat exaggerated the loss to excuse his delay. But struggling to reconstruct the lost material, falling behind with serialization deadlines, and like Whalley himself beset by economic difficulties and nervous fears for his own eyesight, he had already described himself to Ford in a letter of 30 May as being truly 'out of my mind with anxiety . . . at the end of my tether' (CCL vol. 2, 415). The very title of the work was taking over the writing of it.

If for all his gargantuan efforts he could only bring forth 'a ridiculous mouse now and then', he needed to get as much as he could for his mice to keep off the imaginary bailiff. What Conrad called his 'Blackwood period' began in 1897 and ended in 1902, during which time his work was regularly published in *Blackwood's Magazine* ('*Maga*'), a long-established conservative monthly periodical of high literary standing, with interests in imperialism and the colonial world. 'The End of the Tether' was serialized there in the second half of 1902, and Blackwood was indulgent about length and payments. But 'I wish to reach another public than *Maga*'s' (CCL vol. 2, 321). 'Amy Foster' was first published in the *Illustrated London News*, December 1901, as part of a free-bargaining strategy developed when Conrad acquired an agent, J. B. Pinker, from 1900, to loosen his exclusive ties to Blackwood in the search for a wider audience. But Pinker had struggled to find a publisher for 'Amy Foster', eventually earning him £40, and even then Conrad, ever in conflict, hated it on artistic grounds that the story had to be split up into three instalments for serialization, whatever the financial benefit. If 'The Return' had been meant to attract popular interest on account of its sexual subject-matter, it certainly failed to do so. It was the only short story along with the equally controversial 'Falk', with its subject of cannibalism, to be rejected by magazine publishers, according to the supposed standards of middle-class taste. Later, likewise, 'The Duel' proved hard to place, finally appearing, nearly a year after its completion, in *Pall Mall Magazine* in the first half of 1908. The age when high-quality writers such as Dickens and Thackeray and Hardy could also be popular bestsellers was passing. As Gail Fraser has noted, 'Conrad's short fiction played a double role at a transitional point in his career. On the one hand, it helped him push beyond the familiar world of Blackwood's audience; on the other, it provided clear evidence of the gap between artistic endeavour and the marketplace.'[23] Conrad knew that like Henry James he was new and experimental, difficult and modern.

In that vein critics often complained that reading Conrad was a slow business, even the so-called shorter fiction was seen by some as prolix and overloaded. A reviewer in *The Times* wrote of 'The Return', 'Mr Hervey's emotions are then analysed in 18 pages. Then Mrs Hervey returns . . . The pair then make scenes and an abusive use of explanations for 70 pages of psychology' (JCCR vol. 1, 252). Conrad was particularly stung by a one-line dismissal of 'The Duel' in *The Daily Telegraph* as 'tedious through its unnecessary length' (JCCR vol. 2, 454). 'The End of the Tether' was criticized for being diffusely over-length and over-descriptive, 'one long agony' as the reviewer in *The Times of India* put it (JCCR vol. 1, 447). In the publishing house itself, George Blackwood had supported publication of the story of Captain Whalley but at the early stages of its serialization he reported to Conrad's annoyance that 'one can hardly say one has got into the story yet'. 'I know exactly what I am doing . . .' Conrad retorted, 'and in the light of the final incident, the whole story in all its descriptive detail shall fall into its place—acquire its value and its significance' (CCL vol. 2, 416–17). This, he went on, was a method based on his deliberate conviction, to which he clung with the 'fidelity' he often found in his sea-captains. It finally lifts a story onto 'another plane'. Conrad further insisted that instead of simply pushing the narrative forward, he 'depended upon the reader *looking back* upon my story as a whole' as the tale turned round upon itself in a great final rush (CCL vol. 2, 441). *The Illustrated London News* nonetheless characterized Conrad as 'like Wordsworth': 'he has to be waited upon patiently and given his own time and his own way' (JCCR vol. 2, 42).[24]

---

[23] 'The Short Fiction' in *The Cambridge Companion to Joseph Conrad*, ed. J. H. Stape (Cambridge University Press, 1996), 32.

[24] A critical defence of Conrad's slow impressionistic style is found in Ian Watt, *Conrad in the Nineteenth Century* (Chatto & Windus, 1980) in terms of 'delayed decoding': the process of presenting raw and immediate sense-impressions *before* their naming, particularly appropriate to Whalley's own struggles to make sense of what had been a familiar world. Edward Said quoted Rilke that nothing in the world could be imagined in advance, adding 'the retrospective mode of Conrad's shorter works can be understood as the effort to interpret what, at the time of occurrence, would not permit reflection' (*Joseph Conrad and the Fiction of Autobiography*, 87–8). Recently, Yael Levin expands on this defence, which cost Conrad an audience expecting the suspense and momentum of quick linear narrative, in *Slow Modernism* (Oxford University Press, 2020).

In short, it was for psychological as well as financial reasons that Conrad was dismayed not to be a bestseller. 'I suppose there is something in me unsympathetic to the general public —because the novels of Hardy, for instance, are generally tragic enough and gloomily written too and yet they have sold in their time and are selling to the present day.' Writing here in 1908, he adds in vulnerable explanation: 'Foreignness, I suppose' (CCL vol. 4, 9)—evidence of his precarious, vagabond status. For the scream at the shadow of a bailiff falling upon the page in the midst of writing had to do with something else, less literal than money, that Ford himself detected in Conrad's cry. It was the trauma of the immigrant never feeling secure in the world, always in danger of attack or eviction. The look of the bailiff, the knock at the door his father and mother had heard: always, consciously or unconsciously, Conrad feared the outbreak of the psychological within, preying upon the outside world for its existence. 'The occupation of writing to such a nature as Conrad's is terribly engrossing', Ford went on. 'To be suddenly disturbed is apt to cause a second's real madness' (*Joseph Conrad, A Personal Remembrance*, 156). A second in which the clear boundary between reality and unreality was lost. When on a train journey together Ford interrupted him in the absorbed correction of proofs to say they had nearly reached the station, Conrad, said Ford, blindly sprang at his throat. These seconds of real madness were suddenly revealed as in a fault-line between worlds, a crack to which writing itself for Conrad was almost unbearably sensitive and alert. Writing was that strange in-between area which created for Conrad, and then for his readers, an otherwise almost intolerable or impossible place to exist within.

Conrad was always aware of such terrible paradoxes, of inner divisions nonetheless inextricably connected. Being afraid of yourself was another such, making him aware of 'the inseparable being always at your side—master and slave, victim and tormentor—who suffers and causes suffering' (CCL vol. 1, 162). So in these tight amalgams Van Wyk can hardly face being proved right, and Whalley himself chooses not to survive. Yanko cannot understand how his own Amy, after so many years together, seems now turned alien again. The wife in 'The Return' turns back on herself, only for the husband to find that finally he himself cannot bear to stay. It is the closeness of these short fictions to blowing their own mind, in subject-matter and composition, in contradiction, self-destruction and paradox, that is crucial to this selection, a fate that only 'The Duel' narrowly escapes as the strange last story in this selection, when finally D'Hubert can set himself free himself from his symbiotic relation to Feraud and leave the darkness behind with his other. Where D'Hubert can find at last an identity, through a love unwittingly proven to him through Feraud himself, Feraud is left not so much as an empty body but a lost spirit living on without an existence. It is another take in Conrad on how far and in what way life has to be a fight, and what it is if it is not. Must it be true: 'Now that his life was safe it had suddenly lost its special magnificence'?

'Faith is a myth, and beliefs shift like mists on the shore', writes Conrad at his lowest to his idealistic friend, Robert Cunninghame Graham, 14 January 1898. It is near the beginning of the period, 1897 to 1908, that this selection represents: 'Thoughts vanish; words, once pronounced, die; and the memory of yesterday is as shadowy as the hope of tomorrow' (CCL vol. 2, 17). But even here Conrad's work will not let people—least of all himself—live by disbelieving in life, even when it is also all too plausible that beliefs are illusions. That is how D'Hubert represents an alternative version of Van Wyk: his sceptical doubt—about his own worthiness to be truly loved, after a life spent as a soldier—is a thing defeated despite himself.

But Conrad writes again to Cunninghame Graham a few days later on 23 January of his friend's belief in socialism, remembering his own father's fate in Poland and scathingly rejecting a belief that it was politics alone now that could create fundamental solutions for the modern world:

You seem to me tragic with your courage, with your beliefs and your hopes. Every cause is tainted: and you reject this one, espouse that other one as if one were evil and the other good while the same evil is in both, but disguised in different words. . . . You are misguided by the desire of the impossible— and I envy you. (CCL vol. 2, 25)

In that final parenthesis which makes the passage double back upon itself ('—and I envy you'), Conrad knows he can't wholly sustain his sceptically detached position. Unable to live with or without beliefs, this writer of dialectical tales exists within what, in the *Phenomenology of Spirit* (1807), Hegel, master of the dialectic, had prophetically diagnosed for the century to come as the state of 'unhappy consciousness' beyond the defences of stoicism or scepticism: an interlocked state of mind held together only by contradictions that even in their attempted balance threaten eventually to tear each other apart. The short stories and novellas that themselves test out Conrad's own impossibly homeless position thus suffer a splitting and a collapse within themselves, at once alien to humanist accommodations as mere illusions and yet self-avenging for having to be so. 'Beliefs shift like mists on the shore'; 'In the midst of black seas of infinity . . . it was not meant that we should voyage far'; 'If the dam ever broke we should drown in the vast chaotic roar': this is Conradian thinking in that ancient language of the sea which goes beyond even the sea itself. Conrad was not a philosopher, and it was not English philosophy even in the hands of his admirer Bertrand Russell that can offer help in understanding what Conrad stood for—but rather a wider European thinking, including the dark pessimism of Schopenhauer.[25] And above all, it is with Conrad as Nietzsche said in *The Genealogy of Morals* (1887, Chapter 16),[26] that we are like sea-creatures forced to become land-animals in order to survive: beings, now walking on legs where before the sea had carried them, no longer unconsciously at home and in their element, but having to become conscious, adapt their old disinherited instincts, and think and feel separately from inside themselves. That hybrid nature, hardly able to hold itself together, fears there is nothing to support it, and nothing for it at the very end. But crucially, it is not a simple, easy or fashionable nihilism in Conrad that readers will find here. What is vital is, rather, the feeling and the fight with which this nihilism is barely borne, even to the point of near-insanity in these stories.

For the use of manuscript material I gratefully acknowledge the Trustees of the Joseph Conrad Estate; for 'The Return', The Henry W. and Albert A. Berg Collection of English and American Literature, The New York Public Library, Astor, Lenox and Tilden Foundations; for 'The Duel', Rare Book Department, Free Library of Philadelphia; for 'The End of the Tether' and 'The Husband' (the original title of 'Amy Foster'), The Joseph Conrad Collection. General Collection, Beinecke Rare Book and Manuscript Library, Yale University.

Philip Davis

---

[25] On Conrad and Schopenhauer, see Mark Wolaeger, *Joseph Conrad and the Fictions of Skepticism* (Stanford University Press, 1990).

[26] On Conrad and Nietzsche, see Edward Said, *Reflections on Exile* (Harvard University Press, 2000), Chapter 7.

NOTE ON THE TEXT

THE base-texts for all four tales in this edition are those of the first British publication in book form. In addition I have consulted the British serial versions (except for 'The Return' which was never serialized), available at www.conradfirst.net—the archive of magazines and newspapers featuring first and early publications of Conrad's works.

The texts have also been compared with the original manuscript versions, and manuscript alterations, in selected places of importance, in order that Explanatory Notes might include some insight into Conrad's processes of composition, as well as providing necessary information and background. In addition, the Explanatory Notes offer elements of minimal commentary to alert readers to some significant developments or emerging motifs in the process of the tales' unfolding. Sources, letters, and non-fictional writings, prefaces to his works, early reviews, and memories of Conrad by other writers are also included where particularly relevant.

Most other selections of Conrad's stories provide a glossary, especially of nautical terms, at the end of the volume; since there is only one sea-story in this selection, the relevant nautical terms are glossed as they first appear in 'The End of the Tether'.

SELECT BIBLIOGRAPHY

The Works of Conrad

This Introduction has relation to other works by Conrad beyond those chosen for this selection, for further reading.

'Amy Foster' and 'The End of the Tether' belong very much with *Lord Jim* (1900) both chronologically and thematically. 'Typhoon' (1902) offers comparison between the two Captains, Whalley and MacWhirr ('Facing it—always facing it—that's the way to get through'); while Van Wyk is an earlier version of Decoud in Conrad's novel *Nostromo* (1904).

The dialectical form of Conrad's 'The Secret Sharer' (1909) provides an alternative to 'The Duel'. 'An Anarchist' (1905) is another '*homo duplex*' turn-around text: the protagonist, able to escape jail only by being again bound to the anarchists, is sickened by 'the thought of a freedom that could be nothing but a mockery to me'. 'Falk' (1901) belongs with 'The Return' in terms of an alternative Conrad found unacceptable at any rate by the magazine editors to whom those two tales were submitted.

'The Return' may also be compared with Conrad's later account of marital breakdown between the Verlocs in *The Secret Agent* (1907), originally conceived as a short story. James Hanley's *Captain Bottell* (1933), a study in sexual obsession on board ship, would serve as a powerful comparison. Also relevant amidst Conrad's shorter fiction are 'Gasper Ruiz' (1906) and 'A Smile of Fortune' (1910), again undeservedly lesser-known works. In the erotic area, as well as *Victory* (1915), Conrad's *The Rescue* is a strange and much underrated novel, begun in 1896, abandoned, and only finally completed in 1920.

The Shadow Line (1917) is arguably Conrad's greatest story of test, and Henry James (a vital background figure in this selection) offers in 'The Beast in the Jungle' (1903) an almost Conradian novella of venture in extremis.

Conrad: Biographies, Letters and Contemporary Reviews

Ford, Ford Madox, *Joseph Conrad: A Personal Remembrance* (Little, Brown, 1924).

Jasanoff, Maya, *The Dawn Watch: Joseph Conrad in a Global World* (William Collins, 2017).

Karl, Frederick R., *Joseph Conrad: The Three Lives* (Faber, 1979).

Karl, Frederick R., and Davies, Laurence (eds), *The Collected Letters of Joseph Conrad*, 9 vols (Cambridge University Press, 1983–2007).

Najder, Zdzislaw, *Joseph Conrad: A Life*, second revised edition (Camden House, 2007).

Ray, Martin (ed.), *Joseph Conrad: Interviews and Recollections* (Macmillan, 1990).

Sherry, Norman (ed.), *Conrad: The Critical Heritage* (Routledge and Kegan Paul, 1973).

Simmons, Allan H., Peters, John G., and Stape John H. (general eds), *Joseph Conrad: Contemporary Reviews*, 4 vols (Cambridge University Press, 2012).

Stape, John, *The Several Lives of Joseph Conrad* (William Heinemann, 2007).

Conrad: General Criticism

Achebe, Chinua, 'An Image of Africa: Racism in Conrad's "Heart of Darkness"', *Massachusetts Review*, 17.4 (1977), 782–94.

Baxter, Katherine Isobel, and Hampson, Robert (eds), *Conrad and Language* (Edinburgh University Press, 2016).

Carabine, Keith (ed.), *Joseph Conrad: Critical Assessments* (Helm Information, 1992).

Erdinast-Vulcan, Daphna, *Joseph Conrad and the Modern Temper* (Oxford University Press, 1991).

Hampson, Robert, *Joseph Conrad: Betrayal and Identity* (Macmillan, 1992).

Hampson, Robert, *Conrad's Secrets* (Macmillan, 2012).

Hawthorn, Jeremy, *Joseph Conrad: Narrative Technique and Ideological Commitment* (Arnold, 1990).

Knowles, Owen, and Moore, Gene (eds), *The Oxford Reader's Companion to Conrad* (Oxford University Press, 2000).

Levin, Yael, *Slow Modernism* (Oxford University Press, 2020).

Miller, J. Hillis, *Reading Conrad*, ed. J. G. Peters and J. Lothe (Ohio State University Press, 2017).

Miller, Karl, *Doubles* (Oxford University Press, 1985).

Said, Edward, *Joseph Conrad and the Fiction of Autobiography* (Harvard University Press, 1966).

Stape, J. H. (ed.), *The New Cambridge Companion to Joseph Conrad* (Cambridge University Press, 2015).

Watt, Ian, *Conrad in the Nineteenth Century* (Chatto and Windus, 1980).

Woolf, Virginia, 'Joseph Conrad', *The Common Reader* (Hogarth Press, 1925).

There are two journals devoted to Conrad, *The Conradian* and *Conradiana*, including the most recent research.

Conrad: the Stories in this Selection—Background, Critical Reception, and Critical Articles

For an invaluable background account of the sort of venture involved for Conrad in both the content and the writing of the short story, see George Simmel, 'The Adventure' in *Essays on Sociology, Philosophy and Aesthetics*, ed. K. H. Wolff (Harper and Row, 1959), 243–58. The adventure, as a form of vulnerable commitment outside the normal world of mundane boredom, contains the temporary certainty of there being only chance and uncertainty, allowing the risky expectation of the eruption of the unexpected and accidental within itself. Simmel's sense of perilous paradox may be read alongside Walter Benjamin, 'The Storyteller', in *Illuminations* (1955), ed. Hannah Arendt (Schocken Books, 1968), 83–109, where Conrad may be contrastingly seen as offering the anti-humanist threat of ironic anticlimax or deathly negation, in place of traditonally bringing home a moral lesson.

See also Gail Fraser, 'The Short Fiction' in *The New Cambridge Companion to Joseph Conrad*, ed. J. H. Stape (Cambridge University Press, 2015), 25–44, especially on the challenges of these stories to easy bourgeois acceptance.

A. 'THE END OF THE TETHER': THE SAILOR'S STORY

On the Malay background, see Norman Sherry, *Conrad's Eastern World* (Cambridge University Press, 2008), especially 198–205, and J. H. Stape, 'Conrad's "Unreal City": Singapore in "The End of the Tether" ' in *Conrad's Cities: Essays for Hans van Marle*, ed. Gene M. Moore (Brill Rodopi, 1992), 85–96.

On the effect of blindness, compare Kipling's *The Light that Failed* (1891). Conrad was gratified by James Huneker, on a visit in 1912, likening 'The End of the Tether' to other works on old age and the father–daughter relationship, including *King Lear*, Balzac's *Le Père Goriot* (1834), and Turgenev's *Lear of the Steppes* (1880) (*Joseph Conrad: Interviews and Recollections*, ed. Martin Ray, 24).

In terms of its critical reception 'The End of the Tether' was largely overshadowed from the first by 'Youth' and 'Heart of Darkness', although the character of Whalley was admired, especially by American reviewers, as a stalwart Anglo-Saxon type. The reviewer in the *Times Literary Supplement* was an exception in suggesting that 'The End of the Tether' was the best of the three stories and should have been 'at the forefront of the book' (JCCR vol. 1, 396). A notice in *The Monthly Review* probably written by the poet of patriotic and nautical verse, Henry Newbolt, saw it as the 'masterpiece' in the volume (JCCR vol. 1, 406); while the reviewer in *The Spectator* was especially moved by 'the cruel pathos of obscure struggle and unrecorded tragedy' (JCCR vol. 1, 389). No one seems to have noted, however, the importance of the witness given by Van Wyk, the young sceptic.

Daniel R. Shwarz's account of ageing in 'The End of the Tether', *Conrad: Almayer's Folly to Under Western Eyes* (Macmillan, 1980), remains helpful and might prompt further comparison with Ernest Hemingway's *The Old Man and the Sea* (1952). David Mulry offers a useful account of the complexity within apparent simplicity in 'Untethered: Conrad's Narrative Modernity in "The End of the Tether" ', *The Conradian*, 33.2 (Autumn 2008), 18–29.

B. 'AMY FOSTER': THE IMMIGRANT'S STORY

For source material, see Ford Madox Ford's *The Cinque Ports*, quoted at the head of the Explanatory Notes for this tale. In 'Conrad's Polish Literary Background' (*Antemurale*, 10, 224–8), Andrzej Busza identified a tradition of Polish writing on Polish emigrants, especially Henryk Sienkiewicz's novella *After Bread* (1880), Maria Konopnicka's narrative poem *Mr Balcer in Brazil* (1910), and Adolfa Dygasinski's novel *Head Over Heels* (1893). Cedric Watts in his edition of *Typhoon and Other Tales* (World's Classics, 1986) points to other possible influences including Victor Hugo, *Les*

Travailleurs de la Mer ('The Toilers of the Sea', 1866), Flaubert's *Madame Bovary* (1857), and the short stories of Guy de Maupassant such as 'Le Gueux' ('The Beggar', 1884).

In terms of initial critical reception 'Amy Foster' was as overshadowed by being in the same volume as 'Typhoon' as 'The End of the Tether' was by being published alongside 'Youth' and 'Heart of Darkness'. *The Manchester Guardian* spoke of 'an extraordinary tragedy of beings of low organism, for tragedy comes with the great human common measure', but *The Speaker* arguably did better by the story in calling it in its 'power of building up an effect', 'one of the most perfect stories we have ever read' (JCCR vol. 2, 25, 56). The reviewer in *T.P's Weekly* believed the story embodied characteristics of Conrad as a Slav and a Pole: 'a certain capacity for silent endurance, an intense determination to survive, and the restlessness of a race whose home is the wild world' (JCCR vol. 2, 43). In America it was somewhat better noticed, especially for its 'pathos', in being published only with 'Falk', with its attention-catching confession of cannibalism, and 'To-Morrow', and not alongside 'Typhoon'. 'In incident the story is absolutely commonplace, in effect it is the exact opposite' (*The Reader*); 'the little tragedy called "Amy Foster"... the story alone would—or should—make a reputation for any writer' (*Chicago Evening Post*); 'In "Amy Foster" the author, himself an immigrant, has expressed the silent tragedy of the speechless immigrant' (*Boston Evening Transcript*) (JCCR vol. 2, 124, 130, 134). They echo Conrad's own commitment in his 'Preface' to a collection of stories in 1897, to present 'the obscure lives of a few individuals out of all the disregarded multitude of the bewildered, the simple, and the voiceless'.

Robert Andreach, 'The New Narrators of "Amy Foster"', *Studies in Short Fiction*, 2 (1965), 262–9, is still useful. On the link to Conrad's own trauma and his need for distance even through a language, see Sue Finkelstein, 'Hope and Betrayal: A Psychoanalytic Reading of "Amy Foster"', *Conradiana*, 32.1 (2000), 20–31.

A film version, 'Swept from the Sea' (1997), makes Yanko and Amy (played by Vincent Perez and Rachel Weisz) very glamorous, and Dr Kennedy (Ian McKellen) takes a possessive, quasi-sexual interest in Yanko, turning to Amy and her son only at the end in remorse at her loss. The account of Amy's near-dumbness at home is interestingly related to her ill-treatment by her father.

C. 'THE RETURN': THE RICH MAN'S STORY

The story could not find magazine publication, and when published in *Tales of Unrest*, as Conrad's bourgeois tale, it offended middle-class standards of good taste in relation to the sex problem. Even the generally favourable review in *The Literary Gazette* lamented the lack of forgiveness at the end of the story in an extraordinary mixture of thoughts: 'True grace might have suggested to him to give her half a chance. A frank confession on his own part of his previous incompleteness, and of his spiritual development by trial, might have cleared the situation and offered her the opportunity of response. And in any case, there are wives whom we should love, as we love animals and children . . .' (JCCR vol. 1, 249). In America reviews were somewhat more favourable. A reviewer for *The Daily Pioneer Press* subtly described 'the working out of the emotions within emotions that control human action', calling the story 'fiercely analytical', and concluding 'Its strength lies in the fact that a character which we perceive to be limited and bound by conventions to a very marked degree, is still capable of a revolt against the conventional mockeries of life such as few avowedly free spirits are able to make' (JCCR vol. 1, 273).

Modern reception began badly with Albert J. Guerard describing it as not only Conrad's worst story but 'one of the worst ever written by a great novelist' (*Conrad the Novelist*, Harvard University Press, 1958, 96). A fine early counter-account, only odd for claiming that Conrad adopted the sexual subject-matter for its commercial value, is in the book Edward Said made out of his PhD thesis, *Joseph Conrad and the Fiction of Autobiography*, 104–12: 'The predicament in which Hervey finds himself is one that Conrad knew well from his own experience. It was that pressing need to find an unimpeachable starting-point from which to continue life anew' (110). The novelist Colm Tóibín has a short introductory essay in the Hesperus Classics edition of 'The Return' (2004). See also William Bonney, 'Contextualizing and Comprehending Joseph Conrad's "The Return"', *Studies in Short Fiction*, 33.1 (Winter 1996), 77–90.

D. 'THE DUEL': THE SOLDIER'S STORY, DESCRIBED BY CONRAD AS 'A MILITARY TALE'

For sources and manuscript, see the invaluable *Conrad's "The Duel": Sources/Text*, eds J. H. Stape and J. G. Peters (Brill Rodopi, 2015). It was Conrad's first venture into historical fiction.

Dismayed by the reviews, Conrad wrote to Edward Garnett, 21 August 1908, that he had originally thought to call the story 'The Masters of Europe' but 'rejected it as pretentious': the result was that all the early reviewers, he said, missed the 'Napoleonic feeling' by blindly following the mere tale (*Conrad: The Critical Heritage*, ed. Norman Sherry, Routledge and Kegan Paul, 1973, 220). Garnett declared it a masterpiece of style in a review in *The Nation*, but argued that an English audience was temperamentally unsympathetic to its dark and sombre irony (JCCR vol. 2, 471, 474). Other early reviewers saw it as an ironic farce, a satire on duelling, or a whimsical joke made out of caricatures, and some found the irony 'heavy of hand' (JCCR vol. 2, 458). The reviewer in *The Observer*, however, appreciated the variety of tone that was either lost on others, or disturbed and alienated them: 'the amazing feud . . . oscillates delicately between the ludicrous, the dramatic, and the pathetic'—noting that in the end 'our sympathy is no less with the splenetic Feraud in his degradation than with his chivalrous victim' (JCCR vol. 2, 467–8). The tonal mobility of the feelings, and the varying movement of them between the protagonists over the years, made for a different readerly experience than the more direct and individual human emotions felt by Captain Whalley or Yanko Goorall in their separateness. It was only Feraud, wrote the reviewer for the *Birmingham Daily Post*, who was inspired by 'one fixed emotion', in the characteristic Conrad way, and overtaken by it. But the exciting account of the final duel was generally seen as a masterpiece of straight story-telling. 'The Duel' attracted more notice in America, probably because of its publication there as a single volume, 'The Point of Honor'. The way that D'Hubert secretly saves his opponent's life and supports him financially made it a unique story in the history of duelling, said *The New York Times*: 'a gem in its way, being unlike any other duel in print' (JCCR vol. 2, 525).

On the legendary aspect of the story, see Gene M. Moore, 'History and Legend in "The Duel"', *The Conradian*, 41.2 (Autumn 2016), 28–46. In seeking to capture the absurdist feel of the story, Sean Gaston in 'Conrad and the Asymmetrical Duel', *Angelaki, Journal of the Theoretical Humanities*, 15 (2010, issue 2, 39–53) quotes, by way of useful contrast, Dostoevsky's *The Devils* (also translated as *The Demons* or *The Possessed*), 1872 (including a duel in which Gaganov despises the clemency offered by his opponent by firing in the air while Stavrogin replies that he had no intention to insult him: it was not personal, but only the wish not to kill anyone). Gaston also cites the satiric proposal made by an Iraqi vice-president in regard to the Gulf War of 1990: 'that Saddam Hussein and George W. Bush should fight a duel to settle their differences. . . . Mr Bush's spokesman Ari Fleischer rejected the idea saying, "there can be no serious response to an irresponsible statement like that".'

Ridley Scott made an adaptation of 'The Duel' his first film, 'The Duellists' in 1977, starring Harvey Keitel as Feraud and Keith Carradine as D'Hubert. The significance of some of the differences between film and book is discussed in Allan Simmons, 'Cinematic Fidelities in *The Rover* and *The Duellists*' in *Conrad on Film*, ed. Gene M. Moore (Cambridge University Press, 1997), 120–34, and Kit Macfarlane, ' "A Certain Blind Look": Žižek's "absolute undecidability" in Joseph Conrad's "The Duel" and Ridley Scott's *The Duellists*', online at: https://www.sensesofcinema.com/2016/feature-articles/zizek-the-duel-and-the-duellists/

A CHRONOLOGY OF JOSEPH CONRAD

Life	Historical and Cultural Background
The Polish Years: 1857–1873	
1857 3 December: Józef Teodor Konrad Korzeniowski born to Apollo Korzeniowski and Ewa (née Bobrowska) Korzeniowska in Berdyczów (Berdichev), Polish Ukraine	Indian Mutiny; Flaubert, *Madame Bovary* 1859: Darwin, *On the Origin of Species* 1860: Turgenev, *On the Eve*
1861 October: Conrad's father arrested and imprisoned in Warsaw by the Russian authorities for anti-Russian conspiracy	American Civil War begins; emancipation of the serfs in Russia; Dickens, *Great Expectations*
1862 May: Conrad's parents convicted of 'political activities' and exiled to Vologda, Russia; Conrad goes with them	Rise of Bismarck in Prussia; Turgenev, *Fathers and Sons*; Victor Hugo, *Les Misérables*
1863 Exile continues in Chernikhov	Polish insurrection; death of Thackeray
1865 18 April: death of Ewa Korzeniowska	American Civil War ends; Tolstoy, *War and Peace* (1865–72) 1866: Dostoevsky, *Crime and Punishment* 1867: Karl Marx, *Das Kapital*
1868 Korzeniowski permitted to leave Russia; settles with his son in Lwów, Austrian Poland	Dostoevsky, *The Idiot*
1869 February: Conrad and his father move to Cracow; 23 May: death of Apollo Korzeniowski; Conrad's uncle Tadeusz Bobrowski becomes his unofficial guardian	Suez Canal opens; Flaubert, *L'Éducation sentimentale*; Matthew Arnold, *Culture and Anarchy*; J. S. Mill, *The Subjection of Women*
1870–3 Lives in Cracow with his maternal grandmother, Teofila Bobrowska; studies with his tutor, Adam Pulman	Franco-Prussian War; Education Act; death of Dickens 1871: Darwin, *The Descent of Man* 1872: George Eliot, *Middlemarch*
1873 Goes to school in Lwów; May–June: tours Switzerland and N. Italy with his tutor	Death of J. S. Mill, publication of his *Autobiography*

Life	Historical and Cultural Background

The Years at Sea: 1874–1893

1874 September: leaves for Marseille and takes a position with Delestang et Fils, bankers and shippers; December: Conrad's sea-life begins; sails as passenger in the *Mont-Blanc* to Martinique — First Impressionist Exhibition in Paris; Britain extends influence in Malaya

1875 June–December: sails across the Atlantic as apprentice in the *Mont-Blanc* — Tolstoy, *Anna Karenina* (1875–6)

1876–7 July–February: steward in the *Saint-Antoine* sailing from Marseille to South America — Alexander Graham Bell demonstrates the telephone; Wagner's 'The Ring Cycle' performed in Bayreuth; death of George Sand

1877 March–December: possibly involved in Carlist arms smuggling to Spain — Russia declares war on Turkey; Britain annexes Transvaal

1878 March: apparent suicide attempt; April: sails in British steamer *Mavis*; June: lands in England for first time; July: joins British coastal ship *Skimmer of the Sea* as ordinary seaman; October: departs from London in the *Duke of Sutherland* bound for Australia — The Congress of Berlin; James, *The Europeans*

1879–80 October: arrives back in London; December–January: sails in the *Europa* bound for Australia — British Zulu War; Ibsen, *A Doll's House*; James, *Daisy Miller*; Meredith, *The Egoist*

1880 Takes lodgings in London; May: passes second-mate's examination; August: joins the *Loch Etive* bound for Australia as third mate — Edison develops electric lighting; deaths of George Eliot and Flaubert; Dostoevsky, *The Brothers Karamazov*

1881 September: signs on as second mate in the *Palestine* bound for Bangkok — Tsar Alexander II assassinated; deaths of Dostoevsky and Carlyle

1882–3 The *Palestine* repaired in Falmouth but sinks off Sumatra — Married Women's Property Act in Britain; deaths of Darwin and Garibaldi

Life	*Historical and Cultural Background*
1883 July: reunited with his uncle Tadeusz Bobrowski at Marienbad; September: signs on as second mate in the *Riversdale* bound for South Africa and Madras, India	Nietzsche, *Also Sprach Zarathustra*; deaths of Turgenev, Wagner, and Marx
1884 June: sails in the *Narcissus* from Bombay, India, to Dunkirk as second mate; December: passes examination as first mate	Berlin Conference (14 nations), 'The Scramble for Africa'; the Fabian Society founded; Mark Twain, *Huckleberry Finn*
1885 April: sails for Calcutta and Singapore aboard the *Tilkhurst* as second mate	Death of General Gordon at Khartoum; Zola, *Germinal*
1886 August: becomes a naturalized British subject; November: gains his Master's Certificate; briefly signs on as second mate in the *Falconhurst*	Stevenson, *Dr Jekyll and Mr Hyde*; Nietzsche, *Beyond Good and Evil*
1887–8 Makes four voyages to the Malay Archipelago as first mate; February (1887): sails for Java in the *Highland Forest* but is injured and hospitalized in Singapore; August: joins the *Vidar* in Singapore bound for Borneo; January (1888): appointed Master of the *Otago* at Bangkok and sails for Australia	Queen Victoria's Golden Jubilee; Verdi, *Otello* 1888: Wilhelm II becomes Kaiser; British 'protectorate' over Matabeleland, Sarawak, North Borneo, and Brunei; death of Matthew Arnold
1889 Resigns from the *Otago*; March: released from his status as a Russian subject; June: settles briefly in London and in the autumn begins writing *Almayer's Folly*	London Dock Strike; Cecil Rhodes founds the British South Africa Co.; death of Robert Browning
1890 February: returns to Polish Ukraine for the first time in 16 years and visits his uncle Tadeusz Bobrowski; April: in Brussels; appointed by the Société Anonyme Belge pour le Commerce du Haut-Congo;	The Partition of Africa; Ibsen, *Hedda Gabler*; William Morris, *News from Nowhere*; J. G. Frazer, *The Golden Bough* (1890–1914)

Life	*Historical and Cultural Background*
Mid-May: sails for the Congo; August–September: commands the *Roi des Belges* from Stanley Falls to Kinshasa but falls ill with dysentery and malaria; sails for Europe in November	
1891–3 January (1891): back in England; February–March: hospitalized in London; April–May: travels to Champel-les-Bains near Geneva for a cure and returns to London in June, to be temporarily employed by Barr, Moering & Co.; November: joins the *Torrens*, his last sailing ship, and makes four voyages as first mate; meets John Galsworthy and Edward (Ted) Sanderson on one return passage; July (1893): resigns from the *Torrens* but remains on the payroll till mid-October; August–September: visits his uncle in Ukraine; November: briefly joins the *Adowa* at Rouen, France	1891: Hardy, *Tess of the D'Urbervilles*; Wilde, *The Picture of Dorian Gray* 1892: Death of Tennyson 1893: Dvořák, 'New World' Symphony; Verdi, *Falstaff*

Conrad the Writer: 1894–1924

1894 January: leaves the *Adowa* and returns to London; 10 February: Tadeusz Bobrowski dies; April–May: finishes and revises *Almayer's Folly*; August: again at Champel-les-Bains for hydrotherapy; October: meets Edward Garnett; November: meets Jessie George, his future wife	Nicholas II becomes Tsar; 'Dreyfus case' in France; death of Robert Louis Stevenson
1895 April: *Almayer's Folly* published	Crane, *The Red Badge of Courage*; H. G. Wells, *The Time Machine*; death of Engels; Hardy, *Jude the Obscure*

Life	Historical and Cultural Background
1896 March: *An Outcast of the Islands*; marries Jessie George; they live in Stanford-le-Hope, Essex	Puccini, *La Bohème*; death of William Morris
1897 Meets R. B. Cunninghame Graham, Henry James, and Stephen Crane; March: moves to Ivy Walls, Essex; December: *The Nigger of the 'Narcissus'*	Queen Victoria's Diamond Jubilee; H. G. Wells, *The Invisible Man*
1898 Meets Ford Madox (Hueffer) Ford and H. G. Wells; 15 January: Alfred Borys Conrad born; April: *Tales of Unrest*; October: leases Pent Farm, Postling, Kent	Curies discover radium; Wilde, *The Ballad of Reading Gaol*; H. G. Wells, *The War of the Worlds*
1899 February: finishes 'Heart of Darkness'	Boer War begins
1900 September: J. B. Pinker becomes Conrad's literary agent; October: *Lord Jim*	Russia occupies Manchuria; Freud, *The Interpretation of Dreams*; deaths of Wilde, Ruskin, Nietzsche, Crane
1901 June: *The Inheritors* (with Ford)	Death of Queen Victoria; Marconi transmits first transatlantic Morse Code signal; Kipling, *Kim*
1902 November: *Youth: A Narrative and Two Other Stories* ('Heart of Darkness' and 'The End of the Tether')	Balfour's Education Act; death of Zola; Gorky, *The Lower Depths*
1903 April: *Typhoon and Other Stories* October: *Romance* (with Ford)	Wright brothers' first flight; Shaw, *Man and Superman*; James, *The Ambassadors*; Butler, *The Way of All Flesh*
1904 October: *Nostromo*	Russo-Japanese War; Anglo-French *Entente Cordiale*; Chekhov, *The Cherry Orchard*; James, *The Golden Bowl*; death of Chekhov
1905 January–May: resides in Capri, Italy; June: *One Day More* staged in London	Abortive revolution in Russia; beginning of the Women's Suffrage Movement; Freud, *Three Essays on the Theory of Sexuality*; Debussy, *La Mer*

Life	*Historical and Cultural Background*
1906	Meets Arthur Marwood, who becomes a close friend; 2 August: John Conrad born; October: *The Mirror of the Sea: Memories and Impressions*	Anglo-Russian Entente; death of Ibsen; Galsworthy, *The Man of Property*
1907	May–August: at Champel-les-Bains for the children's health; September: *The Secret Agent*; moves to Someries, Luton Hoo, Bedfordshire	Cubist Exhibition in Paris; Shaw, *Major Barbara*
1908	August: *A Set of Six*	Bennett, *The Old Wives' Tale*
1909	February: moves to rented rooms in Aldington, near Hythe, Kent; July: deteriorating relations with Ford culminate in a break	Peary reaches the North Pole; Blériot flies across the Channel; Marinetti launches the Futurist movement
1910	January: quarrels with Pinker; physical and mental breakdown for three months; June: moves to new home, Capel House, Orlestone, Kent	The Union of South Africa created; death of Tolstoy; Post-Impressionist Exhibition, London; E. M. Forster, *Howards End*; Yeats, *The Green Helmet*
1911	October: *Under Western Eyes*	Amundsen reaches the South Pole; the *Blaue Reiter* group formed, Munich
1912	January: *Some Reminiscences* (later retitled *A Personal Record*); October: *'Twixt Land and Sea*	Titanic sinks; Schoenberg, *Pierrot Lunaire*; Pound, *Ripostes*; Mann, *Death in Venice*
1913	March: meets E. N. Doubleday to discuss a collected edition of his work; September: first meets Bertrand Russell	D. H. Lawrence, *Sons and Lovers*; Proust, *A la recherche du temps perdu* (1913–27); Stravinsky, *The Rite of Spring*
1914	January: *Chance*; July–November: visits Poland with his family and is detained for several weeks by the outbreak of the war	Outbreak of First World War; Polish Legion fights Russians; Joyce, *Dubliners*
1915	February: *Within the Tides*; March: *Victory* (USA; September in UK)	Germans sink the Lusitania; Einstein, *General Theory of Relativity*; Pound *Cathay*; D. H. Lawrence, *The Rainbow*; Ford, *The Good Soldier*
1916	March: sits for a bust by the sculptor Jo Davidson; August: visits Foreign Office and Admiralty to discuss propaganda articles	Battles of Verdun and Somme; Joyce, *A Portrait of the Artist as a Young Man*; death of Henry James

Life	*Historical and Cultural Background*
1917 March: The *Shadow-Line*; November: London for a three-month stay	The Russian Revolution; USA enters war; Jung, *The Psychology of the Unconscious*; T. S. Eliot, *Prufrock and Other Observations*; Shaw, *Heartbreak House*
1918 May: first meets G. Jean-Aubry; October: his son Borys hospitalized in Rouen, suffering from shell-shock	Spengler, *The Decline of the West*; death of Wilfred Owen; November, Armistice signed; Polish Republic restored
1919 March: stage version of *Victory* in London; April: *The Arrow of Gold*; May: sells film rights to four of his novels; October: moves to his last home—Oswalds, Bishopsbourne, near Canterbury, Kent	Treaty of Versailles; Keynes, *The Economic Consequences of the Peace*; Walter Gropius founds the *Bauhaus*
1920 May: *The Rescue* (USA; June in UK)	League of Nations founded; Poles rout Russian invaders; D. H. Lawrence, *Women in Love*
1921 February: *Notes on Life and Letters*; The Collected Edition begins publication in England (Heinemann) and the USA (Doubleday)	Irish Free State created; Rutherford and Chadwick work on splitting the atom
1922 November: stage version of *The Secret Agent*, London	Mussolini forms fascist government in Italy; BBC founded; T. S. Eliot, *The Waste Land*; Joyce, *Ulysses*; Woolf, *Jacob's Room*
1923 May–June: visits USA; December: *The Rover*	Yeats wins Nobel Prize for Literature
1924 11 January: birth of first grandson, Philip James; March: sits for sculptor Jacob Epstein; May: declines knighthood; 3 August: dies of a heart attack; buried in Canterbury Cemetery; September: *The Nature of a Crime* (with Ford); October: *Laughing Anne & One Day More: Two Plays*; November: Ford, *Joseph Conrad: A Personal Remembrance*	Death of Lenin; E. M. Forster, *A Passage to India*; Mann, *The Magic Mountain*; Shaw, *St Joan*

Life	*Historical and Cultural Background*
1925 January: *Tales of Hearsay*; September: *Suspense* (unfinished)	Fall of Trotsky, rise of Stalin; Shaw wins the Nobel Prize for Literature; Hitler, *Mein Kampf*; Woolf, *Mrs Dalloway*
1926 March: *Last Essays*	General Strike; Kafka, *The Castle*
1928 June: *The Sisters*	Death of Thomas Hardy; D. H. Lawrence, *Lady Chatterley's Lover*

THE END OF THE TETHER*

I

FOR a long time after the course of the steamer *Sofala** had been altered for the land, the low swampy coast had retained its appearance of a mere smudge of darkness beyond a belt of glitter. The sunrays fell violently upon the calm sea—seemed to shatter themselves upon an adamantine surface into sparkling dust, into a dazzling vapour of light that blinded the eye and wearied the brain with its unsteady brightness.

Captain Whalley did not look at it.* When his Serang,* approaching the roomy cane arm-chair which he filled capably, had informed him in a low voice that the course was to be altered, he had risen at once and had remained on his feet, face forward, while the head of his ship swung through a quarter of a circle. He had not uttered a single word, not even the word to steady the helm. It was the Serang, an elderly, alert, little Malay,* with a very dark skin, who murmured the order to the helmsman.* And then slowly Captain Whalley sat down again in the arm-chair on the bridge* and fixed his eyes on the deck between his feet.

He could not hope to see anything new upon this lane of the sea. He had been on these coasts for the last three years. From Low Cape to Malantan* the distance was fifty miles, six hours' steaming for the old ship with the tide, or seven against. Then you steered straight for the land, and by-and-by three palms would appear on the sky, tall and slim, and with their dishevelled heads in a bunch, as if in confidential criticism of the dark mangroves.* The *Sofala* would be headed towards the sombre strip of the coast, which at a given moment, as the ship closed with it obliquely, would show several clean shining fractures—the brimful estuary of a river. Then on through a brown liquid, three parts water and one part black earth, on and on between the low shores, three parts black earth and one part brackish water, the *Sofala* would plough her way upstream, as she had done once every month for these seven years or more, long before he was aware of her existence, long before he had ever thought of having anything to do with her and her invariable voyages. The old ship ought to have

known the road better than her men, who had not been kept so long
at it without a change; better than the faithful Serang, whom he had
brought over from his last ship to keep the captain's watch; better
than he himself, who had been her captain for the last three years only.
She could always be depended upon to make her courses. Her com-
passes were never out. She was no trouble at all to take about, as if her
great age had given her knowledge, wisdom, and steadiness. She
made her landfalls to a degree of the bearing,* and almost to a minute
of her allowed time. At any moment, as he sat on the bridge without
looking up, or lay sleepless in his bed, simply by reckoning the days
and the hours he could tell where he was—the precise spot of the
beat. He knew it well, too, this monotonous huckster's round,* up
and down the Straits; he knew its order and its sights and its people.
Malacca* to begin with, in at daylight and out at dusk, to cross over
with a rigid phosphorescent wake this highway of the Far East.
Darkness and gleams on the water, clear stars on a black sky, perhaps
the lights of a home steamer keeping her unswerving course in the
middle, or maybe the elusive shadow of a native craft with her mat
sails* flitting by silently—and the low land on the other side in sight
at daylight. At noon the three palms of the next place of call, up
a sluggish river. The only white man residing there was a retired
young sailor,* with whom he had become friendly in the course of
many voyages. Sixty miles farther on there was another place of call,
a deep bay with only a couple of houses on the beach. And so on,
in and out, picking up coastwise cargo here and there, and finishing
with a hundred miles' steady steaming through the maze of an archipelago of small islands up to a large native town at the end of the beat.
There was a three days' rest for the old ship before he started her
again in inverse order, seeing the same shores from another bearing,
hearing the same voices in the same places, back again to the *Sofala*'s
port of registry* on the great highway to the East, where he would
take up a berth nearly opposite the big stone pile of the harbour office
till it was time to start again on the old round of 1,600 miles and thirty
days. Not a very enterprising life, this, for Captain Whalley, Henry
Whalley, otherwise Dare-devil Harry Whalley, of the *Condor*,
a famous clipper* in her day. No. Not a very enterprising life for
a man who had served famous firms, who had sailed famous ships
(more than one or two of them his own); who had made famous passages, had been the pioneer of new routes and new trades; who had

steered across the unsurveyed tracts of the South Seas,* and had seen the sun rise on uncharted islands. Fifty years at sea, and forty out in the East ("a pretty thorough apprenticeship," he used to remark smilingly), had made him honourably known to a generation of ship-owners and merchants in all the ports from Bombay* clear over to where the East merges into the West upon the coast of the two Americas. His fame remained writ, not very large but plain enough, on the Admiralty charts. Was there not somewhere between Australia and China a Whalley Island and a Condor Reef?* On that dangerous coral formation the celebrated clipper had hung stranded for three days, her captain and crew throwing her cargo overboard with one hand and with the other, as it were, keeping off her a flotilla of savage war-canoes. At that time neither the island nor the reef had any offi-cial existence. Later the officers of her Majesty's steam vessel *Fusilier*, despatched to make a survey of the route, recognized in the adoption of these two names the enterprise of the man and the solidity of the ship. Besides, as any one who cares may see, the *General Directory*,* vol. ii. p. 410, begins the description of the "Malotu or Whalley Passage" with the words: "This advantageous route, first discovered in 1850 by Captain Whalley in the ship *Condor*," etc., and ends by recommending it warmly to sailing vessels leaving the China ports for the south in the months from December to April inclusive.

This was the clearest gain he had out of life. Nothing could rob him of this kind of fame. The piercing of the Isthmus of Suez,* like the breaking of a dam, had let in upon the East a flood of new ships, new men, new methods of trade. It had changed the face of the Eastern seas and the very spirit of their life; so that his early experi-ences meant nothing whatever to the new generation of seamen.

In those bygone days he had handled many thousands of pounds of his employers' money and of his own; he had attended faithfully, as by law a shipmaster is expected to do, to the conflicting interests of owners, charterers, and underwriters. He had never lost a ship or consented to a shady transaction; and he had lasted well, outlasting in the end* the conditions that had gone to the making of his name. He had buried his wife (in the Gulf of Petchili*), had married off his daughter to the man of her unlucky choice, and had lost more than an ample competence in the crash of the notorious Travancore and Deccan Banking Corporation,* whose downfall had shaken the East like an earthquake. And he was sixty-seven years old.

II

HIS age sat lightly enough on him; and of his ruin he was not ashamed. He had not been alone to believe in the stability of the Banking Corporation. Men whose judgment in matters of finance was as expert as his seamanship had commended the prudence of his investments, and had themselves lost much money in the great failure. The only difference between him and them was that he had lost his all. And yet not his all. There had remained to him from his lost fortune a very pretty little barque, *Fair Maid*,* which he had bought to occupy his leisure of a retired sailor—"to play with," as he expressed it himself.

He had formally declared himself tired of the sea the year preceding his daughter's marriage. But after the young couple had gone to settle in Melbourne he found out that he could not make himself happy on shore. He was too much of a merchant sea-captain for mere yachting to satisfy him. He wanted the illusion of affairs; and his acquisition of the *Fair Maid* preserved the continuity of his life. He introduced her to his acquaintances in various ports as "my last command." When he grew too old to be trusted with a ship, he would lay her up and go ashore to be buried, leaving directions in his will to have the barque towed out and scuttled* decently in deep water on the day of the funeral. His daughter would not grudge him the satisfaction of knowing that no stranger would handle his last command after him. With the fortune he was able to leave her, the value of a 500-ton barque was neither here nor there. All this would be said with a jocular twinkle in his eye: the vigorous old man had too much vitality for the sentimentalism of regret; and a little wistfully withal, because he was at home in life, taking a genuine pleasure in its feelings and its possessions; in the dignity of his reputation and his wealth, in his love for his daughter, and in his satisfaction with the ship—the plaything of his lonely leisure.

He had the cabin arranged in accordance with his simple ideal of comfort at sea. A big bookcase (he was a great reader) occupied one side of his stateroom; the portrait of his late wife, a flat bituminous oil-painting representing the profile and one long black ringlet of a young woman, faced his bedplace. Three chronometers* ticked him to sleep and greeted him on waking with the tiny competition of their beats. He rose at five every day. The officer of the morning watch,* drinking his early cup of coffee aft* by the wheel, would hear through the wide orifice of the copper ventilators all the splashings, blowings, and splutterings of his captain's toilet. These noises would be followed by a sustained deep murmur of the Lord's Prayer* recited in a loud earnest voice. Five minutes afterwards the head and shoulders of Captain Whalley emerged out of the companion-hatchway.* Invariably he paused for a while on the stairs, looking all round at the horizon; upwards at the trim* of the sails; inhaling deep draughts of the fresh air. Only then he would step out on the poop, acknowledging the hand raised to the peak of the cap with a majestic and benign "Good morning to you." He walked the deck till eight scrupulously. Sometimes, not above twice a year, he had to use a thick cudgel-like stick on account of a stiffness in the hip—a slight touch of rheumatism, he supposed. Otherwise he knew nothing of the ills of the flesh. At the ringing of the breakfast bell he went below to feed his canaries, wind up the chronometers, and take the head of the table. From there he had before his eyes the big carbon photographs* of his daughter, her husband, and two fat-legged babies—his grandchildren—set in black frames into the maple-wood bulkheads of the cuddy.* After breakfast he dusted the glass over these portraits himself with a cloth, and brushed the oil painting of his wife with a plummet* kept suspended from a small brass hook by the side of the heavy gold frame. Then with the door of his state-room shut, he would sit down on the couch under the portrait to read a chapter out of a thick pocket Bible—her Bible. But on some days he only sat there for half an hour with his finger between the leaves and the closed book resting on his knees. Perhaps he had remembered suddenly how fond of boat-sailing she used to be.*

She had been a real shipmate and a true woman, too. It was like an article of faith with him that there never had been, and never could be, a brighter, cheerier home anywhere afloat or ashore than his home under the poop-deck of the *Condor*, with the big main cabin all white and gold, garlanded as if for a perpetual festival with an unfading wreath. She had decorated the centre of every panel with a cluster of home flowers. It took her a twelvemonth to go round the cuddy with this labour of love. To him it had remained a marvel of painting, the highest achievement of taste and skill; and as to old Swinburne, his mate,* every time he came down to his meals he stood transfixed with admiration before the progress of the work. You could almost smell these roses, he declared, sniffing the faint flavour of turpentine which at that time pervaded the saloon, and (as he confessed afterwards) made him somewhat less hearty than usual in tackling his food. But there was nothing of the sort to interfere with his enjoyment of her singing. "Mrs. Whalley is a regular out-and-out nightingale, sir," he would pronounce with a judicial air after listening profoundly over the skylight to the very end of the piece. In fine weather, in the second dog-watch,* the two men could hear her trills and roulades* going on to the accompaniment of the piano in the cabin. On the very day they got engaged he had written to London for the instrument; but they had been married for over a year before it reached them, coming out round the Cape. The big case made part of the first direct general cargo landed in Hongkong* harbour—an event that to the men who walked the busy quays of to-day seemed as hazily remote as the dark ages of history. But Captain Whalley could in a half-hour of solitude live again all his life, with its romance, its idyl, and its sorrow. He had to close her eyes himself. She went away from under the ensign* like a sailor's wife, a sailor herself at heart. He had read the service over her, out of her own prayer-book, without a break in his voice. When he raised his eyes he could see old Swinburne facing him with his cap pressed to his breast, and his rugged, weather-beaten, impassive face streaming with drops of water like a lump of chipped red granite in a shower. It was all very well for that old sea-dog to cry. He had to read on to the end; but after the splash he did not remember much of what happened for the next few days. An elderly sailor of the crew, deft at needlework, put together a mourning frock for the child out of one of her black skirts.

He was not likely to forget; but you cannot dam up life like a slug-gish stream. It will break out and flow over a man's troubles, it will close upon a sorrow like the sea upon a dead body, no matter how much love has gone to the bottom. And the world is not bad. People had been very kind to him; especially Mrs. Gardner, the wife of the senior partner in Gardner, Patteson, & Co., the owners of the *Condor*. It was she who volunteered to look after the little one, and in due course took her to England (something of a journey in those days, even by the overland mail route) with her own girls to finish her education. It was ten years before he saw her again.

As a little child she had never been frightened of bad weather; she would beg to be taken up on deck in the bosom of his oilskin coat to watch the big seas hurling themselves upon the *Condor*. The swirl and crash of the waves seemed to fill her small soul with a breathless delight. "A good boy spoiled," he used to say of her in joke. He had named her Ivy because of the sound of the word, and obscurely fascinated by a vague association of ideas. She had twined herself tightly round his heart, and he intended her to cling close to her father as to a tower of strength; forgetting, while she was little, that in the nature of things she would probably elect to cling to someone else. But he loved life well enough for even that event to give him a certain satisfaction, apart from his more intimate feeling of loss.

After he had purchased the *Fair Maid* to occupy his loneliness, he hastened to accept a rather unprofitable freight* to Australia simply for the opportunity of seeing his daughter in her own home. What made him dissatisfied there was not to see that she clung now to somebody else, but that the prop she had selected seemed on closer examination "a rather poor stick"—even in the matter of health. He disliked his son-in-law's studied civility perhaps more than his method of handling the sum of money he had given Ivy at her marriage. But of his apprehensions he said nothing. Only on the day of his departure, with the hall-door open already, holding her hands and looking steadily into her eyes, he had said, "You know, my dear, all I have is for you and the chicks. Mind you write to me openly." She had answered him by an almost imperceptible movement of her head. She resembled her mother in the colour of her eyes, and in character—and also in this, that she understood him without many words.

Sure enough she had to write; and some of these letters made Captain Whalley lift his white eye-brows. For the rest he considered he was reaping the true reward of his life by being thus able to produce on demand whatever was needed. He had not enjoyed himself so much in a way since his wife had died. Characteristically enough his son-in-law's punctuality in failure caused him at a distance to feel a sort of kindness towards the man. The fellow was so perpetually being jammed on a lee shore* that to charge it all to his reckless navigation would be manifestly unfair. No, no! He knew well what that meant. It was bad luck. His own had been simply marvellous, but he had seen in his life too many good men—seamen and others—go under with the sheer weight of bad luck not to recognize the fatal signs. For all that, he was cogitating on the best way of tying up very strictly every penny he had to leave, when, with a preliminary rumble of rumours (whose first sound reached him in Shanghai* as it happened), the shock of the big failure came; and, after passing through the phases of stupor, of incredulity, of indignation, he had to accept the fact that he had nothing to speak of to leave.

Upon that, as if he had only waited for this catastrophe, the unlucky man, away there in Melbourne, gave up his unprofitable game, and sat down—in an invalid's bath-chair* at that too. "He will never walk again," wrote the wife. For the first time in his life Captain Whalley was a bit staggered.

The *Fair Maid* had to go to work in bitter earnest now. It was no longer a matter of preserving alive the memory of Dare-devil Harry Whalley in the Eastern Seas, or of keeping an old man in pocket-money and clothes, with, perhaps, a bill for a few hundred first-class cigars thrown in at the end of the year. He would have to buckle-to,* and keep her going hard on a scant allowance of gilt for the ginger-bread scrolls at her stem and stern.*

This necessity opened his eyes to the fundamental changes of the world. Of his past only the familiar names remained, here and there, but the things and the men, as he had known them, were gone. The name of Gardner, Patteson & Co. was still displayed on the walls of warehouses by the waterside, on the brass plates and window-panes in the business quarters of more than one Eastern port, but there was no longer a Gardner or a Patteson in the firm. There was no longer for Captain Whalley an arm-chair and a welcome in the private office, with a bit of business ready to be put in the way of an old friend, for the sake of bygone services. The husbands of the Gardner girls sat behind the desks in that room where, long after he had left the employ, he had kept his right of entrance in the old man's time. Their ships now had yellow funnels with black tops, and a time-table of appointed routes like a confounded service of tramways. The winds of December and June were all one to them; their captains (excellent young men he doubted not) were, to be sure, familiar with Whalley Island, because of late years the Government had established a white fixed light on the north end (with a red danger sector over the Condor Reef), but most of them would have been extremely surprised to hear that a flesh-and-blood Whalley still existed—an old man going about the world trying to pick up a cargo here and there for his little bark.

And everywhere it was the same. Departed the men who would have nodded appreciatively at the mention of his name, and would have thought themselves bound in honour to do something for Dare-devil

Harry Whalley. Departed the opportunities which he would have known how to seize; and gone with them the white-winged flock of clippers that lived in the boisterous uncertain life of the winds, skimming big fortunes out of the foam of the sea. In a world that pared down the profits to an irreducible minimum, in a world that was able to count its disengaged tonnage* twice over every day, and in which lean charters* were snapped up by cable* three months in advance, there were no chances of fortune for an individual wandering haphazard with a little barque—hardly indeed any room to exist.

He found it more difficult from year to year. He suffered greatly from the smallness of remittances he was able to send his daughter. Meantime he had given up good cigars, and even in the matter of inferior cheroots limited himself to six a day. He never told her of his difficulties, and she never enlarged upon her struggle to live. Their confidence in each other needed no explanations, and their perfect understanding endured without protestations of gratitude or regret. He would have been shocked if she had taken it into her head to thank him in so many words, but he found it perfectly natural that she should tell him she needed two hundred pounds.

He had come in with the *Fair Maid* in ballast* to look for a freight in the *Sofala*'s port of registry, and her letter met him there. Its tenor was that it was no use mincing matters. Her only resource was in opening a boarding-house, for which the prospects, she judged, were good. Good enough, at any rate, to make her tell him frankly that with two hundred pounds she could make a start. He had torn the envelope open, hastily, on deck, where it was handed to him by the ship-chandler's runner,* who had brought his mail at the moment of anchoring. For the second time in his life he was appalled, and remained stock-still at the cabin door with the paper trembling between his fingers. Open a boarding-house! Two hundred pounds for a start! The only resource! And he did not know where to lay his hands on two hundred pence.

All that night Captain Whalley walked the poop* of his anchored ship, as though he had been about to close with the land in thick weather, and uncertain of his position after a run of many grey days without a sight of sun, moon, or stars. The black night twinkled with the guiding lights of seamen and the steady straight lines of lights on shore; and all around the *Fair Maid* the riding lights of ships cast trembling trails upon the water of the roadstead. Captain Whalley saw not a gleam anywhere till the dawn broke and he found out that his clothing was soaked through with the heavy dew.

His ship was awake. He stopped short, stroked his wet beard, and descended the poop ladder backwards, with tired feet. At the sight of him the chief officer, lounging about sleepily on the quarterdeck, remained open-mouthed in the middle of a great early-morning yawn.

"Good morning to you," pronounced Captain Whalley solemnly, passing into the cabin. But he checked himself in the doorway, and without looking back, "By the bye," he said, "there should be an empty wooden case put away in the lazarette.* It has not been broken up—has it?"

The mate shut his mouth, and then asked as if dazed, "What empty case, sir?"

"A big flat packing-case belonging to that painting in my room. Let it be taken up on deck and tell the carpenter to look it over. I may want to use it before long."

The chief officer did not stir a limb till he had heard the door of the captain's state-room slam within the cuddy. Then he beckoned aft the second mate with his forefinger to tell him that there was something "in the wind."

When the bell rang Captain Whalley's authoritative voice boomed out through a closed door, "Sit down and don't wait for me." And his impressed officers took their places, exchanging looks and whispers across the table. What! No breakfast? And after apparently knocking about all night on deck, too! Clearly, there was something in the wind. In the skylight above their heads, bowed earnestly over the plates, three wire cages rocked and rattled to the restless jumping of the hungry canaries; and they could detect the sounds of their "old man's" deliberate movements within his state-room. Captain Whalley was methodically winding up the chronometers, dusting the portrait of his late wife, getting a clean white shirt out of the drawers, making himself ready in his punctilious unhurried manner to go ashore. He could not have swallowed a single mouthful of food that morning. He had made up his mind to sell the *Fair Maid*.

III

JUST at that time the Japanese were casting far and wide for ships of European build, and he had no difficulty in finding a purchaser, a speculator who drove a hard bargain, but paid cash down for the *Fair Maid*, with a view to a profitable resale. Thus it came about that Captain Whalley found himself on a certain afternoon descending the steps of one of the most important post-offices of the East with a slip of bluish paper in his hand. This was the receipt of a registered letter enclosing a draft for two hundred pounds, and addressed to Melbourne. Captain Whalley pushed the paper into his waistcoat-pocket, took his stick from under his arm, and walked down the street.

It was a recently opened and untidy thoroughfare with rudimentary side-walks and a soft layer of dust cushioning the whole width of the road. One end touched the slummy street of Chinese shops near the harbour, the other drove straight on, without houses, for a couple of miles, through patches of jungle-like vegetation, to the yard gates of the new Consolidated Docks Company.* The crude frontages of the new Government buildings alternated with the blank fencing of vacant plots, and the view of the sky seemed to give an added spaciousness to the broad vista. It was empty and shunned by natives after business hours, as though they had expected to see one of the tigers from the neighbourhood of the New Waterworks* on the hill coming at a loping canter down the middle to get a Chinese shop-keeper for supper. Captain Whalley was not dwarfed by the solitude of the grandly planned street. He had too fine a presence for that. He was only a lonely figure walking purposefully, with a great white beard like a pilgrim, and with a thick stick that resembled a weapon. On one side the new Courts of Justice had a low and unadorned portico* of squat columns half concealed by a few old trees left in the approach. On the other the pavilion wings of the new Colonial Treasury came out to the line of the street. But Captain Whalley, who had now no ship and no home, remembered in passing that on that very site when he first came out from England there had stood a fishing village, a few mat huts erected on piles* between a muddy tidal creek and a miry pathway that went writhing into a tangled wilderness without any docks or waterworks.

No ship—no home. And his poor Ivy away there had no home either. A boarding-house is no sort of home though it may get you a living. His feelings were horribly rasped by the idea of the boarding-house. In his rank of life he had that truly aristocratic temperament characterized by a scorn of vulgar gentility and by prejudiced views as to the derogatory nature of certain occupations. For his own part

he had always preferred sailing merchant ships* (which is a straight-
forward occupation) to buying and selling merchandise, of which the
essence is to get the better of somebody in a bargain—an undignified
trial of wits at best. His father had been Colonel Whalley (retired) of
the H. E. I. Company's service,* with very slender means besides his
pension, but with distinguished connections. He could remember as
a boy how frequently waiters at the inns, country tradesmen and small
people of that sort, used to "My lord" the old warrior on the strength
of his appearance.

Captain Whalley himself (he would have entered the Navy if his
father had not died before he was fourteen) had something of a grand
air which would have suited an old and glorious admiral; but he
became lost like a straw in the eddy of a brook amongst the swarm of
brown and yellow humanity filling a thoroughfare, that by contrast
with the vast and empty avenue he had left seemed as narrow as a lane
and absolutely riotous with life. The walls of the houses were blue; the
shops of the Chinamen yawned like cavernous lairs; heaps of nondescript merchandise overflowed the gloom of the long range of arcades,
and the fiery serenity of sunset took the middle of the street from end
to end with a glow like the reflection of a fire. It fell on the bright
colours and the dark faces of the bare-footed crowd, on the pallid
yellow backs of the half-naked jostling coolies,* on the accoutrements* of a tall Sikh trooper* with a parted beard and fierce moustaches on sentry before the gate of the police compound. Looming
very big above the heads in a red haze of dust, the tightly packed car
of the cable tramway navigated cautiously up the human stream, with
the incessant blare of its horn, in the manner of a steamer groping in
a fog.

Captain Whalley emerged like a diver on the other side, and in the
desert shade between the walls of closed warehouses removed his hat
to cool his brow. A certain disrepute attached to the calling of a landlady of a boarding-house. These women were said to be rapacious,
unscrupulous, untruthful; and though he contemned no class of his
fellow-creatures—God forbid!—these were suspicions to which it
was unseemly that a Whalley should lay herself open. He had not
expostulated with her, however. He was confident she shared his feelings; he was sorry for her; he trusted her judgment; he considered it
a merciful dispensation that he could help her once more—but in his
aristocratic heart of hearts he would have found it more easy to

reconcile himself to the idea of her turning seamstress. Vaguely he remembered reading years ago a touching piece called the "Song of the Shirt."* It was all very well making songs about poor women. The granddaughter of Colonel Whalley, the landlady of a boarding-house! Pooh! He replaced his hat, dived into two pockets, and stopping a moment to apply a flaring match to the end of a cheap cheroot, blew an embittered cloud of smoke at a world that could hold such surprises.

Of one thing he was certain—that she was the own child of a clever mother. Now he had got over the wrench of parting with his ship, he perceived clearly that such a step had been unavoidable. Perhaps he had been growing aware of it all along with an unconfessed know-ledge. But she, far away there, must have had an intuitive perception of it, with the pluck to face that truth and the courage to speak out—all the qualities which had made her mother a woman of such excellent counsel.

It would have had to come to that in the end! It was fortunate she had forced his hand. In another year or two it would have been an utterly barren sale. To keep the ship going he had been involving him-self deeper every year. He was defenceless before the insidious work of adversity, to whose more open assaults he could present a firm front; like a cliff that stands unmoved the open battering of the sea, with a lofty ignorance of the treacherous backwash undermining its base. As it was, every liability satisfied, her request answered, and owing no man a penny, there remained to him from the proceeds a sum of five hundred pounds put away safely. In addition he had upon his person some forty odd dollars—enough to pay his hotel bill, providing he did not linger too long in the modest bedroom where he had taken refuge.

Scantily furnished, and with a waxed floor, it opened into one of the side-verandahs. The straggling building of bricks, as airy as a bird-cage, resounded with the incessant flapping of rattan screens* worried by the wind between the white-washed square pillars of the sea-front. The rooms were lofty, a ripple of sunshine flowed over the ceilings; and the periodical invasions of tourists from some passenger steamer in the harbour flitted through the wind-swept dusk of the apartments with the tumult of their unfamiliar voices and imperman-ent presences, like relays of migratory shades condemned to speed headlong round the earth without leaving a trace. The babble of their

irruptions ebbed out as suddenly as it had arisen; the draughty cor-
ridors and the long chairs of the verandahs knew their sight-seeing
hurry or their prostrate repose no more; and Captain Whalley, substantial and dignified, left well-nigh alone in the vast hotel by each
light-hearted skurry,* felt more and more like a stranded tourist with
no aim in view, like a forlorn traveller without a home. In the solitude
of his room he smoked thoughtfully, gazing at the two sea-chests
which held all that he could call his own in this world. A thick roll of
charts in a sheath of sailcloth leaned in a corner; the flat packing-case
containing the portrait in oils and the three carbon photographs had
been pushed under the bed. He was tired of discussing terms, of
assisting at surveys, of all the routine of the business. What to the
other parties was merely the sale of a ship was to him a momentous
event involving a radically new view of existence. He knew that after
this ship there would be no other; and the hopes of his youth, the
exercise of his abilities, every feeling and achievement of his manhood, had been indissolubly connected with ships. He had served
ships; he had owned ships; and even the years of his actual retirement
from the sea had been made bearable by the idea that he had only to
stretch out his hand full of money to get a ship. He had been at liberty
to feel as though he were the owner of all the ships in the world. The
selling of this one was weary work; but when she passed from him at
last, when he signed the last receipt, it was as though all the ships had
gone out of the world together, leaving him on the shore of inaccessible oceans with seven hundred pounds in his hands.

Striding firmly, without haste, along the quay, Captain Whalley
averted his glances from the familiar roadstead. Two generations of
seamen born since his first day at sea stood between him and all these
ships at the anchorage. His own was sold, and he had been asking
himself, What next?

From the feeling of loneliness, of inward emptiness—and of loss
too, as if his very soul had been taken out of him forcibly—there had
sprung at first a desire to start right off and join his daughter. "Here
are the last pence," he would say to her; "take them, my dear. And
here's your old father: you must take him too."

His soul recoiled, as if afraid of what lay hidden at the bottom of this
impulse. Give up! Never! When one is thoroughly weary all sorts of
nonsense come into one's head. A pretty gift it would have been for
a poor woman—this seven hundred pounds with the incumbrance of

a hale old fellow more than likely to last for years and years to come. Was he not as fit to die in harness as any of the youngsters in charge of these anchored ships out yonder?* He was as solid now as ever he had been. But as to who would give him work to do, that was another matter. Were he, with his appearance and antecedents, to go about looking for a junior's berth,* people, he was afraid, would not take him seriously; or else if he succeeded in impressing them, he would maybe obtain their pity, which would be like stripping yourself naked to be kicked. He was not anxious to give himself away for less than nothing. He had no use for anybody's pity. On the other hand, a command—the only thing he could try for with due regard for common decency—was not likely to be lying in wait for him at the corner of the next street. Commands don't go a-begging nowadays. Ever since he had come ashore to carry out the business of the sale he had kept his ears open, but had heard no hint of one being vacant in the port. And even if there had been one, his successful past itself stood in his way. He had been his own employer too long. The only credential he could produce was the testimony of his whole life. What better recommendation could anyone require? But vaguely he felt that the unique document would be looked upon as an archaic curiosity of the Eastern waters, a screed traced in obsolete words—in a half-forgotten language.

IV

REVOLVING these thoughts, he strolled on near the railings of the quay, broad-chested, without a stoop, as though his big shoulders had never felt the burden of the loads that must be carried between the cradle and the grave. No single betraying fold or line of care disfigured the reposeful modelling of his face. It was full and untanned; and the upper part emerged, massively quiet, out of the downward flow of silvery hair, with the striking delicacy of its clear complexion and the powerful width of the forehead. The first cast of his glance fell on you candid and swift, like a boy's; but because of the ragged snowy thatch of the eyebrows the affability of his attention acquired the character of a dark and searching scrutiny. With age he had put on flesh a little, had increased his girth like an old tree presenting no symptoms of decay; and even the opulent, lustrous ripple of white hairs upon his chest seemed an attribute of unquenchable vitality and vigour.

Once rather proud of his great bodily strength, and even of his personal appearance, conscious of his worth, and firm in his rectitude, there had remained to him, like the heritage of departed prosperity, the tranquil bearing of a man who had proved himself fit in every sort of way for the life of his choice. He strode on squarely under the projecting brim of an ancient Panama hat.* It had a low crown, a crease through its whole diameter, a narrow black ribbon. Imperishable and a little discoloured, this headgear made it easy to pick him out from afar on thronged wharves and in the busy streets. He had never adopted the comparatively modern fashion of pipe-clayed cork helmets.* He disliked the form; and he hoped he could manage to keep a cool head to the end of his life without all these contrivances for hygienic ventilation. His hair was cropped close, his linen always of immaculate whiteness; a suit of thin grey flannel, worn threadbare but scrupulously brushed, floated about his burly limbs, adding to his bulk by the looseness of its cut. The years had mellowed the good-humoured, imperturbable audacity of his prime into a temper carelessly serene; and the leisurely tapping of his iron-shod stick accompanied his footfalls with a self-confident sound on the flagstones. It was impossible to connect such a fine presence and this unruffled aspect with the belittling troubles of poverty; the man's whole existence appeared to pass before you, facile and large, in the freedom of means as ample as the clothing of his body.

The irrational dread of having to break into his five hundred pounds for personal expenses in the hotel disturbed the steady poise of his mind. There was no time to lose. The bill was running up. He nourished the hope that this five hundred would perhaps be the means, if everything else failed, of obtaining some work which, keeping his body and soul together (not a matter of great outlay), would enable him to be of use to his daughter. To his mind it was her own money which he employed, as it were, in backing her father and solely for her benefit. Once at work, he would help her with the greater part of his earnings; he was good for many years yet, and this boarding-house business, he argued to himself, whatever the prospects, could not be much of a gold-mine from the first start. But what work? He was ready to lay hold of anything in an honest way so that it came quickly to his hand; because the five hundred pounds must be preserved intact for eventual use. That was the great point. With the entire five hundred one felt a substance at one's back; but it seemed to him that should he let it dwindle to four-fifty or even four-eighty, all the efficiency would be gone out of the money, as though there were some magic power in the round figure. But what sort of work?

Confronted by that haunting question as by an uneasy ghost, for whom he had no exorcising formula, Captain Whalley stopped short on the apex of a small bridge spanning steeply the bed of a canalized creek with granite shores. Moored between the square blocks a sea-going Malay prau* floated half hidden under the arch of masonry, with her spars* lowered down, without a sound of life on board, and covered from stem to stern with a ridge of palm-leaf mats. He had left behind him the overheated pavements bordered by the stone front-ages that, like the sheer face of cliffs, followed the sweep of the quays; and an unconfined spaciousness of orderly and sylvan aspect opened before him its wide plots of rolled grass, like pieces of green carpet smoothly pegged out, its long ranges of trees lined up in colossal por-ticos of dark shafts roofed with a vault of branches.

Some of these avenues ended at the sea. It was a terraced shore; and beyond, upon the level expanse, profound and glistening like the gaze of a dark-blue eye, an oblique band of stippled purple length-ened itself indefinitely through the gap between a couple of verdant twin islets. The masts and spars of a few ships far away, hull down in the outer roads, sprang straight from the water in a fine maze of rosy lines pencilled on the clear shadow of the eastern board. Captain Whalley gave them a long glance. The ship, once his own, was anchored out there. It was staggering to think that it was open to him no longer to take a boat at the jetty and get himself pulled off to her when the evening came. To no ship. Perhaps never more. Before the sale was concluded, and till the purchase-money had been paid, he had spent daily some time on board the *Fair Maid*. The money had been paid this very morning, and now, all at once, there was positively no ship that he could go on board of when he liked; no ship that would need his presence in order to do her work—to live. It seemed an incredible state of affairs, something too bizarre to last. And the sea was full of craft of all sorts. There was that prau lying so still swathed in her shroud of sewn palm-leaves—she too had her indispensable man. They lived through each other, this Malay he had never seen, and this high-sterned thing of no size that seemed to be resting after a long journey. And of all the ships in sight, near and far, each was provided with a man, the man without whom the finest ship is a dead thing, a floating and purposeless log.

After his one glance at the roadstead he went on, since there was nothing to turn back for, and the time must be got through somehow. The avenues of big trees ran straight over the Esplanade, cutting each other at diverse angles, columnar below and luxuriant above. The interlaced boughs high up there seemed to slumber; not a leaf stirred overhead: and the reedy cast-iron lampposts in the middle of the road, gilt like sceptres, diminished in a long perspective, with their globes of white porcelain atop, resembling a barbarous decoration of ostriches' eggs displayed in a row. The flaming sky kindled a tiny crimson spark upon the glistening surface of each glassy shell.

With his chin sunk a little, his hands behind his back, and the end of his stick marking the gravel with a faint wavering line at his heels, Captain Whalley reflected that if a ship without a man was like a body without a soul, a sailor without a ship was of not much more account in this world than an aimless log adrift upon the sea. The log* might be sound enough by itself, tough of fibre, and hard to destroy—but what of that! And a sudden sense of irremediable idleness weighted his feet like a great fatigue.

A succession of open carriages came bowling along the newly opened sea-road. You could see across the wide grass-plots the discs of vibration made by the spokes. The bright domes of the parasols swayed lightly outwards like full-blown blossoms on the rim of a vase; and the quiet sheet of dark-blue water, crossed by a bar of purple, made a background for the spinning wheels and the high action of the horses, whilst the turbaned heads of the Indian servants elevated above the line of the sea horizon glided rapidly on the paler blue of the sky. In an open space near the little bridge each turn-out* trotted smartly in a wide curve away from the sunset; then pulling up sharp, entered the main alley in a long slow-moving file with the great red stillness of the sky at the back. The trunks of mighty trees stood all touched with red on the same side, the air seemed aflame under the high foliage, the very ground under the hoofs of the horses was red. The wheels turned solemnly; one after another the sunshades drooped, folding their colours like gorgeous flowers shutting their petals at the end of the day. In the whole half-mile of human beings no voice uttered a distinct word, only a faint thudding noise went on mingled with slight jingling sounds, and the motionless heads and shoulders of men and women sitting in couples emerged stolidly above the lowered hoods—as if wooden. But one carriage and pair coming late did not join the line.

It fled along in a noiseless roll; but on entering the avenue one of the dark bays snorted, arching his neck and shying against the steel-tipped pole; a flake of foam fell from the bit upon the point of a satiny shoulder, and the dusky face of the coachman leaned forward at once over the hands taking a fresh grip of the reins. It was a long dark-green landau,* having a dignified and buoyant motion between the sharply curved C-springs,* and a sort of strictly official majesty in its supreme elegance. It seemed more roomy than is usual, its horses seemed slightly bigger, the appointments a shade more perfect, the servants perched somewhat higher on the box. The dresses of three women—two young and pretty, and one, handsome, large, of mature age—seemed to fill completely the shallow body of the carriage. The fourth face was that of a man, heavy lidded, distinguished and sallow, with a sombre, thick, iron-grey imperial* and moustaches, which somehow had the air of solid appendages. His Excellency—*

The rapid motion of that one equipage* made all the others appear utterly inferior, blighted, and reduced to crawl painfully at a snail's pace. The landau distanced the whole file in a sort of sustained rush; the features of the occupant whirling out of sight left behind an impression of fixed stares and impassive vacancy; and after it had vanished in full flight as it were, notwithstanding the long line of vehicles hugging the curb at a walk, the whole lofty vista of the avenue seemed to lie open and emptied of life in the enlarged impression of an august solitude.

Captain Whalley had lifted his head to look, and his mind, disturbed in its meditation, turned with wonder (as men's minds will do) to matters of no importance. It struck him that it was to this port, where he had just sold his last ship, that he had come with the very first he had ever owned, and with his head full of a plan for opening a new trade with a distant part of the Archipelago.* The then governor had given him no end of encouragement. No Excellency he—this Mr. Denham—this governor with his jacket off; a man who tended night and day, so to speak, the growing prosperity of the settlement with the self-forgetful devotion of a nurse for a child she loves; a lone bachelor who lived as in a camp with the few servants and his three dogs in what was called then the Government Bungalow:

a low-roofed structure on the half-cleared slope of a hill, with a new flagstaff in front and a police orderly on the verandah. He remembered toiling up that hill under a heavy sun for his audience; the unfurnished aspect of the cool shaded room; the long table covered at one end with piles of papers, and with two guns, a brass telescope, a small bottle of oil with a feather stuck in the neck at the other—and the flattering attention given to him by the man in power. It was an undertaking full of risk he had come to expound, but a twenty minutes' talk in the Government Bungalow on the hill had made it go smoothly from the start. And as he was retiring Mr. Denham, already seated before the papers, called out after him, "Next month the *Dido** starts for a cruise that way, and I shall request her captain officially to give you a look in and see how you get on." The *Dido* was one of the smart frigates* on the China station—and five-and-thirty years make a big slice of time. Five-and-thirty years ago an enterprise like his had for the colony enough importance to be looked after by a Queen's ship. A big slice of time. Individuals were of some account then. Men like himself; men, too, like poor Evans, for instance, with his red face, his coal-black whiskers, and his restless eyes, who had set up the first patent slip* for repairing small ships, on the edge of the forest, in a lonely bay three miles up the coast. Mr. Denham had encouraged that enterprise too, and yet somehow poor Evans had ended by dying at home deucedly hard up. His son, they said, was squeezing oil out of cocoa-nuts for a living on some God-forsaken islet of the Indian Ocean; but it was from that patent slip in a lonely wooded bay that had sprung the workshops of the Consolidated Docks Company, with its three graving basins* carved out of solid rock, its wharves, its jetties,* its electric-light plant, its steam-power houses—with its gigantic sheer-legs,* fit to lift the heaviest weight ever carried afloat, and whose head could be seen like the top of a queer white monument peeping over bushy points of land and sandy promontories,* as you approached the New Harbour from the west.

There had been a time when men counted: there were not so many carriages in the colony then, though Mr. Denham, he fancied, had a buggy. And Captain Whalley seemed to be swept out of the great avenue by the swirl of a mental backwash. He remembered muddy shores, a harbour without quays,* the one solitary wooden pier (but that was a public work) jutting out crookedly, the first coal-sheds erected on Monkey Point, that caught fire* mysteriously and smouldered for days, so that amazed ships came into a roadstead full of sulphurous smoke, and the sun hung blood-red at midday. He remembered the things, the faces, and something more besides—like the faint flavour of a cup quaffed to the bottom, like a subtle sparkle of the air that was not to be found in the atmosphere of to-day.

In this evocation, swift and full of detail like a flash of magnesium light into the niches of a dark memorial hall, Captain Whalley contemplated things once important, the efforts of small men, the growth of a great place, but now robbed of all consequence by the greatness of accomplished facts, by hopes greater still; and they gave him for a moment such an almost physical grip upon time, such a comprehension of our unchangeable feelings, that he stopped short, struck the ground with his stick, and ejaculated mentally, "What the devil am I doing here!" He seemed lost in a sort of surprise; but he heard his name called out in wheezy tones once, twice—and turned on his heels slowly.

He beheld then, waddling towards him autocratically, a man of an old-fashioned and gouty aspect, with hair as white as his own, but with shaved, florid cheeks, wearing a necktie—almost a neckcloth—whose stiff ends projected far beyond his chin; with round legs, round arms, a round body, a round face—generally producing the effect of his short figure having been distended by means of an air-pump as much as the seams of his clothing would stand. This was the Master-Attendant* of the port. A master-attendant is a superior sort of harbour-master; a person, out in the East, of some consequence in his sphere; a Government official, a magistrate for the waters of the port, and possessed of vast but ill-defined disciplinary authority over seamen of all classes. This particular Master-Attendant was reported to consider it miserably inadequate, on the ground that it did not include the power of life and death. This was a jocular exaggeration. Captain Eliott was fairly satisfied with his position, and nursed no inconsiderable sense of such power as he had. His conceited and tyrannical disposition did not allow him to let it dwindle in his hands for want of use. The uproarious, choleric frankness of his comments on people's character and conduct caused him to be feared at bottom; though in conversation many pretended not to mind him in the least, others would only smile sourly at the mention of his name, and there were even some who dared to pronounce him "a meddlesome old ruffian." But for almost all of them one of Captain Eliott's outbreaks was nearly as distasteful to face as a chance of annihilation.

V

As soon as he had come up quite close he said, mouthing in a growl—

"What's this I hear, Whalley? Is it true you're selling the *Fair Maid*?"

Captain Whalley, looking away, said the thing was done—money had been paid that morning; and the other expressed at once his approbation of such an extremely sensible proceeding. He had got out of his trap to stretch his legs, he explained, on his way home to dinner. Sir Frederick* looked well at the end of his time. Didn't he?

Captain Whalley could not say; had only noticed the carriage going past.

The Master-Attendant, plunging his hands into the pockets of an alpaca jacket* inappropriately short and tight for a man of his age and appearance, strutted with a slight limp, and with his head reaching only to the shoulder of Captain Whalley, who walked easily, staring straight before him. They had been good comrades years ago, almost intimates. At the time when Whalley commanded the renowned *Condor*, Eliott had charge of the nearly as famous *Ringdove** for the same owners; and when the appointment of Master-Attendant was created, Whalley would have been the only other serious candidate. But Captain Whalley, then in the prime of life, was resolved to serve no one but his own auspicious Fortune. Far away, tending his hot irons,* he was glad to hear the other had been successful. There was a worldly suppleness in bluff Ned Eliott that would serve him well in that sort of official appointment. And they were so dissimilar at bottom that as they came slowly to the end of the avenue before the Cathedral, it had never come into Whalley's head that he might have been in that man's place—provided for to the end of his days.

The sacred edifice, standing in solemn isolation amongst the converging avenues of enormous trees, as if to put grave thoughts of heaven into the hours of ease, presented a closed Gothic portal* to the light and glory of the west. The glass of the rosace above the ogive* glowed like fiery coal in the deep carvings of a wheel of stone. The two men faced about.

"I'll tell you what they ought to do next, Whalley," growled Captain Eliott suddenly.

"Well?"

"They ought to send a real live lord out here when Sir Frederick's time is up. Eh?"

Captain Whalley perfunctorily did not see why a lord of the right sort should not do as well as anyone else. But this was not the other's point of view.

"No, no. Place runs itself. Nothing can stop it now. Good enough for a lord," he growled in short sentences. "Look at the changes in our time. We need a lord here now. They have got a lord in Bombay."*

He dined once or twice every year at the Government House— a many-windowed, arcaded palace upon a hill laid out in roads and gardens. And lately he had been taking about a duke in his Master-Attendant's steam-launch to visit the harbour improvements. Before that he had "most obligingly" gone out in person to pick out a good berth for the ducal yacht. Afterwards he had an invitation to lunch on board. The duchess herself lunched with them. A big woman with a red face. Complexion quite sunburnt. He should think ruined. Very gracious manners. They were going on to Japan. . . .

He ejaculated these details for Captain Whalley's edification, pausing to blow out his cheeks as if with a pent-up sense of importance, and repeatedly protruding his thick lips till the blunt crimson end of his nose seemed to dip into the milk of his moustache. The place ran itself; it was fit for any lord; it gave no trouble except in its Marine department—in its Marine department he repeated twice, and after a heavy snort began to relate how the other day her Majesty's Consul-General in French Cochin-China* had cabled to him—in his official capacity—asking for a qualified man to be sent over to take charge of a Glasgow ship whose master had died in Saigon.

"I sent word of it to the officers' quarters in the Sailors' Home,"* he continued, while the limp in his gait seemed to grow more accentuated with the increasing irritation of his voice. "Place's full of them. Twice as many men as there are berths going in the local trade. All hungry for an easy job. Twice as many—and—What d'you think, Whalley? . . ."

He stopped short; his hands clenched and thrust deeply downwards, seemed ready to burst the pockets of his jacket. A slight sigh escaped Captain Whalley.

"Hey? You would think they would be falling over each other. Not a bit of it. Frightened to go home. Nice and warm out here to lie about a verandah waiting for a job. I sit and wait in my office. Nobody. What did they suppose? That I was going to sit there like a dummy with the Consul-General's cable before me? Not likely. So I looked up a list of them I keep by me and sent word for Hamilton*—the worst loafer of them all—and just made him go. Threatened to instruct the steward of the Sailors' Home to have him turned out neck and crop.* He did not think the berth was good enough—if—you—please. 'I've your little records by me,' said I. 'You came ashore here eighteen months ago, and you haven't done six months' work since. You are in debt for your board now at the Home, and I suppose you reckon the Marine Office will pay in the end. Eh? So it shall; but if you don't take this chance, away you go to England, assisted passage, by the first homeward steamer that comes along. You are no better than a pauper. We don't want any white paupers here.' I scared him. But look at the trouble all this gave me."

"You would not have had any trouble," Captain Whalley said almost involuntarily, "if you had sent for me."*

Captain Eliott was immensely amused; he shook with laughter as he walked. But suddenly he stopped laughing. A vague recollection had crossed his mind. Hadn't he heard it said at the time of the Travancore and Deccan smash that poor Whalley had been cleaned out completely. "Fellow's hard up, by heavens!" he thought; and at once he cast a sidelong upward glance at his companion. But Captain Whalley was smiling austerely straight before him, with a carriage of the head inconceivable in a penniless man—and he became reassured. Impossible. Could not have lost everything. That ship had been only a hobby of his. And the reflection that a man who had confessed to receiving that very morning a presumably large sum of money was not likely to spring upon him a demand for a small loan put him entirely at his ease again. There had come a long pause in their talk, however, and not knowing how to begin again, he growled out soberly, "We old fellows ought to take a rest now."

"The best thing for some of us would be to die at the oar," Captain Whalley said negligently.

"Come, now. Aren't you a bit tired by this time of the whole show?" muttered the other sullenly.

"Are you?"

Captain Eliott was. Infernally tired. He only hung on to his berth so long in order to get his pension on the highest scale before he went home. It would be no better than poverty, anyhow; still, it was the only thing between him and the workhouse. And he had a family. Three girls, as Whalley knew. He gave "Harry, old boy," to understand that these three girls were a source of the greatest anxiety and worry to him. Enough to drive a man distracted.

"Why? What have they been doing now?" asked Captain Whalley with a sort of amused absent-mindedness.

"Doing! Doing nothing. That's just it. Lawn-tennis and silly novels from morning to night. . . ."

If one of them at least had been a boy. But all three! And, as ill-luck would have it, there did not seem to be any decent young fellows left in the world. When he looked around in the club he saw only a lot of conceited popinjays* too selfish to think of making a good woman happy. Extreme indigence stared him in the face with all that crowd to keep at home. He had cherished the idea of building himself a little house in the country—in Surrey—to end his days in, but he was afraid it was out of the question, . . . and his staring eyes rolled upwards with such a pathetic anxiety that Captain Whalley charitably nodded down at him, restraining a sort of sickening desire to laugh.

"You must know what it is yourself, Harry. Girls are the very devil for worry and anxiety."

"Ay! But mine is doing well," Captain Whalley pronounced slowly, staring to the end of the avenue.

The Master-Attendant was glad to hear this. Uncommonly glad. He remembered her well. A pretty girl she was.

Captain Whalley, stepping out carelessly, assented as if in a dream. "She was pretty."

The procession of carriages was breaking up.

One after another they left the file to go off at a trot, animating the vast avenue with their scattered life and movement; but soon the aspect of dignified solitude returned and took possession of the straight wide road. A syce* in white stood at the head of a Burmah pony* harnessed to a varnished two-wheel cart; and the whole thing waiting by the curb seemed no bigger than a child's toy forgotten under the soaring trees. Captain Eliott waddled up to it and made as if to clamber in, but refrained; and keeping one hand resting easily on the shaft, he changed the conversation from his pension, his daughters, and his poverty back again to the only other topic in the world—the Marine Office, the men and the ships of the port.

He proceeded to give instances of what was expected of him; and his thick voice drowsed in the still air like the obstinate droning of an enormous bumble-bee. Captain Whalley did not know what was the force or the weakness that prevented him from saying good-night and walking away. It was as though he had been too tired to make the effort. How queer. More queer than any of Ned's instances. Or was it that overpowering sense of idleness alone that made him stand there and listen to these stories. Nothing very real had ever troubled Ned Eliott; and gradually he seemed to detect deep in, as if wrapped up in the gross wheezy rumble, something of the clear hearty voice of the young captain of the *Ringdove*. He wondered if he too had changed to the same extent; and it seemed to him that the voice of his old chum had not changed so very much—that the man was the same. Not a bad fellow the pleasant, jolly Ned Eliott, friendly, well up to his business—and always a bit of a humbug. He remembered how he used to amuse his poor wife. She could read him like an open book. When the *Condor* and the *Ringdove* happened to be in port together, she would frequently ask him to bring Captain Eliott to dinner. They had not met often since those old days. Not once in five years, perhaps. He regarded from under his white eyebrows this man he could not bring himself to take into his confidence at this juncture; and the other went on with his intimate outpourings, and as remote from his hearer as though he had been talking on a hill-top a mile away.

He was in a bit of a quandary now as to the steamer *Sofala*. Ultimately every hitch in the port came into his hands to undo. They would miss him when he was gone in another eighteen months, and most likely some retired naval officer had been pitchforked into the appointment—a man that would understand nothing and care less. That steamer was a coasting craft having a steady trade connection as far north as Tenasserim;* but the trouble was she could get no captain to take her on her regular trip. Nobody would go in her. He really had no power, of course, to order a man to take a job. It was all very well to stretch a point on the demand of a consul-general, but . . .

"What's the matter with the ship?" Captain Whalley interrupted in measured tones.

"Nothing's the matter. Sound old steamer. Her owner has been in my office this afternoon tearing his hair."

"Is he a white man?" asked Whalley in an interested voice.

"He calls himself a white man," answered the Master-Attendant scornfully; "but if so, it's just skin-deep and no more. I told him that to his face too."

"But who is he, then?"

"He's the chief engineer of her. See that, Harry?"

"I see," Captain Whalley said thoughtfully. "The engineer. I see."

How the fellow came to be a shipowner at the same time was quite a tale. He came out third* in a home ship nearly fifteen years ago, Captain Eliott remembered, and got paid off after a bad sort of row both with his skipper and his chief. Anyway, they seemed jolly glad to get rid of him at all costs. Clearly a mutinous sort of chap. Well, he remained out here, a perfect nuisance, everlastingly shipped and unshipped, unable to keep a berth very long; pretty nigh went through every engine-room afloat belonging to the colony. Then suddenly, "What do you think happened, Harry?"

Captain Whalley, who seemed lost in a mental effort as of doing a sum in his head, gave a slight start. He really couldn't imagine. The Master-Attendant's voice vibrated dully with hoarse emphasis. The man actually had the luck to win the second prize in the Manilla lottery.* All these engineers and officers of ships took tickets in that gamble. It seemed to be a perfect mania with them all.

Everybody expected now that he would take himself off home with his money, and go to the devil in his own way. Not at all. The *Sofala*, judged too small and not quite modern enough for the sort of trade she was in, could be got for a moderate price from her owners, who had ordered a new steamer from Europe. He rushed in and bought her. This man had never given any signs of that sort of mental intoxication the mere fact of getting hold of a large sum of money may produce—not till he got a ship of his own; but then he went off his balance all at once: came bouncing into the Marine Office on some transfer business, with his hat hanging over his left eye and switching a little cane in his hand, and told each one of the clerks separately that "Nobody could put him out now. It was his turn. There was no one over him on earth, and there never would be either." He swaggered and strutted between the desks, talking at the top of his voice, and trembling like a leaf all the while, so that the current business of the office was suspended for the time he was in there, and everybody in the big room stood open-mouthed looking at his antics. Afterwards he could be seen during the hottest hours of the day with his face as red as fire rushing along up and down the quays to look at his ship from different points of view: he seemed inclined to stop every stranger he came across just to let them know "that there would be no longer anyone over him; he had bought a ship; nobody on earth could put him out of his engine-room now."

Good bargain as she was, the price of the *Sofala* took up pretty near all the lottery-money. He had left himself no capital to work with. That did not matter so much, for these were the halcyon days of steam coasting trade, before some of the home shipping firms had thought of establishing local fleets to feed their main lines. These, when once organized, took the biggest slices out of that cake, of course; and by-and-by a squad of confounded German tramps* turned up east of Suez Canal and swept up all the crumbs. They prowled on the cheap to and fro along the coast and between the islands, like a lot of sharks in the water ready to snap up anything you let drop. And then the high old times were over for good; for years the *Sofala* had made no more, he judged, than a fair living. Captain Eliott looked upon it as his duty in every way to assist an English ship to hold her own; and it stood to reason that if for want of a captain the *Sofala* began to miss her trips she would very soon lose her trade. There was the quandary. The man was too impracticable. "Too much of a beggar on horseback* from the first," he explained. "Seemed to grow worse as the time went on. In the last three years he's run through eleven skippers; he had tried every single man here, outside of the regular lines. I had warned him before that this would not do. And now, of course, no one will look at the *Sofala*. I had one or two men up at my office and talked to them; but, as they said to me, what was the good of taking the berth to lead a regular dog's life for a month and then get the sack at the end of the first trip? The fellow, of course, told me it was all nonsense; there has been a plot hatching for years against him. And now it had come. All the horrid sailors in the port had conspired to bring him to his knees, because he was an engineer."

Captain Eliott emitted a throaty chuckle.

"And the fact is, that if he misses a couple more trips he need never trouble himself to start again. He won't find any cargo in his old trade. There's too much competition nowadays for people to keep their stuff lying about for a ship that does not turn up when she's expected. It's a bad lookout for him. He swears he will shut himself on board and starve to death in his cabin rather than sell her—even if he could find a buyer. And that's not likely in the least. Not even the Japs would give her insured value for her. It isn't like selling sailing-ships. Steamers do get out of date, besides getting old."

"He must have laid by a good bit of money though," observed Captain Whalley quietly.

The Harbour-master puffed out his purple cheeks to an amazing size.

"Not a stiver,* Harry. Not—a—single—sti-ver."

He waited; but as Captain Whalley, stroking his beard slowly, looked down on the ground without a word, he tapped him on the forearm, tiptoed, and said in a hoarse whisper—

"The Manilla lottery has been eating him up."

He frowned a little, nodding in tiny affirmative jerks. They all were going in for it; a third of the wages paid to ships' officers ("in my port," he snorted) went to Manilla. It was a mania. That fellow Massy had been bitten by it like the rest of them from the first; but after winning once he seemed to have persuaded himself he had only to try again to get another big prize. He had taken dozens and scores of tickets for every drawing since. What with this vice and his ignorance of affairs, ever since he had improvidently bought that steamer he had been more or less short of money.

This, in Captain Eliott's opinion, gave an opening for a sensible sailor-man with a few pounds to step in and save that fool from the consequences of his folly. It was his craze to quarrel with his captains. He had had some really good men too, who would have been too glad to stay if he would only let them. But no. He seemed to think he was no owner unless he was kicking somebody out in the morning and having a row with the new man in the evening. What was wanted for him was a master with a couple of hundred or so to take an interest in the ship on proper conditions. You don't discharge a man for no fault, only because of the fun of telling him to pack up his traps* and go ashore, when you know that in that case you are bound to buy back his share. On the other hand, a fellow with an interest in the ship is not likely to throw up his job in a huff about a trifle. He had told Massy that. He had said: "'This won't do, Mr. Massy. We are getting very sick of you here in the Marine Office. What you must do now is to try whether you could get a sailor to join you as partner. That seems to be the only way.' And that was sound advice, Harry."

Captain Whalley, leaning on his stick, was perfectly still all over, and his hand, arrested in the act of stroking, grasped his whole beard. And what did the fellow say to that?

The fellow had the audacity to fly out at the Master-Attendant. He had received the advice in a most impudent manner. "I didn't come here to be laughed at," he had shrieked. "I appeal to you as an Englishman and a shipowner brought to the verge of ruin by an illegal conspiracy of your beggarly sailors, and all you condescend to do for me is to tell me to go and get a partner!" . . . The fellow had presumed to stamp with rage on the floor of the private office. Where was he going to get a partner? Was he being taken for a fool? Not a single one of that contemptible lot ashore at the "Home" had twopence in his pocket to bless himself with. The very native curs in the bazaar knew that much. . . . "And it's true enough, Harry," rumbled Captain Eliott judicially. "They are much more likely one and all to owe money to the Chinamen in Denham Road for the clothes on their backs. 'Well,' said I, 'you make too much noise over it for my taste, Mr. Massy. Good morning.' He banged the door after him; he dared to bang my door, confound his cheek!"

The head of the Marine department was out of breath with indignation; then recollecting himself as it were, "I'll end by being late to dinner—yarning with you here . . . wife doesn't like it."

He clambered ponderously into the trap; leaned out sideways, and only then wondered wheezily what on earth Captain Whalley could have been doing with himself of late. They had had no sight of each other for years and years till the other day when he had seen him unexpectedly in the office.

What on earth . . .

Captain Whalley seemed to be smiling to himself in his white beard.

"The earth is big," he said vaguely.

The other, as if to test the statement, stared all round from his driving-seat. The Esplanade was very quiet; only from afar, from very far, a long way from the seashore, across the stretches of grass, through the long ranges of trees, came faintly the toot—toot—toot of the cable car beginning to roll before the empty peristyle* of the Public Library on its three-mile journey to the New Harbour Docks.

"Doesn't seem to be so much room on it," growled the Master-Attendant, "since these Germans came along shouldering us at every turn. It was not so in our time."

He fell into deep thought, breathing stertorously, as though he had been taking a nap open-eyed. Perhaps he too, on his side, had detected in the silent pilgrim-like figure, standing there by the wheel, like an arrested wayfarer, the buried lineaments of the features belonging to the young captain of the *Condor*. Good fellow—Harry Whalley—never very talkative. You never knew what he was up to—a bit too off-hand with people of consequence, and apt to take a wrong view of a fellow's actions. Fact was he had a too good opinion of himself. He would have liked to tell him to get in and drive him home to dinner. But one never knew. Wife would not like it.

"And it's funny to think, Harry," he went on in a big, subdued drone, "that of all the people on it there seems only you and I left to remember this part of the world as it used to be . . ."

He was ready to indulge in the sweetness of a sentimental mood had it not struck him suddenly that Captain Whalley, unstirring and without a word, seemed to be awaiting something—perhaps expecting . . . He gathered the reins at once and burst out in bluff, hearty growls—

"Ha! My dear boy. The men we have known—the ships we've sailed—ay! and the things we've done . . ."

The pony plunged—the syce skipped out of the way. Captain Whalley raised his arm.

"Good-bye."

VI

THE sun had set. And when, after drilling a deep hole with his stick, he moved from that spot the night had massed its army of shadows under the trees. They filled the eastern ends of the avenues as if only waiting the signal for a general advance upon the open spaces of the world; they were gathering low between the deep stone-faced banks of the canal. The Malay prau, half-concealed under the arch of the bridge, had not altered its position a quarter of an inch. For a long time Captain Whalley stared down over the parapet, till at last the floating immobility of that beshrouded thing seemed to grow upon him into something inexplicable and alarming. The twilight abandoned the zenith; its reflected gleams left the world below, and the water of the canal seemed to turn into pitch. Captain Whalley crossed it.

The turning to the right, which was his way to his hotel, was only a very few steps farther. He stopped again (all the houses of the sea-front were shut up, the quayside was deserted, but for one or two figures of natives walking in the distance) and began to reckon the amount of his bill. So many days in the hotel at so many dollars a day. To count the days he used his fingers: plunging one hand into his pocket, he jingled a few silver coins. All right for three days more; and then, unless something turned up, he must break into the five hundred—Ivy's money—invested in her father. It seemed to him that the first meal coming out of that reserve would choke him—for certain. Reason was of no use. It was a matter of feeling. His feelings had never played him false.

He did not turn to the right. He walked on, as if there still had been a ship in the roadstead to which he could get himself pulled off in the evening. Far away, beyond the houses, on the slope of an indigo prom-ontory closing the view of the quays, the slim column of a factory-chimney smoked quietly straight up into the clear air. A Chinaman, curled down in the stern of one of the half-dozen sampans* floating off the end of the jetty, caught sight of a beckoning hand. He jumped up, rolled his pigtail* round his head swiftly, tucked in two rapid movements his wide dark trousers high up his yellow thighs, and by a single, noiseless, finlike stir of the oars, sheered the sampan along-side the steps with the ease and precision of a swimming fish.

"*Sofala*," articulated Captain Whalley from above; and the Chinaman, a new emigrant probably, stared upwards with a tense attention as if waiting to see the queer word fall visibly from the white man's lips. "*Sofala*," Captain Whalley repeated; and suddenly his heart failed him. He paused. The shores, the islets, the high ground, the low points, were dark: the horizon had grown sombre; and across the eastern sweep of the shore the white obelisk,* marking the landing-place of the telegraph-cable, stood like a pale ghost on the beach before the dark spread of uneven roofs, intermingled with palms, of the native town. Captain Whalley began again.

"*Sofala*. Savee *So-fa-la*, John?"*

This time the Chinaman made out that bizarre sound, and grunted his assent uncouthly, low down in his bare throat. With the first yellow twinkle of a star that appeared like the head of a pin stabbed deep into the smooth, pale, shimmering fabric of the sky, the edge of a keen chill seemed to cleave through the warm air of the earth. At the moment of stepping into the sampan to go and try for the command of the *Sofala* Captain Whalley shivered a little.

When on his return he landed on the quay again Venus,* like a choice jewel set low on the hem of the sky, cast a faint gold trail behind him upon the roadstead, as level as a floor made of one dark and polished stone. The lofty vaults of the avenues were black—all black overhead—and the porcelain globes on the lamp-posts resembled egg-shaped pearls, gigantic and luminous, displayed in a row whose farther end seemed to sink in the distance, down to the level of his knees. He put his hands behind his back. He would now consider calmly the discretion of it before saying the final word to-morrow. His feet scrunched the gravel loudly—the discretion of it. It would have been easier to appraise had there been a workable alternative. The honesty of it was indubitable: he meant well by the fellow; and periodically his shadow leaped up intense by his side on the trunks of the trees, to lengthen itself, oblique and dim, far over the grass—repeating his stride.

The discretion of it. Was there a choice? He seemed already to have lost something of himself; to have given up to a hungry spectre something of his truth and dignity in order to live. But his life was necessary. Let poverty do its worst in exacting its toll of humiliation. It was certain that Ned Eliott had rendered him, without knowing it, a service for which it would have been impossible to ask. He hoped Ned would not think there had been something underhand in his action. He supposed that now when he heard of it he would understand—or perhaps he would only think Whalley an eccentric old fool. What would have been the good of telling him—any more than of blurting the whole tale to that man Massy? Five hundred pounds ready to invest. Let him make the best of that. Let him wonder. You want a captain—I want a ship. That's enough. B-r-r-r-r. What a disagreeable impression that empty, dark, echoing steamer had made upon him. . . .

A laid-up steamer was a dead thing and no mistake; a sailing-ship* somehow seems always ready to spring into life with the breath of the incorruptible heaven; but a steamer, thought Captain Whalley, with her fires out, without the warm whiffs from below meeting you on her decks, without the hiss of steam, the clangs of iron in her breast—lies there as cold and still and pulseless as a corpse.

In the solitude of the avenue, all black above and lighted below, Captain Whalley, considering the discretion of his course, met, as it were incidentally, the thought of death. He pushed it aside with dislike and contempt. He almost laughed at it; and in the unquenchable vitality of his age only thought with a kind of exultation how little he needed to keep body and soul together. Not a bad investment for the poor woman this solid carcass of her father. And for the rest—in case of anything—the agreement should be clear: the whole five hundred to be paid back to her integrally within three months. Integrally. Every penny. He was not to lose any of her money whatever else had to go— a little dignity—some of his self-respect. He had never before allowed anybody to remain under any sort of false impression as to himself. Well, let that go—for her sake. After all, he had never said anything misleading—and Captain Whalley felt himself corrupt to the marrow of his bones. He laughed a little with the intimate scorn of his worldly prudence. Clearly, with a fellow of that sort, and in the peculiar relation they were to stand to each other, it would not have done to blurt out everything. He did not like the fellow. He did not like his spells of fawning loquacity and bursts of resentfulness. In the end—a poor devil. He would not have liked to stand in his shoes. Men were not evil, after all. He did not like his sleek hair, his queer way of standing at right angles, with his nose in the air, and glancing along his shoulder at you. No. On the whole, men were not bad—they were only silly or unhappy.

Captain Whalley had finished considering the discretion of that step—and there was the whole long night before him. In the full light his long beard would glisten like a silver breastplate covering his heart; in the spaces between the lamps his burly figure passed less distinct, loomed very big, wandering, and mysterious. No; there was not much real harm in men: and all the time a shadow marched with him, slanting on his left hand—which in the East is a presage of evil.*

"Can you make out the clump of palms yet, Serang?" asked Captain Whalley from his chair on the bridge of the *Sofala* approaching the bar of Batu Beru.*

"No, Tuan.* By-and-by see." The old Malay, in a blue dungaree suit, planted on his bony dark feet under the bridge awning,* put his hands behind his back and stared ahead out of the innumerable wrinkles at the corners of his eyes.

Captain Whalley sat still, without lifting his head to look for himself. Three years—thirty-six times. He had made these palms thirty-six times from the southward. They would come into view at the proper time. Thank God, the old ship made her courses and distances trip after trip, as correct as clockwork. At last he murmured again—

"In sight yet?"

"The sun makes a very great glare, Tuan."

"Watch well, Serang."

"Ya,* Tuan."

A white man had ascended the ladder from the deck noiselessly, and had listened quietly to this short colloquy. Then he stepped out on the bridge and began to walk from end to end, holding up the long cherrywood stem of a pipe. His black hair lay plastered in long lanky wisps across the bald summit of his head; he had a furrowed brow, a yellow complexion, and a thick shapeless nose. A scanty growth of whisker did not conceal the contour of his jaw. His aspect was of brooding care; and sucking at a curved black mouthpiece, he presented such a heavy overhanging profile that even the Serang could not help reflecting sometimes upon the extreme unloveliness of some white men.

Captain Whalley seemed to brace himself up in his chair, but gave no recognition whatever to his presence. The other puffed jets of smoke; then suddenly—

"I could never understand that new mania of yours of having this Malay here for your shadow, partner."

Captain Whalley got up from the chair in all his imposing stature and walked across to the binnacle,* holding such an unswerving course that the other had to back away hurriedly, and remained as if intimidated, with the pipe trembling in his hand. "Walk over me now," he muttered in a sort of astounded and discomfited whisper. Then slowly and distinctly he said—

"I—am—not—dirt." And then added defiantly, "As you seem to think."

The Serang jerked out—

"See the palms now, Tuan."

Captain Whalley strode forward to the rail; but his eyes, instead of going straight to the point, with the assured keen glance of a sailor, wandered irresolutely in space, as though he, the discoverer of new routes, had lost his way upon this narrow sea.

Another white man, the mate, came up on the bridge. He was tall, young, lean, with a moustache like a trooper, and something malicious in the eye. He took up a position beside the engineer. Captain Whalley, with his back to them, inquired—

"What's on the log?"

"Eighty-five," answered the mate quickly, and nudged the engineer with his elbow.

Captain Whalley's muscular hands squeezed the iron rail with an extraordinary force; his eyes glared with an enormous effort; he knitted his eyebrows, the perspiration fell from under his hat,—and in a faint voice he murmured, "Steady her, Serang—when she is on the proper bearing."

The silent Malay stepped back, waited a little, and lifted his arm warningly to the helmsman. The wheel revolved rapidly to meet the swing of the ship. Again the mate nudged the engineer. But Massy turned upon him.

"Mr. Sterne," he said violently, "let me tell you—as a shipowner—that you are no better than a confounded fool."

VII

STERNE went down smirking and apparently not at all disconcerted, but the engineer Massy remained on the bridge, moving about with uneasy self-assertion. Everybody on board was his inferior—everyone without exception. He paid their wages and found them in their food. They ate more of his bread and pocketed more of his money than they were worth; and they had no care in the world, while he alone had to meet all the difficulties of shipowning. When he contemplated his position in all its menacing entirety, it seemed to him that he had been for years the prey of a band of parasites: and for years he had scowled at everybody connected with the *Sofala* except, perhaps, at the Chinese firemen who served to get her along. Their use was manifest: they were an indispensable part of the machinery of which he was the master.

When he passed along his decks he shouldered those he came across brutally; but the Malay deck hands had learned to dodge out of his way. He had to bring himself to tolerate them because of the necessary manual labour of the ship which must be done. He had to struggle and plan and scheme to keep the *Sofala* afloat—and what did he get for it? Not even enough respect. They could not have given him enough of that if all their thoughts and all their actions had been directed to that end. The vanity of possession, the vainglory of power, had passed away by this time, and there remained only the material embarrassments, the fear of losing that position which had turned out not worth having, and an anxiety of thought which no abject subservience of men could repay.

He walked up and down. The bridge was his own after all. He had paid for it; and with the stem of the pipe in his hand he would stop short at times as if to listen with a profound and concentrated attention to the deadened beat of the engines (his own engines) and the slight grinding of the steering chains upon the continuous low wash of water alongside. But for these sounds, the ship might have been lying as still as if moored to a bank, and as silent as if abandoned by every living soul; only the coast, the low coast of mud and mangroves with the three palms in a bunch at the back, grew slowly more distinct in its long straight line, without a single feature to arrest attention. The native passengers of the *Sofala* lay about on mats under the awnings; the smoke of her funnel seemed the only sign of her life and connected with her gliding motion in a mysterious manner.

Captain Whalley on his feet, with a pair of binoculars in his hand and the little Malay Serang at his elbow, like an old giant attended by a wizened pigmy, was taking her over the shallow water of the bar.

This submarine ridge of mud, scoured by the stream out of the soft bottom of the river and heaped up far out on the hard bottom of the sea, was difficult to get over. The alluvial coast* having no distinguishing marks, the bearings of the crossing-place had to be taken from the shape of the mountains inland. The guidance of a form flattened and uneven at the top like a grinder tooth,* and of another smooth, saddle-backed summit,* had to be searched for within the great unclouded glare that seemed to shift and float like a dry fiery mist, filling the air, ascending from the water, shrouding the distances, scorching to the eye. In this veil of light the near edge of the shore alone stood out almost coal-black with an opaque and motionless solidity. Thirty miles away the serrated range of the interior stretched across the horizon, its outlines and shades of blue, faint and tremulous like a background painted on airy gossamer on the quivering fabric of an impalpable curtain let down to the plain of alluvial soil; and the openings of the estuary appeared, shining white, like bits of silver let into the square pieces snipped clean and sharp out of the body of the land bordered with mangroves.

On the forepart of the bridge the giant and the pigmy muttered to each other frequently in quiet tones. Behind them Massy stood sideways with an expression of disdain and suspense on his face. His globular eyes were perfectly motionless, and he seemed to have forgotten the long pipe he held in his hand.

On the fore-deck below the bridge, steeply roofed with the white slopes of the awnings, a young lascar* seaman had clambered outside the rail. He adjusted quickly a broad band of sail canvas under his armpits, and throwing his chest against it, leaned out far over the water. The sleeves of his thin cotton shirt, cut off close to the shoulder, bared his brown arm of full rounded form and with a satiny skin like a woman's. He swung it rigidly with the rotary and menacing action of a slinger: the 14-lb. weight hurtled circling in the air, then suddenly flew ahead as far as the curve of the bow.* The wet thin line swished like scratched silk running through the dark fingers of the man, and the plunge of the lead close to the ship's side made a vanishing silvery scar upon the golden glitter; then after an interval the voice of the young Malay uplifted and long-drawn declared the depth of the water in his own language.

"Tiga stengah," he cried after each splash and pause, gathering the line busily for another cast. "Tiga stengah," which means three fathom* and a half. For a mile or so from seaward there was a uniform depth of water right up to the bar. "Half-three. Half-three. Half-three,"—and his modulated cry, returned leisurely and monotonous, like the repeated call of a bird, seemed to float away in sunshine and disappear in the spacious silence of the empty sea and of a lifeless shore lying open, north and south, east and west, without the stir of a single cloud-shadow or the whisper of any other voice.

The owner-engineer of the *Sofala* remained very still behind the two seamen of different race, creed, and colour; the European with the time-defying vigour of his old frame, the little Malay, old, too, but slight and shrunken like a withered brown leaf blown by a chance wind under the mighty shadow of the other. Very busy looking forward at the land, they had not a glance to spare; and Massy, glaring at them from behind, seemed to resent their attention to their duty like a personal slight upon himself.

This was unreasonable; but he had lived in his own world of unreasonable resentments for many years. At last, passing his moist palm over the rare lanky wisps of coarse hair on the top of his yellow head, he began to talk slowly.

"A leadsman,* you want! I suppose that's your correct mail-boat style. Haven't you enough judgment to tell where you are by looking at the land? Why, before I had been a twelvemonth in the trade I was up to that trick—and I am only an engineer. I can point to you from here where the bar is, and I could tell you besides that you are as likely as not to stick her in the mud in about five minutes from now; only you would call it interfering, I suppose. And there's that written agreement of ours, that says I mustn't interfere."

His voice stopped. Captain Whalley, without relaxing the set severity of his features, moved his lips to ask in a quick mumble—

"How near, Serang?"

"Very near now, Tuan," the Malay muttered rapidly.

"Dead slow," said the Captain aloud in a firm tone.

The Serang snatched at the handle of the telegraph.* A gong clanged down below. Massy with a scornful snigger walked off and put his head down the engine-room skylight.

"You may expect some rare fooling with the engines, Jack,"* he bellowed. The space into which he stared was deep and full of gloom; and the grey gleams of steel down there seemed cool after the intense glare of the sea around the ship. The air, however, came up clammy and hot on his face. A short hoot on which it would have been impossible to put any sort of interpretation came from the bottom cavernously. This was the way in which the second engineer answered his chief.

He was a middle-aged man with an inattentive manner, and apparently wrapped up in such a taciturn concern for his engines that he seemed to have lost the use of speech. When addressed directly his only answer would be a grunt or a hoot, according to the distance. For all the years he had been in the *Sofala* he had never been known to exchange as much as a frank Good-morning with any of his shipmates. He did not seem aware that men came and went in the world; he did not seem to see them at all. Indeed he never recognized his ship mates on shore. At table (the four white men of the *Sofala* messed* together) he sat looking into his plate dispassionately, but at the end of the meal would jump up and bolt down below as if a sudden thought had impelled him to rush and see whether somebody had not stolen the engines while he dined. In port at the end of the trip he went ashore regularly, but no one knew where he spent his evenings or in what manner. The local coasting fleet had preserved a wild and incoherent tale of his infatuation for the wife of a sergeant in an Irish infantry regiment. The regiment, however, had done its turn of garrison duty there ages before, and was gone somewhere to the other side of the earth, out of men's knowledge. Twice or perhaps three times in the course of the year he would take too much to drink. On these occasions he returned on board at an earlier hour than usual; ran across the deck balancing himself with his spread arms like a tight-rope walker; and locking the door of his cabin, he would converse and argue with himself the livelong night in an amazing variety of tones; storm, sneer, and whine with an inexhaustible persistence. Massy in his berth next door, raising himself on his elbow, would discover that his second had remembered the name of every white man that had passed through the *Sofala* for years and years back. He remembered the names of men that had died, that had gone home, that had gone to America: he remembered in his cups* the names of men whose connection with the ship had been so short that Massy had almost forgotten its circumstances and could barely recall their faces. The inebriated voice on the other side of the bulkhead commented upon them all with an extraordinary and ingenious venom of scandalous inventions. It seems they had all offended him in some way, and in return he had found them all out. He muttered darkly; he laughed sardonically; he crushed them one after another; but of his chief, Massy, he babbled with an envious and naïve admiration. Clever scoundrel! Don't meet the likes of him every day. Just look at him. Ha! Great! Ship of his own. Wouldn't catch *him* going wrong. No fear—the beast! And Massy, after listening with a gratified smile to these artless tributes to his greatness, would begin to shout, thumping at the bulkhead with both fists—

"Shut up, you lunatic! Won't you let me go to sleep, you fool!"

But a half smile of pride lingered on his lips; outside the solitary lascar told off* for night duty in harbour, perhaps a youth fresh from a forest village, would stand motionless in the shadows of the deck listening to the endless drunken gabble. His heart would be thumping with breathless awe of white men: the arbitrary and obstinate men who pursue inflexibly their incomprehensible purposes,—beings with weird intonations in the voice, moved by unaccountable feelings, actuated by inscrutable motives.

VIII

FOR a while after his second's answering hoot Massy hung over the engine-room gloomily. Captain Whalley, who, by the power of five hundred pounds, had kept his command for three years, might have been suspected of never having seen that coast before. He seemed unable to put down his glasses, as though they had been glued under his contracted eyebrows. This settled frown gave to his face an air of invincible and just severity; but his raised elbow trembled slightly, and the perspiration poured from under his hat as if a second sun had suddenly blazed up at the zenith by the side of the ardent still globe already there, in whose blinding white heat the earth whirled and shone like a mote of dust.

From time to time, still holding up his glasses, he raised his other hand to wipe his streaming face. The drops rolled down his cheeks, fell like rain upon the white hairs of his beard, and brusquely, as if guided by an uncontrollable and anxious impulse, his arm reached out to the stand of the engine-room telegraph.

The gong clanged down below. The balanced vibration of the dead-slow speed ceased together with every sound and tremor in the ship, as if the great stillness that reigned upon the coast had stolen in through her sides of iron and taken possession of her innermost recesses. The illusion of perfect immobility seemed to fall upon her from the luminous blue dome without a stain arching over a flat sea without a stir. The faint breeze she had made for herself expired, as if all at once the air had become too thick to budge; even the slight hiss of the water on her stem died out. The narrow, long hull, carrying its way without a ripple, seemed to approach the shoal* water of the bar by stealth. The plunge of the lead with the mournful, mechanical cry of the lascar came at longer and longer intervals; and the men on her bridge seemed to hold their breath. The Malay at the helm looked fixedly at the compass card,* the Captain and the Serang stared at the coast.

Massy had left the skylight, and, walking flat-footed, had returned softly to the very spot on the bridge he had occupied before. A slow, lingering grin exposed his set of big white teeth: they gleamed evenly in the shade of the awning like the keyboard of a piano in a dusky room.

At last, pretending to talk to himself in excessive astonishment, he said not very loud—

"Stop the engines now. What next, I wonder?"

He waited, stooping from the shoulders, his head bowed, his glance oblique. Then raising his voice a shade—

"If I dared make an absurd remark I would say that you haven't the stomach to . . ."

But a yelling spirit of excitement, like some frantic soul wandering unsuspected in the vast stillness of the coast, had seized upon the body of the lascar at the lead. The languid monotony of his sing-song changed to a swift, sharp clamour. The weight flew after a single whir, the line whistled, splash followed splash in haste. The water had shoaled, and the man, instead of the drowsy tale of fathoms, was calling out the soundings in feet.

"Fifteen feet. Fifteen, fifteen! Fourteen, fourteen . . ."

Captain Whalley lowered the arm holding the glasses. It descended slowly as if by its own weight; no other part of his towering body stirred; and the swift cries with their eager warning note passed him by as though he had been deaf.

Massy, very still, and turning an attentive ear, had fastened his eyes upon the silvery, close-cropped back of the steady old head. The ship herself seemed to be arrested but for the gradual decrease of depth under her keel.*

"Thirteen feet . . . Thirteen! Twelve!" cried the leadsman anxiously below the bridge. And suddenly the barefooted Serang stepped away noiselessly to steal a glance over the side.

Narrow of shoulder, in a suit of faded blue cotton, an old grey felt hat rammed down on his head, with a hollow in the nape of his dark neck, and with his slender limbs, he appeared from the back no bigger than a boy of fourteen. There was a childlike impulsiveness in the curiosity with which he watched the spread of the voluminous, yellowish convolutions rolling up from below to the surface of the blue water like massive clouds driving slowly upwards on the unfathomable sky. He was not startled at the sight in the least. It was not doubt, but the certitude* that the keel of the *Sofala* must be stirring the mud now, which made him peep over the side.

His peering eyes, set aslant in a face of the Chinese type, a little old face, immovable, as if carved in old brown oak, had informed him long before that the ship was not headed at the bar properly. Paid off from the *Fair Maid*, together with the rest of the crew, after the completion of the sale, he had hung, in his faded blue suit and floppy grey hat, about the doors of the Harbour Office, till one day, seeing Captain Whalley coming along to get a crew for the *Sofala*, he had put himself quietly in the way, with his bare feet in the dust and an upward mute glance. The eyes of his old commander had fallen on him favourably—it must have been an auspicious day—and in less than half an hour the white men in the "Ofiss"* had written his name on a document as Serang of the fire-ship* *Sofala*. Since that time he had repeatedly looked at that estuary, upon that coast, from this bridge and from this side of the bar. The record of the visual world fell through his eyes upon his unspeculating mind as on a sensitized plate* through the lens of a camera. His knowledge was absolute and precise; nevertheless, had he been asked his opinion, and especially if questioned in the downright, alarming manner of white men, he would have displayed the hesitation of ignorance. He was certain of his facts—but such a certitude counted for little against the doubt what answer would be pleasing. Fifty years ago, in a jungle village, and before he was a day old, his father (who died without ever seeing a white face) had had his nativity* cast by a man of skill and wisdom in astrology, because in the arrangement of the stars may be read the last word of human destiny. His destiny had been to thrive by the favour of various white men on the sea. He had swept the decks of ships, had tended their helms, had minded their stores, had risen at last to be a Serang; and his placid mind had remained as incapable of penetrating the simplest motives of those he served as they themselves were incapable of detecting* through the crust of the earth the secret nature of its heart, which may be fire or may be stone. But he had no doubt whatever that the *Sofala* was out of the proper track for crossing the bar at Batu Beru.

It was a slight error. The ship could not have been more than twice her own length too far to the northward; and a white man at a loss for a cause (since it was impossible to suspect Captain Whalley of blundering ignorance, of want of skill, or of neglect) would have been inclined to doubt the testimony of his senses. It was some such feeling that kept Massy motionless, with his teeth laid bare by an anxious grin. Not so the Serang. He was not troubled by any intellectual mistrust of his senses. If his captain chose to stir the mud it was well. He had known in his life white men indulge in outbreaks equally strange. He was only genuinely interested to see what would come of it. At last, apparently satisfied, he stepped back from the rail.

He had made no sound: Captain Whalley, however, seemed to have observed the movements of his Serang. Holding his head rigidly, he asked with a mere stir of his lips—

"Going ahead still, Serang?"

"Still going a little, Tuan," answered the Malay. Then added casually, "She is over."

The lead confirmed his words; the depth of water increased at every cast, and the soul of excitement departed suddenly from the lascar swung in the canvas belt over the *Sofala*'s side. Captain Whalley ordered the lead in, set the engines ahead without haste, and averting his eyes from the coast directed the Serang to keep a course for the middle of the entrance.

Massy brought the palm of his hand with a loud smack against his thigh.

"You grazed on the bar. Just look astern* and see if you didn't. Look at the track she left. You can see it plainly. Upon my soul, I thought you would! What made you do that? What on earth made you do that? I believe you are trying to scare me."

He talked slowly, as it were circumspectly, keeping his prominent black eyes on his captain. There was also a slight plaintive note in his rising choler, for, primarily, it was the clear sense of a wrong suffered undeservedly that made him hate the man who, for a beggarly five hundred pounds, claimed a sixth part of the profits under the three years' agreement. Whenever his resentment got the better of the awe the person of Captain Whalley inspired he would positively whimper with fury.

"You don't know what to invent to plague my life out of me. I would not have thought that a man of your sort would condescend . . ."

He paused, half hopefully, half timidly, whenever Captain Whalley made the slightest movement in the deck-chair, as though expecting to be conciliated by a soft speech or else rushed upon and hunted off the bridge.

"I am puzzled," he went on again, with the watchful unsmiling baring of his big teeth. "I don't know what to think. I do believe you are trying to frighten me. You very nearly planted her on the bar for at least twelve hours, besides getting the engines choked with mud. Ships can't afford to lose twelve hours on a trip nowadays—as you ought to know very well, and do know very well to be sure, only . . ."

His slow volubility, the sideways cranings of his neck, the black glances out of the very corners of his eyes, left Captain Whalley unmoved. He looked at the deck with a severe frown. Massy waited for some little time, then began to threaten plaintively.

"You think you've got me bound hand and foot in that agreement. You think you can torment me in any way you please. Ah! But remember it has another six weeks to run yet. There's time for me to dismiss you before the three years are out. You will do yet something that will give me the chance to dismiss you, and make you wait a twelvemonth for your money before you can take yourself off and pull out your five hundred, and leave me without a penny to get the new boilers for her. You gloat over that idea—don't you? I do believe you sit here gloating. It's as if I had sold my soul for five hundred pounds to be everlastingly damned in the end. . . ."

He paused, without apparent exasperation, then continued evenly—

". . . With the boilers worn out and the survey* hanging over my head, Captain Whalley—Captain Whalley, I say, what do you do with your money? You must have stacks of money somewhere—a man like you must. It stands to reason. I am not a fool, you know, Captain Whalley—partner."

Again he paused, as though he had done for good. He passed his tongue over his lips, gave a backward glance at the Serang conning the ship* with quiet whispers and slight signs of the hand. The wash of the propeller sent a swift ripple, crested with dark froth, upon a long flat spit of black slime. The *Sofala* had entered the river; the trail she had stirred up over the bar was a mile astern of her now, out of sight, had disappeared utterly; and the smooth, empty sea along the coast was left behind in the glittering desolation of sunshine. On each side of her, low down, the growth of sombre twisted mangroves covered the semi-liquid banks; and Massy continued in his old tone, with an abrupt start, as if his speech had been ground out of him, like the tune of a music-box, by turning a handle.

"Though if anybody ever got the best of me, it is you. I don't mind saying this. I've said it—there! What more can you want? Isn't that enough for your pride, Captain Whalley. You got over me from the first. It's all of a piece, when I look back at it. You allowed me to insert that clause about intemperance without saying anything, only looking very sick when I made a point of it going in black on white.* How could I tell what was wrong about you. There's generally something wrong somewhere. And, lo and behold! when you come on board it turns out that you've been in the habit of drinking nothing but water for years and years."

His dogmatic reproachful whine stopped. He brooded profoundly, after the manner of crafty and unintelligent men. It seemed inconceivable that Captain Whalley should not laugh at the expression of disgust that overspread the heavy, yellow countenance. But Captain Whalley never raised his eyes—sitting in his arm-chair, outraged, dignified, and motionless.

"Much good it was to me," Massy remonstrated monotonously, "to insert a clause for dismissal for intemperance against a man who drinks nothing but water. And you looked so upset, too, when I read my draft in the lawyer's office that morning, Captain Whalley—you looked so crestfallen, that I made sure I had gone home on your weak spot. A shipowner can't be too careful as to the sort of skipper he gets. You must have been laughing at me in your sleeve all the blessed time. . . . Eh? What are you going to say?"

Captain Whalley had only shuffled his feet slightly. A dull animosity became apparent in Massy's sideways stare.

"But recollect that there are other grounds of dismissal. There's habitual carelessness, amounting to incompetence—there's gross and persistent neglect of duty. I am not quite as big a fool as you try to make me out to be. You have been careless of late—leaving everything to that Serang. Why! I've seen you letting that old fool of a Malay take bearings for you, as if you were too big to attend to your work yourself. And what do you call that silly touch-and-go manner in which you took the ship over the bar just now? You expect me to put up with that?"

Leaning on his elbow against the ladder abaft the bridge, Sterne, the mate, tried to hear, blinking the while from the distance at the second engineer, who had come up for a moment, and stood in the engine-room companion. Wiping his hands on a bunch of cotton waste, he looked about with indifference to the right and left at the river banks slipping astern of the *Sofala* steadily.

Massy turned full at the chair. The character of his whine became again threatening.

"Take care. I may yet dismiss you and freeze to your money for a year. I may . . ."

But before the silent, rigid immobility of the man whose money had come in the nick of time to save him from utter ruin, his voice died out in his throat.

"Not that I want you to go," he resumed after a silence, and in an absurdly insinuating tone. "I want nothing better than to be friends and renew the agreement, if you will consent to find another couple of hundred to help with the new boilers, Captain Whalley. I've told you before. She must have new boilers; you know it as well as I do. Have you thought this over?"

He waited. The slender stem of the pipe with its bulky lump of a bowl at the end hung down from his thick lips. It had gone out. Suddenly he took it from between his teeth and wrung his hands slightly.

"Don't you believe me?" He thrust the pipe bowl into the pocket of his shiny black jacket.

"It's like dealing with the devil," he said. "Why don't you speak? At first you were so high and mighty with me I hardly dared to creep about my own deck. Now I can't get a word from you. You don't seem to see me at all. What does it mean? Upon my soul, you terrify me with this deaf and dumb trick.* What's going on in that head of yours? What are you plotting against me there so hard that you can't say a word? You will never make me believe that you—you—don't know where to lay your hands on a couple of hundred. You have made me curse the day I was born. . . ."

"Mr. Massy," said Captain Whalley suddenly, without stirring.

The engineer started violently.

"If that is so I can only beg you to forgive me."

"Starboard,"* muttered the Serang to the helmsman; and the *Sofala* began to swing round the bend into the second reach.

"Ough!" Massy shuddered. "You make my blood run cold. What made you come here? What made you come aboard that evening all of a sudden, with your high talk and your money—tempting me? I always wondered what was your motive? You fastened yourself on me to have easy times and grow fat on my life blood, I tell you. Was that it? I believe you are the greatest miser in the world, or else why . . ."

"No. I am only poor," interrupted Captain Whalley, stonily.

"Steady," murmured the Serang. Massy turned away with his chin on his shoulder.

"I don't believe it," he said in his dogmatic tone. Captain Whalley made no movement. "There you sit like a gorged vulture—exactly like a vulture."

He embraced the middle of the reach* and both the banks in one blank unseeing circular glance, and left the bridge slowly.

IX

ON turning to descend Massy perceived the head of Sterne the mate
loitering, with his sly confident smile, his red moustaches and blinking
eyes, at the foot of the ladder.

Sterne had been a junior in one of the larger shipping concerns
before joining the *Sofala*. He had thrown up his berth, he said, "on
general principles." The promotion in the employ was very slow, he
complained, and he thought it was time for him to try and get on a bit
in the world. It seemed as though nobody would ever die or leave the
firm; they all stuck fast in their berths till they got mildewed; he was
tired of waiting; and he feared that when a vacancy did occur the best
servants were by no means sure of being treated fairly. Besides, the
captain he had to serve under—Captain Provost—was an unaccountable sort of man, and, he fancied, had taken a dislike to him for some
reason or other. For doing rather more than his bare duty as likely as
not. When he had done anything wrong he could take a talking to, like
a man; but he expected to be treated like a man too, and not to be
addressed invariably as though he were a dog. He had asked Captain
Provost plump and plain to tell him where he was at fault, and Captain
Provost, in a most scornful way, had told him that he was a perfect
officer, and that if he disliked the way he was being spoken to there
was the gangway*—he could take himself off ashore at once. But
everybody knew what sort of man Captain Provost was. It was no use
appealing to the office. Captain Provost had too much influence in the
employ. All the same, they had to give him a good character. He made
bold to say there was nothing in the world against him, and, as he had
happened to hear that the mate of the *Sofala* had been taken to the
hospital that morning with a sunstroke, he thought there would be no
harm in seeing whether he would not do. . . .

He had come to Captain Whalley freshly shaved, red-faced, thin-
flanked, throwing out his lean chest; and had recited his little tale with
an open and manly assurance. Now and then his eyelids quivered
slightly, his hand would steal up to the end of the flaming moustache;
his eyebrows were straight, furry, of a chestnut colour, and the direct-
ness of his frank gaze seemed to tremble on the verge of impudence.
Captain Whalley had engaged him temporarily; then, the other man
having been ordered home by the doctors, he had remained for the
next trip, and then the next. He had now attained permanency, and

the performance of his duties was marked by an air of serious, single-minded application. Directly he was spoken to, he began to smile attentively, with a great deference expressed in his whole attitude; but there was in the rapid winking which went on all the time something quizzical, as though he had possessed the secret of some universal joke cheating all creation and impenetrable to other mortals.

Grave and smiling he watched Massy come down step by step; when the chief engineer had reached the deck he swung about, and they found themselves face to face. Matched as to height and utterly dissimilar, they confronted each other as if there had been something between them—something else than the bright strip of sunlight that, falling through the wide lacing of two awnings, cut crosswise the narrow planking of the deck and separated their feet as it were a stream; something profound and subtle and incalculable, like an unexpressed understanding, a secret mistrust, or some sort of fear.

At last Sterne, blinking his deep-set eyes and sticking forward his scraped, clean-cut chin, as crimson as the rest of his face, murmured—

"You've seen? He grazed! You've seen?"

Massy, contemptuous, and without raising his yellow, fleshy countenance, replied in the same pitch—

"Maybe. But if it had been you we would have been stuck fast in the mud."

"Pardon me, Mr. Massy. I beg to deny it. Of course a shipowner may say what he jolly well pleases on his own deck. That's all right; but I beg to . . ."

"Get out of my way!"

The other had a slight start, the impulse of suppressed indignation perhaps, but held his ground. Massy's downward glance wandered right and left, as though the deck all round Sterne had been bestrewn with eggs that must not be broken, and he had looked irritably for places where he could set his feet in flight. In the end he too did not move, though there was plenty of room to pass on.

"I heard you say up there," went on the mate—"and a very just remark it was too—that there's always something wrong. . . ."

"Eavesdropping is what's wrong with *you*, Mr. Sterne."

"Now, if you would only listen to me for a moment, Mr. Massy, sir, I could . . ."

"You are a sneak," interrupted Massy in a great hurry, and even managed to get so far as to repeat, "a common sneak," before the mate had broken in argumentatively—

"Now, sir, what is it you want? You want . . ."

"I want—I want," stammered Massy, infuriated and astonished—"I want. How do you know that I want anything? How dare you? . . . What do you mean? . . . What are you after—you . . ."

"Promotion." Sterne silenced him with a sort of candid bravado. The engineer's round soft cheeks quivered still, but he said quietly enough—

"You are only worrying my head off," and Sterne met him with a confident little smile.

"A chap in business I know (well up in the world he is now) used to tell me that this was the proper way. 'Always push on to the front,' he would say. 'Keep yourself well before your boss. Interfere whenever you get a chance. Show him what you know. Worry him into seeing you.' That was his advice. Now I know no other boss than you here. You are the owner, and no one else counts for *that* much in my eyes. See, Mr. Massy? I want to get on. I make no secret of it that I am one of the sort that means to get on. These are the men to make use of, sir. You haven't arrived at the top of the tree, sir, without finding that out—I daresay."

"Worry your boss in order to get on," mumbled Massy, as if awestruck by the irreverent originality of the idea. "I shouldn't wonder if this was just what the Blue Anchor* people kicked you out of the employ for. Is that what you call getting on? You shall get on in the same way here if you aren't careful—I can promise you."

At this Sterne hung his head, thoughtful, perplexed, winking hard at the deck. All his attempts to enter into confidential relations with his owner had led of late to nothing better than these dark threats of dismissal; and a threat of dismissal would check him at once into a hesitating silence as though he were not sure that the proper time for defying it had come. On this occasion he seemed to have lost his tongue for a moment, and Massy, getting in motion, heavily passed him by with an abortive attempt at shouldering. Sterne defeated it by stepping aside. He turned then swiftly, opening his mouth very wide as if to shout something after the engineer, but seemed to think better of it.

Always—as he was ready to confess—on the lookout for an opening to get on, it had become an instinct with him to watch the conduct of his immediate superiors for something "that one could lay hold of." It was his belief that no skipper in the world would keep his command for a day if only the owners could be "made to know." This romantic and naïve theory had led him into trouble more than once, but he remained incorrigible; and his character was so instinctively disloyal that whenever he joined a ship the intention of ousting his commander out of the berth and taking his place was always present at the back of his head, as a matter of course. It filled the leisure of his waking hours with the reveries of careful plans and compromising discoveries—the dreams of his sleep with images of lucky turns and favourable accidents. Skippers had been known to sicken and die at sea, than which nothing could be better to give a smart mate a chance of showing what he's made of. They also would tumble overboard sometimes: he had heard of one or two such cases. Others again . . . But, as it were constitutionally, he was faithful to the belief that the conduct of no single one of them would stand the test of careful watching by a man who "knew what's what" and who kept his eyes "skinned pretty well" all the time.

After he had gained a permanent footing on board the *Sofala* he allowed his perennial hope to rise high. To begin with, it was a great advantage to have an old man for captain: the sort of man besides who in the nature of things was likely to give up the job before long from one cause or another. Sterne was greatly chagrined, however, to notice that he did not seem anyway near being past his work yet. Still, these old men go to pieces all at once sometimes. Then there was the owner-engineer close at hand to be impressed by his zeal and steadiness. Sterne never for a moment doubted the obvious nature of his own merits (he was really an excellent officer); only, nowadays, professional merit alone does not take a man along fast enough. A chap must have some push in him, and must keep his wits at work too to help him forward. He made up his mind to inherit the charge of this steamer if it was to be done at all; not indeed estimating the command of the *Sofala* as a very great catch, but for the reason that, out East especially, to make a start is everything, and one command leads to another.

He began by promising himself to behave with great circumspection; Massy's sombre and fantastic humours intimidated him as being outside one's usual sea experience; but he was quite intelligent enough to realize almost from the first that he was there in the presence of an exceptional situation. His peculiar prying imagination penetrated it quickly; the feeling that there was in it an element which eluded his grasp exasperated his impatience to get on. And so one trip came to an end, then another, and he had begun his third before he saw an opening by which he could step in with any sort of effect. It had all been very queer and very obscure; something had been going on near him, as if separated by a chasm from the common life and the working routine of the ship, which was exactly like the life and the routine of any other coasting steamer of that class.

Then one day he made his discovery.

It came to him after all these weeks of watchful observation and puzzled surmises, suddenly, like the long-sought solution of a riddle that suggests itself to the mind in a flash. Not with the same authority, however. Great heavens! Could it be that? And after remaining thunderstruck for a few seconds he tried to shake it off with self-contumely, as though it had been the product of an unhealthy bias towards the Incredible, the Inexplicable, the Unheard-of—the Mad!

This—the illuminating moment—had occurred the trip before, on the return passage. They had just left a place of call on the mainland called Pangu;* they were steaming straight out of a bay. To the east a massive headland closed the view, with the tilted edges of the rocky strata showing through its ragged clothing of rank bushes and thorny creepers. The wind had begun to sing in the rigging; the sea along the coast, green and as if swollen a little above the line of the horizon, seemed to pour itself over, time after time, with a slow and thundering fall, into the shadow of the leeward cape;* and across the wide opening the nearest of a group of small islands stood enveloped in the hazy yellow light of a breezy sunrise; still farther out the hummocky tops of other islets peeped out motionless above the water of the channels between, scoured tumultuously by the breeze.

The usual track of the *Sofala* both going and returning on every trip led her for a few miles along this reef-infested region.* She followed a broad lane of water, dropping astern, one after another, these crumbs of the earth's crust resembling a squadron of dismasted hulks* run in disorder upon a foul ground of rocks and shoals. Some of these fragments of land appeared, indeed, no bigger than a stranded ship; others, quite flat, lay awash like anchored rafts, like ponderous, black rafts of stone; several, heavily timbered and round at the base, emerged in squat domes of deep green foliage that shuddered darkly all over to the flying touch of cloud shadows driven by the sudden gusts of the squally season. The thunderstorms of the coast broke frequently over that cluster; it turned then shadowy in its whole extent; it turned more dark, and as if more still in the play of fire; as if more impenetrably silent in the peals of thunder; its blurred shapes vanished—dissolving utterly at times in the thick rain—to reappear clear-cut and black in the stormy light against the grey sheet of the cloud—scattered on the slaty round table of the sea. Unscathed by storms, resisting the work of years, unfretted by the strife of the world, there it lay unchanged as on that day, four hundred years ago, when first beheld by Western eyes from the deck of a high-pooped caravel.*

It was one of these secluded spots that may be found on the busy sea, as on land you come sometimes upon the clustered houses of a hamlet* untouched by men's restlessness, untouched by their need, by their thought, and as if forgotten by time itself. The lives of uncounted generations had passed it by, and the multitudes of sea-fowl, urging their way from all the points of the horizon to sleep on the outer rocks of the group, unrolled the converging evolutions of their flight in long sombre streamers upon the glow of the sky. The palpitating cloud of their wings soared and stooped over the pinnacles of the rocks, over the rocks slender like spires, squat like martello towers;* over the pyramidal heaps like fallen ruins, over the lines of bald boulders showing like a wall of stones battered to pieces and scorched by lightning—with the sleepy, clear glimmer of water in every breach. The noise of their continuous and violent screaming filled the air.

This great noise would meet the *Sofala* coming up from Batu Beru; it would meet her on quiet evenings, a pitiless and savage clamour enfeebled by distance, the clamour of seabirds settling to rest, and struggling for a footing at the end of the day. No one noticed it especially on board; it was the voice of their ship's unerring landfall, ending the steady stretch of a hundred miles. She had made good her course, she had run her distance till the punctual islets began to emerge one by one, the points of rocks, the hummocks of earth . . . and the cloud of birds hovered—the restless cloud emitting a strident and cruel uproar, the sound of the familiar scene, the living part of the broken land beneath, of the outspread sea, and of the high sky without a flaw.

But when the *Sofala* happened to close with the land after sunset she would find everything very still there under the mantle of the night. All would be still, dumb, almost invisible—but for the blotting out of the low constellations occulted in turns behind the vague masses of the islets whose true outlines eluded the eye amongst the dark spaces of the heaven: and the ship's three lights, resembling three stars—the red and the green with the white above—her three lights, like three companion stars wandering on the earth, held their unswerving course for the passage at the southern end of the group. Sometimes there were human eyes open to watch them come nearer, traveling smoothly in the sombre void; the eyes of a naked fisherman in his canoe floating over a reef. He thought drowsily: "Ha! The fire-ship that once in every moon goes in and comes out of Pangu bay." More he did not know of her. And just as he had detected* the faint rhythm of the propeller beating the calm water a mile and a half away, the time would come for the *Sofala* to alter her course, the lights would swing off him their triple beam—and disappear.

A few miserable, half-naked families, a sort of outcast tribe of long-haired, lean, and wild-eyed people, strove for their living in this lonely wilderness of islets, lying like an abandoned outwork of the land at the gates of the bay. Within the knots and loops of the rocks the water rested more transparent than crystal under their crooked and leaky canoes, scooped out of the trunk of a tree: the forms of the bottom undulated slightly to the dip of a paddle; and the men seemed to hang in the air, they seemed to hang enclosed within the fibres of a dark, sodden log, fishing patiently in a strange, unsteady, pellucid, green air above the shoals.

Their bodies stalked brown and emaciated as if dried up in the sunshine; their lives ran out silently; the homes where they were born, went to rest, and died—flimsy sheds of rushes and coarse grass eked out with a few ragged mats—were hidden out of sight from the open sea. No glow of their household fires ever kindled for a seaman a red spark upon the blind night of the group: and the calms of the coast, the flaming long calms of the equator, the unbreathing, concentrated calms like the deep introspection of a passionate nature, brooded awfully for days and weeks together over the unchangeable inheritance of their children; till at last the stones, hot like live embers, scorched the naked sole, till the water clung warm, and sickly, and as if thickened, about the legs of lean men with girded loins, wading thigh-deep in the pale blaze of the shallows. And it would happen now and then that the *Sofala*, through some delay in one of the ports of call, would heave in sight making for Pangu bay as late as noonday.

Only a blurring cloud at first, the thin mist of her smoke would arise mysteriously from an empty point on the clear line of sea and sky. The taciturn fishermen within the reefs would extend their lean arms towards the offing;* and the brown figures stooping on the tiny beaches, the brown figures of men, women, and children grubbing in the sand in search of turtles' eggs, would rise up, crooked elbow aloft and hand over the eyes, to watch this monthly apparition glide straight on, swerve off—and go by. Their ears caught the panting of that ship; their eyes followed her till she passed between the two capes of the mainland going at full speed as though she hoped to make her way unchecked into the very bosom of the earth.

On such days the luminous sea would give no sign of the dangers lurking on both sides of her path. Everything remained still, crushed by the overwhelming power of the light; and the whole group, opaque in the sunshine,—the rocks resembling pinnacles, the rocks resembling spires, the rocks resembling ruins; the forms of islets resembling beehives, resembling mole-hills, the islets recalling the shapes of haystacks, the contours of ivy-clad towers,—would stand reflected together upside down in the unwrinkled water, like carved toys of ebony disposed on the silvered plate-glass of a mirror.

The first touch of blowing weather would envelop the whole at once in the spume of the windward breakers, as if in a sudden cloud-like burst of steam; and the clear water seemed fairly to boil in all the passages. The provoked sea outlined exactly in a design of angry foam the wide base of the group; the submerged level of broken waste and refuse left over from the building of the coast near by, projecting its dangerous spurs,* all awash, far into the channel, and bristling with wicked long spits often a mile long: with deadly spits made of froth and stones.

And even nothing more than a brisk breeze—as on that morning, the voyage before, when the *Sofala* left Pangu bay early, and Mr. Sterne's discovery was to blossom out like a flower of incredible and evil aspect from the tiny seed of instinctive suspicion,—even such a breeze had enough strength to tear the placid mask from the face of the sea. To Sterne, gazing with indifference, it had been like a revelation to behold for the first time the dangers marked by the hissing livid patches on the water as distinctly as on the engraved paper of a chart. It came into his mind that this was the sort of day most favourable for a stranger attempting the passage: a clear day, just windy enough for the sea to break on every ledge, buoying, as it were, the channel plainly to the sight; whereas during a calm you had nothing to depend on but the compass and the practised judgment of your eye. And yet the successive captains of the *Sofala* had had to take her through at night more than once. Nowadays you could not afford to throw away six or seven hours of a steamer's time. That you couldn't. But then use is everything, and with proper care . . . The channel was broad and safe enough; the main point was to hit upon the entrance correctly in the dark—for if a man got himself involved in that stretch of broken water over yonder he would never get out with a whole ship—if he ever got out at all.

This was Sterne's last train of thought independent of the great discovery. He had just seen to the securing of the anchor, and had remained forward idling away a moment or two. The captain was in charge on the bridge. With a slight yawn he had turned away from his survey of the sea and had leaned his shoulders against the fish davit.*

These, properly speaking, were the very last moments of ease he was to know on board the *Sofala*. All the instants that came after were to be pregnant with purpose and intolerable with perplexity. No more idle, random thoughts; the discovery would put them on the rack, till sometimes he wished to goodness he had been fool enough not to make it at all. And yet, if his chance to get on rested on the discovery of "something wrong," he could not have hoped for a greater stroke of luck.

X

THE knowledge was too disturbing, really. There was "something wrong" with a vengeance, and the moral certitude of it was at first simply frightful to contemplate. Sterne had been looking aft in a mood so idle, that for once he was thinking no harm of anyone. His captain on the bridge presented himself naturally to his sight. How insignificant, how casual was the thought that had started the train of discovery—like an accidental spark that suffices to ignite the charge of a tremendous mine!

Caught under by the breeze, the awnings of the foredeck* bellied upwards and collapsed slowly, and above their heavy flapping the grey stuff of Captain Whalley's roomy coat fluttered incessantly around his arms and trunk. He faced the wind in full light, with his great silvery beard blown forcibly against his chest; the eyebrows overhung heavily the shadows whence his glance appeared to be staring ahead piercingly. Sterne could just detect the twin gleam of the whites shifting under the shaggy arches of the brow. At short range these eyes, for all the man's affable manner, seemed to look you through and through. Sterne never could defend himself from that feeling when he had occasion to speak with his captain. He did not like it. What a big heavy man he appeared up there, with that little shrimp of a Serang in close attendance—as was usual in this extraordinary steamer! Confounded absurd custom that. He resented it. Surely the old fellow could have looked after his ship without that loafing native at his elbow. Sterne wriggled his shoulders with disgust. What was it? Indolence or what?

That old skipper must have been growing lazy for years. They all grew lazy out East here (Sterne was very conscious of his own unimpaired activity); they got slack all over. But he towered very erect on the bridge; and quite low by his side, as you see a small child looking over the edge of a table, the battered soft hat and the brown face of the Serang peeped over the white canvas screen of the rail.

No doubt the Malay was standing back, nearer to the wheel; but the great disparity of size in close association amused Sterne like the observation of a bizarre fact in nature. They were as queer fish out of the sea as any in it.

He saw Captain Whalley turn his head quickly to speak to his Serang; the wind whipped the whole white mass of the beard sideways. He would be directing the chap to look at the compass for him, or what not. Of course. Too much trouble to step over and see for himself. Sterne's scorn for that bodily indolence which overtakes white men in the East increased on reflection. Some of them would be utterly lost if they hadn't all these natives at their beck and call; they grew perfectly shameless about it too. He was not of that sort, thank God! It wasn't in him to make himself dependent for his work on any shrivelled-up little Malay like that. As if one could ever trust a silly native for anything in the world! But that fine old man thought differently, it seems. There they were together, never far apart;

a pair of them, recalling to the mind an old whale attended by a little pilot-fish.*

The fancifulness of the comparison made him smile. A whale with an inseparable pilot-fish! That's what the old man looked like; for it could not be said he looked like a shark, though Mr. Massy had called him that very name. But Mr. Massy did not mind what he said in his savage fits. Sterne smiled to himself—and gradually the ideas evoked by the sound, by the imagined shape of the word pilot-fish; the ideas of aid, of guidance needed and received, came uppermost in his mind: the word pilot awakened the idea of trust, of dependence, the idea of welcome, clear-eyed help brought to the seaman groping for the land in the dark: groping blindly* in fogs: feeling their way in the thick weather of the gales that, filling the air with a salt mist blown up from the sea, contract the range of sight on all sides to a shrunken horizon that seems within reach of the hand.

A pilot sees better than a stranger, because his local knowledge, like a sharper vision, completes the shapes of things hurriedly glimpsed; penetrates the veils of mist spread over the land by the storms of the sea; defines with certitude the outlines of a coast lying under the pall of fog, the forms of landmarks half buried in a starless night as in a shallow grave. He recognizes because he already knows. It is not to his far-reaching eye but to his more extensive knowledge that the pilot looks for certitude; for this certitude of the ship's position on which may depend a man's good fame and the peace of his conscience, the justification of the trust deposited in his hands, with his own life too, which is seldom wholly his to throw away, and the humble lives of others rooted in distant affections, perhaps, and made as weighty as the lives of kings by the burden of the awaiting mystery. The pilot's knowledge brings relief and certitude to the commander of a ship; the Serang, however, in his fanciful suggestion of a pilot-fish attending a whale, could not in any way be credited with a superior knowledge. Why should he have it? These two men had come on that run together—the white and the brown—on the same day: and of course a white man would learn more in a week than the best native would in a month. He was made to stick to the skipper as though he were of some use—as the pilot-fish, they say, is to the whale. But how—it was very marked—how? A pilot-fish—a pilot—a . . . But if not superior knowledge then . . .

Sterne's discovery was made. It was repugnant to his imagination, shocking to his ideas of honesty, shocking to his conception of mankind. This enormity affected one's outlook on what was possible in this world: it was as if for instance the sun had turned blue, throwing a new and sinister light on men and nature. Really in the first moment he had felt sickish, as though he had got a blow below the belt: for a second the very colour of the sea seemed changed—appeared queer to his wandering eye; and he had a passing, unsteady sensation in all his limbs as though the earth had started turning the other way.

A very natural incredulity succeeding this sense of upheaval brought a measure of relief. He had gasped; it was over. But afterwards during all that day sudden paroxysms of wonder would come over him in the midst of his occupations. He would stop and shake his head. The revolt of his incredulity had passed away almost as quick as the first emotion of discovery, and for the next twenty-four hours he had no sleep. That would never do. At meal-times (he took the foot of the table set up for the white men on the bridge) he could not help losing himself in a fascinated contemplation of Captain Whalley opposite. He watched the deliberate upward movements of the arm; the old man put his food to his lips as though he never expected to find any taste in his daily bread, as though he did not know anything about it. He fed himself like a somnambulist. "It's an awful sight," thought Sterne; and he watched the long period of mournful, silent immobility, with a big brown hand lying loosely closed by the side of the plate, till he noticed the two engineers to the right and left looking at him in astonishment. He would close his mouth in a hurry then, and lowering his eyes, wink rapidly at his plate. It was awful to see the old chap sitting there; it was even awful to think that with three words he could blow him up sky-high. All he had to do was to raise his voice and pronounce a single short sentence, and yet that simple act seemed as impossible to attempt as moving the sun out of its place in the sky. The old chap could eat in his terrific mechanical way; but Sterne, from mental excitement, could not—not that evening, at any rate.

He had had ample time since to get accustomed to the strain of the meal-hours. He would never have believed it. But then use is everything; only the very potency of his success prevented anything resembling elation. He felt like a man who, in his legitimate search for a loaded gun to help him on his way through the world, chances to come upon a torpedo—upon a live torpedo with a shattering charge in its head and a pressure of many atmospheres in its tail. It is the sort of weapon to make its possessor careworn and nervous. He had no

mind to be blown up himself; and he could not get rid of the notion
that the explosion was bound to damage him too in some way.

This vague apprehension had restrained him at first. He was able
now to eat and sleep with that fearful weapon by his side, with the
conviction of its power always in mind. It had not been arrived at by
any reflective process; but once the idea had entered his head, the
conviction had followed overwhelmingly in a multitude of observed
little facts to which before he had given only a languid attention. The
abrupt and faltering intonations of the deep voice; the taciturnity put
on like an armour; the deliberate, as if guarded, movements; the long
immobilities, as if the man he watched had been afraid to disturb the
very air: every familiar gesture, every word uttered in his hearing,
every sigh overheard, had acquired a special significance, a confirma-
tory import.

Every day that passed over the *Sofala* appeared to Sterne simply
crammed full with proofs—with incontrovertible proofs. At night,
when off duty, he would steal out of his cabin in pyjamas (for more
proofs) and stand a full hour, perhaps, on his bare feet below the
bridge, as absolutely motionless as the awning stanchion* in its deck
socket near by. On the stretches of easy navigation it is not usual for
a coasting captain to remain on deck all the time of his watch. The
Serang keeps it for him as a matter of custom; in open water, on
a straight course, he is usually trusted to look after the ship by himself. But this old man seemed incapable of remaining quietly down
below. No doubt he could not sleep. And no wonder. This was also
a proof. Suddenly in the silence of the ship panting upon the still,
dark sea, Sterne would hear a low voice above him exclaiming
nervously—

"Serang!"

"Tuan!"

"You are watching the compass well?"

"Yes, I am watching, Tuan."

"The ship is making her course?"

"She is, Tuan. Very straight."

"It is well; and remember, Serang, that the order is that you are to
mind the helmsman and keep a lookout with care, the same as if
I were not on deck."

Then, when the Serang had made his answer, the low tones on the
bridge would cease, and everything round Sterne seemed to become

more still and more profoundly silent. Slightly chilled and with his back aching a little from long immobility, he would steal away to his room on the port side of the deck. He had long since parted with the last vestige of incredulity; of the original emotions, set into a tumult by the discovery, some trace of the first awe alone remained. Not the awe of the man himself—he could blow him up sky-high with six words—rather it was an awestruck indignation at the reckless perversity of avarice (what else could it be?), at the mad and sombre resolution that for the sake of a few dollars more seemed to set at naught the common rule of conscience and pretended to struggle against the very decree of Providence.

You could not find another man like this one in the whole round world—thank God. There was something devilishly dauntless in the character of such a deception which made you pause.

Other considerations occurring to his prudence had kept him tongue-tied from day to day. It seemed to him now that it would yet have been easier to speak out in the first hour of discovery. He almost regretted not having made a row at once. But then the very monstrosity of the disclosure . . . Why! He could hardly face it himself, let alone pointing it out to somebody else. Moreover, with a desperado of that sort one never knew. The object was not to get him out (that was as well as done already), but to step into his place. Bizarre as the thought seemed he might have shown fight. A fellow up to working such a fraud would have enough cheek for anything; a fellow that, as it were, stood up against God Almighty Himself. He was a horrid marvel—that's what he was: he was perfectly capable of brazening out the affair scandalously till he got him (Sterne) kicked out of the ship and everlastingly damaged his prospects in this part of the East. Yet if you want to get on something must be risked. At times Sterne thought he had been unduly timid of taking action in the past; and what was worse, it had come to this, that in the present he did not seem to know what action to take.

Massy's savage moroseness was too disconcerting. It was an incalculable factor of the situation. You could not tell what there was behind that insulting ferocity. How could one trust such a temper; it did not put Sterne in bodily fear for himself, but it frightened him exceedingly as to his prospects.

Though of course inclined to credit himself with exceptional powers of observation, he had by now lived too long with his discovery.

He had gone on looking at nothing else, till at last one day it occurred to him that the thing was so obvious that no one could miss seeing it. There were four white men in all on board the *Sofala*. Jack, the second engineer, was too dull to notice anything that took place out of his engine-room. Remained Massy—the owner—the interested person— nearly going mad with worry. Sterne had heard and seen more than enough on board to know what ailed him; but his exasperation seemed to make him deaf to cautious overtures. If he had only known it, there was the very thing he wanted. But how could you bargain with a man of that sort? It was like going into a tiger's den with a piece of raw meat in your hand. He was as likely as not to rend you for your pains. In fact, he was always threatening to do that very thing; and the urgency of the case, combined with the impossibility of handling it with safety, made Sterne in his watches below toss and mutter open-eyed in his bunk, for hours, as though he had been burning with fever.

Occurrences like the crossing of the bar just now were extremely alarming to his prospects. He did not want to be left behind by some swift catastrophe. Massy being on the bridge, the old man had to brace himself up and make a show, he supposed. But it was getting very bad with him, very bad indeed, now. Even Massy had been emboldened to find fault this time; Sterne, listening at the foot of the ladder, had heard the other's whimpering and artless denunciations. Luckily the beast was very stupid and could not see the why of all this. However, small blame to him; it took a clever man to hit upon the cause. Nevertheless, it was high time to do something. The old man's game could not be kept up for many days more.

"I may yet lose my life at this fooling—let alone my chance," Sterne mumbled angrily to himself, after the stooping back of the chief engineer had disappeared round the corner of the skylight. Yes, no doubt—he thought; but to blurt out his knowledge would not advance his prospects. On the contrary, it would blast them utterly as likely as not. He dreaded another failure. He had a vague conscious-ness of not being much liked by his fellows in this part of the world; inexplicably enough, for he had done nothing to them. Envy, he sup-posed. People were always down on a clever chap who made no bones about his determination to get on. To do your duty and count on the gratitude of that brute Massy would be sheer folly. He was a bad lot. Unmanly! A vicious man! Bad! Bad! A brute! A brute without a spark of anything human about him; without so much as simple curiosity even, or else surely he would have responded in some way to all these hints he had been given. . . . Such insensibility was almost mysterious. Massy's state of exasperation seemed to Sterne to have made him stupid beyond the ordinary silliness of shipowners.

Sterne, meditating on the embarrassments of that stupidity, forgot himself completely. His stony, unwinking stare was fixed on the planks of the deck.

The slight quiver agitating the whole fabric of the ship was more perceptible in the silent river, shaded and still like a forest path. The *Sofala*, gliding with an even motion, had passed beyond the coast-belt of mud and mangroves. The shores rose higher, in firm sloping banks, and the forest of big trees came down to the brink. Where the earth had been crumbled by the floods it showed a steep brown cut, denuding a mass of roots intertwined as if wrestling underground; and in the air, the interlaced boughs, bound and loaded with creepers, carried on the struggle for life,* mingled their foliage in one solid wall of leaves, with here and there the shape of an enormous dark pillar soaring, or a ragged opening, as if torn by the flight of a cannonball, disclosing the impenetrable gloom within, the secular* inviolable shade of the virgin forest. The thump of the engines reverberated regularly like the strokes of a metronome beating the measure of the vast silence, the shadow of the western wall had fallen across the river, and the smoke pouring backwards from the funnel eddied down behind the ship, spread a thin dusky veil over the sombre water, which, checked by the flood-tide, seemed to lie stagnant in the whole straight length of the reaches.

Sterne's body, as if rooted on the spot, trembled slightly from top to toe with the internal vibration of the ship; from under his feet came sometimes a sudden clang of iron, the noisy burst of a shout below; to the right the leaves of the tree-tops caught the rays of the low sun, and seemed to shine with a golden green light of their own shimmering around the highest boughs which stood out black against a smooth blue sky that seemed to droop over the bed of the river like the roof of a tent. The passengers for Batu Beru, kneeling on the planks, were engaged in rolling their bedding of mats busily; they tied up bundles, they snapped the locks of wooden chests. A pockmarked peddler of small wares threw his head back to drain into his throat the last drops out of an earthenware bottle before putting it away in a roll of blankets. Knots of traveling traders standing about the deck conversed in low tones; the followers of a small Rajah* from down the coast, broad-faced, simple young fellows in white drawers and round white cotton caps with their coloured sarongs* twisted across their bronze shoulders, squatted on their hams on the hatch, chewing betel* with bright red mouths as if they had been tasting blood. Their spears, lying piled up together within the circle of their bare toes, resembled a casual bundle of dry bamboos; a thin, livid Chinaman, with a bulky package wrapped up in leaves already thrust under his arm, gazed ahead eagerly; a wandering Kling* rubbed his teeth with a bit of wood, pouring over the side a bright stream of water out of his lips; the fat Rajah dozed in a shabby deck-chair,—and at the turn of every bend the two walls of leaves reappeared running parallel along the banks, with their impenetrable solidity fading at the top to a vaporous mistiness of countless slender twigs growing free, of young delicate branches shooting from the topmost limbs of hoary trunks, of feathery heads of climbers like delicate silver sprays standing up without a quiver. There was not a sign of a clearing anywhere; not a trace of human habitation, except when in one place, on the bare end of a low point under an isolated group of slender tree-ferns, the jagged, tangled remnants of an old hut on piles appeared with that peculiar aspect of ruined bamboo walls that look as if smashed with a club. Farther on, half hidden under the drooping bushes, a canoe containing a man and a woman, together with a dozen green cocoanuts in a heap, rocked helplessly after the *Sofala* had passed, like a navigating contrivance of venturesome insects, of travelling ants; while two glassy folds of water streaming away from each bow of the steamer across the whole width of the river ran with her up stream smoothly, fretting their outer ends into a brown whispering tumble of froth against the miry foot of each bank.

"I must," thought Sterne, "bring that brute Massy to his bearings.* It's getting too absurd in the end. Here's the old man up there buried in his chair—he may just as well be in his grave for all the use he'll ever be in the world—and the Serang's in charge. Because that's what he is. In charge. In the place that's mine by rights. I must bring that savage brute to his bearings. I'll do it at once, too . . ."

When the mate made an abrupt start, a little brown half-naked boy, with large black eyes, and the string of a written charm round his neck, became panic-struck at once. He dropped the banana he had been munching, and ran to the knee of a grave dark Arab in flowing robes, sitting like a Biblical figure, incongruously, on a yellow tin trunk corded with a rope of twisted rattan.* The father, unmoved, put out his hand to pat the little shaven poll* protectingly.

XI

STERNE crossed the deck upon the track of the chief engineer. Jack, the second, retreating backwards down the engine-room ladder, and still wiping his hands, treated him to an incomprehensible grin of white teeth out of his grimy hard face; Massy was nowhere to be seen. He must have gone straight into his berth. Sterne scratched at the door softly, then, putting his lips to the rose of the ventilator, said—

"I must speak to you, Mr. Massy. Just give me a minute or two."

"I am busy. Go away from my door."

"But pray, Mr. Massy . . ."

"You go away. D'you hear? Take yourself off altogether—to the other end of the ship—quite away . . ." The voice inside dropped low. "To the devil."

Sterne paused: then very quietly—

"It's rather pressing. When do you think you will be at liberty, sir?"

The answer to this was an exasperated "Never"; and at once Sterne, with a very firm expression of face, turned the handle.

Mr. Massy's stateroom*—a narrow, one-berth cabin—smelt strongly of soap, and presented to view a swept, dusted, unadorned neatness, not so much bare as barren, not so much severe as starved and lacking in humanity, like the ward of a public hospital, or rather (owing to the small size) like the clean retreat of a desperately poor but exemplary person. Not a single photograph frame ornamented the bulkheads; not a single article of clothing, not as much as a spare cap, hung from the brass hooks. All the inside was painted in one plain tint of pale blue; two big sea-chests in sailcloth covers and with iron padlocks fitted exactly in the space under the bunk. One glance was enough to embrace all the strip of scrubbed planks within the four unconcealed corners. The absence of the usual settee was striking; the teak-wood top of the washing-stand seemed hermetically closed, and so was the lid of the writing-desk, which protruded from the partition at the foot of the bed-place, containing a mattress as thin as a pancake under a threadbare blanket with a faded red stripe, and a folded mosquito-net against the nights spent in harbour. There was not a scrap of paper anywhere in sight, no boots on the floor, no litter of any sort, not a speck of dust anywhere; no traces of pipe-ash even, which, in a heavy smoker, was morally revolting, like a manifestation of extreme hypocrisy; and the bottom of the old wooden arm-chair (the only seat there), polished with much use, shone as if its shabbiness had been waxed. The screen of leaves on the bank, passing as if unrolled endlessly in the round opening of the port, sent a wavering network of light and shade into the place.

Sterne, holding the door open with one hand, had thrust in his head and shoulders. At this amazing intrusion Massy, who was doing absolutely nothing, jumped up speechless.

"Don't call names," murmured Sterne hurriedly. "I won't be called names. I think of nothing but your good, Mr. Massy."

A pause as of extreme astonishment followed. They both seemed to have lost their tongues. Then the mate went on with a discreet glibness.

"You simply couldn't conceive what's going on on board your ship. It wouldn't enter your head for a moment. You are too good—too—too upright, Mr. Massy, to suspect anybody of such a . . . It's enough to make your hair stand on end."

He watched for the effect: Massy seemed dazed, uncomprehending. He only passed the palm of his hand on the coal-black wisps plastered across the top of his head. In a tone suddenly changed to confidential audacity Sterne hastened on.

"Remember that there's only six weeks left to run . . ." The other was looking at him stonily . . . "so anyhow you shall require a captain for the ship before long."

Then only, as if that suggestion had scarified his flesh in the manner of red-hot iron, Massy gave a start and seemed ready to shriek. He contained himself by a great effort.

"Require a captain," he repeated with scathing slowness. "Who requires a captain? You dare to tell me that I need any of you humbugging* sailors to run my ship. You and your likes have been fattening on me for years. It would have hurt me less to throw my money overboard. Pam—pe—red us—e—less f-f-f-frauds. The old ship knows as much as the best of you." He snapped his teeth audibly and growled through them, "The silly law requires a captain."

Sterne had taken heart of grace meantime.

"And the silly insurance people too, as well," he said lightly. "But never mind that. What I want to ask is: Why shouldn't *I* do, sir? I don't say but you could take a steamer about the world as well as any of us sailors. I don't pretend to tell *you* that it is a very great trick . . ." He emitted a short, hollow guffaw, familiarly . . . "I didn't make the law—but there it is; and I am an active young fellow! I quite hold with your ideas; I know your ways by this time, Mr. Massy. I wouldn't try to give myself airs like that—that—er—lazy specimen of an old man up there."

He put a marked emphasis on the last sentence, to lead Massy away from the track in case . . . but he did not doubt of now holding his success. The chief engineer seemed nonplused,* like a slow man invited to catch hold of a whirligig* of some sort.

"What you want, sir, is a chap with no nonsense about him, who would be content to be your sailing-master. Quite right, too. Well, I am fit for the work as much as that Serang. Because that's what it amounts to. Do you know, sir, that a dam' Malay like a monkey is in charge of your ship—and no one else. Just listen to his feet pit-patting above us on the bridge—real officer in charge. He's taking her up the river while the great man is wallowing in the chair—perhaps asleep; and if he is, that would not make it much worse either—take my word for it."

He tried to thrust himself farther in. Massy, with lowered forehead, one hand grasping the back of the arm-chair, did not budge.

"You think, sir, that the man has got you tight in his agreement . . ." Massy raised a heavy snarling face at this . . . "Well, sir, one can't help hearing of it on board. It's no secret. And it has been the talk on shore for years; fellows have been making bets about it. No, sir! It's *you* who have got him at your mercy. You will say that you can't dismiss him for indolence. Difficult to prove in court, and so on. Why, yes. But if you say the word, sir, I can tell you something about his indolence that will give you the clear right to fire him out on the spot and put me in charge for the rest of this very trip—yes, sir, before we leave Batu Beru—and make him pay a dollar a day for his keep till we get back, if you like. Now, what do you think of that? Come, sir. Say the word. It's really well worth your while, and I am quite ready to take your bare word. A definite statement from you would be as good as a bond."

His eyes began to shine. He insisted. A simple statement,—and he thought to himself that he would manage somehow to stick in his berth as long as it suited him. He would make himself indispensable; the ship had a bad name in her port; it would be easy to scare the fellows off. Massy would have to keep him.

"A definite statement from me would be enough," Massy repeated slowly.

"Yes, sir. It would." Sterne stuck out his chin cheerily and blinked at close quarters with that unconscious impudence which had the power to enrage Massy beyond anything.

The engineer spoke very distinctly.

"Listen well to me, then, Mr. Sterne: I wouldn't—d'ye hear?— I wouldn't promise you the value of two pence for anything you can tell me."

He struck Sterne's arm away with a smart blow, and catching hold of the handle pulled the door to. The terrific slam darkened the cabin instantaneously to his eye as if after the flash of an explosion. At once he dropped into the chair. "Oh, no! You don't!" he whispered faintly.

The ship had in that place to shave the bank so close that the gigantic wall of leaves came gliding like a shutter against the port;* the darkness of the primeval forest seemed to flow into that bare cabin with the odour of rotting leaves, of sodden soil—the strong muddy smell of the living earth steaming uncovered after the passing of a deluge. The bushes swished loudly alongside; above there was a series of crackling sounds, with a sharp rain of small broken branches falling on the bridge; a creeper with a great rustle snapped on the head of a boat davit, and a long, luxuriant green twig actually whipped in and out of the open port, leaving behind a few torn leaves that remained suddenly at rest on Mr. Massy's blanket. Then, the ship sheering out in the stream, the light began to return but did not augment beyond a subdued clearness: for the sun was very low already, and the river, wending its sinuous course through a multitude of secular trees as if at the bottom of a precipitous gorge, had been already invaded by a deepening gloom—the swift precursor of the night.

"Oh, no, you don't!" murmured the engineer again. His lips trembled almost imperceptibly; his hands too, a little: and to calm himself he opened the writing-desk, spread out a sheet of thin greyish paper covered with a mass of printed figures and began to scan them attentively for the twentieth time this trip at least.

With his elbows propped, his head between his hands, he seemed to lose himself in the study of an abstruse problem in mathematics. It was the list of the winning numbers from the last drawing of the great lottery which had been the one inspiring fact of so many years of his existence. The conception of a life deprived of that periodical sheet of paper had slipped away from him entirely, as another man, according to his nature, would not have been able to conceive a world without fresh air, without activity, or without affection. A great pile of flimsy sheets had been growing for years in his desk, while the *Sofala*, driven by the faithful Jack, wore out her boilers in tramping up and down the Straits, from cape to cape, from river to river, from bay to bay; accumulating by that hard labour of an overworked, starved ship the blackened mass of these documents. Massy kept them under lock and key like a treasure. There was in them, as in the experience of life, the fascination of hope, the excitement of a half-penetrated mystery, the longing of a half-satisfied desire.

For days together, on a trip, he would shut himself up in his berth with them: the thump of the toiling engines pulsated in his ear; and he would weary his brain poring over the rows of disconnected figures, bewildering by their senseless sequence, resembling the hazards of destiny itself. He nourished a conviction that there must be some logic lurking somewhere in the results of chance. He thought he had seen its very form. His head swam; his limbs ached; he puffed at his pipe mechanically; a contemplative stupor would soothe the fretfulness of his temper, like the passive bodily quietude procured by a drug, while the intellect remains tensely on the stretch. Nine, nine, nought, four, two. He made a note. The next winning number of the great prize was forty-seven thousand and five. These numbers of course would have to be avoided in the future when writing to Manilla for the tickets. He mumbled, pencil in hand . . . "and five. Hm . . . hm." He wetted his finger: the papers rustled. Ha! But what's this? Three years ago, in the September drawing, it was number nine, nought, four, two that took the first prize. Most remarkable. There was a hint there of a definite rule! He was afraid of missing some recondite principle in the overwhelming wealth of his material. What could it be? and for half an hour he would remain dead still, bent low over the desk, without twitching a muscle. At his back the whole berth would be thick with a heavy body of smoke, as if a bomb had burst in there, unnoticed, unheard.

At last he would lock up the desk with the decision of unshaken confidence, jump and go out. He would walk swiftly back and forth

on that part of the foredeck which was kept clear of the lumber* and
of the bodies of the native passengers. They were a great nuisance, but
they were also a source of profit that could not be disdained. He
needed every penny of profit the *Sofala* could make. Little enough it
was, in all conscience! The incertitude of chance gave him no concern, since he had somehow arrived at the conviction that, in the
course of years, every number was bound to have his winning turn. It
was simply a matter of time and of taking as many tickets as he could
afford for every drawing. He generally took rather more; all the earnings of the ship went that way, and also the wages he allowed himself
as chief engineer. It was the wages he paid to others that he begrudged
with a reasoned and at the same time a passionate regret. He scowled
at the lascars with their deck brooms, at the quartermasters* rubbing
the brass rails with greasy rags; he was eager to shake his fist and roar
abuse in bad Malay at the poor carpenter—a timid, sickly, opium-
fuddled Chinaman, in loose blue drawers* for all costume, who
invariably dropped his tools and fled below, with streaming tail* and
shaking all over, before the fury of that "devil." But it was when he
raised up his eyes to the bridge where one of these sailor frauds was
always planted by law in charge of his ship that he felt almost dizzy
with rage. He abominated them all; it was an old feud, from the time
he first went to sea, an unlicked cub with a great opinion of himself,
in the engine-room. The slights that had been put upon him. The
persecutions he had suffered at the hands of skippers—of absolute
nobodies in a steamship after all. And now that he had risen to be
a shipowner they were still a plague to him: he had absolutely to pay
away precious money to the conceited useless loafers:*—As if a fully
qualified engineer—who was the owner as well—were not fit to be
trusted with the whole charge of a ship. Well! he made it pretty warm
for them; but it was a poor consolation. He had come in time to hate
the ship too for the repairs she required, for the coal-bills he had to
pay, for the poor beggarly freights she earned. He would clench his
hand as he walked and hit the rail a sudden blow, viciously, as though
she could be made to feel pain. And yet he could not do without her;
he needed her; he must hang on to her tooth and nail to keep his head
above water till the expected flood of fortune came sweeping up and
landed him safely on the high shore of his ambition.

It was now to do nothing, nothing whatever, and have plenty of
money to do it on. He had tasted of power, the highest form of it his

limited experience was aware of—the power of shipowning. What a deception! Vanity of vanities!* He wondered at his folly. He had thrown away the substance for the shadow. Of the gratification of wealth he did not know enough to excite his imagination with any visions of luxury. How could he—the child of a drunken boiler-maker—going straight from the workshop into the engine-room of a north-country collier!* But the notion of the absolute idleness of wealth he could very well conceive. He revelled in it, to forget his present troubles; he imagined himself walking about the streets of Hull* (he knew their gutters well as a boy) with his pockets full of sovereigns.* He would buy himself a house; his married sisters, their husbands, his old workshop chums, would render him infinite homage. There would be nothing to think of. His word would be law. He had been out of work for a long time before he won his prize, and he remembered how Carlo Mariani (commonly known as Paunchy Charley), the Maltese hotel-keeper at the slummy end of Denham Street, had cringed joyfully before him in the evening, when the news had come. Poor Charley, though he made his living by ministering to various abject vices, gave credit for their food to many a piece of white wreckage. He was naïvely overjoyed at the idea of his old bills being paid, and he reckoned confidently on a spell of festivities in the cavernous grog-shop* downstairs. Massy remembered the curious, respectful looks of the "trashy" white men in the place. His heart had swelled within him. Massy had left Charley's infamous den directly he had realized the possibilities open to him, and with his nose in the air. Afterwards the memory of these adulations was a great sadness.

This was the true power of money—and no trouble with it, nor any thinking required either. He thought with difficulty and felt vividly; to his blunt brain the problems offered by any ordered scheme of life seemed in their cruel toughness to have been put in his way by the obvious malevolence of men. As a shipowner everyone had conspired to make him a nobody. How could he have been such a fool as to purchase that accursed ship. He had been abominably swindled; there was no end to this swindling; and as the difficulties of his improvident ambition gathered thicker round him, he really came to hate everybody he had ever come in contact with. A temper naturally irritable and an amazing sensitiveness to the claims of his own personality had ended by making of life for him a sort of inferno*—a place where his lost soul had been given up to the torment of savage brooding.

But he had never hated anyone so much as that old man who had turned up one evening to save him from an utter disaster——from the conspiracy of the wretched sailors. He seemed to have fallen on board from the sky. His footsteps echoed on the empty steamer, and the strange deep-toned voice on deck repeating interrogatively the words, "Mr. Massy, Mr. Massy there?" had been startling like a wonder. And coming up from the depths of the cold engine-room, where he had been pottering dismally with a candle amongst the enormous shadows, thrown on all sides by the skeleton limbs of machinery, Massy had been struck dumb by astonishment in the presence of that imposing old man with a beard like a silver plate, towering in the dusk rendered lurid by the expiring flames of sunset.

"Want to see me on business? What business? I am doing no business. Can't you see that this ship is laid up?" Massy had turned at bay before the pursuing irony of his disaster. Afterwards he could not believe his ears. What was that old fellow getting at? Things don't happen that way. It was a dream. He would presently wake up and find the man vanished like a shape of mist. The gravity, the dignity, the firm and courteous tone of that athletic old stranger impressed Massy. He was almost afraid. But it was no dream. Five hundred pounds are no dream. At once he became suspicious. What did it mean? Of course it was an offer to catch hold of for dear life. But what could there be behind?

Before they had parted, after appointing a meeting in a solicitor's office early on the morrow, Massy was asking himself, What is his motive? He spent the night in hammering out the clauses of the agreement—a unique instrument of its sort whose tenor got bruited abroad somehow and became the talk and wonder of the port.

Massy's object had been to secure for himself as many ways as possible of getting rid of his partner without being called upon at once to pay back his share. Captain Whalley's efforts were directed to making the money secure. Was it not Ivy's money—a part of her fortune whose only other asset was the time-defying body of her old father? Sure of his forbearance in the strength of his love for her, he accepted, with stately serenity, Massy's stupidly cunning paragraphs against his incompetence, his dishonesty, his drunkenness, for the sake of other stringent stipulations. At the end of three years he was at liberty to withdraw from the partnership, taking his money with him. Provision was made for forming a fund to pay him off. But if he left the *Sofala* before the term, from whatever cause (barring death),

Massy was to have a whole year for paying. "Illness?" the lawyer had suggested: a young man fresh from Europe and not overburdened with business, who was rather amused. Massy began to whine unctuously, "How could he be expected? . . ."

"Let that go," Captain Whalley had said with a superb confidence in his body. "Acts of God," he added. In the midst of life we are in death,* but he trusted his Maker with a still greater fearlessness—his Maker who knew his thoughts, his human affections, and his motives. His Creator knew what use he was making of his health—how much he wanted it . . . "I trust my first illness will be my last. I've never been ill that I can remember," he had remarked. "Let it go."

But at this early stage he had already awakened Massy's hostility by refusing to make it six hundred instead of five. "I cannot do that," was all he had said, simply, but with so much decision that Massy desisted at once from pressing the point, but had thought to himself, "Can't! Old curmudgeon. *Won't!* He must have lots of money, but he would like to get hold of a soft berth and the sixth part of my profits for nothing if he only could."

And during these years Massy's dislike grew under the restraint of something resembling fear. The simplicity of that man appeared dangerous. Of late he had changed, however, had appeared less formidable and with a lessened vigour of life, as though he had received a secret wound. But still he remained incomprehensible in his simplicity, fearlessness, and rectitude. And when Massy learned that he meant to leave him at the end of the time, to leave him confronted with the problem of boilers, his dislike blazed up secretly into hate.

It had made him so clear-eyed that for a long time now Mr. Sterne could have told him nothing he did not know. He had much ado in trying to terrorize that mean sneak into silence; he wanted to deal alone with the situation; and—incredible as it might have appeared to Mr. Sterne—he had not yet given up the desire and the hope of inducing that hated old man to stay. Why! there was nothing else to do, unless he were to abandon his chances of fortune. But now, suddenly, since the crossing of the bar at Batu Beru things seemed to be coming rapidly to a point. It disquieted him so much that the study of the winning numbers failed to soothe his agitation: and the twilight in the cabin deepened, very sombre.

He put the list away, muttering once more, "Oh, no, my boy, you don't. Not if I know it." He did not mean the blinking, eavesdropping humbug to force his action. He took his head again into his hands; his immobility confined in the darkness of this shut-up little place seemed to make him a thing apart infinitely removed from the stir and the sounds of the deck.

He heard them: the passengers were beginning to jabber excitedly; somebody dragged a heavy box past his door. He heard Captain Whalley's voice above—

"Stations,* Mr. Sterne." And the answer from somewhere on deck forward—

"Ay, ay, sir."

"We shall moor head up stream* this time; the ebb has made."

"Head up stream, sir."

"You will see to it, Mr. Sterne."

The answer was covered by the autocratic clang on the engine-room gong. The propeller went on beating slowly: one, two, three; one, two, three—with pauses as if hesitating on the turn. The gong clanged time after time, and the water churned this way and that by the blades was making a great noisy commotion alongside. Mr. Massy did not move. A shore-light on the other bank, a quarter of a mile across the river, drifted, no bigger than a tiny star, passing slowly athwart the circle of the port. Voices from Mr. Van Wyk's jetty answered the hails from the ship; ropes were thrown and missed and thrown again; the swaying flame of a torch carried in a large sampan coming to fetch away in state the Rajah from down the coast cast a sudden ruddy glare into his cabin, over his very person. Mr. Massy did not move. After a few last ponderous turns the engines stopped, and the prolonged clanging of the gong signified that the captain had done with them. A great number of boats and canoes of all sizes boarded the off-side of the *Sofala*. Then after a time the tumult of splashing, of cries, of shuffling feet, of packages dropped with a thump, the noise of the native passengers going away, subsided slowly. On the shore, a voice, cultivated, slightly authoritative, spoke very close alongside—

"Brought any mail for me this time?"

"Yes, Mr. Van Wyk." This was from Sterne, answering over the rail in a tone of respectful cordiality. "Shall I bring it up to you?"

But the voice asked again—

"Where's the captain?"

"Still on the bridge, I believe. He hasn't left his chair. Shall I . . ."

The voice interrupted negligently.

"I will come on board."

"Mr. Van Wyk," Sterne suddenly broke out with an eager effort, "will you do me the favour . . ."

The mate walked away quickly towards the gangway. A silence fell. Mr. Massy in the dark did not move.

He did not move even when he heard slow shuffling footsteps pass his cabin lazily. He contented himself to bellow out through the closed door—

"You—Jack!"

The footsteps came back without haste; the door handle rattled, and the second engineer appeared in the opening, shadowy in the sheen of the skylight at his back, with his face apparently as black as the rest of his figure.

"We have been very long coming up this time," Mr. Massy growled, without changing his attitude.

"What do you expect with half the boiler tubes plugged up for leaks." The second defended himself loquaciously.

"None of your lip," said Massy.

"None of your rotten boilers—I say," retorted his faithful subordinate without animation, huskily. "Go down there and carry a head of steam on them yourself—if you dare. I don't."

"You aren't worth your salt then," Massy said. The other made a faint noise which resembled a laugh but might have been a snarl.

"Better go slow than stop the ship altogether," he admonished his admired superior. Mr. Massy moved at last. He turned in his chair, and grinding his teeth—

"Dam' you and the ship! I wish she were at the bottom of the sea. Then you would have to starve."

The trusty second engineer closed the door gently.

Massy listened. Instead of passing on to the bathroom where he should have gone to clean himself, the second entered his cabin, which was next door. Mr. Massy jumped up and waited. Suddenly he heard the lock snap in there. He rushed out and gave a violent kick to the door.

"I believe you are locking yourself up to get drunk," he shouted.

A muffled answer came after a while.

"My own time."

"If you take to boozing on the trip I'll fire you out," Massy cried.

An obstinate silence followed that threat. Massy moved away perplexed. On the bank two figures appeared, approaching the gangway. He heard a voice tinged with contempt—

"I would rather doubt your word. But I shall certainly speak to him of this."

The other voice, Sterne's, said with a sort of regretful formality—

"Thanks. That's all I want. I must do my duty."

Mr. Massy was surprised. A short, dapper figure leaped lightly on the deck and nearly bounded into him where he stood beyond the circle of light from the gangway lamp. When it had passed towards the bridge, after exchanging a hurried "Good evening," Massy said surlily to Sterne who followed with slow steps—

"What is it you're making up to Mr. Van Wyk for, now?"

"Far from it, Mr. Massy. I am not good enough for Mr. Van Wyk. Neither are you, sir, in his opinion, I am afraid. Captain Whalley is, it seems. He's gone to ask him to dine up at the house this evening."

Then he murmured to himself darkly—

"I hope he will like it."

XII

Mr. Van Wyk, the white man of Batu Beru, an ex-naval officer who, for reasons best known to himself, had thrown away the promise of a brilliant career to become the pioneer of tobacco-planting on that remote part of the coast, had learned to like Captain Whalley. The appearance of the new skipper had attracted his attention. Nothing more unlike all the diverse types he had seen succeeding each other on the bridge of the *Sofala* could be imagined.

At that time Batu Beru was not what it has become since: the centre of a prosperous tobacco-growing district, a tropically suburban-looking little settlement of bungalows in one long street shaded with two rows of trees, embowered by the flowering and trim luxuriance of the gardens, with a three-mile-long carriage-road for the afternoon drives and a first-class Resident with a fat, cheery wife to lead the society of married estate-managers and unmarried young fellows in the service of the big companies.

All this prosperity was not yet; and Mr. Van Wyk prospered alone on the left bank on his deep clearing carved out of the forest, which came down above and below to the water's edge. His lonely bungalow faced across the river the houses of the Sultan: a restless and melancholy old ruler who had done with love and war, for whom life no longer held any savour (except of evil forebodings) and time never had any value. He was afraid of death, and hoped he would die before the white men were ready to take his country from him. He crossed the river frequently (with never less than ten boats crammed full of people), in the wistful hope of extracting some information on the subject from his own white man. There was a certain chair on the verandah he always took: the dignitaries of the court squatted on the rugs and skins between the furniture: the inferior people remained below on the grass plot between the house and the river in rows three or four deep all along the front. Not seldom the visit began at daybreak. Mr. Van Wyk tolerated these inroads. He would nod out of his bedroom window, tooth-brush or razor in hand, or pass through the throng of courtiers in his bathing robe. He appeared and disappeared humming a tune, polished his nails with attention, rubbed his shaved face with eau-de-Cologne, drank his early tea, went out to see his coolies at work: returned, looked through some papers on his desk, read a page or two in a book or sat before his cottage piano* leaning back on the stool, his arms extended, fingers on the keys, his body swaying slightly from side to side. When absolutely forced to speak he gave evasive vaguely soothing answers out of pure compassion: the same feeling perhaps made him so lavishly hospitable with the aerated drinks that more than once he left himself without soda-water for a whole week. That old man had granted him as much land as he cared to have cleared: it was neither more nor less than a fortune.

Whether it was fortune or seclusion from his kind that Mr. Van Wyk sought, he could not have pitched upon a better place. Even the mail-boats of the subsidized company calling on the veriest clusters of palm-thatched hovels along the coast steamed past the mouth of Batu Beru river far away in the offing. The contract was old: perhaps in a few years' time, when it had expired, Batu Beru would be included in the service; meantime all Mr. Van Wyk's mail was addressed to Malacca, whence his agent sent it across once a month by the *Sofala*. It followed that whenever Massy had run short of money (through taking too many lottery tickets), or got into a difficulty about a skipper, Mr. Van Wyk was deprived of his letter and newspapers. In so far he had a personal interest in the fortunes of the *Sofala*. Though he considered himself a hermit (and for no passing whim evidently, since he had stood eight years of it already), he liked to know what went on in the world.

Handy on the verandah upon a walnut *étagère** (it had come last year by the *Sofala*)—everything came by the *Sofala* there lay, piled up under bronze weights, a pile of *The Times'* weekly edition, the large sheets of the *Rotterdam Courant*, the *Graphic* in its world-wide green wrappers, an illustrated Dutch publication without a cover, the numbers of a German magazine with covers of the "Bismarck malade"* colour. There were also parcels of new music—though the piano (it had come years ago by the *Sofala* in the damp atmosphere of the forests was generally out of tune.) It was vexing to be cut off from everything for sixty days at a stretch sometimes, without any means of knowing what was the matter. And when the *Sofala* reappeared Mr. Van Wyk would descend the steps of the verandah and stroll over the grass plot in front of his house, down to the waterside, with a frown on his white brow.

"You've been laid up after an accident, I presume."

He addressed the bridge, but before anybody could answer Massy was sure to have already scrambled ashore over the rail and pushed in, squeezing the palms of his hands together, bowing his sleek head as if gummed all over the top with black threads and tapes. And he would be so enraged at the necessity of having to offer such an explanation that his moaning would be positively pitiful, while all the time he tried to compose his big lips into a smile.

"No, Mr. Van Wyk. You would not believe it. I couldn't get one of those wretches to take the ship out. Not a single one of the lazy beasts could be induced, and the law, you know, Mr. Van Wyk . . ."

He moaned at great length apologetically; the words conspiracy, plot, envy, came out prominently, whined with greater energy. Mr. Van Wyk, examining with a faint grimace his polished finger-nails, would say, "H'm. Very unfortunate," and turn his back on him.

Fastidious, clever, slightly sceptical, accustomed to the best society (he had held a much-envied shore appointment at the Ministry of Marine for a year preceding his retreat from his profession and from Europe), he possessed a latent warmth of feeling and a capacity for sympathy which were concealed by a sort of haughty, arbitrary indifference of manner arising from his early training; and by a something an enemy might have called foppish, in his aspect—like a distorted echo of past elegance. He managed to keep an almost military discipline amongst the coolies of the estate he had dragged into the light of day out of the tangle and shadows of the jungle; and the white shirt he put on every evening with its stiff glossy front and high collar looked as if he had meant to preserve the decent ceremony of evening-dress, but had wound a thick crimson sash above his hips as a concession to the wilderness, once his adversary, now his vanquished companion. Moreover, it was a hygienic precaution. Worn wide open in front, a short jacket of some airy silken stuff floated from his shoulders. His fluffy, fair hair, thin at the top, curled slightly at the sides; a carefully arranged moustache, an ungarnished forehead,* the gleam of low patent shoes peeping under the wide bottom of trousers cut straight from the same stuff as the gossamer coat, completed a figure recalling, with its sash, a pirate chief of romance, and at the same time the elegance of a slightly bald dandy indulging, in seclusion, a taste for unorthodox costume.

It was his evening get-up. The proper time for the *Sofala* to arrive at Batu Beru was an hour before sunset, and he looked picturesque, and somehow quite correct too, walking at the water's edge on the background of grass slope crowned with a low long bungalow with an immensely steep roof of palm thatch, and clad to the eaves in flowering creepers. While the *Sofala* was being made fast he strolled in the shade of the few trees left near the landing-place, waiting till he could go on board. Her white men were not of his kind. The old Sultan (though his wistful invasions were a nuisance) was really much more acceptable to his fastidious taste. But still they were white; the periodical visits of the ship made a break in the well-filled sameness of the days without disturbing his privacy. Moreover, they were necessary from a business point of view; and through a strain of preciseness in his nature he was irritated when she failed to appear at the appointed time.

The cause of the irregularity was too absurd, and Massy, in his opinion, was a contemptible idiot. The first time the *Sofala* reappeared under the new agreement swinging out of the bend below, after he had almost given up all hope of ever seeing her again, he felt so angry that he did not go down at once to the landing-place. His servants had come running to him with the news, and he had dragged a chair close against the front rail of the verandah, spread his elbows out, rested his chin on his hands, and went on glaring at her fixedly while she was being made fast opposite his house. He could make out easily all the white faces on board. Who on earth was that kind of patriarch they had got there on the bridge now?

At last he sprang up and walked down the gravel path. It was a fact that the very gravel for his paths had been imported by the *Sofala*. Exasperated out of his quiet superciliousness, without looking at anyone right or left, he accosted Massy straightway in so determined a manner that the engineer, taken aback, began to stammer unintelligibly. Nothing could be heard but the words: "Mr. Van Wyk . . . Indeed, Mr. Van Wyk . . . For the future, Mr. Van Wyk"—and by the suffusion of blood Massy's vast bilious face acquired an unnatural orange tint, out of which the disconcerted coal-black eyes shone in an extraordinary manner.

"Nonsense. I am tired of this. I wonder you have the impudence to come alongside my jetty as if I had it made for your convenience alone."

Massy tried to protest earnestly. Mr. Van Wyk was very angry. He had a good mind to ask that German firm—those people in Malacca—what was their name?—boats with green funnels. They would be only too glad of the opening to put one of their small steamers on the run. Yes; Schnitzler, Jacob Schnitzler, would in a moment. Yes. He had decided to write without delay.

In his agitation Massy caught up his falling pipe.

"You don't mean it, sir!" he shrieked.

"You shouldn't mismanage your business in this ridiculous manner."

Mr. Van Wyk turned on his heel. The other three whites on the bridge had not stirred during the scene. Massy walked hastily from side to side, puffed out his cheeks, suffocated.

"Stuck up Dutchman!"

And he moaned out feverishly a long tale of griefs. The efforts he had made for all these years to please that man. This was the return you got for it, eh? Pretty. Write to Schnitzler—let in the green-funnel boats—get an old Hamburg Jew to ruin him. No, really he could laugh. . . . He laughed sobbingly. . . . Ha! ha! ha! And make him carry the letter in his own ship presumably.

He stumbled across a grating and swore. He would not hesitate to fling the Dutchman's correspondence overboard—the whole confounded bundle. He had never, never made any charge for that accommodation. But Captain Whalley, his new partner, would not let him probably; besides, it would be only putting off the evil day. For his own part he would make a hole in the water rather than look on tamely at the green funnels overrunning his trade.

He raved aloud. The China boys* hung back with the dishes at the foot of the ladder. He yelled from the bridge down at the deck, "Aren't we going to have any chow* this evening at all?" then turned violently to Captain Whalley, who waited, grave and patient, at the head of the table, smoothing his beard in silence now and then with a forbearing gesture.

"You don't seem to care what happens to me. Don't you see that this affects your interests as much as mine? It's no joking matter."

He took the foot of the table growling between his teeth.

"Unless you have a few thousands put away somewhere. I haven't."

Mr. Van Wyk dined in his thoroughly lit-up bungalow, putting a point of splendour in the night of his clearing above the dark bank of the river. Afterwards he sat down to his piano, and in a pause he became aware of slow footsteps passing on the path along the front. A plank or two creaked under a heavy tread; he swung half round on the music-stool, listening with his fingertips at rest on the keyboard. His little terrier barked violently, backing in from the verandah. A deep voice apologized gravely for "this intrusion." He walked out quickly.

At the head of the steps the patriarchal figure, who was the new captain of the *Sofala* apparently (he had seen a round dozen of them, but not one of that sort), towered without advancing. The little dog barked unceasingly, till a flick of Mr. Van Wyk's handkerchief made him spring aside into silence. Captain Whalley, opening the matter, was met by a punctiliously polite but determined opposition.

They carried on their discussion standing where they had come face to face. Mr. Van Wyk observed his visitor with attention. Then at last, as if forced out of his reserve—

"I am surprised that you should intercede for such a confounded fool."

This outbreak was almost complimentary, as if its meaning had been, "That such a man as you should intercede!" Captain Whalley let it pass by without flinching. One would have thought he had heard nothing. He simply went on to state that he was personally interested in putting things straight between them. Personally . . .

But Mr. Van Wyk, really carried away by his disgust with Massy, became very incisive—

"Indeed—if I am to be frank with you—his whole character does not seem to me particularly estimable or trustworthy . . ."

Captain Whalley, always straight, seemed to grow an inch taller and broader, as if the girth of his chest had suddenly expanded under his beard.

"My dear sir, you don't think I came here to discuss a man with whom I am—I am—h'm—closely associated."

A sort of solemn silence lasted for a moment. He was not used to asking favours, but the importance he attached to this affair had made him willing to try. . . . Mr. Van Wyk, favourably impressed, and suddenly mollified by a desire to laugh, interrupted—

"That's all right if you make it a personal matter; but you can do no less than sit down and smoke a cigar with me."

A slight pause, then Captain Whalley stepped forward heavily. As to the regularity of the service, for the future he made himself responsible for it; and his name was Whalley—perhaps to a sailor (he was speaking to a sailor, was he not?) not altogether unfamiliar. There was a lighthouse now, on an island. Maybe Mr. Van Wyk himself . . .

"Oh yes. Oh indeed." Mr. Van Wyk caught on at once. He indicated a chair. How very interesting. For his own part he had seen some service in the last Acheen War,* but had never been so far East. Whalley Island? Of course. Now that was very interesting. What changes his guest must have seen since.

"I can look further back even—on a whole half-century."

Captain Whalley expanded a bit. The flavour of a good cigar (it was a weakness) had gone straight to his heart, also the civility of that young man. There was something in that accidental contact of which he had been starved in his years of struggle.

The front wall retreating made a square recess furnished like a room. A lamp with a milky glass shade, suspended below the slope of the high roof at the end of a slender brass chain, threw a bright round of light upon a little table bearing an open book and an ivory paper-knife. And, in the translucent shadows beyond, other tables could be seen, a number of easy-chairs of various shapes, with a great profusion of skin rugs strewn on the teakwood planking all over the verandah. The flowering creepers scented the air. Their foliage clipped out between the uprights made as if several frames of thick unstirring leaves reflecting the lamplight in a green glow. Through the opening at his elbow Captain Whalley could see the gangway lantern of the *Sofala* burning dim by the shore, the shadowy masses of the town beyond the open lustrous darkness of the river, and, as if hung along the straight edge of the projecting eaves, a narrow black strip of the night sky full of stars—resplendent. The famous cigar in hand he had a moment of complacency.

"A trifle. Somebody must lead the way. I just showed that the thing could be done; but you men brought up to the use of steam cannot conceive the vast importance of my bit of venturesomeness to the Eastern trade of the time. Why, that new route reduced the average time of a southern passage by eleven days for more than half the year. Eleven days! It's on record. But the remarkable thing—speaking to a sailor—I should say was . . ."

He talked well, without egotism, professionally. The powerful voice, produced without effort, filled the bungalow even into the empty rooms with a deep and limpid resonance, seemed to make a stillness outside; and Mr. Van Wyk was surprised by the serene quality of its tone, like the perfection of manly gentleness. Nursing one small foot, in a silk sock and a patent leather shoe, on his knee, he was immensely entertained. It was as if nobody could talk like this now, and the over-shadowed eyes, the flowing white beard, the big frame, the serenity, the whole temper of the man, were an amazing survival from the prehistoric times of the world coming up to him out of the sea.

Captain Whalley had been also the pioneer of the early trade in the Gulf of Pe-tchi-li. He even found occasion to mention that he had buried his "dear wife" there six-and-twenty years ago. Mr. Van Wyk, impassive, could not help speculating in his mind swiftly as to the sort of woman that would mate with such a man. Did they make an adventurous and well-matched pair? No. Very possible she had been small, frail, no doubt very feminine—or most likely commonplace with domestic instincts, utterly insignificant. But Captain Whalley was no garrulous bore, and shaking his head as if to dissipate the momentary gloom that had settled on his handsome old face, he alluded conversationally to Mr. Van Wyk's solitude.

Mr. Van Wyk affirmed that sometimes he had more company than he wanted. He mentioned smilingly some of the peculiarities of his intercourse with "My Sultan." He made his visits in force. Those people damaged his grass plot in front (it was not easy to obtain some approach to a lawn in the tropics), and the other day had broken down some rare bushes he had planted over there. And Captain Whalley remembered immediately that, in 'forty-seven, the then Sultan, "this man's grandfather," had been notorious as a great protector of the piratical fleets of praus from farther East. They had a safe refuge in the river at Batu Beru. He financed more especially a Balinini chief* called Haji Daman. Captain Whalley, nodding significantly his bushy white eyebrows, had very good reason to know something of that. The world had progressed since that time.

Mr. Van Wyk demurred with unexpected acrimony. Progressed in what? he wanted to know.

Why, in knowledge of truth, in decency, in justice, in order—in honesty too, since men harmed each other mostly from ignorance. It was, Captain Whalley concluded quaintly, more pleasant to live in.

Mr. Van Wyk whimsically would not admit that Mr. Massy, for instance, was more pleasant naturally than the Balinini pirates.

The river had not gained much by the change. They were in their way every bit as honest. Massy was less ferocious than Haji Daman no doubt, but . . .

"And what about you, my good sir?" Captain Whalley laughed a deep soft laugh. "*You* are an improvement, surely."

He continued in a vein of pleasantry. A good cigar was better than a knock on the head—the sort of welcome he would have found on this river forty or fifty years ago. Then leaning forward slightly, he became earnestly serious. It seems as if, outside their own sea-gypsy tribes, these rovers had hated all mankind with an incomprehensible, bloodthirsty hatred. Meantime their depredations had been stopped, and what was the consequence? The new generation was orderly, peaceable, settled in prosperous villages. He could speak from personal knowledge. And even the few survivors of that time—old men now—had changed so much, that it would have been unkind to remember against them that they had ever slit a throat in their lives. He had one especially in his mind's eye: a dignified, venerable headman of a certain large coast village about sixty miles sou'west of Tampasuk.* It did one's heart good to see him—to hear that man speak. He might have been a ferocious savage once. What men wanted was to be checked by superior intelligence, by superior knowledge, by superior force too—yes, by force held in trust from God and sanctified by its use in accordance with His declared will. Captain Whalley believed a disposition for good existed in every man, even if the world were not a very happy place as a whole. In the wisdom of men he had not so much confidence. The disposition had to be helped up pretty sharply sometimes, he admitted. They might be silly, wrongheaded, unhappy; but naturally evil—no. There was at bottom a complete harmlessness at least . . .

"Is there?" Mr. Van Wyk snapped acrimoniously.

Captain Whalley laughed at the interjection, in the good humour of large, tolerating certitude. He could look back at half a century, he pointed out. The smoke oozed placidly through the white hairs hiding his kindly lips.

"At all events," he resumed after a pause, "I am glad that they've had no time to do you much harm as yet."

This allusion to his comparative youthfulness did not offend Mr. Van Wyk, who got up and wriggled his shoulders with an enigmatic half-smile. They walked out together amicably into the starry night towards the river-side. Their footsteps resounded unequally on the dark path. At the shore end of the gangway the lantern, hung low to the handrail, threw a vivid light on the white legs and the big black feet of Mr. Massy waiting about anxiously. From the waist upwards he remained shadowy, with a row of buttons gleaming up to the vague outline of his chin.

"You may thank Captain Whalley for this," Mr. Van Wyk said curtly to him before turning away.

The lamps on the verandah flung three long squares of light between the uprights far over the grass. A bat flitted before his face like a circling flake of velvety blackness. Along the jasmine hedge the night air seemed heavy with the fall of perfumed dew; flowerbeds bordered the path; the clipped bushes uprose in dark rounded clumps here and there before the house; the dense foliage of creepers filtered the sheen of the lamplight within in a soft glow all along the front; and everything near and far stood still in a great immobility, in a great sweetness.

Mr. Van Wyk (a few years before he had had occasion to imagine himself treated more badly than anybody alive had ever been by a woman) felt for Captain Whalley's optimistic views the disdain of a man who had once been credulous himself. His disgust with the world (the woman for a time had filled it for him completely) had taken the form of activity in retirement, because, though capable of great depth of feeling, he was energetic and essentially practical. But there was in that uncommon old sailor, drifting on the outskirts of his busy solitude, something that fascinated his scepticism. His very simplicity (amusing enough) was like a delicate refinement of an upright character. The striking dignity of manner could be nothing else, in a man reduced to such a humble position, but the expression of something essentially noble in the character. With all his trust in mankind he was no fool; the serenity of his temper at the end of so many years, since it could not obviously have been appeased by success, wore an air of profound wisdom. Mr. Van Wyk was amused at it sometimes. Even the very physical traits of the old captain of the *Sofala*, his powerful frame, his reposeful mien, his intelligent, handsome face, the big limbs, the benign courtesy, the touch of rugged severity in the shaggy eyebrows, made up a seductive personality. Mr. Van Wyk disliked littleness of every kind, but there was nothing small about that man, and in the exemplary regularity of many trips an intimacy had grown up between them, a warm feeling at bottom under a kindly stateliness of forms agreeable to his fastidiousness.

They kept their respective opinions on all worldly matters. His other convictions Captain Whalley never intruded. The difference of their ages was like another bond between them. Once, when twitted with the uncharitableness of his youth, Mr. Van Wyk, running his eye over the vast proportions of his interlocutor, retorted in friendly banter—

"Oh. You'll come to my way of thinking yet. You'll have plenty of time. Don't call yourself old: you look good for a round hundred."

But he could not help his stinging incisiveness, and though moderating it by an almost affectionate smile, he added—

"And by then you will probably consent to die from sheer disgust."

Captain Whalley, smiling too, shook his head. "God forbid!"

He thought that perhaps on the whole he deserved something better than to die in such sentiments. The time of course would have to come, and he trusted to his Maker to provide a manner of going out of which he need not be ashamed. For the rest he hoped he would live to a hundred if need be: other men had been known; it would be no miracle. He expected no miracles.

The pronounced, argumentative tone caused Mr. Van Wyk to raise his head and look at him steadily. Captain Whalley was gazing fixedly with a rapt expression, as though he had seen his Creator's favourable decree written in mysterious characters on the wall.* He kept perfectly motionless for a few seconds, then got his vast bulk on to his feet so impetuously that Mr. Van Wyk was startled.

He struck first a heavy blow on his inflated chest: and, throwing out horizontally a big arm that remained steady, extended in the air like the limb of a tree on a windless day—

"Not a pain or an ache there. Can you see this shake in the least?"

His voice was low, in an awing, confident contrast with the headlong emphasis of his movements. He sat down abruptly.

"This isn't to boast of it, you know. I am nothing," he said in his effortless strong voice, that seemed to come out as naturally as a river flows. He picked up the stump of the cigar he had laid aside, and added peacefully, with a slight nod, "As it happens, my life is necessary; it isn't my own, it isn't—God knows."

He did not say much for the rest of the evening, but several times Mr. Van Wyk detected a faint smile of assurance flitting under the heavy moustache.

Later on Captain Whalley would now and then consent to dine "at the house." He could even be induced to drink a glass of wine. "Don't think I am afraid of it, my good sir," he explained. "There was a very good reason why I should give it up."

On another occasion, leaning back at ease, he remarked, "You have treated me most—most humanely, my dear Mr. Van Wyk, from the very first."

"You'll admit there was some merit," Mr. Van Wyk hinted slyly. "An associate of that excellent Massy. . . . Well, well, my dear captain, I won't say a word against him."

"It would be no use your saying anything against him," Captain Whalley affirmed a little moodily. "As I've told you before, my life—my work, is necessary, not for myself alone. I can't choose" . . . He paused, turned the glass before him right round. . . . "I have an only child—a daughter."

The ample downward sweep of his arm over the table seemed to suggest a small girl at a vast distance. "I hope to see her once more before I die. Meantime it's enough to know that she has me sound and solid, thank God. You can't understand how one feels. Bone of my bone, flesh of my flesh;* the very image of my poor wife. Well, she . . ."

Again he paused, then pronounced stoically the words, "She has a hard struggle."

And his head fell on his breast, his eyebrows remained knitted, as by an effort of meditation. But generally his mind seemed steeped in the serenity of boundless trust in a higher power. Mr. Van Wyk wondered sometimes how much of it was due to the splendid vitality of the man, to the bodily vigour which seems to impart something of its force to the soul. But he had learned to like him very much.

XIII

THIS was the reason why Mr. Sterne's confidential communication, delivered hurriedly on the shore alongside the dark silent ship, had disturbed his equanimity. It was the most incomprehensible and unexpected thing that could happen; and the perturbation of his spirit was so great that, forgetting all about his letters, he ran rapidly up the bridge ladder.

The portable table was being put together for dinner to the left of the wheel by two pig-tailed "boys," who as usual snarled at each other over the job, while another, a doleful, burly, very yellow Chinaman, resembling Mr. Massy, waited apathetically with the cloth over his arm and a pile of thick dinner-plates against his chest. A common cabin lamp with its globe missing, brought up from below, had been hooked to the wooden framework of the awning; the side-screens had been lowered all round; Captain Whalley filling the depths of the wicker-chair seemed to sit benumbed in a canvas tent crudely lighted, and used for the storing of nautical objects; a shabby steering-wheel, a battered brass binnacle on a stout mahogany stand, two dingy life-buoys,* an old cork fender* lying in a corner, dilapidated deck-lockers* with loops of thin rope instead of door-handles.

He shook off the appearance of numbness to return Mr. Van Wyk's unusually brisk greeting, but relapsed directly afterwards. To accept a pressing invitation to dinner "up at the house" cost him another very visible physical effort. Mr. Van Wyk, perplexed, folded his arms, and leaning back against the rail, with his little, black, shiny feet well out, examined him covertly.

"I've noticed of late that you are not quite yourself, old friend."

He put an affectionate gentleness into the last two words. The real intimacy of their intercourse had never been so vividly expressed before.

"Tut, tut, tut!"

The wicker-chair creaked heavily.

"Irritable," commented Mr. Van Wyk to himself; and aloud, "I'll expect to see you in half an hour, then," he said negligently, moving off.

"In half an hour," Captain Whalley's rigid silvery head repeated behind him as if out of a trance.

Amidships, below, two voices, close against the engine-room, could be heard answering each other—one angry and slow, the other alert.

"I tell you the beast has locked himself in to get drunk."

"Can't help it now, Mr. Massy. After all, a man has a right to shut himself up in his cabin in his own time."

"Not to get drunk."

"I heard him swear that the worry with the boilers was enough to drive any man to drink," Sterne said maliciously.

Massy hissed out something about bursting the door in. Mr. Van Wyk, to avoid them, crossed in the dark to the other side of the deserted deck. The planking of the little wharf rattled faintly under his hasty feet.

"Mr. Van Wyk! Mr. Van Wyk!"

He walked on: somebody was running on the path. "You've forgotten to get your mail."

Sterne, holding a bundle of papers in his hand, caught up with him.

"Oh, thanks."

But, as the other continued at his elbow, Mr. Van Wyk stopped short. The overhanging eaves, descending low upon the lighted front of the bungalow, threw their black straight-edged shadow into the great body of the night on that side. Everything was very still. A tinkle of cutlery and a slight jingle of glasses were heard. Mr. Van Wyk's servants were laying the table for two on the verandah.

"I'm afraid you give me no credit whatever for my good intentions in the matter I've spoken to you about," said Sterne.

"I simply don't understand you."

"Captain Whalley is a very audacious man, but he will understand that his game is up. That's all that anybody need ever know of it from me. Believe me, I am very considerate in this, but duty is duty. I don't want to make a fuss. All I ask you, as his friend, is to tell him from me that the game's up. That will be sufficient."

Mr. Van Wyk felt a loathsome dismay at this queer privilege of friendship. He would not demean himself by asking for the slightest explanation; to drive the other away with contumely he did not think prudent—as yet, at any rate. So much assurance staggered him. Who could tell what there could be in it, he thought? His regard for Captain

Whalley had the tenacity of a disinterested sentiment, and his practical instinct coming to his aid, he concealed his scorn.

"I gather, then, that this is something grave."

"Very grave," Sterne assented solemnly, delighted at having produced an effect at last. He was ready to add some effusive protestations of regret at the "unavoidable necessity," but Mr. Van Wyk cut him short—very civilly, however.

Once on the verandah Mr. Van Wyk put his hands in his pockets, and, straddling his legs, stared down at a black panther skin lying on the floor before a rocking-chair. "It looks as if the fellow had not the pluck to play his own precious game openly," he thought.

This was true enough. In the face of Massy's last rebuff Sterne dared not declare his knowledge. His object was simply to get charge of the steamer and keep it for some time. Massy would never forgive him for forcing himself on; but if Captain Whalley left the ship of his own accord, the command would devolve upon him for the rest of the trip; so he hit upon the brilliant idea of scaring the old man away. A vague menace, a mere hint, would be enough in such a brazen case; and, with a strange admixture of compassion, he thought that Batu Beru was a very good place for throwing up the sponge. The skipper could go ashore quietly, and stay with that Dutchman of his. Weren't these two as thick as thieves together? And on reflection he seemed to see that there was a way to work the whole thing through that great friend of the old man's. This was another brilliant idea. He had an inborn preference for circuitous methods. In this particular case he desired to remain in the background as much as possible, to avoid exasperating Massy needlessly. No fuss! Let it all happen naturally.

Mr. Van Wyk all through the dinner was conscious of a sense of isolation that invades sometimes the closeness of human intercourse. Captain Whalley failed lamentably and obviously in his attempts to eat something. He seemed overcome by a strange absentmindedness. His hand would hover irresolutely, as if left without guidance by a preoccupied mind. Mr. Van Wyk had heard him coming up from a long way off in the profound stillness of the river-side, and had noticed the irresolute character of the footfalls. The toe of his boot had struck the bottom stair as though he had come along mooning with his head in the air right up to the steps of the verandah. Had the captain of the *Sofala* been another sort of man he would have suspected the work of age there. But one glance at him was enough.

Time—after, indeed, marking him for its own—had given him up to his usefulness, in which his simple faith would see a proof of Divine mercy. "How could I contrive to warn him?" Mr. Van Wyk wondered, as if Captain Whalley had been miles and miles away, out of sight and earshot of all evil. He was sickened by an immense disgust of Sterne. To even mention his threat to a man like Whalley would be positively indecent. There was something more vile and insulting in its hint than in a definite charge of crime—the debasing taint of blackmailing. "What could anyone bring against him?" he asked himself. This was a limpid* personality. "And for what object?" The Power that man trusted had thought fit to leave him nothing on earth that envy could lay hold of, except a bare crust of bread.

"Won't you try some of this?" he asked, pushing a dish slightly. Suddenly it seemed to Mr. Van Wyk that Sterne might possibly be coveting the command of the *Sofala*. His cynicism was quite startled by what looked like a proof that no man may count himself safe from his kind unless in the very abyss of misery. An intrigue of that sort was hardly worth troubling about, he judged; but still, with such a fool as Massy to deal with, Whalley ought to and must be warned.

At this moment Captain Whalley, bolt upright, the deep cavities of the eyes overhung by a bushy frown, and one large brown hand resting on each side of his empty plate, spoke across the tablecloth abruptly—"Mr. Van Wyk, you've always treated me with the most humane consideration."

"My dear captain, you make too much of a simple fact that I am not a savage." Mr. Van Wyk, utterly revolted by the thought of Sterne's obscure attempt, raised his voice incisively, as if the mate had been hiding somewhere within earshot. "Any consideration I have been able to show was no more than the rightful due of a character I've learned to regard by this time with an esteem that nothing can shake."

A slight ring of glass made him lift his eyes from the slice of pineapple he was cutting into small pieces on his plate. In changing his position Captain Whalley had contrived to upset an empty tumbler.

Without looking that way, leaning sideways on his elbow, his other hand shading his brow, he groped shakily for it, then desisted. Van Wyk stared blankly, as if something momentous had happened all at once. He did not know why he should feel so startled; but he forgot Sterne utterly for the moment.

"Why, what's the matter?"

And Captain Whalley, half-averted, in a deadened, agitated voice, muttered—

"Esteem!"

"And I may add something more," Mr. Van Wyk, very steady-eyed, pronounced slowly.

"Hold! Enough!" Captain Whalley did not change his attitude or raise his voice. "Say no more! I can make you no return. I am too poor even for that now. Your esteem is worth having. You are not a man that would stoop to deceive the poorest sort of devil on earth, or make a ship unseaworthy every time he takes her to sea."

Mr. Van Wyk, leaning forward, his face gone pink all over, with the starched table-napkin over his knees, was inclined to mistrust his senses, his power of comprehension, the sanity of his guest.

"Where? Why? In the name of God!—what's this? What ship? I don't understand who . . ."

"Then, in the name of God, it is I! A ship's unseaworthy when her captain can't see. I am going blind."

Mr. Van Wyk made a slight movement, and sat very still afterwards for a few seconds; then, with the thought of Sterne's "The game's up," he ducked under the table to pick up the napkin which had slipped off his knees. This was the game that was up. And at the same time the muffled voice of Captain Whalley passed over him—

"I've deceived them all. Nobody knows."

He emerged flushed to the eyes. Captain Whalley, motionless under the full blaze of the lamp, shaded his face with his hand.

"And you had that courage?"

"Call it by what name you like. But you are a humane man—a—a—gentleman, Mr. Van Wyk. You may have asked me what I had done with my conscience."

He seemed to muse, profoundly silent, very still in his mournful pose.

"I began to tamper with it in my pride. You begin to see a lot of things when you are going blind. I could not be frank with an old chum even. I was not frank with Massy—no, not altogether. I knew he took me for a wealthy sailor fool, and I let him. I wanted to keep up my importance—because there was poor Ivy away there—my daughter. What did I want to trade on his misery for? I did trade on it—for her. And now, what mercy could I expect from him? He would trade on mine if he knew it. He would hunt the old fraud out, and stick to the money for a year. Ivy's money. And I haven't kept a penny for myself. How am I going to live for a year. A year! In a year there will be no sun in the sky for her father."

His deep voice came out, awfully veiled, as though he had been overwhelmed by the earth of a landslide, and talking to you of the thoughts that haunt the dead in their graves. A cold shudder ran down Mr. Van Wyk's back.

"And how long is it since you have . . .?" he began.

"It was a long time before I could bring myself to believe in this—this visitation." Captain Whalley spoke with gloomy patience from under his hand.

He had not thought he had deserved it. He had begun by deceiving himself from day to day, from week to week. He had the Serang at hand there—an old servant. It came on gradually, and when he could no longer deceive himself . . .

His voice died out almost.

"Rather than give her up I set myself to deceive you all."

"It's incredible," whispered Mr. Van Wyk. Captain Whalley's appalling murmur flowed on.

"Not even the sign of God's anger could make me forget her. How could I forsake my child, feeling my vigour all the time—the blood warm within me? Warm as yours. It seems to me that, like the blinded Samson,* I would find the strength to shake down a temple upon my head. She's a struggling woman—my own child that we used to pray over together, my poor wife and I. Do you remember that day I as well as told you that I believed God would let me live to a hundred for her sake? What sin is there in loving your child? Do you see it? I was ready for her sake to live for ever. I half believed I would. I've been praying for death since. Ha! Presumptuous man—you wanted to live . . ."

A tremendous, shuddering upheaval of that big frame, shaken by a gasping sob, set the glasses jingling all over the table, seemed to make the whole house tremble to the roof-tree. And Mr. Van Wyk, whose feeling of outraged love had been translated into a form of struggle with nature, understood very well that, for that man whose whole life had been conditioned by action, there could exist no other expression for all the emotions; that, to voluntarily cease venturing, doing, enduring, for his child's sake, would have been exactly like plucking his warm love for her out of his living heart. Something too monstrous, too impossible, even to conceive.

Captain Whalley had not changed his attitude, that seemed to express something of shame, sorrow, and defiance.

"I have even deceived you. If it had not been for that word 'esteem.' These are not the words for me. I would have lied to you. Haven't I lied to you? Weren't you going to trust your property on board this very trip?"

"I have a floating yearly policy,"* Mr. Van Wyk said almost unwittingly, and was amazed at the sudden cropping up of a commercial detail.

"The ship is unseaworthy, I tell you. The policy would be invalid if it were known . . ."

"We shall share the guilt, then."

"Nothing could make mine less," said Captain Whalley.

He had not dared to consult a doctor; the man would have perhaps asked who he was, what he was doing; Massy might have heard something. He had lived on without any help, human or divine. The very prayers stuck in his throat. What was there to pray for? and death seemed as far as ever. Once he got into his cabin he dared not come out again; when he sat down he dared not get up; he dared not raise his eyes to anybody's face; he felt reluctant to look upon the sea or up to the sky. The world was fading before his great fear of giving himself away. The old ship was his last friend; he was not afraid of her; he knew every inch of her deck; but at her too he hardly dared to look, for fear of finding he could see less than the day before. A great incertitude enveloped him. The horizon was gone; the sky mingled darkly with the sea. Who was this figure standing over yonder? what was this thing lying down there? And a frightful doubt of the reality of what he could see made even the remnant of sight* that remained to him an added torment, a pitfall always open for his miserable pretence. He was afraid to stumble inexcusably over something—to say a fatal Yes or No* to a question. The hand of God was upon him, but it could not tear him away from his child. And, as if in a nightmare of humiliation, every featureless man seemed an enemy.

He let his hand fall heavily on the table. Mr. Van Wyk, arms down, chin on breast, with a gleam of white teeth pressing on the lower lip, meditated on Sterne's "The game's up."

"The Serang of course does not know."

"Nobody," said Captain Whalley, with assurance.*

"Ah yes. Nobody. Very well. Can you keep it up to the end of the trip? That is the last under the agreement with Massy."

Captain Whalley got up and stood erect, very stately, with the great white beard lying like a silver breastplate over the awful secret of his heart. Yes; that was the only hope there was for him of ever seeing her again, of securing the money, the last he could do for her, before he crept away somewhere—useless, a burden, a reproach to himself. His voice faltered.

"Think of it! Never see her any more: the only human being besides myself now on earth that can remember my wife. She's just like her mother. Lucky the poor woman is where there are no tears shed over those they loved on earth and that remain to pray not to be led into temptation—because, I suppose, the blessed know the secret of grace in God's dealings with His created children."

He swayed a little, said with austere dignity—

"I don't. I know only the child He has given me."

And he began to walk. Mr. Van Wyk, jumping up, saw the full meaning of the rigid head, the hesitating feet,* the vaguely extended hand. His heart was beating fast; he moved a chair aside, and instinctively advanced as if to offer his arm. But Captain Whalley passed him by, making for the stairs quite straight.

"He could not see me at all out of his line," Van Wyk thought, with a sort of awe. Then going to the head of the stairs, he asked a little tremulously—

"What is it like—like a mist—like . . ."

Captain Whalley, half-way down, stopped, and turned round undismayed to answer.

"It is as if the light were ebbing out of the world.* Have you ever watched the ebbing sea on an open stretch of sands withdrawing farther and farther away from you? It is like this—only there will be no flood to follow. Never. It is as if the sun were growing smaller, the stars going out one by one. There can't be many left that I can see by this. But I haven't had the courage to look of late . . ." He must have been able to make out Mr. Van Wyk, because he checked him by an authoritative gesture and a stoical—

"I can get about alone yet."

It was as if he had taken his line, and would accept no help from men, after having been cast out, like a presumptuous Titan,* from his heaven. Mr. Van Wyk, arrested, seemed to count the footsteps right out of earshot. He walked between the tables, tapping smartly with his heels, took up a paper-knife, dropped it after a vague glance along the blade; then happening upon the piano, struck a few chords again and again, vigorously, standing up before the keyboard with an attentive poise of the head like a piano-tuner; closing it, he pivoted on his heels brusquely, avoided the little terrier sleeping trustfully on crossed forepaws, came upon the stairs next, and, as though he had lost his balance on the top step, ran down headlong out of the house. His servants, beginning to clear the table, heard him mutter to himself (evil words no doubt) down there, and then after a pause go away with a strolling gait in the direction of the wharf.

The bulwarks* of the *Sofala* lying alongside the bank made a low, black wall on the undulating contour of the shore. Two masts and a funnel uprose from behind it with a great rake, as if about to fall: a solid, square elevation in the middle bore the ghostly shapes of white boats, the curves of davits,* lines of rail and stanchions, all confused and mingling darkly everywhere; but low down, amidships, a single lighted port stared out on the night, perfectly round, like a small, full moon, whose yellow beam caught a patch of wet mud, the edge of trodden grass, two turns of heavy cable wound round the foot of a thick wooden post in the ground.

Mr. Van Wyk, peering alongside, heard a muzzy* boastful voice apparently jeering at a person called Prendergast. It mouthed abuse thickly, choked; then pronounced very distinctly the word "Murphy," and chuckled. Glass tinkled tremulously. All these sounds came from the lighted port. Mr. Van Wyk hesitated, stooped; it was impossible to look through unless he went down into the mud.

"Sterne," he said, half aloud.

The drunken voice within said gladly—

"Sterne—of course. Look at him blink. Look at him! Sterne, Whalley, Massy. Massy, Whalley, Sterne. But Massy's the best. You can't come over him. He would just love to see you starve."

Mr. Van Wyk moved away, made out farther forward a shadowy head stuck out from under the awnings as if on the watch, and spoke quietly in Malay, "Is the mate asleep?"

"No. Here, at your service."

In a moment Sterne appeared, walking as noiselessly as a cat on the wharf.

"It's so jolly dark, and I had no idea you would be down to-night."

"What's this horrible raving?" asked Mr. Van Wyk, as if to explain the cause of a shudder that ran over him audibly.

"Jack's broken out on a drunk. That's our second. It's his way. He will be right enough by to-morrow afternoon, only Mr. Massy will keep on worrying up and down the deck. We had better get away."

He muttered suggestively of a talk "up at the house." He had long desired to effect an entrance there, but Mr. Van Wyk nonchalantly demurred: it would not, he feared, be quite prudent, perhaps; and the opaque black shadow under one of the two big trees left at the landing-place swallowed them up, impenetrably dense, by the side of the wide river, that seemed to spin into threads of glitter the light of a few big stars dropped here and there upon its outspread and flowing stillness.

"The situation is grave beyond doubt," Mr. Van Wyk said. Ghost-like in their white clothes they could not distinguish each others' features, and their feet made no sound on the soft earth. A sort of purring was heard. Mr. Sterne felt gratified by such a beginning.

"I thought, Mr. Van Wyk, a gentleman of your sort would see at once how awkwardly I was situated."

"Yes, very. Obviously his health is bad. Perhaps he's breaking up. I see, and he himself is well aware—I assume I am speaking to a man of sense—he is well aware that his legs are giving out."

"His legs—ah!" Mr. Sterne was disconcerted, and then turned sulky. "You may call it his legs if you like; what I want to know is whether he intends to clear out quietly. That's a good one, too! His legs! Pooh!"

"Why, yes. Only look at the way he walks." Mr. Van Wyk took him up in a perfectly cool and undoubting tone. "The question, however, is whether your sense of duty does not carry you too far from your true interest. After all, I too could do something to serve you. You know who I am."

"Everybody along the Straits has heard of you, sir."

Mr. Van Wyk presumed that this meant something favorable. Sterne had a soft laugh at this pleasantry. He should think so! To the opening statement, that the partnership agreement was to expire at the end of this very trip, he gave an attentive assent. He was aware. One heard of nothing else on board all the blessed day long. As to Massy, it was no secret that he was in a jolly deep hole with these worn-out boilers. He would have to borrow somewhere a couple of hundred first of all to pay off the captain; and then he would have to raise money on mortgage upon the ship for the new boilers—that is, if he could find a lender at all. At best it meant loss of time, a break in the trade, short earnings for the year—and there was always the danger of having his connection filched away from him by the Germans. It was whispered about that he had already tried two firms. Neither would have anything to do with him. Ship too old, and the man too well known in the place. . . . Mr. Sterne's final rapid winking remained buried in the deep darkness sibilating with his whispers.

"Supposing, then, he got the loan," Mr. Van Wyk resumed in a deliberate undertone, "on your own showing he's more than likely to get a mortgagee's man thrust upon him as captain. For my part, I know that I would make that very stipulation myself if I had to find the money. And as a matter of fact I am thinking of doing so. It would be worth my while in many ways. Do you see how this would bear on the case under discussion?"

"Thank you, sir. I am sure you couldn't get anybody that would care more for your interests."

"Well, it suits my interest that Captain Whalley should finish his time. I shall probably take a passage with you down the Straits. If that can be done, I'll be on the spot when all these changes take place, and in a position to look after your interests."

"Mr. Van Wyk, I want nothing better. I am sure I am infinitely . . ."

"I take it, then, that this may be done without any trouble."

"Well, sir, what risk there is can't be helped; but (speaking to you as my employer now) the thing is more safe than it looks. If anybody had told me of it I wouldn't have believed it, but I have been looking on myself. That old Serang has been trained up to the game. There's nothing the matter with his—his—limbs, sir. He's got used to doing things himself in a remarkable way. And let me tell you, sir, that Captain Whalley, poor man, is by no means useless. Fact. Let me explain to you, sir. He stiffens up that old monkey of a Malay, who knows well enough what to do. Why, he must have kept captain's watches in all sorts of country ships off and on for the last five-and-twenty years. These natives, sir, as long as they have a white man close at the back, will go on doing the right thing most surprisingly well—even if left quite to themselves. Only the white man must be of the sort to put starch into them, and the captain is just the one for that. Why, sir, he has drilled him so well that now he needs hardly speak at all. I have seen that little wrinkled ape made to take the ship out of Pangu Bay on a blowy morning and on all through the islands; take her out first-rate, sir, dodging under the old man's elbow, and in such quiet style that you could not have told for the life of you which of the two was doing the work up there. That's where our poor friend would be still of use to the ship even if—if—he could no longer lift a foot, sir. Provided the Serang does not know that there's anything wrong."

"He doesn't."

"Naturally not. Quite beyond his apprehension. They aren't capable of finding out anything about us, sir."

"You seem to be a shrewd man," said Mr. Van Wyk in a choked mutter, as though he were feeling sick.

"You'll find me a good enough servant, sir."

Mr. Sterne hoped now for a handshake at least, but unexpectedly, with a "What's this? Better not to be seen together," Mr. Van Wyk's white shape wavered, and instantly seemed to melt away in the black air under the roof of boughs. The mate was startled. Yes. There was that faint thumping clatter.

He stole out silently from under the shade. The lighted port-hole shone from afar. His head swam with the intoxication of sudden success. What a thing it was to have a gentleman to deal with! He crept aboard, and there was something weird in the shadowy stretch of empty decks, echoing with shouts and blows proceeding from a darker part amidships. Mr. Massy was raging before the door of the berth: the drunken voice within flowed on undisturbed in the violent racket of kicks.

"Shut up! Put your light out and turn in, you confounded swilling pig—you! D'you hear me, you beast?"

The kicking stopped, and in the pause the muzzy oracular voice announced from within—

"Ah! Massy, now—that's another thing. Massy's deep."

"Who's that aft there? You, Sterne? He'll drink himself into a fit of horrors." The chief engineer appeared vague and big at the corner of the engine-room.

"He will be good enough for duty to-morrow. I would let him be, Mr. Massy."

Sterne slipped away into his berth, and at once had to sit down. His head swam with exultation. He got into his bunk as if in a dream. A feeling of profound peace, of pacific joy, came over him. On deck all was quiet.

Mr. Massy, with his ear against the door of Jack's cabin, listened critically to a deep stertorous breathing within. This was a dead-drunk sleep. The bout was over: tranquilized on that score, he too went in, and with slow wriggles got out of his old tweed jacket. It was a garment with many pockets, which he used to put on at odd times of the day, being subject to sudden chilly fits, and when he felt warmed he would take it off and hang it about anywhere all over the ship. It would be seen swinging on belaying-pins,* thrown over the heads of winches,* suspended on people's very door-handles for that matter. Was he not the owner? But his favourite place was a hook on a wooden awning stanchion on the bridge, almost against the binnacle. He had even in the early days more than one tussle on that point with Captain Whalley, who desired the bridge to be kept tidy. He had been overawed then. Of late, though, he had been able to defy his partner with impunity. Captain Whalley never seemed to notice anything now. As to the Malays, in their awe of that scowling man not one of the crew would dream of laying a hand on the thing, no matter where or what it swung from.

With an unexpectedness which made Mr. Massy jump and drop the coat at his feet, there came from the next berth the crash and thud of a headlong, jingling, clattering fall. The faithful Jack must have dropped to sleep suddenly as he sat at his revels, and now had gone over chair and all, breaking, as it seemed by the sound, every single glass and bottle in the place. After the terrific smash all was still for a time in there, as though he had killed himself outright on the spot. Mr. Massy held his breath. At last a sleepy uneasy groaning sigh was exhaled slowly on the other side of the bulkhead.

"I hope to goodness he's too drunk to wake up now," muttered Mr. Massy.

The sound of a softly knowing laugh nearly drove him to despair. He swore violently under his breath. The fool would keep him awake all night now for certain. He cursed his luck. He wanted to forget his maddening troubles in sleep sometimes. He could detect no movements. Without apparently making the slightest attempt to get up, Jack went on sniggering to himself where he lay; then began to speak, where he had left off as it were—

"Massy! I love the dirty rascal. He would like to see his poor old Jack starve—but just you look where he has climbed to." . . . He hiccoughed in a superior, leisurely manner. . . . "Ship-owning it with the best. A lottery ticket you want. Ha! ha! I will give you lottery tickets, my boy. Let the old ship sink and the old chum starve—that's right. He don't go wrong—Massy don't. Not he. He's a genius—that man is. That's the way to win your money. Ship and chum must go."

"The silly fool has taken it to heart," muttered Massy to himself. And, listening with a softened expression of face for any slight sign of returning drowsiness, he was discouraged profoundly by a burst of laughter full of joyful irony.

"Would like to see her at the bottom of the sea! Oh, you clever, clever devil! Wish her sunk, eh? I should think you would, my boy; the damned old thing and all your troubles with her. Rake in the insurance money—turn your back on your old chum—all's well—gentleman again."

A grim stillness had come over Massy's face. Only his big black eyes rolled uneasily. The raving fool. And yet it was all true. Yes. Lottery tickets, too. All true. What? Beginning again? He wished he wouldn't. . . .

But it was even so. The imaginative drunkard on the other side of the bulkhead* shook off the deathlike stillness that after his last words had fallen on the dark ship moored to a silent shore.

"Don't you dare to say anything against George Massy, Esquire. When he's tired of waiting he will do away with her. Look out! Down she goes—chum and all. He'll know how to . . ."

The voice hesitated, weary, dreamy, lost, as if dying away in a vast open space.

". . . Find a trick that will work. He's up to it—never fear . . ."

He must have been very drunk, for at last the heavy sleep gripped him with the suddenness of a magic spell, and the last word lengthened itself into an interminable, noisy, in-drawn snore. And then even the snoring stopped, and all was still.

But it seemed as though Mr. Massy had suddenly come to doubt the efficacy of sleep as against a man's troubles; or perhaps he had found the relief he needed in the stillness of a calm contemplation that may contain the vivid thoughts of wealth, of a stroke of luck, of long idleness, and may bring before you the imagined form of every desire; for, turning about and throwing his arms over the edge of his bunk, he stood there with his feet on his favourite old coat, looking out through the round port into the night over the river. Sometimes a breath of wind would enter and touch his face, a cool breath charged with the damp, fresh feel from a vast body of water. A glimmer here and there was all he could see of it; and once he might after all suppose he had dozed off, since there appeared before his vision, unexpectedly and connected with no dream, a row of flaming and gigantic figures—three nought seven one two—making up a number such as you may see on a lottery ticket. And then all at once the port was no longer black: it was pearly grey, framing a shore crowded with houses, thatched roof beyond thatched roof, walls of mats and bamboo, gables of carved teak timber. Rows of dwellings raised on a forest of piles lined the steely band of the river, brimful and still, with the tide at the turn. This was Batu Beru—and the day had come.

Mr. Massy shook himself, put on the tweed coat, and, shivering nervously as if from some great shock, made a note of the number. A fortunate, rare hint that. Yes; but to pursue fortune one wanted money—ready cash.

Then he went out and prepared to descend into the engine-room. Several small jobs had to be seen to, and Jack was lying dead drunk on the floor of his cabin, with the door locked at that. His gorge rose at the thought of work. Ay! But if you wanted to do nothing you had to get first a good bit of money. A ship won't save you. He cursed the *Sofala*. True, all true. He was tired of waiting for some chance that would rid him at last of that ship that had turned out a curse on his life.

XIV

THE deep, interminable hoot of the steam-whistle had, in its grave, vibrating note, something intolerable, which sent a slight shudder down Mr. Van Wyk's back. It was the early afternoon; the *Sofala* was leaving Batu Beru for Pangu, the next place of call. She swung in the stream, scantily attended by a few canoes, and, gliding on the broad river, became lost to view from the Van Wyk bungalow.

Its owner had not gone this time to see her off. Generally he came down to the wharf, exchanged a few words with the bridge while she cast off, and waved his hand to Captain Whalley at the last moment. This day he did not even go as far as the balustrade of the verandah. "He couldn't see me if I did," he said to himself. "I wonder whether he can make out the house at all." And this thought somehow made him feel more alone than he had ever felt for all these years. What was it? six or seven? Seven. A long time.

He sat on the verandah with a closed book on his knee, and, as it were, looked out upon his solitude, as if the fact of Captain Whalley's blindness had opened his eyes to his own. There were many sorts of heartaches and troubles, and there was no place where they could not find a man out. And he felt ashamed, as though he had for six years behaved like a peevish boy.

His thought followed the *Sofala* on her way. On the spur of the moment he had acted impulsively, turning to the thing most pressing. And what else could he have done? Later on he should see. It seemed necessary that he should come out into the world, for a time at least. He had money—something could be arranged; he would grudge no time, no trouble, no loss of his solitude. It weighed on him now—and Captain Whalley appeared to him as he had sat shading his eyes, as if, being deceived in the trust of his faith, he were beyond all the good and evil that can be wrought by the hands of men.

Mr. Van Wyk's thoughts followed the *Sofala* down the river, winding about through the belt of the coast forest, between the buttressed shafts of the big trees, through the mangrove strip, and over the bar. The ship crossed it easily in broad daylight, piloted, as it happened, by Mr. Sterne, who took the watch from four to six, and then went below to hug himself with delight at the prospect of being virtually employed by a rich man—like Mr. Van Wyk. He could not see how any hitch could occur now. He did not seem able to get over the feeling of being "fixed up at last." From six to eight, in the course of duty, the Serang looked alone after the ship. She had a clear road before her now till about three in the morning, when she would close with the Pangu group. At eight Mr. Sterne came out cheerily to take charge again till midnight. At ten he was still chirruping and humming to himself on the bridge, and about that time Mr. Van Wyk's thought abandoned the *Sofala*. Mr. Van Wyk had fallen asleep at last.

Massy, blocking the engine-room companion, jerked himself into his tweed jacket surlily, while the second waited with a scowl.

"Oh. You came out? You sot! Well, what have you got to say for yourself?"

He had been in charge of the engines till then. A sombre fury darkened his mind: a hot anger against the ship, against the facts of life, against the men for their cheating, against himself too—because of an inward tremor of his heart.

An incomprehensible growl answered him.

"What? Can't you open your mouth now? You yelp out your infernal rot loud enough when you are drunk. What do you mean by abusing people in that way?—you old useless boozer, you!"

"Can't help it. Don't remember anything about it. You shouldn't listen."

"You dare to tell me! What do you mean by going on a drunk like this!"

"Don't ask me. Sick of the dam' boilers—you would be. Sick of life."

"I wish you were dead, then. You've made me sick of you. Don't you remember the uproar you made last night? You miserable old soaker!"*

"No; I don't. Don't want to. Drink is drink."

"I wonder what prevents me from kicking you out. What do you want here?"

"Relieve you. You've been long enough down there, George."

"Don't you George me—you tippling old rascal, you! If I were to die to-morrow you would starve. Remember that. Say Mr. Massy."

"Mr. Massy," repeated the other stolidly.

Dishevelled, with dull blood-shot eyes, a snuffy, grimy shirt, greasy trousers, naked feet thrust into ragged slippers, he bolted in head down directly Massy had made way for him.

The chief engineer looked around. The deck was empty as far as the taffrail.* All the native passengers had left in Batu Beru this time, and no others had joined. The dial of the patent log* tinkled periodically in the dark at the end of the ship. It was a dead calm, and, under the clouded sky, through the still air that seemed to cling warm, with a seaweed smell, to her slim hull,* on a sea of sombre grey and unwrinkled, the ship moved on an even keel,* as if floating detached in empty space. But Mr. Massy slapped his forehead, tottered a little, caught hold of a belaying-pin at the foot of the mast.

"I shall go mad," he muttered, walking across the deck unsteadily. A shovel was scraping loose coal down below—a fire-door clanged. Sterne on the bridge began whistling a new tune.

Captain Whalley, sitting on the couch, awake and fully dressed, heard the door of his cabin open. He did not move in the least, waiting to recognize the voice, with an appalling strain of prudence.

A bulkhead lamp blazed on the white paint, the crimson plush, the brown varnish of mahogany tops. The white wood packing-case under the bed-place had remained unopened for three years now, as though Captain Whalley had felt that, after the *Fair Maid* was gone, there could be no abiding-place on earth for his affections. His hands rested on his knees; his handsome head with big eyebrows presented a rigid profile to the doorway. The expected voice spoke out at last.

"Once more, then. What am I to call you?"

Ha! Massy. Again. The weariness of it crushed his heart—and the pain of shame was almost more than he could bear without crying out.

"Well. Is it to be 'partner' still?"

"You don't know what you ask."

"I know what I want . . ."

Massy stepped in and closed the door.

". . . And I am going to have a try for it with you once more."

His whine was half persuasive, half menacing.

"For it's no manner of use to tell me that you are poor. You don't spend anything on yourself, that's true enough; but there's another name for that. You think you are going to have what you want out of me for three years, and then cast me off without hearing what I think of you. You think I would have submitted to your airs if I had known you had only a beggarly five hundred pounds in the world. You ought to have told me."

"Perhaps," said Captain Whalley, bowing his head. "And yet it has saved you." . . . Massy laughed scornfully. . . . "I have told you often enough since."

"And I don't believe you now. When I think how I let you lord it over my ship! Do you remember how you used to bullyrag* me about my coat and your bridge? It was in his way. His bridge! 'And I won't be a party to this—and I couldn't think of doing that.' Honest man! And now it all comes out. 'I am poor, and I can't. I have only this five hundred in the world.' "

He contemplated the immobility of Captain Whalley, that seemed to present an inconquerable obstacle in his path. His face took a mournful cast.

"You are a hard man."

"Enough," said Captain Whalley, turning upon him. "You shall get nothing from me, because I have nothing of mine to give away now."

"Tell that to the marines!"*

Mr. Massy, going out, looked back once; then the door closed, and Captain Whalley, alone, sat as still as before. He had nothing of his own—even his past of honour, of truth, of just pride, was gone. All his spotless life had fallen into the abyss. He had said his last good-bye to it. But what belonged to *her*, that he meant to save. Only a little money. He would take it to her in his own hands—this last gift of a man that had lasted too long. And an immense and fierce impulse, the very passion of paternity, flamed up with all the unquenched vigour of his worthless life in a desire to see her face.

Just across the deck Massy had gone straight to his cabin, struck a light, and hunted up the note of the dreamed number whose figures had flamed up also with the fierceness of another passion. He must contrive somehow not to miss a drawing. That number meant something. But what expedient* could he contrive to keep himself going?

"Wretched miser!" he mumbled.

If Mr. Sterne could at no time have told him anything new about his partner, he could have told Mr. Sterne that another use could be made of a man's affliction than just to kick him out, and thus defer the term of a difficult payment for a year. To keep the secret of the affliction and induce him to stay was a better move. If without means, he would be anxious to remain; and that settled the question of refunding him his share. He did not know exactly how much Captain Whalley was disabled; but if it so happened that he put the ship ashore somewhere for good and all, it was not the owner's fault—was it? He was not obliged to know that there was anything wrong. But probably nobody would raise such a point, and the ship was fully insured. He had had enough self-restraint to pay up the premiums. But this was not all. He could not believe Captain Whalley to be so confoundedly destitute as not to have some more money put away somewhere. If he, Massy, could get hold of it, that would pay for the boilers, and everything went on as before. And if she got lost in the end, so much the better. He hated her: he loathed the troubles that took his mind off the chances of fortune. He wished her at the bottom of the sea, and the insurance money in his pocket. And as, baffled, he left Captain Whalley's cabin, he enveloped in the same hatred the ship with the worn-out boilers and the man with the dimmed eyes.

And our conduct after all is so much a matter of outside suggestion, that had it not been for his Jack's drunken gabble he would have there and then had it out with this miserable man, who would neither help, nor stay, nor yet lose the ship. The old fraud! He longed to kick him out. But he restrained himself. Time enough for that—when he liked. There was a fearful new thought put into his head. Wasn't he up to it after all? How that beast Jack had raved! "Find a safe trick to get rid of her." Well, Jack was not so far wrong. A very clever trick had occurred to him. Aye! But what of the risk?

A feeling of pride—the pride of superiority to common prejudices—crept into his breast, made his heart beat fast, his mouth turn dry. Not everybody would dare; but he was Massy, and he was up to it!

Six bells* were struck on deck. Eleven! He drank a glass of water, and sat down for ten minutes or so to calm himself. Then he got out of his chest a small bull's-eye lantern* of his own and lit it.

Almost opposite his berth, across the narrow passage under the bridge, there was, in the iron deck-structure covering the stokehold fiddle* and the boiler-space, a storeroom with iron sides, iron roof, iron-plated floor, too, on account of the heat below. All sorts of rubbish was shot there: it had a mound of scrap-iron in a corner; rows of empty oil-cans; sacks of cotton-waste, with a heap of charcoal, a deck-forge,* fragments of an old hencoop, winch-covers all in rags, remnants of lamps, and a brown felt hat, discarded by a man dead now (of a fever on the Brazil coast), who had been once mate of the *Sofala*, had remained for years jammed forcibly behind a length of burst copper pipe, flung at some time or other out of the engine-room. A complete and imperious blackness pervaded that Capharnaum* of forgotten things. A small shaft of light from Mr. Massy's bull's-eye fell slanting right through it.

His coat was unbuttoned; he shot the bolt of the door (there was no other opening), and, squatting before the scrap-heap, began to pack his pockets with pieces of iron. He packed them carefully, as if the rusty nuts, the broken bolts, the links of cargo chain, had been so much gold he had that one chance to carry away. He packed his side-pockets till they bulged, the breast pocket, the pockets inside. He turned over the pieces. Some he rejected. A small mist of powdered rust began to rise about his busy hands. Mr. Massy knew something of the scientific basis of his clever trick. If you want to deflect the magnetic needle of a ship's compass, soft iron is the best; likewise many small pieces in the pockets of a jacket would have more effect than a few large ones, because in that way you obtain a greater amount of surface for weight in your iron, and it's surface that tells.

He slipped out swiftly—two strides sufficed—and in his cabin he perceived that his hands were all red—red with rust. It disconcerted him, as though he had found them covered with blood: he looked himself over hastily. Why, his trousers too! He had been rubbing his rusty palms on his legs.

He tore off the waistband button in his haste, brushed his coat, washed his hands. Then the air of guilt left him, and he sat down to wait.

He sat bolt upright and weighted with iron in his chair. He had a hard, lumpy bulk against each hip, felt the scrappy iron in his pockets touch his ribs at every breath, the downward drag of all these pounds hanging upon his shoulders. He looked very dull too, sitting idle there, and his yellow face, with motionless black eyes, had something passive and sad in its quietness.

When he heard eight bells* struck above his head, he rose and made ready to go out. His movements seemed aimless, his lower lip had dropped a little, his eyes roamed about the cabin, and the tremendous tension of his will had robbed them of every vestige of intelligence.

With the last stroke of the bell the Serang appeared noiselessly on the bridge to relieve the mate. Sterne overflowed with good nature, since he had nothing more to desire.

"Got your eyes well open yet, Serang? It's middling dark; I'll wait till you get your sight properly."

The old Malay murmured, looked up with his worn eyes, sidled away into the light of the binnacle, and, crossing his hands behind his back, fixed his eyes on the compass-card.

"You'll have to keep a good look-out ahead for land, about half-past three. It's fairly clear, though. You have looked in on the captain as you came along—eh? He knows the time? Well, then, I am off."

At the foot of the ladder he stood aside for the captain. He watched him go up with an even, certain tread, and remained thoughtful for a moment. "It's funny," he said to himself, "but you can never tell whether that man has seen you or not. He might have heard me breathe this time."

He was a wonderful man when all was said and done. They said he had had a name in his day. Mr. Sterne could well believe it; and he concluded serenely that Captain Whalley must be able to see people more or less—as himself just now, for instance—but not being certain of anybody, had to keep up that unnoticing silence of manner for fear of giving himself away. Mr. Sterne was a shrewd guesser.

This necessity of every moment brought home to Captain Whalley's heart the humiliation of his falsehood. He had drifted into it from paternal love, from incredulity, from boundless trust in divine justice meted out to men's feelings on this earth. He would give his poor Ivy the benefit of another month's work; perhaps the affliction was only temporary. Surely God would not rob his child of his power to help, and cast him naked into a night without end. He had caught at every hope; and when the evidence of his misfortune was stronger than hope, he tried not to believe the manifest thing.

In vain. In the steadily darkening universe a sinister clearness fell upon his ideas. In the illuminating moments of suffering he saw life, men, all things, the whole earth with all her burden of created nature, as he had never seen them before.*

Sometimes he was seized with a sudden vertigo and an overwhelming terror; and then the image of his daughter appeared. Her, too, he had never seen so clearly before. Was it possible that he should ever be unable to do anything whatever for her? Nothing. And not see her any more? Never.

Why? The punishment was too great for a little presumption, for a little pride. And at last he came to cling to his deception with a fierce determination to carry it out to the end, to save her money intact, and behold her once more with his own eyes. Afterwards—what? The idea of suicide was revolting to the vigour of his manhood. He had prayed for death till the prayers had stuck in his throat. All the days of his life he had prayed for daily bread, and not to be led into temptation,* in a childlike humility of spirit. Did words mean anything? Whence did the gift of speech come? The violent beating of his heart reverberated in his head—seemed to shake his brain to pieces.

He sat down heavily in the deck-chair to keep the pretence of his watch. The night was dark. All the nights were dark now.

"Serang," he said, half aloud.

"Ada, Tuan.* I am here."

"There are clouds on the sky?"

"There are, Tuan."

"Let her be steered straight. North."

"She is going north, Tuan."

The Serang stepped back. Captain Whalley recognized Massy's footfalls on the bridge.

The engineer walked over to port and returned, passing behind the chair several times. Captain Whalley detected* an unusual character as of prudent care in this prowling. The near presence of that man brought with it always a recrudescence of moral suffering for Captain Whalley. It was not remorse. After all, he had done nothing but good to the poor devil. There was also a sense of danger—the necessity of a greater care.

Massy stopped and said—

"So you still say you must go?"

"I must indeed."

"And you couldn't at least leave the money for a term of years?"

"Impossible."

"Can't trust it with me without your care, eh?"

Captain Whalley remained silent. Massy sighed deeply over the back of the chair.

"It would just do to save me," he said in a tremulous voice.

"I've saved you once."

The chief engineer took off his coat with careful movements, and proceeded to feel for the brass hook screwed into the wooden stanchion. For this purpose he placed himself right in front of the binnacle, thus hiding completely the compass-card from the quarter-master at the wheel. "Tuan!" the lascar at last murmured softly, meaning to let the white man know that he could not see to steer.

Mr. Massy had accomplished his purpose. The coat was hanging from the nail, within six inches of the binnacle. And directly he had stepped aside the quartermaster, a middle-aged, pock-marked, Sumatra Malay, almost as dark as a negro, perceived with amazement that in that short time, in this smooth water, with no wind at all, the ship had gone swinging far out of her course. He had never known her get away like this before. With a slight grunt of astonishment he turned the wheel hastily to bring her head back north, which was the course. The grinding of the steering-chains,* the chiding murmurs of the *Serang*, who had come over to the wheel, made a slight stir, which attracted Captain Whalley's anxious attention. He said, "Take better care." Then everything settled to the usual quiet on the bridge. Mr. Massy had disappeared.

But the iron in the pockets of the coat had done its work; and the *Sofala*, heading north by the compass, made untrue by this simple device, was no longer making a safe course for Pangu Bay.

The hiss of water parted by her stem, the throb of her engines, all the sounds of her faithful and laborious life, went on uninterrupted in the great calm of the sea joining on all sides the motionless layer of cloud over the sky. A gentle stillness as vast as the world seemed to wait upon her path, enveloping her lovingly in a supreme caress. Mr. Massy thought there could be no better night for an arranged shipwreck.

Run up high and dry on one of the reefs east of Pangu—wait for daylight—hole in the bottom—out boats—Pangu Bay same evening. That's about it. As soon as she touched he would hasten on the bridge, get hold of the coat (nobody would notice in the dark), and shake it upside-down over the side, or even fling it into the sea. A detail. Who could guess? Coat been seen hanging there from that hook hundreds of times. Nevertheless, when he sat down on the lower step of the bridge-ladder his knees knocked together a little. The waiting part was the worst of it. At times he would begin to pant quickly, as though he had been running, and then breathe largely, swelling with the intimate sense of a mastered fate. Now and then he would hear the shuffle of the Serang's bare feet up there: quiet, low voices would exchange a few words, and lapse almost at once into silence. . . .

"Tell me directly you see any land, Serang."

"Yes, Tuan. Not yet."

"No, not yet," Captain Whalley would agree.

The ship had been the best friend of his decline. He had sent all the money he had made by and in the *Sofala* to his daughter. His thought lingered on the name. How often he and his wife had talked over the cot of the child in the big stern-cabin of the *Condor*; she would grow up, she would marry, she would love them, they would live near her and look at her happiness—it would go on without end. Well, his wife was dead, to the child he had given all he had to give; he wished he could come near her, see her, see her face once, live in the sound of her voice, that could make the darkness of the living grave ready for him supportable. He had been starved of love too long. He imagined her tenderness.

The Serang had been peering forward, and now and then glancing at the chair. He fidgeted restlessly, and suddenly burst out close to Captain Whalley—

"Tuan, do you see anything of the land?"

The alarmed voice brought Captain Whalley to his feet at once. He! See! And at the question, the curse of his blindness seemed to fall on him with a hundredfold force.

"What's the time?" he cried.

"Half-past three, Tuan."

"We are close. You *must* see. Look, I say. Look."

Mr. Massy, awakened by the sudden sound of talking from a short doze on the lowest step, wondered why he was there. Ah! A faintness came over him. It is one thing to sow the seed of an accident and another to see the monstrous fruit hanging over your head ready to fall in the sound of agitated voices.

"There's no danger," he muttered thickly.

The horror of incertitude had seized upon Captain Whalley, the miserable mistrust of men, of things—of the very earth. He had steered that very course thirty-six times by the same compass—if anything was certain in this world it was its absolute, unerring correctness. Then what had happened? Did the Serang lie? Why lie? Why? Was he going blind too?

"Is there a mist? Look low on the water. Low down, I say."

"Tuan, there's no mist. See for yourself."

Captain Whalley steadied the trembling of his limbs by an effort. Should he stop the engines at once and give himself away. A gust of irresolution swayed all sorts of bizarre notions in his mind. The unusual had come, and he was not fit to deal with it. In this passage of inexpressible anguish he saw her face—the face of a young girl—with an amazing strength of illusion. No, he must not give himself away after having gone so far for her sake. "You steered the course? You made it? Speak the truth."

"Ya, Tuan. On the course now. Look."

Captain Whalley strode to the binnacle, which to him made such a dim spot of light in an infinity of shapeless shadow. By bending his face right down to the glass he had been able before . . .

Having to stoop so low, he put out, instinctively, his arm to where he knew there was a stanchion to steady himself against. His hand closed on something that was not wood but cloth. The slight pull adding to the weight, the loop broke, and Mr. Massy's coat falling, struck the deck heavily with a dull thump, accompanied by a lot of clicks.

"What's this?"

Captain Whalley fell on his knees, with groping hands extended in a frank gesture of blindness. They trembled, these hands feeling for the truth. He saw it. Iron near the compass. Wrong course. Wreck her! His ship. Oh no. Not that.

"Jump and stop her!" he roared out in a voice not his own.

He ran himself—hands forward, a blind man, and while the clanging of the gong echoed still all over the ship, she seemed to butt full tilt into the side of a mountain.

It was low water along the north side of the strait. Mr. Massy had not reckoned on that. Instead of running aground for half her length, the *Sofala* butted the sheer ridge of a stone reef which would have been awash at high water. This made the shock absolutely terrific. Everybody in the ship that was standing was thrown down headlong: the shaken rigging made a great rattling to the very trucks. All the lights went out: several chain-guys,* snapping, clattered against the funnel: there were crashes, pings of parted wire-rope, splintering sounds, loud cracks, the masthead lamp flew over the bows,* and all the doors about the deck began to bang heavily. Then, after having hit, she rebounded, hit the second time the very same spot like a battering-ram. This completed the havoc: the funnel, with all the guys gone, fell over with a hollow sound of thunder, smashing the wheel to bits, crushing the frame of the awnings, breaking the lockers, filling the bridge with a mass of splinters, sticks, and broken wood. Captain Whalley picked himself up and stood knee-deep in wreckage, torn, bleeding, knowing the nature of the danger he had escaped mostly by the sound, and holding Mr. Massy's coat in his arms.

By this time Sterne (he had been flung out of his bunk) had set the engines astern. They worked for a few turns, then a voice bawled out, "Get out of the damned engine-room, Jack!"—and they stopped; but the ship had gone clear of the reef and lay still, with a heavy cloud of steam issuing from the broken deck-pipes, and vanishing in wispy shapes into the night. Notwithstanding the suddenness of the disaster there was no shouting, as if the very violence of the shock had half-stunned the shadowy lot of people swaying here and there about her decks. The voice of the Serang pronounced distinctly above the confused murmurs—

"Eight fathom."* He had heaved the lead.

Mr. Sterne cried out next in a strained pitch—

"Where the devil has she got to? Where are we?"

Captain Whalley replied in a calm bass—

"Amongst the reefs to the eastward."

"You know it, sir? Then she will never get out again."

"She will be sunk in five minutes. Boats, Sterne. Even one will save you all in this calm."

The Chinaman stokers* went in a disorderly rush for the port boats. Nobody tried to check them. The Malays, after a moment of confusion, became quiet, and Mr. Sterne showed a good countenance.* Captain Whalley had not moved. His thoughts were darker than this night in which he had lost his first ship.

"He made me lose a ship."

Another tall figure standing before him amongst the litter of the smash on the bridge whispered insanely—

"Say nothing of it."

Massy stumbled closer. Captain Whalley heard the chattering of his teeth.

"I have the coat."

"Throw it down and come along," urged the chattering voice. "B-b-b-b-boat!"

"You will get fifteen years for this."

Mr. Massy had lost his voice. His speech was a mere dry rustling in his throat.

"Have mercy!"

"Had you any when you made me lose my ship? Mr. Massy, you shall get fifteen years for this!"

"I wanted money! Money! My own money! I will give you some money. Take half of it. You love money yourself."

"There's a justice . . ."

Massy made an awful effort, and in a strange, half choked utterance—

"You blind devil! It's you that drove me to it."

Captain Whalley, hugging the coat to his breast, made no sound. The light had ebbed for ever from the world—let everything go. But this man should not escape scot-free.

Sterne's voice commanded—

"Lower away!"

The blocks* rattled.

"Now then," he cried, "over with you. This way. You, Jack, here. Mr. Massy! Mr. Massy! Captain! Quick, sir! Let's get—

"I shall go to prison for trying to cheat the insurance, but you'll get exposed; you, honest man, who has been cheating me. You are poor. Aren't you? You've nothing but the five hundred pounds. Well, you have nothing at all now. The ship's lost, and the insurance won't be paid."

Captain Whalley did not move. True! Ivy's money! Gone in this wreck. Again he had a flash of insight. He was indeed at the end of his tether.

Urgent voices cried out together alongside. Massy did not seem able to tear himself away from the bridge. He chattered and hissed despairingly—

"Give it up to me! Give it up!"

"No," said Captain Whalley; "I could not give it up. You had better go. Don't wait, man, if you want to live. She's settling down by the head fast. No; I shall keep it, but I shall stay on board."

Massy did not seem to understand; but the love of life, awakened suddenly, drove him away from the bridge.

Captain Whalley laid the coat down, and stumbled amongst the heaps of wreckage to the side.

"Is Mr. Massy in with you?" he called out into the night.

Sterne from the boat shouted—

"Yes; we've got him. Come along, sir. It's madness to stay longer."

Captain Whalley felt along the rail carefully, and, without a word, cast off the painter.* They were expecting him still down there. They were waiting, till a voice suddenly exclaimed—

"We are adrift! Shove off!"

"Captain Whalley! Leap! . . . pull up a little . . . leap! You can swim."

In that old heart, in that vigorous body, there was, that nothing should be wanting, a horror of death that apparently could not be overcome by the horror of blindness. But after all, for Ivy he had carried his point, walking in his darkness to the very verge of a crime. God had not listened to his prayers. The light had finished ebbing out of the world; not a glimmer. It was a dark waste; but it was unseemly that a Whalley who had gone so far to carry a point should continue to live. He must pay the price.

"Leap as far as you can, sir; we will pick you up."

They did not hear him answer. But their shouting seemed to remind him of something. He groped his way back, and sought for Mr. Massy's coat. He could swim indeed; people sucked down by the whirlpool of a sinking ship do come up sometimes to the surface, and it was unseemly that a Whalley, who had made up his mind to die, should be beguiled by chance into a struggle. He would put all these pieces of iron into his own pockets.*

They, looking from the boat, saw the *Sofala*, a black mass upon a black sea, lying still at an appalling cant.* No sound came from her. Then, with a great bizarre shuffling noise, as if the boilers had broken through the bulkheads, and with a faint muffled detonation, where the ship had been there appeared for a moment something standing upright and narrow, like a rock out of the sea. Then that too disappeared.

When the *Sofala* failed to come back to Batu Beru at the proper time, Mr. Van Wyk understood at once that he would never see her any more. But he did not know what had happened till some months afterwards, when, in a native craft lent him by his Sultan, he had made his way to the *Sofala*'s port of registry, where already her existence and the official inquiry into her loss was beginning to be forgotten.

It had not been a very remarkable or interesting case, except for the fact that the captain had gone down with his sinking ship. It was the only life lost; and Mr. Van Wyk would not have been able to learn any details had it not been for Sterne, whom he met one day on the quay near the bridge over the creek, almost on the very spot where Captain Whalley, to preserve his daughter's five hundred pounds intact, had turned to get a sampan which would take him on board the *Sofala*.

From afar Mr. Van Wyk saw Sterne blink straight at him and raise his hand to his hat. They drew into the shade of a building (it was a bank), and the mate related how the boat with the crew got into Pangu Bay about six hours after the accident, and how they had lived for a fortnight in a state of destitution before they found an opportunity to get away from that beastly place. The inquiry had exonerated everybody from all blame. The loss of the ship was put down to an unusual set of the current. Indeed, it could not have been anything else: there was no other way to account for the ship being set seven miles to the eastward of her position during the middle watch.

"A piece of bad luck for me, sir."

Sterne passed his tongue on his lips, and glanced aside. "I lost the advantage of being employed by you, sir. I can never be sorry enough. But here it is: one man's poison, another man's meat.* This could not have been handier for Mr. Massy if he had arranged that shipwreck himself. The most timely total loss I've ever heard of."

"What became of that Massy?" asked Mr. Van Wyk.

"He, sir? Ha! ha! He would keep on telling me that he meant to buy another ship; but as soon as he had the money in his pocket he cleared out for Manilla by mail-boat early in the morning. I gave him chase right aboard, and he told me then he was going to make his fortune dead sure in Manilla. I could go to the devil for all he cared. And yet he as good as promised to give me the command if I didn't talk too much."

"You never said anything . . ." Mr. Van Wyk began.

"Not I, sir. Why should I? I mean to get on, but the dead aren't in my way," said Sterne. His eyelids were beating rapidly, then drooped for an instant. "Besides, sir, it would have been an awkward business. You made me hold my tongue just a bit too long."

"Do you know how it was that Captain Whalley remained on board? Did he really refuse to leave? Come now! Or was it perhaps an accidental . . .?"

"Nothing!" Sterne interrupted with energy. "I tell you I yelled for him to leap overboard. He simply must have cast off the painter of the boat himself. We all yelled to him—that is, Jack and I. He wouldn't even answer us. The ship was as silent as a grave to the last. Then the boilers fetched away, and down she went. Accident! Not it! The game was up, sir, I tell you."

This was all that Sterne had to say.

Mr. Van Wyk had been of course made the guest of the club for a fortnight, and it was there that he met the lawyer in whose office had been signed the agreement between Massy and Captain Whalley.

"Extraordinary old man," he said. "He came into my office from nowhere in particular as you may say, with his five hundred pounds to place, and that engineer fellow following him anxiously. And now he is gone out a little inexplicably, just as he came. I could never understand him quite. There was no mystery at all about that Massy, eh? I wonder whether Whalley refused to leave the ship. It would have been foolish. He was blameless, as the court found."

Mr. Van Wyk had known him well, he said, and he could not believe in suicide. Such an act would not have been in character with what he knew of the man.

"It is my opinion, too," the lawyer agreed. The general theory was that the captain had remained too long on board trying to save something of importance. Perhaps the chart which would clear him, or else something of value in his cabin. The painter of the boat had come adrift of itself it was supposed. However, strange to say, some little time before that voyage poor Whalley had called in his office and had left with him a sealed envelope addressed to his daughter, to be forwarded to her in case of his death. Still it was nothing very unusual, especially in a man of his age. Mr. Van Wyk shook his head. Captain Whalley looked good for a hundred years.

"Perfectly true," assented the lawyer. "The old fellow looked as though he had come into the world full-grown and with that long beard. I could never, somehow, imagine him either younger or older—don't you know. There was a sense of physical power about that man too. And perhaps that was the secret of that something peculiar in his person which struck everybody who came in contact with him. He looked indestructible by any ordinary means that put an end to the rest of us. His deliberate, stately courtesy of manner was full of significance. It was as though he were certain of having plenty of time for everything. Yes, there was something indestructible about him; and the way he talked sometimes you might have thought he believed it himself. When he called on me last with that letter he wanted me to take charge of, he was not depressed at all. Perhaps a shade more deliberate in his talk and manner. Not depressed in the least. Had he a presentiment, I wonder? Perhaps! Still it seems a miserable end for such a striking figure."

"Oh yes! It was a miserable end," Mr. Van Wyk said, with so much fervour that the lawyer looked up at him curiously; and afterwards, after parting with him, he remarked to an acquaintance—

"Queer person that Dutch tobacco-planter from Batu Beru. Know anything of him?"

"Heaps of money," answered the bank manager. "I hear he's going home by the next mail to form a company to take over his estates. Another tobacco district thrown open. He's wise, I think. These good times won't last for ever."

In the southern hemisphere Captain Whalley's daughter had no presentiment of evil when she opened the envelope addressed to her in the lawyer's handwriting. She had received it in the afternoon; all the boarders had gone out, her boys were at school, her husband sat upstairs in his big arm-chair with a book, thin-faced, wrapped up in rugs to the waist. The house was still, and the greyness of a cloudy day lay against the panes of three lofty windows.

In a shabby dining-room, where a faint cold smell of dishes lingered all the year round, sitting at the end of a long table surrounded by many chairs pushed in with their backs close against the edge of the perpetually laid table-cloth, she read the opening sentence: "Most profound regret—painful duty—your father is no more—in accordance with his instructions—fatal casualty—consolation—no blame attached to his memory. . . ."

Her face was thin, her temples a little sunk under the smooth bands of black hair, her lips remained resolutely compressed, while her dark eyes grew larger, till at last, with a low cry, she stood up, and instantly stooped to pick up another envelope which had slipped off her knees on to the floor.

She tore it open, snatched out the enclosure. . . .

"My dearest child," it said, "I am writing this while I am able yet to write legibly. I am trying hard to save for you all the money that is left; I have only kept it to serve you better. It is yours. It shall not be lost: it shall not be touched. There's five hundred pounds. Of what I have earned I have kept nothing back till now. For the future, if I live, I must keep back some—a little—to bring me to you. I must come to you. I must see you once more.

"It is hard to believe that you will ever look on these lines. God seems to have forgotten me. I want to see you—and yet death would be a greater favour. If you ever read these words, I charge you to begin by thanking a God merciful at last, for I shall be dead then, and it will be well. My dear, I am at the end of my tether."

The next paragraph began with the words: "My sight is going . . ."*

She read no more that day. The hand holding up the paper to her eyes fell slowly, and her slender figure in a plain black dress walked rigidly to the window. Her eyes were dry: no cry of sorrow or whisper of thanks went up to heaven from her lips. Life had been too hard, for all the efforts of his love. It had silenced her emotions. But for the first time in all these years its sting had departed, the carking care of poverty, the meanness of a hard struggle for bread. Even the image of her husband and of her children seemed to glide away from her into the grey twilight; it was her father's face alone that she saw, as though he had come to see her, always quiet and big, as she had seen him last, but with something more august and tender in his aspect.

She slipped his folded letter between the two buttons of her plain black bodice, and leaning her forehead against a window-pane remained there till dusk, perfectly motionless, giving him all the time she could spare. Gone! Was it possible? My God, was it possible! The blow had come softened by the spaces of the earth, by the years of absence. There had been whole days when she had not thought of him at all—had no time. But she had loved him, she felt she had loved him, after all.*

AMY FOSTER

KENNEDY is a country doctor, and lives in Colebrook, on the shores of Eastbay.* The high ground rising abruptly behind the red roofs of the little town crowds the quaint High Street against the wall which defends it from the sea. Beyond the sea-wall there curves for miles in a vast and regular sweep the barren beach of shingle, with the village of Brenzett standing out darkly across the water, a spire in a clump of trees; and still further out the perpendicular column of a light house, looking in the distance no bigger than a lead-pencil, marks the vanishing-point of the land. The country at the back of Brenzett is low and flat; but the bay is fairly well sheltered from the seas, and occasionally a big ship, windbound or through stress of weather, makes use of the anchoring ground a mile and a half due north from you as you stand at the back door of the Ship Inn in Brenzett.* A dilapidated windmill near by lifting its shattered arms from a mound no loftier than a rubbish-heap, and a Martello tower* squatting at the water's edge half a mile to the south of the Coastguard cottages, are familiar to the skippers of small craft. These are the official seamarks for the patch of trustworthy bottom represented on the Admiralty charts* by an irregular oval of dots enclosing several figures six, with a tiny anchor engraved among them, and the legend "mud and shells" over all.

The brow of the upland overtops the square tower of the Colebrook Church. The slope is green and looped by a white road. Ascending along this road, you open a valley broad and shallow, a wide green trough of pastures and hedges merging inland into a vista of purple tints and flowing lines closing the view.

In this valley down to Brenzett and Colebrook and up to Darnford, the market town fourteen miles away, lies the practice of my friend Kennedy. He had begun life as surgeon in the Navy, and afterwards had been the companion of a famous traveller, in the days when there were continents with unexplored interiors. His papers on the fauna and flora made him known to scientific societies. And now he had come to a country practice—from choice.* The penetrating power of his mind, acting like a corrosive fluid, had destroyed his ambition,

I fancy. His intelligence is of a scientific order, of an investigating habit, and of that unappeasable curiosity which believes that there is a particle of a general truth in every mystery.

A good many years ago now, on my return from abroad, he invited me to stay with him. I came readily enough, and as he could not neglect his patients to keep me company, he took me on his rounds—thirty miles or so of an afternoon, sometimes. I waited for him on the roads; the horse reached after the leafy twigs, and, sitting high in the dogcart, I could hear Kennedy's laugh through the half-open door of some cottage. He had a big, hearty laugh that would have fitted a man twice his size, a brisk manner, a bronzed face, and a pair of grey, profoundly attentive eyes. He had the talent of making people talk to him freely, and an inexhaustible patience in listening to their tales.

One day, as we trotted out of a large village into a shady bit of road, I saw on our left hand a low, brick cottage, with diamond panes in the windows, a creeper on the end wall, a roof of shingle, and some roses climbing on the rickety trellis-work of the tiny porch. Kennedy pulled up to a walk. A woman, in full sunlight, was throwing a dripping blanket over a line stretched between two old apple-trees. And as the bob-tailed, long-necked chestnut,* trying to get his head, jerked the left hand, covered by a thick dogskin glove, the doctor raised his voice over the hedge: "How's your child, Amy?"

I had the time to see her dull face, red, not with a mantling blush, but as if her flat cheeks had been vigorously slapped, and to take in the squat figure, the scanty, dusty brown hair drawn into a tight knot at the back of the head. She looked quite young. With a distinct catch in her breath, her voice sounded low and timid.

"He's well, thank you."

We trotted again. "A young patient of yours," I said; and the doctor, flicking the chestnut absently, muttered, "Her husband used to be."

"She seems a dull creature," I remarked listlessly.

"Precisely," said Kennedy. "She is very passive. It's enough to look at the red hands hanging at the end of those short arms, at those slow, prominent brown eyes, to know the inertness of her mind—an inertness that one would think made it everlastingly safe from all the surprises of imagination. And yet which of us is safe?* At any rate, such as you see her, she had enough imagination to fall in love. She's the daughter of one Isaac Foster, who from a small farmer has sunk into a shepherd; the beginning of his misfortunes dating from his runaway marriage with the cook of his widowed father—a well-to-do, apoplectic grazier,* who passionately struck his name off his will, and had been heard to utter threats against his life. But this old affair, scandalous enough to serve as a motive for a Greek tragedy, arose from the similarity of their characters. There are other tragedies, less scandalous and of a subtler poignancy, arising from irreconcilable differences and from that fear of the Incomprehensible that hangs over all our heads—over all our heads. . . ."

The tired chestnut dropped into a walk; and the rim of the sun, all red in a speckless sky, touched familiarly the smooth top of a ploughed rise near the road as I had seen it times innumerable touch the distant horizon of the sea. The uniform brownness of the harrowed field glowed with a rosy tinge, as though the powdered clods had sweated out in minute pearls of blood the toil of uncounted ploughmen. From the edge of a copse a waggon with two horses was rolling gently along the ridge. Raised above our heads upon the skyline, it loomed up against the red sun, triumphantly big, enormous, like a chariot of giants drawn by two slow-stepping steeds of legendary proportions. And the clumsy figure of the man plodding at the head of the leading horse projected itself on the background of the Infinite with a heroic uncouthness. The end of his carter's whip quivered high up in the blue. Kennedy discoursed.

"She's the eldest of a large family. At the age of fifteen they put her out to service at the New Barns Farm. I attended Mrs. Smith, the tenant's wife, and saw that girl there for the first time. Mrs. Smith, a genteel person with a sharp nose, made her put on a black dress every afternoon. I don't know what induced me to notice her at all. There are faces that call your attention by a curious want of definiteness in their whole aspect, as, walking in a mist, you peer attentively at a vague shape which, after all, may be nothing more curious or strange than a signpost. The only peculiarity I perceived in her was a slight hesitation in her utterance, a sort of preliminary stammer which passes away with the first word. When sharply spoken to, she was apt to lose her head at once; but her heart was of the kindest. She had never been heard to express a dislike for a single human being, and she was tender to every living creature. She was devoted to Mrs. Smith, to Mr. Smith, to their dogs, cats, canaries; and as to Mrs. Smith's grey parrot, its peculiarities exercised upon her a positive fascination. Nevertheless, when that outlandish bird, attacked by the cat, shrieked for help in human accents, she ran out into the yard stopping her ears, and did not prevent the crime.* For Mrs. Smith this was another evidence of her stupidity; on the other hand, her want of charm, in view of Smith's well-known frivolousness, was a great recommendation. Her short-sighted eyes would swim with pity for a poor mouse in a trap, and she had been seen once by some boys on her knees in the wet grass helping a toad in difficulties. If it's true, as some German fellow* has said, that without phosphorus there is no thought, it is still more true that there is no kindness of heart without a certain amount of imagination. She had some. She had even more than is necessary to understand suffering and to be moved by pity. She fell in love under circumstances that leave no room for doubt in the matter; for you need imagination to form a notion of beauty at all, and still more to discover your ideal in an unfamiliar shape.

"How this aptitude came to her, what it did feed upon, is an inscrutable mystery. She was born in the village, and had never been further away from it than Colebrook or perhaps Darnford. She lived for four years with the Smiths. New Barns is an isolated farmhouse a mile away from the road, and she was content to look day after day at the same fields, hollows, rises; at the trees and the hedgerows; at the faces of the four men about the farm, always the same—day after day, month after month, year after year. She never showed a desire for conversation, and, as it seemed to me, she did not know how to smile. Sometimes of a fine Sunday afternoon she would put on her best dress, a pair of stout boots, a large grey hat trimmed with a black feather (I've seen her in that finery), seize an absurdly slender parasol, climb over two stiles, tramp over three fields and along two hundred yards of road—never further. There stood Foster's cottage. She would help her mother to give their tea to the younger children, wash up the crockery, kiss the little ones, and go back to the farm. That was all. All the rest, all the change, all the relaxation. She never seemed to wish for anything more. And then she fell in love. She fell in love silently, obstinately—perhaps helplessly. It came slowly, but when it came it worked like a powerful spell; it was love as the Ancients* understood it: an irresistible and fateful impulse—a possession! Yes, it was in her to become haunted and possessed by a face, by a presence, fatally, as though she had been a pagan worshipper of form under a joyous sky—and to be awakened at last from that mysterious forgetfulness of self, from that enchantment, from that transport, by a fear resembling the unaccountable terror of a brute. . . ."

With the sun hanging low on its western limit, the expanse of the grass-lands framed in the counter-scarps of the rising ground took on a gorgeous and sombre aspect. A sense of penetrating sadness, like that inspired by a grave strain of music, disengaged itself from the silence of the fields. The men we met walked past, slow, unsmiling, with downcast eyes, as if the melancholy of an over-burdened earth had weighted their feet, bowed their shoulders, borne down their glances.

"Yes," said the doctor to my remark, "one would think the earth is under a curse, since of all her children these that cling to her the closest are uncouth in body and as leaden of gait as if their very hearts were loaded with chains. But here on this same road you might have seen amongst these heavy men a being lithe, supple and long-limbed, straight like a pine, with something striving upwards in his appearance as though the heart within him had been buoyant. Perhaps it was only the force of the contrast, but when he was passing one of these villagers here, the soles of his feet did not seem to me to touch the dust of the road. He vaulted over the stiles, paced these slopes with a long elastic stride that made him noticeable at a great distance, and had lustrous black eyes. He was so different from the mankind around that, with his freedom of movement, his soft—a little startled—glance, his olive complexion and graceful bearing, his humanity suggested to me the nature of a woodland creature. He came from there."

The doctor pointed with his whip, and from the summit of the descent seen over the rolling tops of the trees in a park by the side of the road, appeared the level sea far below us, like the floor of an immense edifice inlaid with bands of dark ripple, with still trails of glitter, ending in a belt of glassy water at the foot of the sky. The light blur of smoke, from an invisible steamer, faded on the great clearness of the horizon like the mist of a breath on a mirror; and, inshore, the white sails of a coaster, with the appearance of disentangling themselves slowly from under the branches, floated clear of the foliage of the trees.

"Shipwrecked in the bay?" I said.

"Yes; he was a castaway.* A poor emigrant* from Central Europe bound to America and washed ashore here in a storm. And for him, who knew nothing of the earth, England was an undiscovered country. It was some time before he learned its name; and for all I know he might have expected to find wild beasts or wild men here, when, crawling in the dark over the sea-wall, he rolled down the other side into a dyke, where it was another miracle he didn't get drowned. But he struggled instinctively like an animal under a net, and this blind struggle threw him out into a field. He must have been, indeed, of a tougher fibre than he looked to withstand without expiring such buffetings, the violence of his exertions, and so much fear. Later on, in his broken English that resembled curiously the speech of a young child, he told me himself that he put his trust in God,* believing he was no longer in this world. And truly—he would add—how was he to know? He fought his way against the rain and the gale on all fours, and crawled at last among some sheep huddled close under the lee of a hedge. They ran off in all directions, bleating in the darkness, and he welcomed the first familiar sound he heard on these shores. It must have been two in the morning then. And this is all we know of the manner of his landing, though he did not arrive unattended by any means. Only his grisly company did not begin to come ashore till much later in the day. . . ."

The doctor gathered the reins, clicked his tongue; we trotted down the hill. Then turning, almost directly, a sharp corner into the High Street, we rattled over the stones and were home.

Late in the evening Kennedy, breaking a spell of moodiness that had come over him, returned to the story. Smoking his pipe, he paced the long room from end to end. A reading-lamp concentrated all its light upon the papers on his desk; and, sitting by the open window, I saw, after the windless, scorching day, the frigid splendour of a hazy sea lying motionless under the moon. Not a whisper, not a splash, not a stir of the shingle, not a footstep, not a sigh came up from the earth below—never a sign of life but the scent of climbing jasmine: and Kennedy's voice, speaking behind me, passed through the wide casement,* to vanish outside in a chill and sumptuous stillness.

". . . . The relations of shipwrecks in the olden time tell us of much suffering. Often the castaways were only saved from drowning to die miserably from starvation on a barren coast; others suffered violent death or else slavery, passing through years of precarious existence with people to whom their strangeness was an object of suspicion, dislike or fear. We read about these things, and they are very pitiful. It is indeed hard upon a man to find himself a lost stranger, helpless, incomprehensible, and of a mysterious origin, in some obscure corner of the earth. Yet amongst all the adventurers shipwrecked in all the wild parts of the world, there is not one, it seems to me, that ever had to suffer a fate so simply tragic as the man I am speaking of, the most innocent of adventurers cast out by the sea in the bight of this bay, almost within sight from this very window.

"He did not know the name of his ship. Indeed, in the course of time we discovered he did not even know that ships had names—'like Christian people'; and when, one day, from the top of the Talfourd Hill, he beheld the sea lying open to his view, his eyes roamed afar, lost in an air of wild surprise, as though he had never seen such a sight before. And probably he had not. As far as I could make out, he had been hustled together with many others on board an emigrant-ship lying at the mouth of the Elbe,* too bewildered to take note of his surroundings, too weary to see anything, too anxious to care. They were driven below into the 'tween-deck* and battened down* from the very start. It was a low timber dwelling—he would say—with wooden beams overhead, like the houses in his country, but you went into it down a ladder. It was very large, very cold, damp and sombre, with places in the manner of wooden boxes where people had to sleep one above another, and it kept on rocking all ways at once all the time.* He crept into one of these boxes and lay down there in the clothes in which he had left his home many days before, keeping his bundle and his stick by his side. People groaned, children cried, water dripped, the lights went out, the walls of the place creaked, and everything was being shaken so that in one's little box one dared not lift one's head. He had lost touch with his only companion (a young man from the same valley, he said), and all the time a great noise of wind went on outside and heavy blows fell—boom! boom! An awful sickness overcame him, even to the point of making him neglect his prayers. Besides, one could not tell whether it was morning or evening. It seemed always to be night in that place.

"Before that he had been travelling a long, long time on the iron track.* He looked out of the window, which had a wonderfully clear glass in it, and the trees, the houses, the fields, and the long roads seemed to fly round and round about him till his head swam. He gave me to understand that he had on his passage beheld uncounted multitudes of people—whole nations—all dressed in such clothes as the rich wear. Once he was made to get out of the carriage, and slept through a night on a bench in a house of bricks with his bundle under his head; and once for many hours he had to sit on a floor of flat stones dozing, with his knees up and with his bundle between his feet. There was a roof over him, which seemed made of glass, and was so high that the tallest mountain-pine he had ever seen would have had room to grow under it. Steam-machines rolled in at one end and out at the other. People swarmed more than you can see on a feast-day round the miraculous Holy Image in the yard of the Carmelite Convent* down in the plains where, before he left his home, he drove his mother in a wooden cart:—a pious old woman who wanted to offer prayers and make a vow for his safety. He could not give me an idea of how large and lofty and full of noise and smoke and gloom, and clang of iron, the place was, but some one had told him it was called Berlin.* Then they rang a bell, and another steam-machine came in, and again he was taken on and on through a land that wearied his eyes by its flatness without a single bit of a hill to be seen anywhere. One more night he spent shut up in a building like a good stable with a litter of straw on the floor, guarding his bundle amongst a lot of men, of whom not one could understand a single word he said. In the morning they were all led down to the stony shores of an extremely broad muddy river, flowing not between hills but between houses that seemed immense. There was a steam-machine that went on the water,* and they all stood upon it packed tight, only now there were with them many women and children who made much noise.* A cold rain fell, the wind blew in his face; he was wet through, and his teeth chattered. He and the young man from the same valley took each other by the hand.

"They thought they were being taken to America straight away, but suddenly the steam-machine bumped against the side of a thing like a great house on the water.* The walls were smooth and black, and there uprose, growing from the roof as it were, bare trees in the shape of crosses, extremely high. That's how it appeared to him then, for he had never seen a ship before. This was the ship that was going to swim all the way to America. Voices shouted, everything swayed; there was a ladder dipping up and down. He went up on his hands and knees in mortal fear of falling into the water below, which made a great splashing. He got separated from his companion, and when he descended into the bottom of that ship his heart seemed to melt suddenly within him.

"It was then also, as he told me, that he lost contact for good and all with one of those three men who the summer before had been going about through all the little towns in the foothills of his country. They would arrive on market-days driving in a peasant's cart, and would set up an office in an inn or some other Jew's house. There were three of them, of whom one with a long beard looked venerable; and they had red cloth collars round their necks and gold lace on their sleeves like Government officials. They sat proudly behind a long table; and in the next room, so that the common people shouldn't hear, they kept a cunning telegraph machine, through which they could talk to the Emperor of America. The fathers hung about the door, but the young men of the mountains would crowd up to the table asking many questions, for there was work to be got all the year round at three dollars a day in America, and no military service to do.

"But the American Kaiser* would not take everybody. Oh no! He himself had a great difficulty in getting accepted, and the venerable man in uniform had to go out of the room several times to work the telegraph on his behalf. The American Kaiser engaged him at last at three dollars, he being young and strong. However, many able young men backed out, afraid of the great distance; besides, those only who had some money could be taken. There were some who sold their huts and their land because it cost a lot of money to get to America; but then, once there, you had three dollars a day, and if you were clever you could find places where true gold could be picked up on the ground. His father's house was getting overfull. Two of his brothers were married and had children. He promised to send money home from America by post twice a year. His father sold an old cow, a pair of piebald mountain ponies of his own raising, and a cleared plot of fair pasture land on the sunny slope of a pine-clad pass to a Jew inn-keeper, in order to pay the people of the ship that took men to America to get rich in a short time.

"He must have been a real adventurer at heart, for how many of the greatest enterprises in the conquest of the earth had for their beginning just such a bargaining away of the paternal cow for the mirage of true gold far away! I have been telling you more or less in my own words what I learned fragmentarily in the course of two or three years, during which I seldom missed an opportunity of a friendly chat with him. He told me this story of his adventure with many flashes of white teeth and lively glances of black eyes, at first in a sort of anxious baby-talk, then, as he acquired the language, with great fluency, but always with that singing, soft, and at the same time vibrating intonation that instilled a strangely penetrating power into the sound of the most familiar English words, as if they had been the words of an unearthly language. And he always would come to an end, with many emphatic shakes of his head, upon that awful sensation of his heart melting within him directly he set foot on board that ship. Afterwards there seemed to come for him a period of blank ignorance, at any rate as to facts. No doubt he must have been abominably seasick and abominably unhappy—this soft and passionate adventurer, taken thus out of his knowledge, and feeling bitterly as he lay in his emigrant bunk his utter loneliness; for his was a highly sensitive nature. The next thing we know of him for certain is that he had been hiding in Hammond's pig-pound by the side of the road to Norton, six miles, as the crow flies, from the sea. Of these experiences he was unwilling to speak: they seemed to have seared into his soul a sombre sort of wonder and indignation. Through the rumours of the countryside, which lasted for a good many days after his arrival, we know that the fisherman of West Colebrook had been disturbed and startled by heavy knocks against the walls of weather-board cottages, and by a voice crying piercingly strange words in the night. Several of them turned out even, but, no doubt, he had fled in sudden alarm at their rough angry tones hailing each other in the darkness. A sort of frenzy must have helped him up the steep Norton hill. It was he, no doubt, who early the following morning had seen lying (in a swoon, I should say) on the roadside grass by the Brenzett carrier, who actually got down to have a nearer look, but drew back, intimidated by the perfect immobility, and by something queer in the aspect of that tramp, sleeping so still under the showers. As the day advanced, some children came dashing into school at Norton in such a fright that the schoolmistress went out and spoke indignantly to a 'horrid-looking man' on the road. He edged away, hanging his head, for a few steps, and then suddenly ran off with extraordinary fleetness. The driver of Mr. Bradley's milk-cart made no secret of it that he had lashed with his whip at a hairy sort of gipsy fellow who, jumping up at a turn of the road by the Vents, made a snatch at the pony's bridle. And he caught him a good one too, right over the face, he said, that made him drop down in the mud a jolly sight quicker than he had jumped up; but it was a good half a mile before he could stop the pony. Maybe that in his desperate endeavours to get help, and in his need to get in touch with some one, the poor devil had tried to stop the cart. Also three boys confessed afterwards to throwing stones at a funny tramp, knocking about all wet and muddy, and, it seemed, very drunk, in the narrow deep lane by the limekilns. All this was the talk of three villages for days; but we have Mrs. Finn's (the wife of Smith's waggoner) unimpeachable testimony that she saw him get over the low wall of Hammond's pig-pound and lurch straight at her, babbling aloud in a voice that was enough to make one die of fright. Having the baby with her in a perambulator, Mrs. Finn called out to him to go away, and as he persisted in coming nearer, she hit him courageously with her umbrella over the head, and, without once looking back, ran like the wind with the perambulator as far as the first house in the village. She stopped then, out of breath, and spoke to old Lewis, hammering there at a heap of stones; and the old chap, taking off his immense black wire goggles, got up on his shaky legs to look where she pointed. Together they followed with their eyes the figure of the man running over a field; they saw him fall down, pick himself up, and run on again, staggering and waving his long arms above his head, in the direction of the New Barns Farm. From that moment he is plainly in the toils of his obscure and touching destiny. There is no doubt after this of what happened to him. All is certain now: Mrs. Smith's intense terror; Amy Foster's stolid conviction held against the other's nervous attack, that the man 'meant no harm'; Smith's exasperation (on his return from Darnford Market) at finding the dog barking himself into a fit, the back-door locked, his wife in hysterics; and all for an unfortunate dirty tramp, supposed to be even then lurking in his stackyard. Was he? He would teach him to frighten women.

"Smith is notoriously hot-tempered, but the sight of some nondescript and miry creature sitting cross-legged amongst a lot of loose straw, and swinging itself to and fro like a bear in a cage, made him pause. Then this tramp stood up silently before him, one mass of mud and filth from head to foot. Smith, alone amongst his stacks with this apparition, in the stormy twilight ringing with the infuriated barking of the dog, felt the dread of an inexplicable strangeness. But when that being, parting with his black hands the long matted locks that hung before his face, as you part the two halves of a curtain, looked out at him with glistening, wild, black-and-white eyes, the weirdness of this silent encounter fairly staggered him. He has admitted since (for the story has been a legitimate subject of conversation about here for years) that he made more than one step backwards. Then a sudden burst of rapid, senseless speech persuaded him at once that he had to do with an escaped lunatic. In fact, that impression never wore off completely. Smith has not in his heart given up his secret conviction of the man's essential insanity to this very day.

"As the creature approached him, jabbering in a most discomposing manner, Smith (unaware that he was being addressed as 'gracious lord,'* and adjured in God's name to afford food and shelter) kept on speaking firmly but gently to it, and retreating all the time into the other yard. At last, watching his chance, by a sudden charge he bundled him headlong into the wood-lodge, and instantly shot the bolt. Thereupon he wiped his brow, though the day was cold. He had done his duty to the community by shutting up a wandering and probably dangerous maniac. Smith isn't a hard man at all, but he had room in his brain only for that one idea of lunacy. He was not imaginative enough to ask himself whether the man might not be perishing with cold and hunger. Meantime, at first, the maniac made a great deal of noise in the lodge. Mrs. Smith was screaming upstairs, where she had locked herself in her bedroom; but Amy Foster sobbed piteously at the kitchen-door, wringing her hands and muttering, 'Don't! don't!' I daresay Smith had a rough time of it that evening with one noise and another, and this insane, disturbing voice crying obstinately through the door only added to his irritation. He couldn't possibly have connected this troublesome lunatic with the sinking of a ship in Eastbay, of which there had been a rumour in the Darnford market-place. And I daresay the man inside had been very near to insanity on that night. Before his excitement collapsed and he became unconscious he was throwing himself violently about in the dark, rolling on some dirty sacks, and biting his fists with rage, cold, hunger, amazement, and despair.

"He was a mountaineer of the eastern range of the Carpathians,* and the vessel sunk the night before in Eastbay was the Hamburg emigrant-ship *Herzogin Sophia-Dorothea*,* of appalling memory.

"A few months later we could read in the papers the accounts of the bogus 'Emigration Agencies' among the Sclavonian peasantry* in the more remote provinces of Austria. The object of these scoundrels was to get hold of the poor ignorant people's homesteads, and they were in league with the local usurers. They exported their victims through

Hamburg mostly. As to the ship, I had watched her out of this very window, reaching close-hauled under short canvas into the bay on a dark, threatening afternoon. She came to an anchor, correctly by the chart, off the Brenzett Coastguard station. I remember before the night fell looking out again at the outlines of her spars and rigging that stood out dark and pointed on a background of ragged, slaty clouds like another and a slighter spire to the left of the Brenzett church-tower. In the evening the wind rose. At midnight I could hear in my bed the terrific gusts and the sounds of a driving deluge.

"About that time the Coastguardmen thought they saw the lights of a steamer over the anchoring-ground. In a moment they vanished; but it is clear that another vessel of some sort had tried for shelter in the bay on that awful, blind night, had rammed the German ship amidships* (a breach—as one of the divers told me afterwards—'that you could sail a Thames barge through'), and then had gone out either scathless or damaged, who shall say; but had gone out, unknown, unseen, and fatal, to perish mysteriously at sea. Of her nothing ever came to light, and yet the hue and cry that was raised all over the world would have found her out if she had been in existence anywhere on the face of the waters.

"A completeness without a clue, and a stealthy silence as of a neatly executed crime, characterize this murderous disaster, which, as you may remember, had its gruesome celebrity. The wind would have prevented the loudest outcries from reaching the shore; there had been evidently no time for signals of distress. It was death without any sort of fuss. The Hamburg ship, filling all at once, capsized as she sank, and at daylight there was not even the end of a spar* to be seen above water. She was missed, of course, and at first the Coastguardmen surmised that she had either dragged her anchor or parted her cable some time during the night, and had been blown out to sea. Then, after the tide turned, the wreck must have shifted a little and released some of the bodies, because a child—a little fairhaired child in a red frock—came ashore abreast of the Martello tower. By the afternoon you could see along three miles of beach dark figures with bare legs dashing in and out of the tumbling foam, and rough-looking men, women with hard faces, children, mostly fair-haired, were being carried, stiff and dripping, on stretchers, on wattles, on ladders, in a long procession past the door of the Ship Inn, to be laid out in a row under the north wall of the Brenzett Church.

"Officially, the body of the little girl in the red frock is the first thing that came ashore from that ship. But I have patients amongst the seafaring population of West Colebrook, and, unofficially, I am informed that very early that morning two brothers, who went down to look after their cobble* hauled up on the beach, found, a good way from Brenzett, an ordinary ship's hencoop lying high and dry on the shore, with eleven drowned ducks inside. Their families ate the birds, and the hencoop was split into firewood with a hatchet. It is possible that a man (supposing he happened to be on deck at the time of the accident) might have floated ashore on that hencoop. He might. I admit it is improbable, but there was the man—and for days, nay, for weeks—it didn't enter our heads that we had amongst us the only living soul that had escaped from that disaster. The man himself, even when he learned to speak intelligibly, could tell us very little. He remembered he had felt better (after the ship had anchored, I suppose), and that the darkness, the wind, and the rain took his breath away. This looks as if he had been on deck some time during that night. But we mustn't forget he had been taken out of his knowledge, that he had been sea-sick and battened down below for four days, that he had no general notion of a ship or of the sea, and therefore could have no definite idea of what was happening to him. The rain, the wind, the darkness he knew; he understood the bleating of the sheep, and he remembered the pain of his wretchedness and misery, his heartbroken astonishment that it was neither seen nor understood, his dismay at finding all the men angry and all the women fierce. He had approached them as a beggar, it is true, he said; but in his country, even if they gave nothing, they spoke gently to beggars. The children in his country were not taught to throw stones at those who asked for compassion. Smith's strategy overcame him completely. The wood-lodge presented the horrible aspect of a dungeon. What would be done to him next? . . . No wonder that Amy Foster appeared to his eyes with the aureole of an angel of light. The girl had not been able to sleep for thinking of the poor man, and in the morning, before the Smiths were up, she slipped out across the back yard. Holding the door of the wood-lodge ajar, she looked in and extended to him half a loaf of white bread—'such bread as the rich eat in my country,' he used to say.

"At this he got up slowly from amongst all sorts of rubbish, stiff, hungry, trembling, miserable, and doubtful. 'Can you eat this?' she asked in her soft and timid voice. He must have taken her for a 'gracious lady.' He devoured ferociously, and tears were falling on the crust. Suddenly he dropped the bread, seized her wrist, and imprinted a kiss on her hand. She was not frightened. Through his forlorn condition she had observed that he was good-looking. She shut the door and walked back slowly to the kitchen. Much later on, she told Mrs. Smith, who shuddered at the bare idea of being touched by that creature.

"Through this act of impulsive pity he was brought back again within the pale of human relations with his new surroundings. He never forgot it—never.

"That very same morning old Mr. Swaffer (Smith's nearest neighbour) came over to give his advice, and ended by carrying him off. He stood, unsteady on his legs, meek, and caked over in halfdried mud, while the two men talked around him in an incomprehensible tongue. Mrs. Smith had refused to come downstairs till the madman was off the premises; Amy Foster, far from within the dark kitchen, watched through the open back door; and he obeyed the signs that were made to him to the best of his ability. But Smith was full of mistrust. 'Mind, sir! It may be all his cunning,' he cried repeatedly in a tone of warning. When Mr. Swaffer started the mare, the deplorable being sitting humbly by his side, through weakness, nearly fell out over the back of the high two-wheeled cart. Swaffer took him straight home. And it is then that I come upon the scene.

"I was called in by the simple process of the old man beckoning to me with his forefinger over the gate of his house as I happened to be driving past. I got down, of course.

"'I've got something here,' he mumbled, leading the way to an outhouse at a little distance from his other farm-buildings.

"It was there that I saw him first, in a long low room taken upon the space of that sort of coach-house. It was bare and whitewashed, with a small square aperture glazed with one cracked, dusty pane at its further end. He was lying on his back upon a straw pallet; they had given him a couple of horse-blankets, and he seemed to have spent the remainder of his strength in the exertion of cleaning himself. He was almost speechless; his quick breathing under the blankets pulled up to his chin, his glittering, restless black eyes reminded me of a wild bird caught in a snare. While I was examining him, old Swaffer stood silently by the door, passing the tips of his fingers along his shaven upper lip. I gave some directions, promised to send a bottle of medicine, and naturally made some inquiries.

"'Smith caught him in the stackyard at New Barns,' said the old chap in his deliberate, unmoved manner, and as if the other had been indeed a sort of wild animal, 'That's how I came by him. Quite a curiosity, isn't he? Now tell me, doctor—you've been all over the world—don't you think that's a bit of a Hindoo* we've got hold of here?'

"I was greatly surprised. His long black hair scattered over the straw bolster contrasted with the olive pallor of his face. It occurred to me he might be a Basque.* It didn't necessarily follow that he should understand Spanish; but I tried him with the few words I know, and also with some French. The whispered sounds I caught by bending my ear to his lips puzzled me utterly. That afternoon the young ladies from the Rectory (one of them read Goethe* with a dictionary, and the other had struggled with Dante* for years), coming to see Miss Swaffer, tried their German and Italian on him from the doorway. They retreated, just the least bit scared by the flood of passionate speech which, turning on his pallet,* he let out at them. They admitted that the sound was pleasant, soft, musical—but, in conjunction with his looks perhaps, it was startling—so excitable, so utterly unlike anything one had ever heard. The village boys climbed up the bank to have a peep through the little square aperture. Everybody was wondering what Mr. Swaffer would do with him.

"He simply kept him.

"Swaffer would be called eccentric were he not so much respected. They will tell you that Mr. Swaffer sits up as late as ten o'clock at night to read books, and they will tell you also that he can write a cheque for two hundred pounds without thinking twice about it. He himself would tell you that the Swaffers had owned land between this and Darnford for these three hundred years. He must be eighty-five today, but he does not look a bit older than when I first came here. He is a great breeder of sheep, and deals extensively in cattle. He attends market days for miles around in every sort of weather, and drives sitting bowed low over the reins, his lank grey hair curling over the collar of his warm coat, and with a green plaid rug round his legs. The calmness of advanced age gives a solemnity to his manner. He is clean-shaved; his lips are thin and sensitive; something rigid and monachal in the set of his features lends a certain elevation to the character of his face. He has been known to drive miles in the rain to see a new kind of rose in somebody's garden, or a monstrous cabbage grown by a cottager. He loves to hear tell of or to be shown something what he calls 'outlandish.' Perhaps it was just that outlandishness of the man which influenced old Swaffer. Perhaps it was only an inexplicable caprice. All I know is that at the end of three weeks I caught sight of Smith's lunatic digging in Swaffer's kitchen garden. They had found out he could use a spade. He dug barefooted.

"His black hair flowed over his shoulders. I suppose it was Swaffer who had given him the striped old cotton shirt; but he wore still the national brown cloth trousers (in which he had been washed ashore) fitting to the leg almost like tights; was belted with a broad leathern belt studded with little brass discs; and had never yet ventured into the village. The land he looked upon seemed to him kept neatly, like the grounds round a landowner's house; the size of the cart-horses struck him with astonishment; the roads resembled garden walks, and the aspect of the people, especially on Sundays, spoke of opulence. He wondered what made them so hardhearted and their children so bold. He got his food at the back door, carried it in both hands, carefully, to his outhouse, and, sitting alone on his pallet, would make the sign of the cross before he began. Beside the same pallet, kneeling in the early darkness of the short days, he recited aloud the Lord's Prayer before he slept. Whenever he saw old Swaffer he would bow with veneration from the waist, and stand erect while the old man, with his fingers over his upper lip, surveyed him silently. He bowed also to Miss Swaffer, who kept house frugally for her father—a broad-shouldered, big-boned woman of forty-five, with the pocket of her dress full of keys, and a grey, steady eye. She was Church—as people said (while her father was one of the trustees of the Baptist Chapel)—and wore a little steel cross at her waist. She dressed severely in black, in memory of one of the innumerable Bradleys of the neighbourhood, to whom she had been engaged some twenty-five years ago—a young farmer who broke his neck out hunting on the eve of the wedding-day. She had the unmoved countenance of the deaf, spoke very seldom, and her lips, thin like her father's, astonished one sometimes by a mysteriously ironic curl.

"These were the people to whom he owed allegiance, and an overwhelming loneliness seemed to fall from the leaden sky of that winter without sunshine. All the faces were sad. He could talk to no one, and had no hope of ever understanding anybody. It was as if these had been the faces of people from the other world—dead people—he used to tell me years afterwards. Upon my word, I wonder he did not go mad. He didn't know where he was. Somewhere very far from his mountains—somewhere over the water. Was this America, he wondered?

"If it hadn't been for the steel cross at Miss Swaffer's belt he would not, he confessed, have known whether he was in a Christian country at all. He used to cast stealthy glances at it, and feel comforted. There was nothing here the same as in his country! The earth and the water were different; there were no images of the Redeemer by the roadside. The very grass was different, and the trees. All the trees but the three old Norway pines on the bit of lawn before Swaffer's house, and these reminded him of his country. He had been detected once, after dusk, with his forehead against the trunk of one of them, sobbing, and talking to himself. They had been like brothers to him at that time, he affirmed. Everything else was strange. Conceive you* the kind of an existence over-shadowed, oppressed, by the everyday material appearances, as if by the visions of a nightmare. At night, when he could not sleep, he kept on thinking of the girl who gave him the first piece of bread he had eaten in this foreign land. She had been neither fierce nor angry, nor frightened. Her face he remembered as the only comprehensible face amongst all these faces that were as closed, as mysterious, and as mute as the faces of the dead who are possessed of a knowledge beyond the comprehension of the living. I wonder whether the memory of her compassion prevented him from cutting his throat. But there! I suppose I am an old sentimentalist, and forget the instinctive love of life which it takes all the strength of an uncommon despair to overcome.

"He did the work which was given him with an intelligence which surprised old Swaffer. By-and-by it was discovered that he could help at the ploughing, could milk the cows, feed the bullocks in the cattle-yard, and was of some use with the sheep. He began to pick up words, too, very fast; and suddenly, one fine morning in spring, he rescued from an untimely death a grand-child of old Swaffer.

"Swaffer's younger daughter is married to Willcox, a solicitor and the Town Clerk of Colebrook. Regularly twice a year they come to stay with the old man for a few days. Their only child, a little girl not three years old at the time, ran out of the house alone in her little white pinafore, and, toddling across the grass of a terraced garden, pitched herself over a low wall head first into the horsepond in the yard below.

"Our man was out with the waggoner and the plough in the field nearest to the house, and as he was leading the team round to begin a fresh furrow, he saw, through the gap of a gate, what for anybody else would have been a mere flutter of something white. But he had straight-glancing, quick, far-reaching eyes, that only seemed to flinch and lose their amazing power before the immensity of the sea. He was barefooted, and looking as outlandish as the heart of Swaffer could desire. Leaving the horses on the turn, to the inexpressible disgust of the waggoner he bounded off, going over the ploughed ground in long leaps, and suddenly appeared before the mother, thrust the child into her arms, and strode away.

"The pond was not very deep; but still, if he had not had such good eyes, the child would have perished—miserably suffocated in the foot or so of sticky mud at the bottom. Old Swaffer walked out slowly into the field, waited till the plough came over to his side, had a good look at him, and without saying a word went back to the house. But from that time they laid out his meals on the kitchen table; and at first, Miss Swaffer, all in black and with an inscrutable face, would come and stand in the doorway of the living-room to see him make a big sign of the cross before he fell to. I believe that from that day, too, Swaffer began to pay him regular wages.

"I can't follow step by step his development. He cut his hair short, was seen in the village and along the road going to and fro to his work like any other man. Children ceased to shout after him. He became aware of social differences, but remained for a long time surprised at the bare poverty of the churches among so much wealth. He couldn't understand either why they were kept shut up on weekdays. There was nothing to steal in them. Was it to keep people from praying too often?* The rectory took much notice of him about that time, and I believe the young ladies attempted to prepare the ground for his conversion. They could not, however, break him of his habit of crossing himself, but he went so far as to take off the string with a couple of brass medals the size of a sixpence, a tiny metal cross, and a square sort of scapulary* which he wore round his neck. He hung them on the wall by the side of his bed, and he was still to be heard every evening reciting the Lord's Prayer, in incomprehensible words and in a slow, fervent tone, as he had heard his old father do at the head of all the kneeling family, big and little, on every evening of his life. And though he wore corduroys at work, and a slop-made pepper-and-salt suit on Sundays,* strangers would turn round to look after him on the road. His foreignness had a peculiar and indelible stamp. At last people became used to seeing him. But they never became used to him. His rapid, skimming walk; his swarthy complexion; his hat cocked on the left ear; his habit, on warm evenings, of wearing his coat over one shoulder, like a hussar's dolman;* his manner of leaping over the stiles, not as a feat of agility, but in the ordinary course of progression—all these peculiarities were, as one may say, so many causes of scorn and offence to the inhabitants of the village. They wouldn't in their dinner hour lie flat on their backs on the grass to stare at the sky. Neither did they go about the fields screaming dismal tunes. Many times have I heard his high-pitched voice from behind the ridge of some sloping sheep-walk, a voice light and soaring, like a lark's, but with a melancholy human note, over our fields that hear only the song of birds.* And I would be startled myself Ah! He was different: innocent of heart, and full of good will, which nobody wanted, this castaway, that, like a man transplanted into another planet, was separated by an immense space from his past and by an immense ignorance from his future. His quick, fervent utterance positively shocked everybody. 'An excitable devil,' they called him. One evening, in the tap-room of the Coach and Horses (having drunk some whisky), he upset them all by singing a love-song of his country. They hooted him down, and he was pained; but Preble, the lame wheelwright, and Vincent, the fat blacksmith, and the other notables too, wanted to drink their evening beer in peace. On another occasion he tried to show them how to dance. The dust rose in clouds from the sanded floor; he leaped straight up amongst the deal tables, struck his heels together, squatted on one heel in front of old Preble, shooting out the other leg, uttered wild and exulting cries, jumped up to whirl on one foot, snapping his fingers above his head—and a strange carter who was having a drink in there began to swear, and cleared out with his half-pint in his hand into the bar. But when suddenly he sprang upon a table and continued to dance among the glasses, the landlord interfered. He didn't want any 'acrobat tricks in the tap-room.'* They laid their hands on him. Having had a glass or two, Mr. Swaffer's foreigner tried to expostulate: was ejected forcibly: got a black eye.

"I believe he felt the hostility of his human surroundings. But he was tough—tough in spirit, too, as well as in body. Only the memory of the sea frightened him, with that vague terror that is left by a bad dream. His home was far away; and he did not want now to go to America. I had often explained to him that there is no place on earth where true gold can be found lying ready and to be got for the trouble of the picking up. How then, he asked, could he ever return home with empty hands when there had been sold a cow, two ponies, and a bit of land to pay for his going? His eyes would fill with tears, and, averting them from the immense shimmer of the sea, he would throw himself face down on the grass. But sometimes, cocking his hat with a little conquering air, he would defy my wisdom. He had found his bit of true gold. That was Amy Foster's heart; which was 'a golden heart, and soft to people's misery,' he would say in the accents of overwhelming conviction.

"He was called Yanko.* He had explained that this meant Little John; but as he would also repeat very often that he was a mountaineer (some word sounding in the dialect of his country like Goorall)* he got it for his surname. And this is the only trace of him that the succeeding ages may find in the marriage register of the parish. There it stands—Yanko Goorall—in the rector's handwriting. The crooked cross made by the castaway, a cross whose tracing no doubt seemed to him the most solemn part of the whole ceremony, is all that remains now to perpetuate the memory of his name.

"His courtship had lasted some time—ever since he got his precarious footing in the community. It began by his buying for Amy Foster a green satin ribbon in Darnford. This was what you did in his country. You bought a ribbon at a Jew's stall on a fair-day. I don't suppose the girl knew what to do with it, but he seemed to think that his honourable intentions could not be mistaken.

"It was only when he declared his purpose to get married that I fully understood how, for a hundred futile and inappreciable reasons, how—shall I say odious?—he was to all the countryside. Every old woman in the village was up in arms. Smith, coming upon him near the farm, promised to break his head for him if he found him about again. But he twisted his little black moustache with such a bellicose air and rolled such big, black fierce eyes at Smith that this promise came to nothing. Smith, however, told the girl that she must be mad to take up with a man who was surely wrong in his head. All the same, when she heard him in the gloaming whistle from beyond the orchard a couple of bars of a weird and mournful tune, she would drop whatever she had in her hand—she would leave Mrs. Smith in the middle of a sentence—and she would run out to his call. Mrs. Smith called her a shameless hussy. She answered nothing. She said nothing at all to anybody, and went on her way as if she had been deaf. She and I alone in all the land, I fancy, could see his very real beauty. He was very good-looking, and most graceful in his bearing, with that something wild as of a woodland creature in his aspect. Her mother moaned over her dismally whenever the girl came to see her on her day out. The father was surly, but pretended not to know; and Mrs. Finn once told her plainly that 'this man, my dear, will do you some harm some day yet.' And so it went on. They could be seen on the roads, she tramping stolidly in her finery—grey dress, black feather, stout boots, prominent white cotton gloves that caught your eye a hundred yards away; and he, his coat slung picturesquely over one shoulder, pacing by her side, gallant of bearing and casting tender glances upon the girl with the golden heart. I wonder whether he saw how plain she was. Perhaps among types so different from what he had ever seen, he had not the power to judge; or perhaps he was seduced by the divine quality of her pity.

"Yanko was in great trouble meantime. In his country you get an old man for an ambassador in marriage affairs. He did not know how to proceed. However, one day in the midst of sheep in a field (he was now Swaffer's under-shepherd with Foster) he took off his hat to the father and declared himself humbly. 'I daresay she's fool enough to marry you,' was all Foster said. 'And then,' he used to relate, 'he puts his hat on his head, looks black at me as if he wanted to cut my throat, whistles the dog, and off he goes, leaving me to do the work.' The Fosters, of course, didn't like to lose the wages the girl earned: Amy used to give all her money to her mother. But there was in Foster a very genuine aversion to that match. He contended that the fellow was very good with sheep, but was not fit for any girl to marry. For one thing, he used to go along the hedges muttering to himself like a dam' fool; and then, these foreigners behave very queerly to women sometimes. And perhaps he would want to carry her off somewhere—or run off himself. It was not safe. He preached it to his daughter that the fellow might ill-use her in some way. She made no answer. It was, they said in the village, as if the man had done something to her. People discussed the matter. It was quite an excitement, and the two went on 'walking out' together* in the face of opposition. Then something unexpected happened.

"I don't know whether old Swaffer ever understood how much he was regarded in the light of a father by his foreign retainer. Anyway the relation was curiously feudal. So when Yanko asked formally for an interview—'and the Miss too' (he called the severe, deaf Miss Swaffer simply *Miss*)—it was to obtain their permission to marry. Swaffer heard him unmoved, dismissed him by a nod, and then shouted the intelligence into Miss Swaffer's best ear. She showed no surprise, and only remarked grimly, in a veiled blank voice, 'He certainly won't get any other girl to marry him.'

"It is Miss Swaffer who has all the credit of the munificence: but in a very few days it came out that Mr. Swaffer had presented Yanko with a cottage (the cottage you've seen this morning) and something like an acre of ground—had made it over to him in absolute property. Willcox expedited the deed, and I remember him telling me he had a great pleasure in making it ready. It recited: 'In consideration of saving the life of my beloved grandchild, Bertha Willcox.'

"Of course, after that no power on earth could prevent them from getting married.

"Her infatuation endured. People saw her going out to meet him in the evening. She stared with unblinking, fascinated eyes up the road where he was expected to appear, walking freely, with a swing from the hip, and humming one of the love-tunes of his country. When the boy was born, he got elevated* at the Coach and Horses, essayed again a song and a dance, and was again ejected. People expressed their commiseration for a woman married to that Jack-in-the-box.* He didn't care. There was a man now (he told me boastfully) to whom he could sing and talk in the language of his country, and show how to dance by-and-by.

"But I don't know. To me he appeared to have grown less springy of step, heavier in body, less keen of eye. Imagination, no doubt; but it seems to me now as if the net of fate had been drawn closer round him already.

"One day I met him on the footpath over the Talfourd Hill. He told me that 'women were funny.' I had heard already of domestic differences. People were saying that Amy Foster was beginning to find out what sort of man she had married. He looked upon the sea with indifferent, unseeing eyes. His wife had snatched the child out of his arms one day as he sat on the doorstep crooning to it a song such as the mothers sing to babies in his mountains. She seemed to think he was doing it some harm. Women are funny. And she had objected to him praying aloud in the evening. Why? He expected the boy to repeat the prayer aloud after him by-and-by, as he used to do after his old father when he was a child—in his own country. And I discovered he longed for their boy to grow up so that he could have a man to talk with in that language that to our ears sounded so disturbing, so passionate, and so bizarre. Why his wife should dislike the idea he couldn't tell. But that would pass, he said. And tilting his head knowingly, he tapped his breastbone to indicate that she had a good heart: not hard, not fierce, open to compassion, charitable to the poor!

"I walked away thoughtfully; I wondered whether his difference, his strangeness, were not penetrating with repulsion that dull nature* they had begun by irresistibly attracting. I wondered. . . ."

The Doctor came to the window and looked out at the frigid splendour of the sea, immense in the haze, as if enclosing all the earth with all the hearts lost among the passions of love and fear.

"Physiologically, now," he said, turning away abruptly, "it was possible. It was possible."

He remained silent. Then went on—

"At all events, the next time I saw him he was ill—lung trouble. He was tough, but I daresay he was not acclimatized as well as I had supposed. It was a bad winter; and, of course, these mountaineers do get fits of home sickness; and a state of depression would make him vulnerable. He was lying half dressed on a couch downstairs.

"A table covered with a dark oilcloth took up all the middle of the little room. There was a wicker cradle on the floor, a kettle spouting steam on the hob, and some child's linen lay drying on the fender. The room was warm, but the door opens right into the garden, as you noticed perhaps.

"He was very feverish, and kept on muttering to himself. She sat on a chair and looked at him fixedly across the table with her brown, blurred eyes. 'Why don't you have him upstairs?' I asked. With a start and a confused stammer she said, 'Oh! ah! I couldn't sit with him upstairs, sir.'

"I gave her certain directions; and going outside, I said again that he ought to be in bed upstairs. She wrung her hands. 'I couldn't. I couldn't.

He keeps on saying something—I don't know what.' With the memory of all the talk against the man that had been dinned into her ears, I looked at her narrowly. I looked into her short-sighted eyes, at her dumb eyes that once in her life had seen an enticing shape, but seemed, staring at me, to see nothing at all now. But I saw she was uneasy.

"'What's the matter with him?' she asked in a sort of vacant trepidation. 'He doesn't look very ill. I never did see anybody look like this before. . . .'

"'Do you think,' I asked indignantly, 'he is shamming?'

"'I can't help it, sir,' she said stolidly. And suddenly she clapped her hands and looked right and left. 'And there's the baby. I am so frightened. He wanted me just now to give him the baby. I can't understand what he says to it.'

"'Can't you ask a neighbour to come in tonight?' I asked.

"'Please, sir, nobody seems to care to come,' she muttered, dully resigned all at once.

"I impressed upon her the necessity of the greatest care, and then had to go. There was a good deal of sickness that winter. 'Oh, I hope he won't talk!' she exclaimed softly just as I was going away.

"I don't know how it is I did not see—but I didn't. And yet, turning in my trap, I saw her lingering before the door, very still, and as if meditating a flight up the miry road.

"Towards the night his fever increased.

"He tossed, moaned, and now and then muttered a complaint. And she sat with the table between her and the couch, watching every movement and every sound, with the terror, the unreasonable terror, of that man she could not understand creeping over her. She had drawn the wicker cradle close to her feet. There was nothing in her now but the maternal instinct and that unaccountable fear.

"Suddenly coming to himself, parched, he demanded a drink of water. She did not move. She had not understood, though he may have thought he was speaking in English.* He waited, looking at her, burning with fever, amazed at her silence and immobility, and then he shouted impatiently, 'Water! Give me water!'

"She jumped to her feet, snatched up the child, and stood still. He spoke to her, and his passionate remonstrances only increased her fear of that strange man. I believe he spoke to her for a long time, entreating, wondering, pleading, ordering, I suppose. She says she bore it as long as she could. And then a gust of rage came over him.

"He sat up and called out terribly one word—some word.* Then he got up as though he hadn't been ill at all, she says. And as in fevered dismay, indignation, and wonder he tried to get to her round the table, she simply opened the door and ran out with the child in her arms. She heard him call twice after her down the road in a terrible voice—and fled. . . . Ah! but you should have seen stirring behind the dull, blurred glance of these eyes the spectre of the fear which had hunted her on that night three miles and a half to the door of Foster's cottage! I did the next day.

"And it was I who found him lying face down and his body in a puddle, just outside the little wicket gate.

"I had been called out that night to an urgent case in the village, and on my way home at daybreak passed by the cottage. The door stood open. My man helped me to carry him in. We laid him on the couch. The lamp smoked, the fire was out, the chill of the stormy night oozed from the cheerless yellow paper on the wall. 'Amy!' I called aloud, and my voice seemed to lose itself in the emptiness of this tiny house as if I had cried in a desert. He opened his eyes. 'Gone!' he said distinctly. 'I had only asked for water—only for a little water. . . .'

"He was muddy.* I covered him up and stood waiting in silence, catching a painfully gasped word now and then. They were no longer in his own language. The fever had left him, taking with it the heat of life. And with his panting breast and lustrous eyes he reminded me again of a wild creature under the net; of a bird caught in a snare. She had left him. She had left him—sick—helpless—thirsty. The spear of the hunter had entered his very soul. 'Why?' he cried in the penetrating and indignant voice of a man calling to a responsible Maker. A gust of wind and a swish of rain answered.

"And as I turned away to shut the door he pronounced the word 'Merciful!' and expired.

"Eventually I certified heart-failure as the immediate cause of death. His heart must have indeed failed him, or else he might have stood this night of storm and exposure, too. I closed his eyes and drove away. Not very far from the cottage I met Foster walking sturdily between the dripping hedges with his collie at his heels.

"'Do you know where your daughter is?' I asked.

"'Don't I!' he cried. 'I am going to talk to him a bit. Frightening a poor woman like this.'

"'He won't frighten her any more,' I said. 'He is dead.'

"He struck with his stick at the mud.

"'And there's the child.'

"Then, after thinking deeply for a while—

"'I don't know that it isn't for the best.'

"That's what he said. And she says nothing at all now. Not a word of him. Never. Is his image as utterly gone from her mind as his lithe and striding figure, his carolling voice are gone from our fields? He is no longer before her eyes to excite her imagination into a passion of love or fear; and his memory seems to have vanished from her dull brain as a shadow passes away upon a white screen. She lives in the cottage and works for Miss Swaffer. She is Amy Foster for everybody, and the child is 'Amy Foster's boy.' She calls him Johnny—which means Little John.

"It is impossible to say whether this name recalls anything to her. Does she ever think of the past? I have seen her hanging over the boy's cot in a very passion of maternal tenderness. The little fellow was lying on his back, a little frightened at me, but very still, with his big black eyes, with his fluttered air of a bird in a snare. And looking at him I seemed to see again the other one*—the father, cast out mysteriously by the sea to perish in the supreme disaster of loneliness and despair."

THE RETURN

THE inner circle train* from the City rushed impetuously out of a black hole and pulled up with a discordant, grinding racket in the smirched twilight of a West-End station. A line of doors flew open and a lot of men stepped out headlong. They had high hats, healthy pale faces, dark overcoats and shiny boots; they held in their gloved hands thin umbrellas and hastily folded evening papers that resembled stiff, dirty rags of greenish, pinkish, or whitish colour. Alvan Hervey stepped out with the rest, a smouldering cigar between his teeth. A disregarded little woman in rusty black, with both arms full of parcels, ran along in distress, bolted suddenly into a third-class compartment* and the train went on. The slamming of carriage doors burst out sharp and spiteful like a fusillade;* an icy draught mingled with acrid fumes swept the whole length of the platform and made a tottering old man, wrapped up to his ears in a woollen comforter,* stop short in the moving throng to cough violently over his stick. No one spared him a glance.

Alvan Hervey passed through the ticket gate. Between the bare walls of a sordid staircase men clambered rapidly; their backs appeared alike—almost as if they had been wearing a uniform; their indifferent faces were varied but somehow suggested kinship, like the faces of a band of brothers who through prudence, dignity, disgust, or foresight would resolutely ignore each other; and their eyes, quick or slow; their eyes gazing up the dusty steps; their eyes brown, black, grey, blue, had all the same stare, concentrated and empty, satisfied and unthinking.

Outside the big doorway of the street they scattered in all directions, walking away fast from one another with the hurried air of men fleeing from something compromising; from familiarity or confidences; from something suspected and concealed—like truth or pestilence. Alvan Hervey hesitated, standing alone in the doorway for a moment; then decided to walk home.

He strode firmly. A misty rain settled like silvery dust on clothes, on moustaches; wetted the faces, varnished the flagstones, darkened the walls, dripped from umbrellas. And he moved on in the rain with careless serenity, with the tranquil ease of someone successful and disdainful, very sure of himself—a man with lots of money and friends. He was tall, well set-up, good-looking and healthy; and his clear pale face had under its commonplace refinement that slight tinge of overbearing brutality which is given by the possession of only partly difficult accomplishments; by excelling in games, or in the art of making money; by the easy mastery over animals and over needy men.

He was going home much earlier than usual, straight from the City and without calling at his club.* He considered himself well connected, well educated and intelligent. Who doesn't? But his connections, education and intelligence were strictly on a par with those of the men with whom he did business or amused himself.* He had married five years ago. At the time all his acquaintances had said he was very much in love; and he had said so himself, frankly, because it is very well understood that every man falls in love once in his life—unless his wife dies, when it may be quite praiseworthy to fall in love again. The girl was healthy, tall, fair, and in his opinion was well connected, well educated and intelligent. She was also intensely bored with her home where, as if packed in a tight box, her individuality—of which she was very conscious—had no play. She strode like a grenadier,* was strong and upright like an obelisk,* had a beautiful face, a candid brow, pure eyes, and not a thought of her own in her head. He surrendered quickly to all those charms, and she appeared to him so unquestionably of the right sort that he did not hesitate for a moment to declare himself in love. Under the cover of that sacred and poetical fiction he desired her masterfully, for various reasons; but principally for the satisfaction of having his own way. He was very dull and solemn about it—for no earthly reason, unless to conceal his feelings—which is an eminently proper thing to do. Nobody, however, would have been shocked had he neglected that duty, for the feeling he experienced really was a longing—a longing stronger and a little more complex no doubt,* but no more reprehensible in its nature than a hungry man's appetite for his dinner.

After their marriage they busied themselves, with marked success, in enlarging the circle of their acquaintance. Thirty people knew them by sight; twenty more with smiling demonstrations tolerated their occasional presence within hospitable thresholds; at least fifty others became aware of their existence. They moved in their enlarged world amongst perfectly delightful men and women who feared emotion, enthusiasm, or failure, more than fire, war, or mortal disease;

who tolerated only the commonest formulas of commonest thoughts, and recognized only profitable facts. It was an extremely charming sphere, the abode of all the virtues, where nothing is realized and where all joys and sorrows are cautiously toned down into pleasures and annoyances. In that serene region, then, where noble sentiments are cultivated in sufficient profusion to conceal the pitiless material-ism* of thoughts and aspirations Alvan Hervey and his wife spent five years of prudent bliss unclouded by any doubt as to the moral propri-ety of their existence. She, to give her individuality fair play, took up all manner of philanthropic work and became a member of various rescuing and reforming societies patronized or presided over by ladies of title. He took an active interest in politics; and having met quite by chance a literary man—who nevertheless was related to an earl—he was induced to finance a moribund society paper. It was a semi-political, and wholly scandalous publication, redeemed by excessive dulness; and as it was utterly faithless, as it contained no new thought, as it never by any chance had a flash of wit, satire, or indignation in its pages, he judged it respectable enough, at first sight. Afterwards, when it paid, he promptly perceived that upon the whole it was a virtuous undertaking. It paved the way of his ambition; and he enjoyed also the special kind of importance he derived from this connection with what he imagined to be literature.

This connection still further enlarged their world. Men who wrote or drew prettily for the public came at times to their house, and his editor came very often. He thought him rather an ass because he had such big front teeth (the proper thing is to have small, even teeth) and wore his hair a trifle longer than most men do. However, some dukes wear their hair long, and the fellow indubitably knew his business. The worst was that his gravity, though perfectly portentous, could not be trusted. He sat, elegant and bulky, in the drawing-room, the head of his stick hovering in front of his big teeth, and talked for hours with a thick-lipped smile (he said nothing that could be considered objectionable and not quite the thing), talked in an unusual manner—not obviously—irritatingly. His forehead was too lofty—unusually so—and under it there was a straight nose, lost between the hairless cheeks, that in a smooth curve ran into a chin shaped like the end of a snow-shoe. And in this face that resembled the face of a fat and fiendishly knowing baby there glittered a pair of clever, peering, unbelieving black eyes. He wrote verses too. Rather an ass. But the band of men who trailed at the skirts of his monumental frock-coat* seemed to perceive wonderful things in what he said. Alvan Hervey put it down to affectation. Those artist chaps, upon the whole, were so affected. Still, all this was highly proper—very useful to him—and his wife seemed to like it—as if she also had derived some distinct and secret advantage from this intellectual connection. She received her mixed and decorous guests with a kind of tall, ponderous grace, peculiarly her own and which awakened in the mind of intimidated strangers incongruous and improper reminiscences of an elephant, a giraffe, a gazelle; of a Gothic tower*—of an overgrown angel. Her Thursdays were becoming famous in their world; and their world grew steadily, annexing street after street. It included also Somebody's Gardens, a Crescent—a couple of Squares.

Thus Alvan Hervey and his wife for five prosperous years lived by the side of one another. In time they came to know each other sufficiently well for all the practical purposes of such an existence, but they were no more capable of real intimacy than two animals feeding at the same manger, under the same roof, in a luxurious stable. His longing was appeased and became a habit; and she had her desire—the desire to get away from under the paternal roof, to assert her individuality, to move in her own set (so much smarter than the parental one); to have a home of her own, and her own share of the world's respect, envy, and applause. They understood each other warily, tacitly, like a pair of cautious conspirators in a profitable plot; because they were both unable to look at a fact, a sentiment, a principle, or a belief otherwise than in the light of their own dignity, of their own glorification, of their own advantage. They skimmed over the surface of life* hand in hand, in a pure and frosty atmosphere— like two skilful skaters cutting figures on thick ice for the admiration of the beholders, and disdainfully ignoring the hidden stream, the stream restless and dark; the stream of life, profound and unfrozen.*

Alvan Hervey turned twice to the left, once to the right, walked along two sides of a square, in the middle of which groups of tame-looking trees stood in respectable captivity behind iron railings, and rang at his door. A parlourmaid opened. A fad of his wife's, this, to have only women servants. That girl, while she took his hat and overcoat, said something which made him look at his watch. It was five o'clock, and his wife not at home. There was nothing unusual in that. He said, "No; no tea," and went upstairs.

He ascended without footfalls. Brass rods glimmered all up the red carpet. On the first-floor landing a marble woman, decently covered from neck to instep with stone draperies, advanced a row of lifeless toes to the edge of the pedestal, and thrust out blindly a rigid white arm holding a cluster of lights. He had artistic tastes—at home. Heavy curtains caught back, half concealed dark corners. On the rich, stamped paper of the walls hung sketches, water-colours, engravings. His tastes were distinctly artistic. Old church towers peeped above green masses of foliage; the hills were purple, the sands yellow, the seas sunny, the skies blue. A young lady sprawled with dreamy eyes in a moored boat, in company of a lunch basket, a champagne bottle, and an enamoured man in a blazer. Bare-legged boys flirted sweetly with ragged maidens, slept on stone steps, gambolled with dogs. A pathetically lean girl flattened against a blank wall, turned up expiring eyes and tendered a flower for sale; while, near by, the large photographs of some famous and mutilated bas-reliefs seemed to represent a massacre turned into stone.

He looked, of course, at nothing, ascended another flight of stairs and went straight into the dressing room. A bronze dragon nailed by the tail to a bracket writhed away from the wall in calm convolutions, and held, between the conventional fury of its jaws, a crude gas flame that resembled a butterfly. The room was empty, of course; but, as he stepped in, it became filled all at once with a stir of many people; because the strips of glass on the doors of wardrobes and his wife's large pier-glass reflected him from head to foot, and multiplied his image into a crowd of gentlemanly and slavish imitators, who were dressed exactly like himself; had the same restrained and rare gestures; who moved when he moved, stood still with him in an obsequious immobility, and had just such appearances of life and feeling as he thought it dignified and safe for any man to manifest. And like real people who are slaves of common thoughts, that are not even their own, they affected a shadowy independence by the superficial variety of their movements. They moved together with him; but they either advanced to meet him, or walked away from him; they appeared, disappeared; they seemed to dodge behind walnut furniture, to be seen again, far within the polished panes, stepping about distinct and unreal in the convincing illusion of a room. And like the men he respected they could be trusted to do nothing individual, original, or startling—nothing unforeseen and nothing improper.

He moved for a time aimlessly in that good company, humming a popular but refined tune, and thinking vaguely of a business letter from abroad, which had to be answered on the morrow with cautious prevarication. Then, as he walked towards a wardrobe, he saw appearing at his back, in the high mirror, the corner of his wife's dressing-table, and amongst the glitter of silver-mounted objects on it, the square white patch of an envelope. It was such an unusual thing to be seen there that he spun round almost before he realized his surprise; and all the sham men about him pivoted on their heels; all appeared surprised; and all moved rapidly towards envelopes on dressing-tables.

He recognized his wife's handwriting and saw that the envelope was addressed to himself. He muttered, "How very odd," and felt annoyed. Apart from any odd action being essentially an indecent thing in itself, the fact of his wife indulging in it made it doubly offensive. That she should write to him at all, when she knew he would be home for dinner, was perfectly ridiculous; but that she should leave it like this—in evidence for chance discovery—struck him as so outrageous that, thinking of it, he experienced suddenly a staggering sense of insecurity, an absurd and bizarre flash of a notion that the house had moved a little under his feet.* He tore the envelope open, glanced at the letter, and sat down in a chair near by.

He held the paper before his eyes and looked at half a dozen lines scrawled on the page, while he was stunned by a noise meaningless and violent, like the clash of gongs or the beating of drums; a great aimless uproar that, in a manner, prevented him from hearing himself think* and made his mind an absolute blank. This absurd and distracting tumult seemed to ooze out of the written words, to issue from between his very fingers that trembled, holding the paper. And suddenly he dropped the letter as though it had been something hot, or venomous, or filthy; and rushing to the window with the unreflecting precipitation of a man anxious to raise an alarm of fire or murder, he threw it up and put his head out.

A chill gust of wind, wandering through the damp and sooty obscurity over the waste of roofs and chimney-pots, touched his face with a clammy flick. He saw an illimitable darkness, in which stood a black jumble of walls, and, between them, the many rows of gas-lights* stretched far away in long lines, like strung-up beads of fire. A sinister loom as of a hidden conflagration lit up faintly from below the mist, falling upon a billowy and motionless sea of tiles and bricks. At the rattle of the opened window the world seemed to leap out of the night and confront him, while floating up to his ears there came a sound vast and faint; the deep mutter of something immense and alive. It penetrated him* with a feeling of dismay and he gasped silently. From the cab-stand in the square came distinct hoarse voices and a jeering laugh which sounded ominously harsh and cruel. It sounded threatening. He drew his head in, as if before an aimed blow, and flung the window down quickly. He made a few steps, stumbled against a chair, and with a great effort, pulled himself together to lay hold of a certain thought that was whizzing about loose in his head.

He got it at last, after more exertion than he expected; he was flushed and puffed a little as though he had been catching it with his hands, but his mental hold on it was weak, so weak that he judged it necessary to repeat it aloud*—to hear it spoken firmly—in order to insure a perfect measure of possession. But he was unwilling to hear his own voice—to hear any sound whatever—owing to a vague belief, shaping itself slowly within him, that solitude and silence are the greatest felicities of mankind. The next moment it dawned upon him that they are perfectly unattainable—that faces must be seen, words spoken, thoughts heard. All the words—all the thoughts!

He said very distinctly, and looking at the carpet, "She's gone."

It was terrible—not the fact but the words;* the words charged with the shadowy might of a meaning, that seemed to possess the tremendous power to call Fate down upon the earth, like those strange and appalling words that sometimes are heard in sleep. They vibrated round him* in a metallic atmosphere, in a space that had the hardness of iron and the resonance of a bell of bronze. Looking down between the toes of his boots he seemed to listen thoughtfully to the receding wave of sound; to the wave spreading out in a widening circle, embracing streets, roofs, church-steeples, fields—and travelling away, widening endlessly, far, very far, where he could not hear—where he could not imagine anything—where . . .

"And—with that . . . ass," he said again without stirring in the least. And there was nothing but humiliation. Nothing else. He could derive no moral solace from any aspect of the situation, which radiated pain only on every side. Pain. What kind of pain? It occurred to him that he ought to be heart-broken; but in an exceedingly short moment he perceived that his suffering was nothing of so trifling and dignified a kind. It was altogether a more serious matter, and partook rather of the nature of those subtle and cruel feelings which are awakened by a kick or a horse-whipping.

He felt very sick—physically sick—as though he had bitten through something nauseous. Life, that to a well-ordered mind should be a matter of congratulation, appeared to him, for a second or so, perfectly intolerable. He picked up the paper at his feet, and sat down with the wish to think it out, to understand why his wife—his wife!—should leave him, should throw away respect, comfort, peace, decency, position—throw away everything for nothing! He set himself to think out the hidden logic of her action—a mental undertaking fit for the leisure hours of a madhouse, though he couldn't see it. And he thought of his wife in every relation except the only fundamental one. He thought of her as a well-bred girl, as a wife, as a cultured person, as the mistress of a house, as a lady; but he never for a moment thought of her simply as a woman.

Then a fresh wave, a raging wave of humiliation, swept through his mind, and left nothing there but a personal sense of undeserved abasement. Why should he be mixed up with such a horrid exposure! It annihilated all the advantages of his well-ordered past, by a truth effective and unjust like a calumny—and the past was wasted. Its failure was disclosed—a distinct failure, on his part, to see, to guard, to understand. It could not be denied; it could not be explained away, hustled out of sight. He could not sit on it and look solemn. Now—if she had only died!

If she had only died! He was driven to envy such a respectable bereavement, and one so perfectly free from any taint of misfortune that even his best friend or his best enemy would not have felt the slightest thrill of exultation. No one would have cared. He sought comfort in clinging to the contemplation of the only fact of life that the resolute efforts of mankind had never failed to disguise in the clatter and glamour of phrases. And nothing lends itself more to lies than death. If she had only died! Certain words would have been said to him in a sad tone, and he, with proper fortitude, would have made appropriate answers. There were precedents for such an occasion. And no one would have cared. If she had only died! The promises, the terrors, the hopes of eternity, are the concern of the corrupt dead; but the obvious sweetness of life belongs to living, healthy men. And life was his concern: that sane and gratifying existence untroubled by too much love or by too much regret. She had interfered with it; she had defaced it. And suddenly it occurred to him he must have been mad to marry. It was too much in the nature of giving yourself away, of wearing—if for a moment—your heart on your sleeve. But every one married. Was all mankind mad!

In the shock of that startling thought he looked up, and saw to the left, to the right, in front, men sitting far off in chairs and looking at him with wild eyes—emissaries of a distracted mankind intruding to spy upon his pain and his humiliation. It was not to be borne. He rose quickly, and the others jumped up, too, on all sides. He stood still in the middle of the room as if discouraged by their vigilance. No escape! He felt something akin to despair. Everybody must know. The servants must know to-night. He ground his teeth . . . And he had never noticed, never guessed anything. Every one will know. He thought: The woman's a monster, but everybody will think me a fool; and standing still in the midst of severe walnut-wood furniture, he felt such a tempest of anguish within him that he seemed to see himself rolling on the carpet, beating his head against the wall. He was disgusted with himself, with the loathsome rush of emotion breaking through all the reserves that guarded his manhood. Something unknown, withering and poisonous, had entered his life, passed near him, touched him, and he was deteriorating. He was appalled. What was it? She was gone. Why? His head was ready to burst with the endeavour to understand her act and his subtle horror of it. Everything was changed. Why? Only a woman gone, after all; and yet he had a vision, a vision quick and distinct as a dream: the vision of everything he had thought indestructible and safe in the world crashing down about him, like solid walls do before the fierce breath of a hurricane. He stared, shaking in every limb, while he felt the destructive breath, the mysterious breath, the breath of passion, stir the profound peace of the house. He looked round in fear. Yes. Crime may be forgiven; uncalculating sacrifice, blind trust, burning faith, other follies, may be turned to account; suffering, death itself, may with a grin or a frown be explained away; but passion is the unpardonable and secret infamy of our hearts, a thing to curse, to hide and to deny; a shameless and forlorn thing that tramples upon the smiling promises, that tears off the placid mask, that strips the body of life. And it had come to him! It had laid its unclean hand upon the spotless draperies of his existence, and he had to face it alone with all the world looking on. All the world! And he thought that even the bare suspicion of such an adversary within his house carried with it a taint and a condemnation. He put both his hands out as if to ward off the reproach of a defiling truth; and, instantly, the appalled conclave of unreal men, standing about mutely beyond the clear lustre of mirrors, made at him the same gesture of rejection and horror.

He glanced vainly here and there, like a man looking in desperation for a weapon or for a hiding place, and understood at last that he was disarmed and cornered by the enemy that, without any squeamishness, would strike so as to lay open his heart. He could get help nowhere, or even take counsel with himself, because in the sudden shock of her desertion the sentiments which he knew that in fidelity to his bringing up, to his prejudices and his surroundings, he ought to experience, were so mixed up with the novelty of real feelings, of fundamental feelings that know nothing of creed, class, or education, that he was unable to distinguish clearly between what is and what ought to be; between the inexcusable truth and the valid pretences. And he knew instinctively that truth would be of no use to him.* Some kind of concealment seemed a necessity because one cannot explain. Of course not! Who would listen? One had simply to be without stain and without reproach to keep one's place in the forefront of life.

He said to himself, "I must get over it the best I can," and began to walk up and down the room. What next? What ought to be done? He thought: I will travel—no I won't. I shall face it out.* And after that resolve he was greatly cheered by the reflection that it would be a mute and an easy part to play, for no one would be likely to converse with him about the abominable conduct of—that woman. He argued to himself that decent people—and he knew no others—did not care to talk about such indelicate affairs. She had gone off—with that unhealthy, fat ass of a journalist. Why? He had been all a husband ought to be. He had given her a good position—she shared his prospects—he had treated her invariably with great consideration. He reviewed his conduct with a kind of dismal pride. It had been irreproachable. Then, why? For love? Profanation! There could be no love there. A shameful impulse of passion. Yes, passion. His own wife! Good God! . . . And the indelicate aspect of his domestic misfortune struck him with such shame that, next moment, he caught himself in the act of pondering absurdly over the notion whether it would not be more dignified for him to induce a general belief that he had been in the habit of beating his wife. Some fellows do ... and anything would be better than the filthy fact; for it was clear he had lived with the root of it for five years—and it was too shameful. Anything! Anything! Brutality ... But he gave it up directly, and began to think of the Divorce Court.* It did not present itself to him, notwithstanding his respect for law and usage, as a proper refuge for dignified grief. It appeared rather as an unclean and sinister cavern where men and women are haled by adverse fate to writhe ridiculously in the presence of uncompromising truth. It should not be allowed. That woman! Five ... years ... married five years ... and never to see anything. Not to the very last day ... not till she coolly went off. And he pictured to himself all the people he knew engaged in speculating as to whether all that time he had been blind, foolish, or infatuated. What a woman! Blind! ... Not at all. Could a clean-minded man imagine such depravity? Evidently not. He drew a free breath. That was the attitude to take; it was dignified enough; it gave him the advantage, and he could not help perceiving that it was moral. He yearned unaffectedly to see morality (in his person) triumphant before the world. As to her she would be forgotten. Let her be forgotten—buried in oblivion—lost! No one would allude ... Refined people—and every man and woman he knew could be so described—had, of course, a horror of such topics. Had they? Oh, yes. No one would allude to her ... in his hearing. He stamped his foot, tore the letter across, then again and again. The thought of sympathizing friends excited in him a fury of mistrust. He flung down the small bits of paper. They settled, fluttering at his feet, and looked very white on the dark carpet, like a scattered handful of snow-flakes.

This fit of hot anger was succeeded by a sudden sadness, by the darkening passage of a thought that ran over the scorched surface of his heart, like upon a barren plain, and after a fiercer assault of sun-rays, the melancholy and cooling shadow of a cloud. He realized that he had had a shock*—not a violent or rending blow, that can be seen, resisted, returned, forgotten, but a thrust, insidious and penetrating, that had stirred all those feelings, concealed and cruel, which the arts of the devil, the fears of mankind—God's infinite compassion, perhaps—keep chained deep down in the inscrutable twilight of our breasts. A dark curtain seemed to rise before him, and for less than a second he looked upon the mysterious universe of moral suffering.

As a landscape is seen complete, and vast, and vivid, under a flash of lightning, so he could see disclosed in a moment all the immensity of pain that can be contained in one short moment of human thought. Then the curtain fell again, but his rapid vision left in Alvan Hervey's mind a trail of invincible sadness, a sense of loss and bitter solitude, as though he had been robbed and exiled. For a moment he ceased to be a member of society with a position, a career, and a name attached to all this, like a descriptive label of some complicated compound. He was a simple human being removed from the delightful world of crescents and squares. He stood alone, naked and afraid, like the first man on the first day of evil.* There are in life events, contacts, glimpses, that seem brutally to bring all the past to a close. There is a shock and a crash, as of a gate flung to behind one by the perfidious hand of fate. Go and seek another paradise, fool or sage. There is a moment of dumb dismay, and the wanderings must begin again; the painful explaining away of facts, the feverish raking up of illusions, the cultivation of a fresh crop of lies in the sweat of one's brow, to sustain life, to make it supportable, to make it fair, so as to hand intact to another generation of blind wanderers the charming legend of a heartless country, of a promised land, all flowers and blessings . . .

He came to himself with a slight start, and became aware of an oppressive, crushing desolation. It was only a feeling, it is true, but it produced on him a physical effect, as though his chest had been squeezed in a vice. He perceived himself so extremely forlorn and lamentable, and was moved so deeply by the oppressive sorrow, that another turn of the screw,* he felt, would bring tears out of his eyes. He was deteriorating. Five years of life in common had appeased his longing. Yes, long-time ago. The first five months did that—but . . . There was the habit—the habit of her person, of her smile, of her gestures, of her voice, of her silence. She had a pure brow and good hair. How utterly wretched all this was. Good hair and fine eyes—remarkably fine. He was surprised by the number of details that intruded upon his unwilling memory. He could not help remembering her footsteps, the rustle of her dress, her way of holding her head, her decisive manner of saying "Alvan," the quiver of her nostrils when she was annoyed. All that had been so much his property, so intimately and specially his! He raged in a mournful, silent way, as he took stock of his losses. He was like a man counting the cost of an unlucky speculation—irritated, depressed—exasperated with himself and with others, with the fortunate, with the indifferent, with the callous; yet the wrong done him appeared so cruel that he would perhaps have dropped a tear over that spoliation if it had not been for his conviction that men do not weep. Foreigners do; they also kill sometimes in such circumstances. And to his horror he felt himself driven to regret almost that the usages of a society ready to forgive the shooting of a burglar forbade him, under the circumstances, even as much as a thought of murder. Nevertheless, he clenched his fists and set his teeth hard. And he was afraid at the same time. He was afraid with that penetrating faltering fear that seems, in the very middle of a beat, to turn one's heart into a handful of dust. The contamination of her crime spread out, tainted the universe, tainted himself; woke up all the dormant infamies of the world; caused a ghastly kind of clairvoyance in which he could see the towns and fields of the earth, its sacred places, its temples and its houses, peopled by monsters—by monsters of duplicity, lust, and murder. She was a monster—he himself was thinking monstrous thoughts . . . and yet he was like other people. How many men and women at this very moment were plunged in abominations—meditated crimes. It was frightful to think of. He remembered all the streets—the well-to-do streets he had passed on his way home; all the innumerable houses with closed doors and curtained windows. Each seemed now an abode of anguish and folly. And his thought, as if appalled, stood still, recalling with dismay the decorous and frightful silence that was like a conspiracy; the grim, impenetrable silence of miles of walls concealing passions, misery, thoughts of crime. Surely he was not the only man; his was not the only house . . . and yet no one knew—no one guessed. But he knew. He knew with unerring certitude that could not be deceived by the correct silence of walls, of closed doors, of curtained windows. He was beside himself with a despairing agitation, like a man informed of a deadly secret—the secret of a calamity threatening the safety of mankind—the sacredness, the peace of life.

He caught sight of himself in one of the looking-glasses. It was a relief. The anguish of his feeling had been so powerful that he more than half expected to see some distorted wild face there, and he was pleasantly surprised to see nothing of the kind. His aspect, at any rate, would let no one into the secret of his pain. He examined himself with attention. His trousers were turned up, and his boots a little muddy, but he looked very much as usual. Only his hair was slightly ruffled, and that disorder, somehow, was so suggestive of trouble that he went quickly to the table, and began to use the brushes, in an anxious desire to obliterate the compromising trace, that only vestige of his emotion. He brushed with care, watching the effect of his smoothing; and another face, slightly pale and more tense than was perhaps desirable, peered back at him from the toilet glass. He laid the brushes down, and was not satisfied. He took them up again and brushed, brushed mechanically—forgot himself in that occupation. The tumult of his thoughts ended in a sluggish flow of reflection, such as, after the outburst of a volcano, the almost imperceptible progress of a stream of lava, creeping languidly over a convulsed land and pitilessly obliterating any landmark left by the shock of the earthquake. It is a destructive but, by comparison, it is a peaceful phenomenon. Alvan Hervey was almost soothed by the deliberate pace of his thoughts. His moral landmarks were going one by one, consumed in the fire of his experience, buried in hot mud, in ashes. He was cooling—on the surface; but there was enough heat left somewhere to make him slap the brushes on the table, and turning away, say in a fierce whisper: "I wish him joy . . . Damn the woman."

He felt himself utterly corrupted by her wickedness, and the most significant symptom of his moral downfall was the bitter, acrid satisfaction with which he recognized it. He, deliberately, swore in his thoughts; he meditated sneers; he shaped in profound silence words of cynical unbelief, and his most cherished convictions stood revealed finally as the narrow prejudices of fools. A crowd of shapeless, unclean thoughts crossed his mind in a stealthy rush, like a band of veiled malefactors hastening to a crime. He put his hands deep into his pockets. He heard a faint ringing somewhere, and muttered to himself: "I am not the only one . . . not the only one." There was another ring. Front door!

His heart leaped up into his throat, and forthwith descended as low as his boots. A call! Who? Why? He wanted to rush out on the landing and shout to the servant: "Not at home! Gone away abroad!" . . . Any excuse. He could not face a visitor. Not this evening. No. To-morrow. . . . Before he could break out of the numbness that enveloped him like a sheet of lead, he heard far below, as if in the entrails of the earth, a door close heavily. The house vibrated to it more than to a clap of thunder. He stood still, wishing himself invisible. The room was very chilly. He did not think he would ever feel like that. But people must be met—they must be faced—talked to—smiled at. He heard another door, much nearer—the door of the drawing-room—being opened and flung to again. He imagined for a moment he would faint. How absurd! That kind of thing had to be gone through. A voice spoke. He could not catch the words. Then the voice spoke again, and footsteps were heard on the first floor landing. Hang it all! Was he to hear that voice and those footsteps whenever any one spoke or moved. He thought: "This is like being haunted—I suppose it will last for a week or so, at least. Till I forget. Forget! Forget!" Someone was coming up the second flight of stairs. Servant? He listened, then, suddenly, as though an incredible, frightful revelation had been shouted to him from a distance, he bellowed out in the empty room: "What! What!" in such a fiendish tone as to astonish himself. The footsteps stopped outside the door. He stood openmouthed, maddened and still, as if in the midst of a catastrophe. The door-handle rattled lightly. It seemed to him that the walls were coming apart, that the furniture swayed at him; the ceiling slanted queerly for a moment, a tall wardrobe tried to topple over. He caught hold of something and it was the back of a chair. So he had reeled against a chair! Oh! Confound it! He gripped hard.

The flaming butterfly poised between the jaws of the bronze dragon radiated a glare, a glare that seemed to leap up all at once into a crude, blinding fierceness, and made it difficult for him to distinguish plainly the figure of his wife standing upright with her back to the closed door. He looked at her and could not detect her breathing. The harsh and violent light was beating on her, and he was amazed to see her preserve so well the composure of her upright attitude in that scorching brilliance which, to his eyes, enveloped her like a hot and consuming mist. He would not have been surprised if she had vanished in it as suddenly as she had appeared. He stared and listened; listened for some sound, but the silence round him was absolute*—as though he had in a moment grown completely deaf as well as dim-eyed. Then his hearing returned, preternaturally sharp. He heard the patter of a rain-shower on the window panes behind the lowered blinds, and below, far below, in the artificial abyss of the square, the deadened roll of wheels and the splashy trotting of a horse. He heard a groan also—very distinct—in the room—close to his ear.

He thought with alarm: "I must have made that noise myself;" and at the same instant the woman left the door, stepped firmly across the floor before him, and sat down in a chair. He knew that step. There was no doubt about it. She had come back! And he very nearly said aloud "Of course!"—such was his sudden and masterful perception of the indestructible character of her being. Nothing could destroy her—and nothing but his own destruction could keep her away. She was the incarnation of all the short moments which every man spares out of his life for dreams, for precious dreams that concrete the most cherished, the most profitable of his illusions. He peered at her with inward trepidation. She was mysterious, significant, full of obscure meaning —like a symbol. He peered, bending forward, as though he had been discovering about her things he had never seen before. Unconsciously he made a step towards her—then another. He saw her arm make an ample, decided movement and he stopped. She had lifted her veil. It was like the lifting of a vizor.

The spell was broken. He experienced a shock as though he had been called out of a trance by the sudden noise of an explosion. It was even more startling and more distinct; it was an infinitely more intimate change, for he had the sensation of having come into this room only that very moment; of having returned from very far; he was made aware that some essential part of himself had in a flash returned into his body, returned finally* from a fierce and lamentable region, from the dwelling-place of unveiled hearts. He woke up to an amazing infinity of contempt, to a droll bitterness of wonder, to a disenchanted conviction of safety. He had a glimpse of the irresistible force, and he saw also the barrenness of his convictions—of her convictions. It seemed to him that he could never make a mistake as long as he lived. It was morally impossible to go wrong. He was not elated by that certitude; he was dimly uneasy about its price; there was a chill as of death in this triumph of sound principles, in this victory snatched under the very shadow of disaster.

The last trace of his previous state of mind vanished, as the instantaneous and elusive trail of a bursting meteor vanishes on the profound blackness of the sky; it was the faint flicker of a painful thought, gone as soon as perceived, that nothing but her presence—after all—had the power to recall him to himself. He stared at her. She sat with her hands on her lap, looking down; and he noticed that her boots were dirty, her skirts wet and splashed, as though she had been driven back there by a blind fear through a waste of mud. He was indignant, amazed and shocked, but in a natural, healthy way now; so that he could control those unprofitable sentiments by the dictates of cautious self-restraint. The light in the room had no unusual brilliance now; it was a good light in which he could easily observe the expression of her face. It was that of dull fatigue. And the silence that surrounded them was the normal silence* of any quiet house, hardly disturbed by the faint noises of a respectable quarter of the town. He was very cool—and it was quite coolly that he thought how much better it would be if neither of them ever spoke again. She sat with closed lips, with an air of lassitude in the stony forgetfulness of her pose, but after a moment she lifted her drooping eyelids and met his tense and inquisitive stare by a look that had all the formless eloquence of a cry. It penetrated, it stirred without informing; it was the very essence of anguish stripped of words that can be smiled at, argued away, shouted down, disdained. It was anguish naked and unashamed, the bare pain of existence let loose upon the world in the fleeting unreserve of a look that had in it an immensity of fatigue, the scornful sincerity, the black impudence of an extorted confession. Alvan Hervey was seized with wonder, as though he had seen something inconceivable; and some obscure part of his being was ready to exclaim with him: "I would never have believed it!" but an instantaneous revulsion of wounded susceptibilities checked the unfinished thought.

He felt full of rancorous indignation against the woman who could look like this at one. This look probed him; it tampered with him. It was dangerous to one as would be a hint of unbelief whispered by a priest in the august decorum of a temple; and at the same time it was impure, it was disturbing, like a cynical consolation muttered in the dark, tainting the sorrow, corroding the thought, poisoning the heart. He wanted to ask her furiously: "Who do you take me for? How dare you look at me like this?" He felt himself helpless before the hidden meaning of that look; he resented it with pained and futile violence as an injury so secret that it could never, never be redressed. His wish was to crush her by a single sentence. He was stainless. Opinion was on his side; morality, men and gods were on his side; law, conscience—all the world! She had nothing but that look. And he could only say:

"How long do you intend to stay here?"

Her eyes did not waver, her lips remained closed; and for any effect of his words he might have spoken to a dead woman, only that this one breathed quickly. He was profoundly disappointed by what he had said.* It was a great deception, something in the nature of treason. He had deceived himself. It should have been altogether different—other words—another sensation. And before his eyes, so fixed that at times they saw nothing, she sat apparently as unconscious as though she had been alone, sending that look of brazen confession straight at him—with an air of staring into empty space. He said significantly:

"Must I go then?" And he knew he meant nothing of what he implied.

One of her hands on her lap moved slightly as though his words had fallen there and she had thrown them off on the floor. But her silence encouraged him. Possibly it meant remorse—perhaps fear. Was she thunderstruck by his attitude? . . . Her eyelids dropped. He seemed to understand ever so much—everything! Very well—but she must be made to suffer. It was due to him. He understood everything, yet he judged it indispensable to say with an obvious affectation of civility:

"I don't understand—be so good as to . . ."

She stood up. For a second he believed she intended to go away, and it was as though someone had jerked a string attached to his heart. It hurt. He remained open-mouthed and silent. But she made an irresolute step towards him, and instinctively he moved aside. They stood before one another, and the fragments of the torn letter lay between them—at their feet—like an insurmountable obstacle, like a sign of eternal separation! Around them three other couples stood still and face to face, as if waiting for a signal to begin some action—a struggle, a dispute, or a dance.

She said: "Don't—Alvan!" and there was something that resembled a warning in the pain of her tone. He narrowed his eyes as if trying to pierce her with his gaze. Her voice touched him. He had aspirations after magnanimity, generosity, superiority—interrupted, however, by flashes of indignation and anxiety—frightful anxiety to know how far she had gone. She looked down at the torn paper. Then she looked up, and their eyes met again, remained fastened together, like an unbreakable bond, like a clasp of eternal complicity;* and the decorous silence, the pervading quietude of the house which enveloped this meeting of their glances became for a moment inexpressibly vile, for he was afraid she would say too much and make magnanimity impossible, while behind the profound mournfulness of her face there was a regret—a regret of things done—the regret of delay—the thought that if she had only turned back a week sooner—a day sooner—only an hour sooner. . . . They were afraid to hear again the sound of their voices; they did not know what they might say—perhaps something that could not be recalled; and words are more terrible than facts. But the tricky fatality that lurks in obscure impulses spoke through Alvan Hervey's lips suddenly; and he heard his own voice with the excited and sceptical curiosity with which one listens to actors' voices speaking on the stage in the strain of a poignant situation.

"If you have forgotten anything . . . of course . . . I . . ."

Her eyes blazed at him for an instant; her lips trembled—and then she also became the mouth-piece of the mysterious force forever hovering near us; of that perverse inspiration, wandering capricious and uncontrollable, like a gust of wind.

"What is the good of this, Alvan? . . . You know why I came back. . . . You know that I could not . . ."

He interrupted her with irritation.

"Then—what's this?" he asked, pointing downwards at the torn letter.

"That's a mistake," she said hurriedly, in a muffled voice.

This answer amazed him. He remained speechless, staring at her. He had half a mind to burst into a laugh. It ended in a smile as involuntary as a grimace of pain.

"A mistake . . ." he began, slowly, and then found himself unable to say another word.

"Yes . . . it was honest," she said very low, as if speaking to the memory of a feeling in a remote past.

He exploded.

"Curse your honesty! . . . Is there any honesty in all this! . . . When did you begin to be honest? Why are you here? What are you now? . . . Still honest? . . ."

He walked at her, raging, as if blind; during these three quick strides he lost touch of the material world and was whirled interminably through a kind of empty universe* made up of nothing but fury and anguish, till he came suddenly upon her face—very close to his. He stopped short, and all at once seemed to remember something heard ages ago.

"You don't know the meaning of the word," he shouted.

She did not flinch. He perceived with fear that everything around him was still. She did not move a hair's breadth; his own body did not stir. An imperturbable calm enveloped their two motionless figures, the house, the town, all the world—and the trifling tempest of his feelings. The violence of the short tumult within him had been such as could well have shattered all creation; and yet nothing was changed. He faced his wife in the familiar room in his own house. It had not fallen. And right and left all the innumerable dwellings, standing shoulder to shoulder, had resisted the shock of his passion, had presented, unmoved, to the loneliness of his trouble, the grim silence of walls, the impenetrable and polished discretion of closed doors and curtained windows. Immobility and silence pressed on him, assailed him, like two accomplices of the immovable and mute woman before his eyes.* He was suddenly vanquished. He was shown his impotence. He was soothed by the breath of a corrupt resignation coming to him through the subtle irony of the surrounding peace.

He said with villainous composure:

"At any rate it isn't enough for me. I want to know more—if you're going to stay."

"There is nothing more to tell," she answered, sadly.

It struck him as so very true that he did not say anything. She went on:

"You wouldn't understand. . . ."

"No?" he said, quietly. He held himself tight not to burst into howls and imprecations.

"I tried to be faithful . . ." she began again.

"And this?" he exclaimed, pointing at the fragments of her letter.

"This—this is a failure," she said.

"I should think so," he muttered, bitterly.

"I tried to be faithful to myself—Alvan—and . . . and honest to you. . . ."

"If you had tried to be faithful to me it would have been more to the purpose," he interrupted, angrily. "I've been faithful to you and you have spoiled my life—both our lives . . ." Then after a pause the unconquerable preoccupation of self came out, and he raised his voice to ask resentfully, "And, pray, for how long have you been making a fool of me?"

She seemed horribly shocked by that question. He did not wait for an answer, but went on moving about all the time; now and then coming up to her, then wandering off restlessly to the other end of the room.

"I want to know. Everybody knows, I suppose, but myself—and that's your honesty!"

"I have told you there is nothing to know," she said, speaking unsteadily as if in pain. "Nothing of what you suppose. You don't understand me. This letter is the beginning—and the end."

"The end—this thing has no end," he clamoured, unexpectedly. "Can't you understand that? I can . . . The beginning . . ."

He stopped and looked into her eyes with concentrated intensity, with a desire to see, to penetrate, to understand, that made him positively hold his breath till he gasped.

"By Heavens!" he said, standing perfectly still in a peering attitude and within less than a foot from her.

"By Heavens!" he repeated, slowly, and in a tone whose involuntary strangeness was a complete mystery to himself. "By Heavens —I could believe you—I could believe anything—now!"

He turned short on his heel and began to walk up and down the room with an air of having disburdened himself of the final pronouncement of his life—of having said something on which he would not go back, even if he could. She remained as if rooted to the carpet. Her eyes followed the restless movements of the man, who avoided looking at her. Her wide stare clung to him, inquiring, wondering and doubtful.

"But the fellow was forever sticking in here," he burst out, distractedly. "He made love to you,* I suppose—and, and . . ." He lowered his voice. "And—you let him."

"And I let him," she murmured, catching his intonation, so that her voice sounded unconscious, sounded far off and slavish, like an echo.

He said twice, "You! You!" violently, then calmed down. "What could you see in the fellow?" he asked, with unaffected wonder. "An effeminate, fat ass. What could you . . . Weren't you happy? Didn't you have all you wanted? Now—frankly; did I deceive your expectations in any way? Were you disappointed with our position—or with our prospects—perhaps? You know you couldn't be—they are much better than you could hope for when you married me. . . ."

He forgot himself so far as to gesticulate a little while he went on with animation:

"What could you expect from such a fellow? He's an outsider—a rank outsider. . . . If it hadn't been for my money . . . do you hear? . . . for my money, he wouldn't know where to turn. His people won't have anything to do with him. The fellow's no class—no class at all. He's useful, certainly, that's why I . . . I thought you had enough intelligence to see it. . . . And you . . . No! It's incredible! What did he tell you? Do you care for no one's opinion—is there no restraining influence in the world for you—women? Did you ever give me a thought? I tried to be a good husband. Did I fail? Tell me—what have I done?"

Carried away by his feelings he took his head in both his hands and repeated wildly:

"What have I done? . . . Tell me! What? . . ."

"Nothing," she said.*

"Ah! You see . . . you can't . . ." he began, triumphantly, walking away; then suddenly, as though he had been flung back at her by something invisible he had met, he spun round and shouted with exasperation:

"What on earth did you expect me to do?"

Without a word she moved slowly towards the table, and, sitting down, leaned on her elbow, shading her eyes with her hand. All that time he glared at her watchfully as if expecting every moment to find in her deliberate movements an answer to his question. But he could not read anything, he could gather no hint of her thought. He tried to suppress his desire to shout, and after waiting awhile, said with incisive scorn:

"Did you want me to write absurd verses; to sit and look at you for hours—to talk to you about your soul? You ought to have known I wasn't that sort. . . . I had something better to do. But if you think I was totally blind . . ."

He perceived in a flash that he could remember an infinity of enlightening occurrences. He could recall ever so many distinct occasions when he came upon them; he remembered the absurdly interrupted gesture of his fat, white hand, the rapt expression of her face, the glitter of unbelieving eyes; snatches of incomprehensible conversations not worth listening to, silences that had meant nothing at the time and seemed now illuminating like a burst of sunshine. He remembered all that. He had not been blind. Oh! No! And to know this was an exquisite relief: it brought back all his composure.

"I thought it beneath me to suspect you," he said, loftily.

The sound of that sentence* evidently possessed some magical power, because, as soon as he had spoken, he felt wonderfully at ease; and directly afterwards he experienced a flash of joyful amazement at the discovery that he could be inspired to such noble and truthful utterance. He watched the effect of his words. They caused her to glance to him quickly over her shoulder. He caught a glimpse of wet eyelashes, of a red cheek with a tear running down swiftly; and then she turned away again and sat as before, covering her face with her hands.

"You ought to be perfectly frank with me," he said, slowly.

"You know everything," she answered, indistinctly, through her fingers.

"This letter. . . . Yes . . . but . . ."

"And I came back," she exclaimed in a stifled voice; "you know everything."

"I am glad of it—for your sake," he said with impressive gravity. He listened to himself with solemn emotion.* It seemed to him that something inexpressibly momentous was in progress within the room, that every word and every gesture had the importance of events preordained from the beginning of all things, and summing up in their finality the whole purpose of creation.

"For your sake," he repeated.

Her shoulders shook as though she had been sobbing, and he forgot himself in the contemplation of her hair. Suddenly he gave a start, as if waking up, and asked very gently and not much above a whisper—

"Have you been meeting him often?"

"Never!" she cried into the palms of her hands.

This answer seemed for a moment to take from him the power of speech. His lips moved for some time before any sound came.

"You preferred to make love here—under my very nose," he said, furiously. He calmed down instantly, and felt regretfully uneasy, as though he had let himself down in her estimation by that outburst. She rose, and with her hand on the back of the chair confronted him with eyes that were perfectly dry now. There was a red spot on each of her cheeks.

"When I made up my mind to go to him—I wrote," she said.

"But you didn't go to him," he took up in the same tone. "How far did you go? What made you come back?"

"I didn't know myself," she murmured. Nothing of her moved but her lips. He fixed her sternly.

"Did he expect this? Was he waiting for you?" he asked.

She answered him by an almost imperceptible nod, and he continued to look at her for a good while without making a sound. Then, at last—

"And I suppose he is waiting yet?" he asked, quickly.

Again she seemed to nod at him. For some reason* he felt he must know the time. He consulted his watch gloomily. Half-past seven.

"Is he?" he muttered, putting the watch in his pocket. He looked up at her, and, as if suddenly overcome by a sense of sinister fun, gave a short, harsh laugh, directly repressed.

"No! It's the most unheard! . . ." he mumbled while she stood before him biting her lower lip, as if plunged in deep thought. He laughed again in one low burst that was as spiteful as an imprecation. He did not know why he felt such an overpowering and sudden distaste for the facts of existence—for facts in general—such an immense disgust at the thought of all the many days already lived through. He was wearied. Thinking seemed a labour beyond his strength. He said—

"You deceived me—now you make a fool of him . . . It's awful! Why?"

"I deceived myself!" she exclaimed.

"Oh! Nonsense!" he said, impatiently.

"I am ready to go if you wish it," she went on, quickly. "It was due to you—to be told—to know. No! I could not!" she cried, and stood still wringing her hands stealthily.

"I am glad you repented before it was too late," he said in a dull tone and looking at his boots. "I am glad . . . some spark of better feeling," he muttered, as if to himself. He lifted up his head after a moment of brooding silence. "I am glad to see that there is some sense of decency left in you," he added a little louder. Looking at her he appeared to hesitate, as if estimating the possible consequences of what he wished to say, and at last blurted out—

"After all, I loved you. . . ."

"I did not know," she whispered.

"Good God!" he cried. "Why do you imagine I married you?"

The indelicacy of his obtuseness angered her.

"Ah—why?" she said through her teeth.

He appeared overcome with horror, and watched her lips intently as though in fear.

"I imagined many things," she said, slowly, and paused. He watched, holding his breath. At last she went on musingly, as if thinking aloud, "I tried to understand. I tried honestly. . . . Why? . . . To do the usual thing—I suppose. . . . To please yourself."

He walked away smartly, and when he came back, close to her, he had a flushed face.

"You seemed pretty well pleased, too—at the time," he hissed, with scathing fury. "I needn't ask whether you loved me."

"I know now I was perfectly incapable of such a thing," she said, calmly, "If I had, perhaps you would not have married me."

"It's very clear I would not have done it if I had known you—as I know you now."

He seemed to see himself proposing to her—ages ago. They were strolling up the slope of a lawn. Groups of people were scattered in sunshine. The shadows of leafy boughs lay still on the short grass. The coloured sunshades far off, passing between trees, resembled deliberate and brilliant butterflies moving without a flutter. Men smiling amiably, or else very grave, within the impeccable shelter of their black coats, stood by the side of women who, clustered in clear summer toilettes, recalled all the fabulous tales of enchanted gardens where animated flowers smile at bewitched knights. There was a sumptuous serenity in it all, a thin, vibrating excitement, the perfect security, as of an invincible ignorance, that evoked within him a transcendent belief in felicity as the lot of all mankind, a recklessly picturesque desire to get promptly something for himself only, out of that splendour unmarred by any shadow of a thought. The girl walked by his side across an open space; no one was near, and suddenly he stood still, as if inspired, and spoke. He remembered looking at her pure eyes, at her candid brow; he remembered glancing about quickly to see if they were being observed, and thinking that nothing could go wrong in a world of so much charm, purity, and distinction. He was proud of it. He was one of its makers, of its possessors, of its guardians, of its extollers. He wanted to grasp it solidly, to get as much gratification as he could out of it; and in view of its incomparable quality, of its unstained atmosphere, of its nearness to the heaven of its choice, this gust of brutal desire seemed the most noble of aspirations. In a second he lived again through all these moments, and then all the pathos of his failure presented itself to him with such vividness that there was a suspicion of tears in his tone when he said almost unthinkingly, "My God! I did love you!"

She seemed touched by the emotion of his voice. Her lips quivered a little, and she made one faltering step towards him, putting out her hands in a beseeching gesture, when she perceived, just in time, that being absorbed by the tragedy of his life he had absolutely forgotten her very existence. She stopped, and her outstretched arms fell slowly. He, with his features distorted by the bitterness of his thought, saw neither her movement nor her gesture. He stamped his foot in vexation, rubbed his head—then exploded.

"What the devil am I to do now?"

He was still again. She seemed to understand, and moved to the door firmly.

"It's very simple—I'm going," she said aloud.

At the sound of her voice he gave a start of surprise, looked at her wildly, and asked in a piercing tone—

"You. . . . Where? To him?"

"No—alone—good-bye."

The door-handle rattled under her groping hand as though she had been trying to get out of some dark place.

"No—stay!" he cried.

She heard him faintly. He saw her shoulder touch the lintel of the door. She swayed as if dazed. There was less than a second of suspense while they both felt as if poised on the very edge of moral annihilation, ready to fall into some devouring nowhere. Then, almost simultaneously, he shouted, "Come back!" and she let go the handle of the door. She turned round in peaceful desperation like one who deliberately has thrown away the last chance of life; and, for a moment, the room she faced appeared terrible, and dark, and safe—like a grave.

He said, very hoarse and abrupt: "It can't end like this. . . . Sit down;" and while she crossed the room again to the low-backed chair before the dressing-table, he opened the door and put his head out to look and listen. The house was quiet. He came back pacified, and asked—

"Do you speak the truth?"

She nodded.

"You have lived a lie, though," he said, suspiciously.

"Ah! You made it so easy," she answered.

"You reproach me—me!"

"How could I?" she said; "I would have you no other—now."

"What do you mean by . . ." he began, then checked himself, and without waiting for an answer went on, "I won't ask any questions. Is this letter the worst of it?"

She had a nervous movement of her hands.

"I must have a plain answer," he said, hotly.

"Then, no! The worst is my coming back."

There followed a period of dead silence,* during which they exchanged searching glances.

He said authoritatively—

"You don't know what you are saying. Your mind is unhinged. You are beside yourself, or you would not say such things. You can't control yourself. Even in your remorse . . ." He paused a moment, then said with a doctoral air: "Self-restraint is everything in life, you know. It's happiness, it's dignity . . . it's everything."

She was pulling nervously at her handkerchief while he went on watching anxiously to see the effect of his words. Nothing satisfactory happened. Only, as he began to speak again, she covered her face with both her hands.

"You see where the want of self-restraint leads to. Pain—humiliation—loss of respect—of friends, of everything that ennobles life, that . . . All kinds of horrors," he concluded, abruptly.

She made no stir. He looked at her pensively for some time as though he had been concentrating the melancholy thoughts evoked by the sight of that abased woman. His eyes became fixed and dull. He was profoundly penetrated by the solemnity of the moment; he felt deeply the greatness of the occasion. And more than ever the walls of his house seemed to enclose the sacredness of ideals to which he was about to offer a magnificent sacrifice. He was the high priest of that temple, the severe guardian of formulas, of rites, of the pure ceremonial concealing the black doubts of life. And he was not alone. Other men, too—the best of them—kept watch and ward by the hearthstones that were the altars of that profitable persuasion. He understood confusedly that he was part of an immense and beneficent power, which had a reward ready for every discretion. He dwelt within the invincible wisdom of silence; he was protected by an indestructible faith that would last forever, that would withstand unshaken all the assaults—the loud execrations of apostates, and the secret weariness of its confessors! He was in league with a universe of untold advantages. He represented the moral strength of a beautiful reticence that could vanquish all the deplorable crudities of life—fear, disaster, sin—even death itself. It seemed to him he was on the point of sweeping triumphantly away all the illusory mysteries of existence. It was simplicity itself.

"I hope you see now the folly—the utter folly of wickedness," he began in a dull, solemn manner. "You must respect the conditions of your life or lose all it can give you. All! Everything!"

He waved his arm once, and three exact replicas of his face,* of his clothes, of his dull severity, of his solemn grief, repeated the wide gesture that in its comprehensive sweep indicated an infinity of moral sweetness, embraced the walls, the hangings, the whole house, all the crowd of houses outside, all the flimsy and inscrutable graves of the living, with their doors numbered like the doors of prison-cells, and as impenetrable as the granite of tombstones.

"Yes! Restraint, duty, fidelity—unswerving fidelity to what is expected of you. This—only this—secures the reward, the peace. Everything else we should labour to subdue—to destroy. It's misfortune; it's disease. It is terrible—terrible. We must not know anything about it—we needn't. It is our duty to ourselves—to others. You do not live all alone in the world—and if you have no respect for the dignity of life, others have. Life is a serious matter. If you don't conform to the highest standards you are no one—it's a kind of death. Didn't this occur to you? You've only to look round you to see the truth of what I am saying. Did you live without noticing anything, without understanding anything? From a child you had examples before your eyes—you could see daily the beauty, the blessings of morality, of principles. . . ."

His voice rose and fell pompously in a strange chant. His eyes were still, his stare exalted and sullen; his face was set, was hard, was woodenly exulting over the grim inspiration that secretly possessed him, seethed within him, lifted him up into a stealthy frenzy of belief. Now and then he would stretch out his right arm over her head, as it were, and he spoke down at that sinner from a height, and with a sense of avenging virtue, with a profound and pure joy as though he could from his steep pinnacle see every weighty word strike and hurt like a punishing stone.

"Rigid principles—adherence to what is right," he finished after a pause.

"What is right?" she said, distinctly, without uncovering her face.

"Your mind is diseased!" he cried, upright and austere. "Such a question is rot—utter rot. Look round you—there's your answer, if you only care to see. Nothing that outrages the received beliefs can be right. Your conscience tells you that. They are the received beliefs because they are the best, the noblest, the only possible. They survive. . . ."

He could not help noticing with pleasure the philosophic breadth of his view, but he could not pause to enjoy it, for his inspiration, the call of august truth, carried him on.

"You must respect the moral foundations of a society that has made you what you are. Be true to it. That's duty—that's honour—that's honesty."

He felt a great glow within him, as though he had swallowed something hot. He made a step nearer. She sat up and looked at him with an ardour of expectation that stimulated his sense of the supreme importance of that moment. And as if forgetting himself he raised his voice very much.

"'What's right?' you ask me. Think only. What would you have been if you had gone off with that infernal vagabond? . . . What would you have been? . . . You! My wife! . . ."

He caught sight of himself in the pier glass, drawn up to his full height, and with a face so white that his eyes, at the distance, resembled the black cavities in a skull. He saw himself as if about to launch imprecations, with arms uplifted above her bowed head. He was ashamed of that unseemly posture,* and put his hands in his pockets hurriedly. She murmured faintly, as if to herself—

"Ah! What am I now?"

"As it happens you are still Mrs. Alvan Hervey*—uncommonly lucky for you, let me tell you," he said in a conversational tone. He walked up to the furthest corner of the room, and, turning back, saw her sitting very upright, her hands clasped on her lap, and with a lost, unswerving gaze of her eyes which stared unwinking like the eyes of the blind, at the crude gas flame, blazing and still, between the jaws of the bronze dragon.

He came up quite close to her, and straddling his legs a little, stood looking down at her face for some time without taking his hands out of his pockets. He seemed to be turning over in his mind a heap of words, piecing his next speech out of an overpowering abundance of thoughts.

"You've tried me to the utmost," he said at last; and as soon as he said these words he lost his moral footing, and felt himself swept away from his pinnacle by a flood of passionate resentment against the bungling creature that had come so near to spoiling his life. "Yes; I've been tried more than any man ought to be," he went on with righteous bitterness. "It was unfair. What possessed you to? . . . What possessed you? . . . Write such a . . . After five years of perfect happiness! 'Pon my word, no one would believe. . . . Didn't you feel you couldn't? Because you couldn't . . . it was impossible—you know. Wasn't it? Think. Wasn't it?"

"It was impossible," she whispered, obediently.

This submissive assent given with such readiness* did not soothe him, did not elate him; it gave him, inexplicably, that sense of terror we experience when in the midst of conditions we had learned to think absolutely safe* we discover all at once the presence of a near and unsuspected danger. It was impossible, of course! He knew it. She knew it. She confessed it. It was impossible! That man knew it, too—as well as any one; couldn't help knowing it. And yet those two had been engaged in a conspiracy against his peace—in a criminal enterprise for which there could be no sanction of belief within themselves. There could not be! There could not be! And yet how near to . . . With a short thrill he saw himself an exiled forlorn figure in a realm of ungovernable, of unrestrained folly. Nothing could be foreseen, foretold—guarded against. And the sensation was intolerable, had something of the withering horror that may be conceived as following upon the utter extinction of all hope. In the flash of thought the dishonouring episode seemed to disengage itself from everything actual, from earthly conditions, and even from earthly suffering; it became purely a terrifying knowledge, an annihilating knowledge of a blind and infernal force. Something desperate and vague, a flicker of an insane desire to abase himself before the mysterious impulses of evil, to ask for mercy in some way, passed through his mind; and then came the idea, the persuasion, the certitude, that the evil must be forgotten—must be resolutely ignored to make life possible; that the knowledge must be kept out of mind, out of sight, like the knowledge of certain death is kept out of the daily existence of men. He stiffened himself inwardly for the effort, and next moment it appeared very easy, amazingly feasible, if one only kept strictly to facts, gave one's mind to their perplexities and not to their meaning. Becoming conscious of a long silence, he cleared his throat warningly, and said in a steady voice—

"I am glad you feel this . . . uncommonly glad . . . you felt this in time. For, don't you see . . ." Unexpectedly he hesitated.

"Yes . . . I see," she murmured.

"Of course you would," he said, looking at the carpet and speaking like one who thinks of something else. He lifted his head. "I cannot believe—even after this—even after this—that you are altogether—altogether . . . other than what I thought you. It seems impossible—to me."

"And to me," she breathed out.

"Now—yes," he said, "but this morning? And to-morrow? . . . This is what . . ."

He started at the drift of his words and broke off abruptly. Every train of thought seemed to lead into the hopeless realm of ungovernable folly, to recall the knowledge and the terror of forces that must be ignored. He said rapidly—

"My position is very painful—difficult . . . I feel . . ."

He looked at her fixedly with a pained air, as though frightfully oppressed by a sudden inability to express his pent-up ideas.

"I am ready to go," she said very low. "I have forfeited everything . . . to learn . . . to learn . . ."

Her chin fell on her breast; her voice died out in a sigh. He made a slight gesture of impatient assent.

"Yes! Yes! It's all very well . . . of course. Forfeited—ah! Morally forfeited—only morally forfeited . . . if I am to believe you . . ."

She startled him by jumping up.

"Oh! I believe, I believe," he said, hastily, and she sat down as suddenly as she had got up. He went on gloomily—

"I've suffered—I suffer now. You can't understand how much. So much that when you propose a parting I almost think. . . . But no. There is duty. You've forgotten it; I never did. Before heaven, I never did. But in a horrid exposure like this the judgment of mankind goes astray—at least for a time. You see, you and I—at least I feel that—you and I are one before the world. It is as it should be. The world is right—in the main—or else it couldn't be—couldn't be—what it is. And we are part of it. We have our duty to—to our fellow beings who don't want to . . . to . . . er."

He stammered. She looked up at him with wide eyes, and her lips were slightly parted. He went on mumbling—

". . . Pain. . . . Indignation. . . . Sure to misunderstand. I've suffered enough. And if there has been nothing irreparable—as you assure me . . . then . . ."

"Alvan!" she cried.

"What?" he said, morosely. He gazed down at her for a moment with a sombre stare, as one looks at ruins, at the devastation of some natural disaster.

"Then," he continued after a short pause, "the best thing is . . . the best for us . . . for every one. . . . Yes . . . least pain—most unselfish. . . ." His voice faltered, and she heard only detached words. ". . . Duty. . . . Burden. . . . Ourselves. . . . Silence."

A moment of perfect stillness ensued.

"This is an appeal I am making to your conscience," he said, suddenly, in an explanatory tone, "not to add to the wretchedness of all this: to try loyally and help me to live it down somehow. Without any reservations—you know. Loyally! You can't deny I've been cruelly wronged and—after all—my affection deserves . . ." He paused with evident anxiety to hear her speak.

"I make no reservations," she said, mournfully. "How could I? I found myself out and came back to . . ." her eyes flashed scornfully for an instant ". . . to what—to what you propose. You see . . . I . . . I can be trusted . . . now."

He listened to every word with profound attention, and when she ceased seemed to wait for more.

"Is that all you've got to say?" he asked.

She was startled by his tone, and said faintly—

"I spoke the truth. What more can I say?"

"Confound it! You might say something human," he burst out. "It isn't being truthful; it's being brazen—if you want to know. Not a word to show you feel your position, and—and mine. Not a single word of acknowledgment, or regret—or remorse . . . or . . . something."

"Words!"* she whispered in a tone that irritated him. He stamped his foot.

"This is awful!" he exclaimed. "Words? Yes, words. Words mean something—yes—they do—for all this infernal affectation. They mean something to me—to everybody—to you. What the devil did you use to express those sentiments—sentiments—pah!—which made you forget me, duty, shame!" . . . He foamed at the mouth while she stared at him, appalled by this sudden fury. "Did you two talk only with your eyes?" he spluttered savagely. She rose.

"I can't bear this," she said, trembling from head to foot. "I am going."

They stood facing one another for a moment.

"Not you," he said, with conscious roughness, and began to walk up and down the room. She remained very still with an air of listening anxiously to her own heart-beats, then sank down on the chair slowly, and sighed, as if giving up a task beyond her strength.

"You misunderstand everything I say," he began quietly, "but I prefer to think that—just now—you are not accountable for your actions." He stopped again before her. "Your mind is unhinged," he said, with unction. "To go now would be adding crime—yes, crime—to folly. I'll have no scandal in my life, no matter what's the cost. And why? You are sure to misunderstand me—but I'll tell you. As a matter of duty. Yes. But you're sure to misunderstand me—recklessly. Women always do—they are too—too narrow-minded."

He waited for a while, but she made no sound, didn't even look at him; he felt uneasy, painfully uneasy, like a man who suspects he is unreasonably mistrusted. To combat that exasperating sensation he recommenced talking very fast. The sound of his words excited his thoughts, and in the play of darting thoughts he had glimpses now and then of the inexpugnable rock of his convictions, towering in solitary grandeur above the unprofitable waste of errors and passions.

"For it is self-evident," he went on with anxious vivacity, "it is self-evident that, on the highest ground we haven't the right—no, we haven't the right to intrude our miseries upon those who—who naturally expect better things from us. Every one wishes his own life and the life around him to be beautiful and pure. Now, a scandal amongst people of our position is disastrous for the morality—a fatal influence—don't you see—upon the general tone of the class—very important—the most important, I verily believe, in—in the community. I feel this—profoundly. This is the broad view. In time you'll give me . . . when you become again the woman I loved—and trusted. . . ."

He stopped short, as though unexpectedly suffocated, then in a completely changed voice said, "For I did love and trust you"—and again was silent for a moment. She put her handkerchief to her eyes.

"You'll give me credit for—for—my motives. It's mainly loyalty to—to the larger conditions of our life—where you—you! of all women—failed. One doesn't usually talk like this—of course—but in this case you'll admit . . . And consider—the innocent suffer with the guilty. The world is pitiless in its judgments. Unfortunately there are always those in it who are only too eager to misunderstand. Before you and before my conscience I am guiltless, but any—any disclosure would impair my usefulness in the sphere—in the larger sphere in which I hope soon to . . . I believe you fully shared my views in that matter—I don't want to say any more . . . on—on that point—but, believe me, true unselfishness is to bear one's burdens in—in silence. The ideal must—must be preserved—for others, at least. It's clear as daylight. If I've a—a loathsome sore, to gratuitously display it would be abominable—abominable! And often in life—in the highest conception of life—outspokenness in certain circumstances is nothing less than criminal. Temptation, you know, excuses no one. There is no such thing really if one looks steadily to one's welfare—which is grounded in duty. But there are the weak." . . . His tone became ferocious for an instant . . . "And there are the fools and the envious—especially for people in our position. I am guiltless of this terrible—terrible . . . estrangement; but if there has been nothing irreparable." . . . Something gloomy, like a deep shadow passed over his face. . . . "Nothing irreparable—you see even now I am ready to trust you implicitly—then our duty is clear."

He looked down. A change came over his expression and straightway from the outward impetus of his loquacity he passed into the dull contemplation of all the appeasing truths that, not without some wonder,* he had so recently been able to discover within himself. During this profound and soothing communion with his innermost beliefs he remained staring at the carpet, with a portentously solemn face and with a dull vacuity of eyes that seemed to gaze into the blankness of an empty hole. Then, without stirring in the least, he continued:

"Yes. Perfectly clear. I've been tried to the utmost, and I can't pretend that, for a time, the old feelings—the old feelings are not. . . ." He sighed. . . . "But I forgive you. . . ."

She made a slight movement without uncovering her eyes. In his profound scrutiny of the carpet he noticed nothing. And there was silence, silence within and silence without, as though his words had stilled the beat and tremor of all the surrounding life, and the house had stood alone—the only dwelling upon a deserted earth.

He lifted his head and repeated solemnly:

"I forgive you . . . from a sense of duty—and in the hope . . . ."

He heard a laugh, and it not only interrupted his words but also destroyed the peace of his self-absorption with the vile pain of a reality intruding upon the beauty of a dream. He couldn't understand whence the sound came. He could see, foreshortened, the tear-stained, dolorous face of the woman stretched out, and with her head thrown over the back of the seat. He thought the piercing noise was a delusion. But another shrill peal followed by a deep sob and succeeded by another shriek of mirth positively seemed to tear him out from where he stood. He bounded to the door. It was closed. He turned the key and thought: that's no good. . . . "Stop this!" he cried, and perceived with alarm that he could hardly hear his own voice in the midst of her screaming. He darted back with the idea of stifling that unbearable noise with his hands, but stood still distracted, finding himself as unable to touch her as though she had been on fire. He shouted, "Enough of this!" like men shout in the tumult of a riot, with a red face and starting eyes; then, as if swept away before another burst of laughter, he disappeared in a flash out of three looking-glasses, vanished suddenly from before her. For a time the woman gasped and laughed at no one in the luminous stillness of the empty room.

He reappeared, striding at her, and with a tumbler of water in his hand. He stammered: "Hysterics—Stop—They will hear—Drink this." She laughed at the ceiling. "Stop this!" he cried. "Ah!"

He flung the water in her face, putting into the action all the secret brutality of his spite, yet still felt that it would have been perfectly excusable—in any one—to send the tumbler after the water. He restrained himself, but at the same time was so convinced nothing could stop the horror of those mad shrieks that, when the first sensation of relief came, it did not even occur to him to doubt the impression of having become suddenly deaf. When, next moment, he became sure that she was sitting up, and really very quiet, it was as though everything—men, things, sensations, had come to a rest. He was prepared to be grateful. He could not take his eyes off her, fearing, yet unwilling to admit, the possibility of her beginning again; for, the experience, however contemptuously he tried to think of it, had left the bewilderment of a mysterious terror. Her face was streaming with water and tears; there was a wisp of hair on her forehead, another stuck to her cheek; her hat was on one side, undecorously tilted; her soaked veil resembled a sordid rag festooning her forehead. There was an utter unreserve in her aspect, an abandonment of safeguards, that ugliness of truth which can only be kept out of daily life by unremitting care for appearances. He did not know why, looking at her, he thought suddenly of to-morrow, and why the thought called out a deep feeling of unutterable, discouraged weariness—a fear of facing the succession of days. To-morrow! It was as far as yesterday. Ages elapsed between sunrises—sometimes. He scanned her features like one looks at a forgotten country. They were not distorted—he recognized landmarks, so to speak; but it was only a resemblance that he could see, not the woman of yesterday—or was it, perhaps, more than the woman of yesterday? Who could tell? Was it something new? A new expression—or a new shade of expression? or something deep—an old truth unveiled, a fundamental and hidden truth—some unnecessary, accursed certitude? He became aware that he was trembling very much, that he had an empty tumbler in his hand—that time was passing. Still looking at her with lingering mistrust he reached towards the table to put the glass down and was startled to feel it apparently go through the wood. He had missed the edge.* The surprise, the slight jingling noise of the accident annoyed him beyond expression. He turned to her irritated.

"What's the meaning of this?" he asked, grimly.

She passed her hand over her face and made an attempt to get up.

"You're not going to be absurd again," he said. " 'Pon my soul, I did not know you could forget yourself to that extent." He didn't try to conceal his physical disgust, because he believed it to be a purely moral reprobation of every unreserve, of anything in the nature of a scene. "I assure you—it was revolting," he went on. He stared for a moment at her. "Positively degrading," he added with insistence.

She stood up quickly as if moved by a spring and tottered. He started forward instinctively. She caught hold of the back of the chair and steadied herself. This arrested him, and they faced each other wide-eyed, uncertain, and yet coming back slowly to the reality of things with relief and wonder, as though just awakened after tossing through a long night of fevered dreams.

"Pray, don't begin again," he said, hurriedly, seeing her open her lips. "I deserve some little consideration—and such unaccountable behaviour is painful to me. I expect better things. . . . I have the right. . . ."

She pressed both her hands to her temples.

"Oh, nonsense!" he said, sharply. "You are perfectly capable of coming down to dinner. No one should even suspect; not even the servants. No one! No one! . . . I am sure you can."

She dropped her arms; her face twitched. She looked straight into his eyes and seemed incapable of pronouncing a word. He frowned at her.

"I—wish—it," he said, tyrannically. "For your own sake also. . . ." He meant to carry that point without any pity. Why didn't she speak? He feared passive resistance. She must. . . . Make her come. His frown deepened, and he began to think of some effectual violence, when most unexpectedly she said in a firm voice, "Yes, I can," and clutched the chair-back again. He was relieved, and all at once her attitude ceased to interest him. The important thing was that their life would begin again with an every-day act—with something that could not be misunderstood, that, thank God, had no moral meaning, no perplexity—and yet was symbolic of their uninterrupted communion in the past—in all the future. That morning, at that table, they had breakfast together; and now they would dine. It was all over! What had happened between could be forgotten—must be forgotten, like things that can only happen once—death for instance.

"I will wait for you," he said, going to the door. He had some difficulty with it, for he did not remember he had turned the key. He hated that delay, and his checked impatience to be gone out of the room made him feel quite ill as, with the consciousness of her presence behind his back, he fumbled at the lock. He managed it at last; then in the doorway he glanced over his shoulder to say, "It's rather late—you know—" and saw her standing where he had left her, with a face white as alabaster and perfectly still, like a woman in a trance.

He was afraid she would keep him waiting, but without any breathing time, he hardly knew how, he found himself sitting at table with her. He had made up his mind to eat, to talk, to be natural. It seemed to him necessary that deception should begin at home. The servants must not know—must not suspect. This intense desire of secrecy; of secrecy dark, destroying, profound, discreet like a grave, possessed him with the strength of a hallucination—seemed to spread itself to inanimate objects that had been the daily companions of his life, affected with a taint of enmity every single thing within the faithful walls that would stand forever between the shamelessness of facts and the indignation of mankind. Even when—as it happened once or twice—both the servants left the room together he remained carefully natural, industriously hungry, laboriously at his ease, as though he had wanted to cheat the black oak sideboard, the heavy curtains, the stiff-backed chairs, into the belief of an unstained happiness. He was mistrustful of his wife's self-control, unwilling to look at her and reluctant to speak, for it seemed to him inconceivable that she should not betray herself by the slightest movement, by the very first word spoken. Then he thought the silence in the room was becoming dangerous, and so excessive as to produce the effect of an intolerable uproar. He wanted to end it, as one is anxious to interrupt an indiscreet confession; but with the memory of that laugh upstairs he dared not give her an occasion to open her lips. Presently he heard her voice pronouncing in a calm tone some unimportant remark. He detached his eyes from the centre of his plate and felt excited as if on the point of looking at a wonder. And nothing could be more wonderful than her composure. He was looking at the candid eyes, at the pure brow, at what he had seen every evening for years in that place; he listened to the voice that for five years he had heard every day. Perhaps she was a little pale—but a healthy pallor had always been for him one of her chief attractions. Perhaps her face was rigidly set—but that marmoreal impassiveness, that magnificent stolidity, as of a wonderful statue by some great sculptor working under the curse of the gods; that imposing, unthinking stillness of her features, had till then mirrored for him the tranquil dignity of a soul of which he had thought himself—as a matter of course—the inexpugnable possessor. Those were the outward signs of her difference from the ignoble herd that feels, suffers, fails, errs—but has no distinct value in the world except as a moral contrast to the prosperity of the elect. He had been proud of her appearance. It had the perfectly proper frankness of perfection—and now he was shocked to see it unchanged.* She looked like this, spoke like this, exactly like this, a year ago, a month ago—only yesterday when she. . . . What went on within made no difference. What did she think? What meant the pallor, the placid face, the candid brow, the pure eyes? What did she think during all these years? What did she think yesterday—to-day; what would she think to-morrow? He must find out. . . . And yet how could he get to know? She had been false to him, to that man, to herself; she was ready to be false—for him. Always false. She looked lies, breathed lies, lived lies—would tell lies—always—to the end of life! And he would never know what she meant. Never! Never! No one could. Impossible to know.

He dropped his knife and fork, brusquely, as though by the virtue of a sudden illumination he had been made aware of poison in his plate, and became positive in his mind that he could never swallow another morsel of food as long as he lived. The dinner went on in a room that had been steadily growing, from some cause, hotter than a furnace. He had to drink. He drank time after time, and, at last, recollecting himself, was frightened at the quantity, till he perceived that what he had been drinking was water—out of two different wine glasses; and the discovered unconsciousness of his actions affected him painfully. He was disturbed to find himself in such an unhealthy state of mind. Excess of feeling—excess of feeling; and it was part of his creed that any excess of feeling was unhealthy—morally unprofitable; a taint on practical manhood. Her fault. Entirely her fault. Her sinful self-forgetfulness was contagious. It made him think thoughts he had never had before;* thoughts disintegrating, tormenting, sapping to the very core of life—like mortal disease; thoughts that bred the fear of air, of sunshine, of men—like the whispered news of a pestilence.

The maids served without noise; and to avoid looking at his wife and looking within himself, he followed with his eyes first one and then the other without being able to distinguish between them. They moved silently about, without one being able to see by what means, for their skirts touched the carpet all round; they glided here and there, receded, approached, rigid in black and white, with precise gestures, and no life in their faces, like a pair of marionettes in mourning; and their air of wooden unconcern struck him as unnatural, suspicious, irremediably hostile. That such people's feelings or judgment could affect one in any way, had never occurred to him before. He understood they had no prospects, no principles—no refinement and no power. But now he had become so debased that he could not even attempt to disguise from himself his yearning to know the secret thoughts of his servants. Several times he looked up covertly at the faces of those girls. Impossible to know. They changed his plates and utterly ignored his existence. What impenetrable duplicity. Women— nothing but women round him. Impossible to know. He experienced that heart-probing, fiery sense of dangerous loneliness, which some- times assails the courage of a solitary adventurer in an unexplored country. The sight of a man's face—he felt—of any man's face, would have been a profound relief. One would know then—some- thing—could understand. . . . He would engage a butler as soon as possible. And then the end of that dinner—which had seemed to have been going on for hours—the end came, taking him violently by sur- prise, as though he had expected in the natural course of events to sit at that table for ever and ever.

But upstairs in the drawing-room he became the victim of a restless fate, that would, on no account, permit him to sit down. She had sunk on a low easy-chair, and taking up from a small table at her elbow a fan with ivory leaves, shaded her face from the fire. The coals glowed without a flame; and upon the red glow the vertical bars of the grate stood out at her feet, black and curved, like the charred ribs of a consumed sacrifice. Far off, a lamp perched on a slim brass rod, burned under a wide shade of crimson silk: the centre, within the shadows of the large room, of a fiery twilight that had in the warm quality of its tint something delicate, refined and infernal. His soft footfalls and the subdued beat of the clock on the high mantel-piece answered each other regularly—as if time and himself, engaged in a measured contest, had been pacing together through the infernal delicacy of twilight towards a mysterious goal.

He walked from one end of the room to the other without a pause, like a traveller who, at night, hastens doggedly upon an interminable journey. Now and then he glanced at her. Impossible to know. The gross precision of that thought expressed to his practical mind some- thing illimitable and infinitely profound, the all-embracing subtlety of a feeling, the eternal origin of his pain. This woman had accepted him, had abandoned him—had returned to him. And of all this he would never know the truth. Never. Not till death—not after—not on judgment day when all shall be disclosed, thoughts and deeds, rewards and punishments, but the secret of hearts alone shall return, forever unknown,* to the Inscrutable Creator of good and evil, to the Master of doubts and impulses.

He stood still to look at her. Thrown back and with her face turned away from him, she did not stir—as if asleep. What did she think? What did she feel? And in the presence of her perfect stillness, in the breathless silence, he felt himself insignificant and powerless before her, like a prisoner in chains. The fury of his impotence called out sinister images, that faculty of tormenting vision, which in a moment of anguishing sense of wrong induces a man to mutter threats or make a menacing gesture in the solitude of an empty room. But the gust of passion passed at once, left him trembling a little, with the wondering, reflective fear of a man who has paused on the very verge of suicide. The serenity of truth and the peace of death can be only secured through a largeness of contempt embracing all the profitable servitudes of life. He found he did not want to know. Better not. It was all over. It was as if it hadn't been.* And it was very necessary for both of them, it was morally right, that nobody should know.

He spoke suddenly, as if concluding a discussion.

"The best thing for us is to forget all this."

She started a little and shut the fan with a click.

"Yes, forgive—and forget," he repeated, as if to himself.

"I'll never forget," she said in a vibrating voice. "And I'll never forgive myself. . . ."

"But I, who have nothing to reproach myself . . ." He began, making a step towards her. She jumped up.

"I did not come back for your forgiveness," she exclaimed, passionately, as if clamouring against an unjust aspersion.

He only said "oh!" and became silent. He could not understand this unprovoked aggressiveness of her attitude, and certainly was very far from thinking that an unpremeditated hint of something resembling emotion in the tone of his last words had caused that uncontrollable burst of sincerity. It completed his bewilderment, but he was not at all angry now. He was as if benumbed by the fascination of the incomprehensible. She stood before him, tall and indistinct, like a black phantom in the red twilight. At last poignantly uncertain as to what would happen if he opened his lips, he muttered:

"But if my love is strong enough . . ." and hesitated.

He heard something snap loudly in the fiery stillness. She had broken her fan. Two thin pieces of ivory fell, one after another, without a sound, on the thick carpet, and instinctively he stooped to pick them up. While he groped at her feet it occurred to him that the woman there had in her hands an indispensable gift which nothing else on earth could give; and when he stood up he was penetrated by an irresistible belief in an enigma, by the conviction that within his reach and passing away from him was the very secret of existence—its certitude, immaterial and precious! She moved to the door, and he followed at her elbow, casting about for a magic word that would make the enigma clear, that would compel the surrender of the gift. And there is no such word! The enigma is only made clear by sacrifice, and the gift of heaven is in the hands of every man. But they had lived in a world that abhors enigmas, and cares for no gifts but such as can be obtained in the street. She was nearing the door. He said hurriedly:

"'Pon my word, I loved you—I love you now."

She stopped for an almost imperceptible moment to give him an indignant glance, and then moved on. That feminine penetration—so clever and so tainted by the eternal instinct of self-defence, so ready to see an obvious evil in everything it cannot understand—filled her with bitter resentment against both the men who could offer to the spiritual and tragic strife of her feelings nothing but the coarseness of their abominable materialism. In her anger against her own ineffectual self-deception she found hate enough for them both. What did they want? What more did this one want? And as her husband faced her again, with his hand on the door-handle, she asked herself whether he was unpardonably stupid, or simply ignoble.

She said nervously, and very fast:

"You are deceiving yourself. You never loved me. You wanted a wife—some woman—any woman that would think, speak, and behave in a certain way—in a way you approved. You loved yourself."

"You won't believe me?" he asked, slowly.

"If I had believed you loved me," she began, passionately, then drew in a long breath; and during that pause he heard the steady beat of blood in his ears. "If I had believed it . . . I would never have come back," she finished recklessly.

He stood looking down as though he had not heard. She waited. After a moment he opened the door, and, on the landing, the sightless woman of marble appeared, draped to the chin, thrusting blindly at them a cluster of lights.

He seemed to have forgotten himself in a meditation so deep that on the point of going out she stopped to look at him in surprise. While she had been speaking he had wandered on the track of the enigma, out of the world of senses into the region of feeling. What did it matter what she had done, what she had said, if through the pain of her acts and words he had obtained the word of the enigma! There can be no life without faith and love—faith in a human heart, love of a human being! That touch of grace, whose help once in life is the privilege of the most undeserving, flung open for him the portals of beyond, and in contemplating there the certitude immaterial and precious he forgot all the meaningless accidents of existence: the bliss of getting, the delight of enjoying; all the protean and enticing forms of the cupidity that rules a material world* of foolish joys, of contemptible sorrows. Faith!—Love!—the undoubting, clear faith in the truth of a soul—the great tenderness, deep as the ocean, serene and eternal, like the infinite peace of space above the short tempests of the earth. It was what he had wanted all his life—but he understood it only then for the first time. It was through the pain of losing her that the knowledge had come. She had the gift! She had the gift! And in all the world she was the only human being that could surrender it to his immense desire. He made a step forward, putting his arms out, as if to take her to his breast, and, lifting his head, was met by such a look of blank consternation that his arms fell as though they had been struck down by a blow. She started away from him, stumbled over the threshold, and once on the landing turned, swift and crouching. The train of her gown swished as it flew round her feet. It was an undisguised panic. She panted, showing her teeth, and the hate of strength, the disdain of weakness, the eternal preoccupation of sex came out like a toy demon out of a box.

"This is odious," she screamed.

He did not stir; but her look, her agitated movements, the sound of her voice were like a mist of facts thickening between him and the vision of love and faith. It vanished; and looking at that face triumphant and scornful, at that white face, stealthy and unexpected, as if discovered staring from an ambush, he was coming back slowly to the world of senses.* His first clear thought was: I am married to that woman; and the next: she will give nothing but what I see. He felt the need not to see. But the memory of the vision, the memory that abides forever within the seer made him say to her with the naive austerity of a convert awed by the touch of a new creed, "You haven't the gift." He turned his back on her, leaving her completely mystified. And she went upstairs slowly, struggling with a distasteful suspicion of having been confronted by something more subtle than herself—more profound than the misunderstood and tragic contest of her feelings.

He shut the door of the drawing-room and moved at hazard, alone amongst the heavy shadows and in the fiery twilight as of an elegant place of perdition. She hadn't the gift—no one had. . . . He stepped on a book that had fallen off one of the crowded little tables. He picked up the slender volume, and holding it, approached the crimson-shaded lamp. The fiery tint deepened on the cover, and contorted gold letters sprawling all over it in an intricate maze, came out, gleaming redly. "Thorns and Arabesques."* He read it twice, "Thorns and Ar. . . ." The other's book of verses. He dropped it at his feet, but did not feel the slightest pang of jealousy or indignation. What did he know? . . . What? . . . The mass of hot coals tumbled down in the grate, and he turned to look at them . . . Ah! That one was ready to give up everything he had for that woman—who did not come—who had not the faith, the love, the courage to come. What did that man expect, what did he hope, what did he want? The woman—or the certitude immaterial and precious! The first unselfish thought he had ever given to any human being was for that man who had tried to do him a terrible wrong. He was not angry. He was saddened by an impersonal sorrow, by a vast melancholy as of all mankind longing for what cannot be attained. He felt his fellowship with every man—even with that man—especially with that man. What did he think now? Had he ceased to wait—and hope? Would he ever cease to wait and hope? Would he understand that the woman, who had no courage, had not the gift—had not the gift!

The clock began to strike, and the deep-toned vibration filled the room as though with the sound of an enormous bell tolling far away. He counted the strokes. Twelve. Another day had begun. To-morrow had come; the mysterious and lying to-morrow that lures men, disdainful of love and faith, on and on through the poignant futilities of life to the fitting reward of a grave. He counted the strokes, and gazing at the grate seemed to wait for more. Then, as if called out, left the room, walking firmly.

When outside he heard footsteps in the hall and stood still. A bolt was shot—then another. They were locking up—shutting out his desire and his deception from the indignant criticism of a world full of noble gifts for those who proclaim themselves without stain and without reproach. He was safe; and on all sides of his dwelling servile fears and servile hopes slept, dreaming of success, behind the severe discretion of doors as impenetrable to the truth within as the granite of tombstones. A lock snapped—a short chain rattled. Nobody shall know!*

Why* was this assurance of safety heavier than a burden of fear, and why the day that began presented itself obstinately like the last day of all—like a to-day without a to-morrow? Yet nothing was changed, for nobody would know; and all would go on as before—the getting, the enjoying, the blessing of hunger that is appeased every day; the noble incentives of unappeasable ambitions. All—all the blessings of life. All—but the certitude immaterial and precious—the certitude of love and faith. He believed the shadow of it had been with him as long as he could remember; that invisible presence had ruled his life. And now the shadow had appeared and faded he could not extinguish his longing for the truth of its substance. His desire of it was naive; it was masterful like the material aspirations that are the groundwork of existence, but, unlike these, it was unconquerable. It was the subtle despotism of an idea that suffers no rivals, that is lonely, inconsolable, and dangerous. He went slowly up the stairs. Nobody shall know. The days would go on and he would go far—very far. If the idea could not be mastered, fortune could be, man could be—the whole world. He was dazzled by the greatness of the prospect; the brutality of a practical instinct shouted to him that only that which could be had was worth having. He lingered on the steps. The lights were out in the hall, and a small yellow flame flitted about down there. He felt a sudden contempt for himself which braced him up. He went on, but at the door of their room and with his arm advanced to open it, he faltered. On the flight of stairs below the head of the girl who had been locking up appeared. His arm fell. He thought, "I'll wait till she is gone"—and stepped back within the perpendicular folds of a *portière.**

He saw her come up gradually, as if ascending from a well. At every step the feeble flame of the candle swayed before her tired, young face, and the darkness of the hall seemed to cling to her black skirt, followed her, rising like a silent flood, as though the great night of the world* had broken through the discreet reserve of walls, of closed doors, of curtained windows. It rose over the steps, it leaped up the walls like an angry wave, it flowed over the blue skies, over the yellow sands, over the sunshine of landscapes, and over the pretty pathos of ragged innocence and of meek starvation. It swallowed up the delicious idyll in a boat and the mutilated immortality of famous basreliefs. It flowed from outside—it rose higher, in a destructive silence. And, above it, the woman of marble, composed and blind on the high pedestal, seemed to ward off the devouring night with a cluster of lights.

He watched the rising tide of impenetrable gloom with impatience, as if anxious for the coming of a darkness black enough to conceal a shameful surrender. It came nearer. The cluster of lights went out. The girl ascended facing him. Behind her the shadow of a colossal woman danced lightly on the wall. He held his breath while she passed by, noiseless and with heavy eyelids. And on her track the flowing tide of a tenebrous sea* filled the house, seemed to swirl about his feet, and rising unchecked, closed silently above his head.

The time had come but he did not open the door. All was still; and instead of surrendering to the reasonable exigencies of life he stepped out, with a rebelling heart, into the darkness of the house. It was the abode of an impenetrable night; as though indeed the last day had come and gone, leaving him alone in a darkness that has no to-morrow. And looming vaguely below the woman of marble, livid and still like a patient phantom, held out in the night a cluster of extinguished lights.

His obedient thought traced for him the image of an uninterrupted life, the dignity and the advantages of an uninterrupted success; while his rebellious heart beat violently within his breast, as if maddened by the desire of a certitude immaterial and precious—the certitude of love and faith. What of the night within his dwelling if outside he could find the sunshine in which men sow, in which men reap! Nobody would know. The days, the years would pass, and . . . He remembered that he had loved her. The years would pass . . . And then he thought of her as we think of the dead—in a tender immensity of regret, in a passionate longing for the return of idealized perfections.* He had loved her—he had loved her—and he never knew the truth . . . The years would pass in the anguish of doubt . . . He remembered her smile, her eyes, her voice, her silence, as though he had lost her forever. The years would pass and he would always mistrust her smile, suspect her eyes; he would always misbelieve her voice, he would never have faith in her silence. She had no gift—she had no gift! What was she? Who was she? . . . The years would pass; the memory of this hour would grow faint—and she would share the material serenity* of an unblemished life. She had no love and no faith for any one. To give her your thought, your belief, was like whispering your confession over the edge of the world.* Nothing came back—not even an echo.

In the pain of that thought was born his conscience; not that fear of remorse which grows slowly, and slowly decays amongst the complicated facts of life, but a Divine wisdom springing full-grown, armed and severe out of a tried heart, to combat the secret baseness of motives. It came to him in a flash that morality is not a method of happiness. The revelation was terrible. He saw at once that nothing of what he knew mattered in the least. The acts of men and women, success, humiliation, dignity, failure—nothing mattered. It was not a question of more or less pain, of this joy, of that sorrow. It was a question of truth or falsehood—it was a question of life or death.

He stood in the revealing night—in the darkness that tries the hearts, in the night useless for the work of men, but in which their gaze, undazzled by the sunshine of covetous days, wanders sometimes as far as the stars. The perfect stillness around him had something solemn in it, but he felt it was the lying solemnity of a temple devoted to the rites of a debasing persuasion. The silence within the discreet walls was eloquent of safety but it appeared to him exciting and sinister, like the discretion of a profitable infamy; it was the prudent peace of a den of coiners*—of a house of ill-fame!* The years would pass—and nobody would know. Never! Not till death—not after . . .

"Never!" he said aloud to the revealing night.

And he hesitated. The secret of hearts, too terrible for the timid eyes of men, shall return, veiled forever, to the Inscrutable Creator of good and evil, to the Master of doubts and impulses. His conscience was born—he heard its voice, and he hesitated, ignoring the strength within, the fateful power, the secret of his heart! It was an awful sacrifice to cast all one's life into the flame of a new belief. He wanted help against himself, against the cruel decree of salvation. The need of tacit complicity, where it had never failed him, the habit of years affirmed itself. Perhaps she would help . . . He flung the door open and rushed in like a fugitive.

He was in the middle of the room before he could see anything but the dazzling brilliance of the light; and then, as if detached and floating in it on the level of his eyes, appeared the head of a woman. She had jumped up when he burst into the room.

For a moment they contemplated each other as if struck dumb with amazement. Her hair streaming on her shoulders glinted like burnished gold. He looked into the unfathomable candour of her eyes. Nothing within—nothing—nothing.

He stammered distractedly.

"I want . . . I want . . . to . . . to . . . know . . ."

On the candid light of the eyes flitted shadows; shadows of doubt, of suspicion, the ready suspicion of an unquenchable antagonism, the pitiless mistrust of an eternal instinct of defence; the hate,* the profound, frightened hate of an incomprehensible—of an abominable emotion intruding its coarse materialism upon the spiritual and tragic contest of her feelings.

"Alvan . . . I won't bear this . . ." She began to pant suddenly, "I've a right—a right to—to—myself . . ."

He lifted one arm, and appeared so menacing that she stopped in a fright and shrank back a little.

He stood with uplifted hand . . . The years would pass—and he would have to live with that unfathomable candour where flit shadows of suspicions and hate . . . The years would pass—and he would never know—never trust . . . The years would pass without faith and love. . . .

"Can you stand it?" he shouted, as though she could have heard all his thoughts.

He looked menacing. She thought of violence, of danger—and, just for an instant, she doubted whether there were splendours enough on earth to pay the price of such a brutal experience. He cried again.

"Can you stand it?" and glared as if insane. Her eyes blazed, too. She could not hear the appalling clamour of his thoughts. She suspected in him a sudden regret, a fresh fit of jealousy, a dishonest desire of evasion. She shouted back angrily—

"Yes!"

He was shaken where he stood as if by a struggle to break out of invisible bonds. She trembled from head to foot.

"Well, I can't!" He flung both his arms out, as if to push her away, and strode from the room. The door swung to with a click. She made three quick steps towards it and stood still, looking at the white and gold panels. No sound came from beyond, not a whisper, not a sigh;

not even a footstep was heard outside on the thick carpet. It was as though no sooner gone he had suddenly expired—as though he had died there and his body had vanished on the instant together with his soul.* She listened, with parted lips and irresolute eyes. Then below, far below her, as if in the entrails of the earth, a door slammed heavily;* and the quiet house vibrated to it from roof to foundations, more than to a clap of thunder.

He never returned.

THE DUEL

I

NAPOLEON I.,* whose career had the quality of a duel against the whole of Europe, disliked duelling between the officers of his army. The great military emperor was not a swashbuckler, and had little respect for tradition.

Nevertheless, a story of duelling, which became a legend in the army, runs through the epic of imperial wars. To the surprise and admiration of their fellows, two officers, like insane artists trying to gild refined gold or paint the lily,* pursued a private contest through the years of universal carnage. They were officers of cavalry, and their connection with the high-spirited but fanciful animal which carries men into battle seems particularly appropriate. It would be difficult to imagine for heroes of this legend two officers of infantry of the line,* for example, whose fantasy is tamed by much walking exercise, and whose valour necessarily must be of a more plodding kind. As to gunners or engineers, whose heads are kept cool on a diet of mathematics, it is simply unthinkable.

The names of the two officers were Feraud and D'Hubert,* and they were both lieutenants in a regiment of hussars,* but not in the same regiment.

Feraud was doing regimental work, but Lieut.* D'Hubert had the good fortune to be attached to the person of the general commanding the division, as *officier d'ordonnance*.* It was in Strasbourg,* and in this agreeable and important garrison they were enjoying greatly a short interval of peace.* They were enjoying it, though both intensely warlike, because it was a sword-sharpening, firelock-cleaning peace, dear to a military heart and undamaging to military prestige, inasmuch that no one believed in its sincerity or duration.

Under those historical circumstances, so favourable to the proper appreciation of military leisure, Lieut. D'Hubert, one fine afternoon, made his way along a quiet street of a cheerful suburb towards Lieut. Feraud's quarters, which were in a private house with a garden at the back, belonging to an old maiden lady.

His knock at the door was answered instantly by a young maid in Alsatian costume.* Her fresh complexion and her long eyelashes, lowered demurely at the sight of the tall officer, caused Lieut. D'Hubert, who was accessible to esthetic impressions, to relax the cold, severe gravity of his face. At the same time he observed that the girl had over her arm a pair of hussars breeches, blue with a red stripe.

"Lieut. Feraud in?" he inquired, benevolently.

"Oh, no, sir! He went out at six this morning."

The pretty maid tried to close the door. Lieut. D'Hubert, opposing this move with gentle firmness, stepped into the ante-room, jingling his spurs.

"Come, my dear! You don't mean to say he has not been home since six o'clock this morning?"

Saying these words, Lieut. D'Hubert opened without ceremony the door of a room so comfortably and neatly ordered that only from internal evidence in the shape of boots, uniforms, and military accoutrements did he acquire the conviction that it was Lieut. Feraud's room. And he saw also that Lieut. Feraud was not at home. The truthful maid had followed him, and raised her candid eyes to his face.

"H'm!" said Lieut. D'Hubert, greatly disappointed, for he had already visited all the haunts where a lieutenant of hussars could be found of a fine afternoon. "So he's out? And do you happen to know, my dear, why he went out at six this morning?"

"No," she answered, readily. "He came home late last night, and snored. I heard him when I got up at five. Then he dressed himself in his oldest uniform and went out. Service, I suppose."

"Service? Not a bit of it!" cried Lieut. D'Hubert. "Learn, my angel, that he went out thus early to fight a duel with a civilian."

She heard this news without a quiver of her dark eyelashes. It was very obvious that the actions of Lieut. Feraud were generally above criticism. She only looked up for a moment in mute surprise, and Lieut. D'Hubert concluded from this absence of emotion that she must have seen Lieut. Feraud since the morning. He looked around the room.

"Come!" he insisted, with confidential familiarity. "He's perhaps somewhere in the house now?"

She shook her head.

"So much the worse for him!" continued Lieut. D'Hubert, in a tone of anxious conviction. "But he has been home this morning."

This time the pretty maid nodded slightly.

"He has!" cried Lieut. D'Hubert. "And went out again? What for? Couldn't he keep quietly indoors! What a lunatic! My dear girl——"

Lieut. D'Hubert's natural kindness of disposition and strong sense of comradeship helped his powers of observation. He changed his tone to a most insinuating softness, and, gazing at the hussars breeches hanging over the arm of the girl, he appealed to the interest she took in Lieut. Feraud's comfort and happiness. He was pressing and persuasive. He used his eyes, which were kind and fine, with excellent effect. His anxiety to get hold at once of Lieut. Feraud, for Lieut. Feraud's own good, seemed so genuine that at last it overcame the girl's unwillingness to speak. Unluckily she had not much to tell. Lieut. Feraud had returned home shortly before ten, had walked straight into his room, and had thrown himself on his bed to resume his slumbers. She had heard him snore rather louder than before far into the afternoon. Then he got up, put on his best uniform, and went out. That was all she knew.

She raised her eyes, and Lieut. D'Hubert stared into them incredulously.

"It's incredible. Gone parading the town in his best uniform! My dear child, don't you know he ran that civilian through this morning? Clean through, as you spit a hare."

The pretty maid heard the gruesome intelligence without any signs of distress. But she pressed her lips together thoughtfully.

"He isn't parading the town," she remarked in a low tone. "Far from it."

"The civilian's family is making an awful row," continued Lieut. D'Hubert, pursuing his train of thought. "And the general is very angry. It's one of the best families in the town. Feraud ought to have kept close at least——"

"What will the general do to him?" inquired the girl, anxiously.

"He won't have his head cut off, to be sure," grumbled Lieut. D'Hubert. "His conduct is positively indecent. He's making no end of trouble for himself by this sort of bravado."

"But he isn't parading the town," the maid insisted in a shy murmur.

"Why, yes! Now I think of it, I haven't seen him anywhere about. What on earth has he done with himself?"

"He's gone to pay a call," suggested the maid, after a moment of silence.

Lieut. D'Hubert started.

"A call! Do you mean a call on a lady? The cheek of the man! And how do you know this, my dear?"

Without concealing her woman's scorn for the denseness of the masculine mind, the pretty maid reminded him that Lieut. Feraud had arrayed himself in his best uniform before going out. He had also put on his newest dolman,* she added, in a tone as if this conversation were getting on her nerves, and turned away brusquely.

Lieut. D'Hubert, without questioning the accuracy of the deduction, did not see that it advanced him much on his official quest. For his quest after Lieut. Feraud had an official character. He did not know any of the women this fellow, who had run a man through in the morning, was likely to visit in the afternoon. The two young men knew each other but slightly. He bit his gloved finger in perplexity.

"Call!" he exclaimed. "Call on the devil!"

The girl, with her back to him, and folding the hussars breeches on a chair, protested with a vexed little laugh:

"Oh, dear, no! On Madame de Lionne."

Lieut. D'Hubert whistled softly. Madame de Lionne was the wife of a high official who had a well-known *salon** and some pretensions to sensibility and elegance. The husband was a civilian, and old; but the society of the *salon* was young and military. Lieut. D'Hubert had whistled, not because the idea of pursuing Lieut. Feraud into that very *salon* was disagreeable to him, but because, having arrived in Strasbourg only lately, he had not had the time as yet to get an introduction to Madame de Lionne. And what was that swashbuckler Feraud doing there, he wondered. He did not seem the sort of man who—

"Are you certain of what you say?" asked Lieut. D'Hubert.

The girl was perfectly certain. Without turning round to look at him, she explained that the coachman of their next door neighbours knew the *maître-d'hôtel** of Madame de Lionne. In this way she had her information. And she was perfectly certain. In giving this assurance she sighed. Lieut. Feraud called there nearly every afternoon, she added.

"Ah, bah!" exclaimed D'Hubert, ironically. His opinion of Madame de Lionne went down several degrees. Lieut. Feraud did not seem to him specially worthy of attention on the part of a woman with a reputation for sensibility and elegance. But there was no saying. At bottom they were all alike—very practical rather than idealistic. Lieut. D'Hubert, however, did not allow his mind to dwell on these considerations.

"By thunder!" he reflected aloud. "The general goes there sometimes. If he happens to find the fellow making eyes at the lady there will be the devil to pay! Our general is not a very accommodating person, I can tell you."

"Go quickly, then! Don't stand here now I've told you where he is!" cried the girl, colouring to the eyes.

"Thanks, my dear! I don't know what I would have done without you."

After manifesting his gratitude in an aggressive way, which at first was repulsed violently, and then submitted to with a sudden and still more repellent indifference, Lieut. D'Hubert took his departure.

He clanked and jingled along the streets with a martial swagger. To run a comrade to earth in a drawing-room where he was not known did not trouble him in the least. A uniform is a passport. His position as *officier d'ordonnance* of the general added to his assurance. Moreover, now that he knew where to find Lieut. Feraud, he had no option. It was a service matter.

Madame de Lionne's house had an excellent appearance. A man in livery, opening the door of a large drawing-room with a waxed floor, shouted his name and stood aside to let him pass. It was a reception day. The ladies wore big hats surcharged with a profusion of feathers; their bodies sheathed in clinging white gowns, from the armpits to the tips of the low satin shoes, looked sylph-like and cool in a great display of bare necks and arms. The men who talked with them, on the contrary, were arrayed heavily in multi-coloured garments with collars up to their ears and thick sashes round their waists. Lieut. D'Hubert made his unabashed way across the room and, bowing low before a sylph-like form reclining on a couch, offered his apologies for this intrusion, which nothing could excuse but the extreme urgency of the service order he had to communicate to his comrade Feraud. He proposed to himself to return presently in a more regular manner and beg forgiveness for interrupting the interesting conversation . . .

A bare arm was extended towards him with gracious nonchalance even before he had finished speaking. He pressed the hand respectfully to his lips, and made the mental remark that it was bony. Madame de Lionne was a blonde, with too fine a skin and a long face.

"*C'est ça!*"* she said, with an ethereal smile, disclosing a set of large teeth. "Come this evening to plead for your forgiveness."

"I will not fail, madame."

Meantime, Lieut. Feraud, splendid in his new dolman and the extremely polished boots of his calling, sat on a chair within a foot of the couch, one hand resting on his thigh, the other twirling his moustache to a point. At a significant glance from D'Hubert he rose without alacrity, and followed him into the recess of a window.

"What is it you want with me?" he asked, with astonishing indifference.* Lieut. D'Hubert could not imagine that in the innocence of his heart and simplicity of his conscience Lieut. Feraud took a view of his duel in which neither remorse nor yet a rational apprehension of consequences had any place. Though he had no clear recollection how the quarrel had originated (it was begun in an establishment where beer and wine are drunk late at night), he had not the slightest doubt of being himself the outraged party. He had had two experienced friends for his seconds. Everything had been done according to the rules governing that sort of adventures. And a duel is obviously fought for the purpose of someone being at least hurt, if not killed outright. The civilian got hurt. That also was in order. Lieut. Feraud was perfectly tranquil; but Lieut. D'Hubert took it for affectation, and spoke with a certain vivacity.

"I am directed by the general to give you the order to go at once to your quarters, and remain there under close arrest."

It was now the turn of Lieut. Feraud to be astonished. "What the devil are you telling me there?" he murmured, faintly, and fell into such profound wonder that he could only follow mechanically the motions of Lieut. D'Hubert. The two officers, one tall, with an interesting face and a moustache the colour of ripe corn, the other, short and sturdy, with a hooked nose and a thick crop of black curly hair, approached the mistress of the house to take their leave. Madame de Lionne, a woman of eclectic taste, smiled upon these armed young men with impartial sensibility and an equal share of interest. Madame de Lionne took her delight in the infinite variety of the human species. All the other eyes in the drawing-room followed the departing officers; and when they had gone out one or two men, who had already heard of the duel, imparted the information to the sylph-like ladies, who received it with faint shrieks of humane concern.

Meantime, the two hussars walked side by side, Lieut. Feraud trying to master the hidden reason of things which in this instance eluded the grasp of his intellect, Lieut. D'Hubert feeling annoyed at the part he had to play, because the general's instructions were that he should see personally that Lieut. Feraud carried out his orders to the letter, and at once.

"The chief seems to know this animal," he thought, eyeing his companion, whose round face, the round eyes, and even the twisted-up jet black little moustache seemed animated by a mental exasperation against the incomprehensible. And aloud he observed rather reproachfully, "The general is in a devilish fury with you!"

Lieut. Feraud stopped short on the edge of the pavement, and cried in accents of unmistakable sincerity, "What on earth for?" The innocence of the fiery Gascon* soul was depicted in the manner in which he seized his head in both hands as if to prevent it bursting with perplexity.

"For the duel," said Lieut. D'Hubert, curtly. He was annoyed greatly by this sort of perverse fooling.

"The duel! The ..."

Lieut. Feraud passed from one paroxysm of astonishment into another. He dropped his hands and walked on slowly, trying to reconcile this information with the state of his own feelings. It was impossible. He burst out indignantly, "Was I to let that sauerkraut-eating* civilian wipe his boots on the uniform of the 7th Hussars?"

Lieut. D'Hubert could not remain altogether unmoved by that simple sentiment. This little fellow was a lunatic, he thought to himself, but there was something in what he said.

"Of course, I don't know how far you were justified," he began, soothingly. "And the general himself may not be exactly informed. Those people have been deafening him with their lamentations."

"Ah! the general is not exactly informed," mumbled Lieut. Feraud, walking faster and faster as his choler at the injustice of his fate began to rise. "He is not exactly ... And he orders me under close arrest, with God knows what afterwards!"

"Don't excite yourself like this," remonstrated the other. "Your adversary's people are very influential, you know, and it looks bad enough on the face of it. The general had to take notice of their complaint at once. I don't think he means to be over-severe with you. It's the best thing for you to be kept out of sight for a while."

"I am very much obliged to the general," muttered Lieut. Feraud through his teeth. "And perhaps you would say I ought to be grateful to you, too, for the trouble you have taken to hunt me up in the drawing-room of a lady who—"

"Frankly," interrupted Lieut. D'Hubert, with an innocent laugh, "I think you ought to be. I had no end of trouble to find out where you were. It wasn't exactly the place for you to disport yourself in under the circumstances. If the general had caught you there making eyes at the goddess of the temple . . . oh, my word! . . . He hates to be bothered with complaints against his officers, you know. And it looked uncommonly like sheer bravado."

The two officers had arrived now at the street door of Lieut. Feraud's lodgings. The latter turned towards his companion. "Lieut. D'Hubert," he said, "I have something to say to you, which can't be said very well in the street. You can't refuse to come up."

The pretty maid had opened the door. Lieut. Feraud brushed past her brusquely, and she raised her scared and questioning eyes to Lieut. D'Hubert, who could do nothing but shrug his shoulders slightly as he followed with marked reluctance.

In his room Lieut. Feraud unhooked the clasp, flung his new dolman on the bed, and, folding his arms across his chest, turned to the other hussar.

"Do you imagine I am a man to submit tamely to injustice?"* he inquired, in a boisterous voice.

"Oh, do be reasonable!" remonstrated Lieut. D'Hubert.

"I am reasonable! I am perfectly reasonable!" retorted the other with ominous restraint. "I can't call the general to account for his behaviour, but you are going to answer me for yours."

"I can't listen to this nonsense," murmured Lieut. D'Hubert, making a slightly contemptuous grimace.

"You call this nonsense? It seems to me a perfectly plain statement. Unless you don't understand French."

"What on earth do you mean?"

"I mean," screamed suddenly Lieut. Feraud, "to cut off your ears to teach you to disturb me with the general's orders when I am talking to a lady!"

A profound silence followed this mad declaration; and through the open window Lieut. D'Hubert heard the little birds singing sanely in the garden. He said, preserving his calm, "Why! If you take that tone, of course I shall hold myself at your disposition whenever you are at liberty to attend to this affair; but I don't think you will cut my ears off."

"I am going to attend to it at once," declared Lieut. Feraud, with extreme truculence. "If you are thinking of displaying your airs and graces to-night in Madame de Lionne's *salon* you are very much mistaken."

"Really!" said Lieut. D'Hubert, who was beginning to feel irritated, "you are an impracticable sort of fellow. The general's orders to me were to put you under arrest, not to carve you into small pieces. Good-morning!" And turning his back on the little Gascon, who, always sober in his potations, was as though born intoxicated with the sunshine of his vine-ripening country, the Northman, who could drink hard on occasion, but was born sober under the watery skies of Picardy,* made for the door. Hearing, however, the unmistakable sound behind his back of a sword drawn from the scabbard, he had no option but to stop.

"Devil take this mad Southerner!" he thought, spinning round and surveying with composure the warlike posture of Lieut. Feraud, with a bare sword in his hand.

"At once!—at once!" stuttered Feraud, beside himself.

"You had my answer," said the other, keeping his temper very well.

At first he had been only vexed, and somewhat amused; but now his face got clouded. He was asking himself seriously how he could manage to get away. It was impossible to run from a man with a sword, and as to fighting him, it seemed completely out of the question. He waited awhile, then said exactly what was in his heart.

"Drop this! I won't fight with you. I won't be made ridiculous."

"Ah, you won't?" hissed the Gascon. "I suppose you prefer to be made infamous. Do you hear what I say? . . . Infamous! Infamous! Infamous!" he shrieked, rising and falling on his toes and getting very red in the face.

Lieut. D'Hubert, on the contrary, became very pale at the sound of the unsavoury word for a moment, then flushed pink to the roots of his fair hair. "But you can't go out to fight; you are under arrest, you lunatic!" he objected, with angry scorn.

"There's the garden: it's big enough to lay out your long carcass in," spluttered the other with such ardour that somehow the anger of the cooler man subsided.

"This is perfectly absurd,"* he said, glad enough to think he had found a way out of it for the moment. "We shall never get any of our comrades to serve as seconds. It's preposterous."

"Seconds! Damn the seconds! We don't want any seconds. Don't you worry about any seconds. I shall send word to your friends to come and bury you when I am done. And if you want any witnesses, I'll send word to the old girl to put her head out of a window at the back. Stay! There's the gardener. He'll do. He's as deaf as a post, but he has two eyes in his head. Come along! I will teach you, my staff officer, that the carrying about of a general's orders is not always child's play."

While thus discoursing he had unbuckled his empty scabbard. He sent it flying under the bed, and, lowering the point of the sword, brushed past the perplexed Lieut. D'Hubert, exclaiming, "Follow me!" Directly he had flung open the door a faint shriek was heard and the pretty maid, who had been listening at the keyhole, staggered away, putting the backs of her hands over her eyes. Feraud did not seem to see her, but she ran after him and seized his left arm. He shook her off, and then she rushed towards Lieut. D'Hubert and clawed at the sleeve of his uniform.

"Wretched man!" she sobbed. "Is this what you wanted to find him for?"

"Let me go," entreated Lieut. D'Hubert, trying to disengage himself gently. "It's like being in a madhouse," he protested, with exasperation. "Do let me go! I won't do him any harm."

A fiendish laugh from Lieut. Feraud commented that assurance.* "Come along!" he shouted, with a stamp of his foot.

And Lieut. D'Hubert did follow. He could do nothing else. Yet in vindication of his sanity it must be recorded that as he passed through the ante-room the notion of opening the street door and bolting out presented itself to this brave youth, only of course to be instantly dismissed, for he felt sure that the other would pursue him without shame or compunction. And the prospect of an officer of hussars being chased along the street by another officer of hussars with a naked sword could not be for a moment entertained. Therefore he followed into the garden. Behind them the girl tottered out, too. With ashy lips and wild, scared eyes, she surrendered herself to a dreadful curiosity. She had also the notion of rushing if need be between Lieut. Feraud and death.

The deaf gardener, utterly unconscious of approaching footsteps, went on watering his flowers till Lieut. Feraud thumped him on the back. Beholding suddenly an enraged man flourishing a big sabre, the old chap trembling in all his limbs dropped the watering-pot. At once Lieut. Feraud kicked it away with great animosity, and, seizing the gardener by the throat, backed him against a tree. He held him there, shouting in his ear, "Stay here, and look on! You understand? You've got to look on! Don't dare budge from the spot!"

Lieut. D'Hubert came slowly down the walk, unclasping his dolman with unconcealed disgust. Even then, with his hand already on the hilt of his sword, he hesitated to draw till a roar, "*En garde, fichtre!** What do you think you came here for?" and the rush of his adversary forced him to put himself as quickly as possible in a posture of defence.

The clash of arms filled that prim garden, which hitherto had known no more warlike sound than the click of clipping shears; and presently the upper part of an old lady's body was projected out of a window upstairs. She tossed her arms above her white cap, scolding in a cracked voice. The gardener remained glued to the tree, his toothless mouth open in idiotic astonishment, and a little farther up the path the pretty girl, as if spellbound to a small grass plot, ran a few steps this way and that, wringing her hands and muttering crazily. She did not rush between the combatants: the onslaughts of Lieut. Feraud were so fierce that her heart failed her. Lieut. D'Hubert, his faculties concentrated upon defence, needed all his skill and science of the sword to stop the rushes of his adversary. Twice already he had to break ground.* It bothered him to feel his foothold made insecure by the round, dry gravel of the path rolling under the hard soles of his boots. This was most unsuitable ground, he thought, keeping a watchful, narrowed gaze, shaded by long eyelashes, upon the fiery stare of his thick-set adversary. This absurd affair would ruin his reputation of a sensible, well-behaved, promising young officer. It would damage, at any rate, his immediate prospects, and lose him the good-will of his general. These worldly preoccupations were no doubt misplaced in view of the solemnity of the moment. A duel, whether regarded as a ceremony in the cult of honour, or even when reduced in its moral essence to a form of manly sport, demands a perfect singleness of intention, a homicidal austerity of mood. On the other hand, this vivid concern for his future had not a bad effect inasmuch as it began to rouse the anger of Lieut. D'Hubert. Some seventy seconds had elapsed since they had crossed blades, and Lieut. D'Hubert had to break ground again in order to avoid impaling his reckless adversary like a beetle for a cabinet of specimens. The result was that misapprehending the motive, Lieut. Feraud with a triumphant sort of snarl pressed his attack.

"This enraged animal will have me against the wall directly," thought Lieut. D'Hubert. He imagined himself much closer to the house than he was, and he dared not turn his head; it seemed to him that he was keeping his adversary off with his eyes rather more than with his point. Lieut. Feraud crouched and bounded with a fierce tigerish agility fit to trouble the stoutest heart. But what was more appalling than the fury of a wild beast, accomplishing in all innocence of heart a natural function, was the fixity of savage purpose man alone is capable of displaying. Lieut. D'Hubert in the midst of his worldly preoccupations perceived it at last. It was an absurd and damaging affair to be drawn into, but whatever silly intention the fellow had started with, it was clear enough that by this time he meant to kill—nothing less. He meant it with an intensity of will utterly beyond the inferior faculties of a tiger.

As is the case with constitutionally brave men, the full view of the danger interested Lieut. D'Hubert. And directly he got properly interested, the length of his arm and the coolness of his head told in his favour. It was the turn of Lieut. Feraud to recoil, with a bloodcurdling grunt of baffled rage. He made a swift feint, and then rushed straight forward.

"Ah! you would, would you?" Lieut. D'Hubert exclaimed, mentally. The combat had lasted nearly two minutes, time enough for any man to get embittered, apart from the merits of the quarrel. And all at once it was over. Trying to close breast to breast under his adversary's guard Lieut. Feraud received a slash on his shortened arm. He did not feel it in the least, but it checked his rush, and his feet slipping on the gravel he fell backwards with great violence. The shock jarred his boiling brain into the perfect quietude of insensibility. Simultaneously with his fall the pretty servant-girl shrieked; but the old maiden lady at the window ceased her scolding, and began to cross herself piously.

Beholding his adversary stretched out perfectly still, his face to the sky, Lieut. D'Hubert thought he had killed him outright. The impression of having slashed hard enough to cut his man clean in two abode with him for a while in an exaggerated memory of the right good-will he had put into the blow. He dropped on his knees hastily by the side of the prostrate body. Discovering that not even the arm was severed, a slight sense of disappointment mingled with the feeling of relief. The fellow deserved the worst. But truly he did not want the death of that sinner. The affair was ugly enough as it stood, and Lieut. D'Hubert addressed himself at once to the task of stopping the bleeding. In this task it was his fate to be ridiculously impeded by the pretty maid. Rending the air with screams of horror, she attacked him from behind and, twining her fingers in his hair, tugged back at his head. Why she should choose to hinder him at this precise moment he could not in the least understand. He did not try. It was all like a very wicked and harassing dream. Twice to save himself from being pulled over he had to rise and fling her off. He did this stoically, without a word, kneeling down again at once to go on with his work. But the third time, his work being done, he seized her and held her arms pinned to her body. Her cap was half off, her face was red, her eyes blazed with crazy boldness. He looked mildly into them while she called him a wretch, a traitor, and a murderer many times in succession. This did not annoy him so much as the conviction that she had managed to scratch his face abundantly. Ridicule would be added to the scandal of the story. He imagined the adorned tale making its way through the garrison of the town, through the whole army on the frontier, with every possible distortion of motive and sentiment and circumstance, spreading a doubt upon the sanity of his conduct and the distinction of his taste even to the very ears of his honourable family. It was all very well for that fellow Feraud, who had no connections, no family to speak of, and no quality but courage, which, anyhow, was a matter of course, and possessed by every single trooper in the whole mass of French cavalry. Still holding down the arms of the girl in a strong grip, Lieut. D'Hubert glanced over his shoulder. Lieut. Feraud had opened his eyes. He did not move. Like a man just waking from a deep sleep he stared without any expression at the evening sky.

Lieut. D'Hubert's urgent shouts to the old gardener produced no effect—not so much as to make him shut his toothless mouth. Then he remembered that the man was stone deaf. All that time the girl struggled, not with maidenly coyness, but like a pretty, dumb fury,* kicking his shins now and then. He continued to hold her as if in a vice, his instinct telling him that were he to let her go she would fly at his eyes. But he was greatly humiliated by his position. At last she gave up. She was more exhausted than appeased, he feared. Nevertheless, he attempted to get out of this wicked dream by way of negotiation.

"Listen to me," he said, as calmly as he could. "Will you promise to run for a surgeon if I let you go?"

With real affliction he heard her declare that she would do nothing of the kind. On the contrary, her sobbed out intention was to remain in the garden, and fight tooth and nail for the protection of the vanquished man. This was shocking.

"My dear child!" he cried in despair, "is it possible that you think me capable of murdering a wounded adversary? Is it. . . . Be quiet, you little wild cat, you!"

They struggled. A thick, drowsy voice said behind him, "What are you after with that girl?"

Lieut. Feraud had raised himself on his good arm. He was looking sleepily at his other arm, at the mess of blood on his uniform, at a small red pool on the ground, at his sabre lying a foot away on the path. Then he laid himself down gently again to think it all out, as far as a thundering headache would permit of mental operations.

Lieut. D'Hubert released the girl who crouched at once by the side of the other lieutenant. The shades of night were falling on the little trim garden with this touching group, whence proceeded low murmurs of sorrow and compassion, with other feeble sounds of a different character, as if an imperfectly awake invalid were trying to swear. Lieut. D'Hubert went away.

He passed through the silent house, and congratulated himself upon the dusk concealing his gory hands and scratched face from the passers-by. But this story could by no means be concealed. He dreaded the discredit and ridicule above everything, and was painfully aware of sneaking through the back streets in the manner of a murderer.* Presently the sounds of a flute coming out of the open window of a lighted upstairs room in a modest house interrupted his dismal reflections. It was being played with a persevering virtuosity, and through the *fioritures** of the tune one could hear the regular thumping of the foot beating time on the floor.

Lieut. D'Hubert shouted a name, which was that of an army surgeon whom he knew fairly well. The sounds of the flute ceased, and the musician appeared at the window, his instrument still in his hand, peering into the street.

"Who calls? You, D'Hubert? What brings you this way?"

He did not like to be disturbed at the hour when he was playing the flute. He was a man whose hair had turned grey already in the thankless task of tying up wounds on battlefields where others reaped advancement and glory.

"I want you to go at once and see Feraud. You know Lieut. Feraud? He lives down the second street. It's but a step from here."

"What's the matter with him?"

"Wounded."

"Are you sure?"

"Sure!" cried D'Hubert. "I come from there."

"That's amusing," said the elderly surgeon. Amusing was his favourite word; but the expression of his face when he pronounced it never corresponded. He was a stolid man. "Come in," he added. "I'll get ready in a moment."

"Thanks! I will. I want to wash my hands in your room."

Lieut. D'Hubert found the surgeon occupied in unscrewing his flute, and packing the pieces methodically in a case. He turned his head.

"Water there—in the corner. Your hands do want washing."

"I've stopped the bleeding," said Lieut. D'Hubert. "But you had better make haste. It's rather more than ten minutes ago, you know."

The surgeon did not hurry his movements.

"What's the matter? Dressing came off? That's amusing. I've been at work in the hospital all day but I've been told this morning by somebody that he had come off without a scratch."

"Not the same duel probably," growled moodily Lieut. D'Hubert, wiping his hands on a coarse towel.

"Not the same. . . . What? Another. It would take the very devil to make me go out twice in one day." The surgeon looked narrowly at Lieut. D'Hubert. "How did you come by that scratched face? Both sides, too—and symmetrical. It's amusing."

"Very!" snarled Lieut. D'Hubert. "And you will find his slashed arm amusing, too. It will keep both of you amused for quite a long time."

The doctor was mystified and impressed by the brusque bitterness of Lieut. D'Hubert's tone. They left the house together, and in the street he was still more mystified by his conduct.

"Aren't you coming with me?" he asked.

"No," said Lieut. D'Hubert. "You can find the house by yourself. The front door will be standing open very likely."

"All right. Where's his room?"

"Ground floor. But you had better go right through and look in the garden first."

This astonishing piece of information made the surgeon go off without further parley. Lieut. D'Hubert regained his quarters nursing a hot and uneasy indignation. He dreaded the chaff of his comrades almost as much as the anger of his superiors. The truth was confoundedly grotesque and embarrassing, even putting aside the irregularity of the combat itself, which made it come abominably near a criminal offence. Like all men without much imagination, a faculty which helps the process of reflective thought, Lieut. D'Hubert became frightfully harassed by the obvious aspects of his predicament. He was certainly glad that he had not killed Lieut. Feraud outside all rules, and without the regular witnesses proper to such a transaction. Uncommonly glad. At the same time he felt as though he would have liked to wring his neck for him without ceremony.

He was still under the sway of these contradictory sentiments when the surgeon amateur of the flute came to see him. More than three days had elapsed. Lieut. D'Hubert was no longer *officier d'ordonnance* to the general commanding the division. He had been sent back to his regiment. And he was resuming his connection with the soldiers' military family by being shut up in close confinement, not at his own quarters in town, but in a room in the barracks. Owing to the gravity of the incident, he was forbidden to see any one. He did not know what had happened, what was being said, or what was being thought. The arrival of the surgeon was a most unexpected thing to the worried captive. The amateur of the flute began by explaining that he was there only by a special favour of the colonel.

"I represented to him that it would be only fair to let you have some authentic news of your adversary," he continued. "You'll be glad to hear he's getting better fast."

Lieut. D'Hubert's face exhibited no conventional signs of gladness. He continued to walk the floor of the dusty bare room.

"Take this chair, doctor," he mumbled.

The doctor sat down.

"This affair is variously appreciated—in town and in the army. In fact, the diversity of opinions is amusing."

"Is it!" mumbled Lieut. D'Hubert, tramping steadily from wall to wall. But within himself he marvelled that there could be two opinions on the matter. The surgeon continued.

"Of course, as the real facts are not known—"

"I should have thought," interrupted D'Hubert, "that the fellow would have put you in possession of facts."

"He said something," admitted the other, "the first time I saw him. And, by the bye, I did find him in the garden. The thump on the back of his head had made him a little incoherent then. Afterwards he was rather reticent than otherwise."

"Didn't think he would have the grace to be ashamed!" mumbled D'Hubert, resuming his pacing while the doctor murmured, "It's very amusing. Ashamed! Shame was not exactly his frame of mind. However, you may look at the matter otherwise."

"What are you talking about? What matter?" asked D'Hubert, with a sidelong look at the heavy-faced, grey-haired figure seated on a wooden chair.

"Whatever it is," said the surgeon a little impatiently, "I don't want to pronounce any opinion on your conduct—"

"By heavens, you had better not!" burst out D'Hubert.

"There!—there! Don't be so quick in flourishing the sword. It doesn't pay in the long run. Understand once for all that I would not carve any of you youngsters except with the tools of my trade. But my advice is good. If you go on like this you will make for yourself an ugly reputation."

"Go on like what?" demanded Lieut. D'Hubert, stopping short, quite startled. "I!—I!—make for myself a reputation. . . . What do you imagine?"

"I told you I don't wish to judge of the rights and wrongs of this incident. It's not my business. Nevertheless—"

"What on earth has he been telling you?" interrupted Lieut. D'Hubert, in a sort of awed scare.

"I told you already, that at first, when I picked him up in the garden, he was incoherent. Afterwards he was naturally reticent. But I gather at least that he could not help himself."

"He couldn't?" shouted Lieut. D'Hubert in a great voice. Then, lowering his tone impressively, "And what about me? Could I help myself?"

The surgeon stood up. His thoughts were running upon the flute, his constant companion with a consoling voice. In the vicinity of field

ambulances, after twenty-four hours' hard work, he had been known
to trouble with its sweet sounds the horrible stillness of battlefields,
given over to silence and the dead. The solacing hour of his daily life
was approaching, and in peace time he held on to the minutes as
a miser to his hoard.

"Of course!—of course!" he said, perfunctorily. "You would think
so. It's amusing. However, being perfectly neutral and friendly to you
both, I have consented to deliver his message to you. Say that I am
humouring an invalid if you like. He wants you to know that this affair
is by no means at an end. He intends to send you his seconds directly
he has regained his strength—providing, of course, the army is not in
the field at that time."*

"He intends, does he? Why, certainly," spluttered Lieut. D'Hubert
in a passion.

The secret of his exasperation was not apparent to the visitor; but
this passion confirmed the surgeon in the belief which was gaining
ground outside that some very serious difference had arisen between
these two young men, something serious enough to wear an air of
mystery, some fact of the utmost gravity. To settle their urgent difference about that fact, those two young men had risked being broken
and disgraced at the outset almost of their career. The surgeon feared
that the forthcoming inquiry would fail to satisfy the public curiosity.
They would not take the public into their confidence as to that something which had passed between them of a nature so outrageous as to
make them face a charge of murder—neither more nor less. But what
could it be?

The surgeon was not very curious by temperament; but that question haunting his mind caused him twice that evening to hold the
instrument off his lips and sit silent for a whole minute—right in the
middle of a tune—trying to form a plausible conjecture.

II

HE succeeded in this object no better than the rest of the garrison
and the whole of society. The two young officers, of no especial consequence till then, became distinguished by the universal curiosity as
to the origin of their quarrel. Madame de Lionne's *salon* was the
centre of ingenious surmises; that lady herself was for a time assailed

by inquiries as being the last person known to have spoken to these unhappy and reckless young men before they went out together from her house to a savage encounter with swords, at dusk, in a private garden. She protested she had not observed anything unusual in their demeanour. Lieut. Feraud had been visibly annoyed at being called away. That was natural enough; no man likes to be disturbed in a conversation with a lady famed for her elegance and sensibility. But in truth the subject bored Madame de Lionne, since her personality could by no stretch of reckless gossip be connected with this affair. And it irritated her to hear it advanced that there might have been some woman in the case. This irritation arose, not from her elegance or sensibility, but from a more instinctive side of her nature. It became so great at last that she peremptorily forbade the subject to be mentioned under her roof. Near her couch the prohibition was obeyed, but farther off in the *salon* the pall of the imposed silence continued to be lifted more or less. A personage with a long, pale face, resembling the countenance of a sheep, opined, shaking his head, that it was a quarrel of long standing envenomed by time. It was objected to him that the men themselves were too young for such a theory. They belonged also to different and distant parts of France. There were other physical impossibilities, too. A sub-commissary of the Intendance,* an agreeable and cultivated bachelor in kerseymere breeches, Hessian boots,* and a blue coat embroidered with silver lace, who affected to believe in the transmigration of souls,* suggested that the two had met perhaps in some previous existence. The feud was in the forgotten past. It might have been something quite inconceivable in the present state of their being; but their souls remembered the animosity, and manifested an instinctive antagonism. He developed this theme jocularly. Yet the affair was so absurd from the worldly, the military, the honourable, or the prudential point of view, that this weird explanation seemed rather more reasonable than any other.

The two officers had confided nothing definite to any one. Humiliation at having been worsted arms in hand, and an uneasy feeling of having been involved in a scrape by the injustice of fate, kept Lieut. Feraud savagely dumb. He mistrusted the sympathy of mankind. That would, of course, go to that dandified staff officer. Lying in bed, he raved aloud to the pretty maid who administered to his needs with devotion, and listened to his horrible imprecations with alarm. That Lieut. D'Hubert should be made to "pay for it," seemed to her just and natural. Her principal care was that Lieut. Feraud should not excite himself. He appeared so wholly admirable and fascinating to the humility of her heart that her only concern was to see him get well quickly, even if it were only to resume his visits to Madame de Lionne's *salon*.

Lieut. D'Hubert kept silent for the immediate reason that there was no one, except a stupid young soldier servant, to speak to. Further, he was aware that the episode, so grave professionally, had its comic side. When reflecting upon it, he still felt that he would like to wring Lieut. Feraud's neck for him. But this formula was figurative rather than precise, and expressed more a state of mind than an actual physical impulse. At the same time, there was in that young man a feeling of comradeship and kindness which made him unwilling to make the position of Lieut. Feraud worse than it was. He did not want to talk at large about this wretched affair. At the inquiry he would have, of course, to speak the truth in self-defence. This prospect vexed him.

But no inquiry took place. The army took the field instead. Lieut. D'Hubert, liberated without remark, took up his regimental duties; and Lieut. Feraud, his arm just out of the sling, rode unquestioned with his squadron to complete his convalescence in the smoke of battlefields and the fresh air of night bivouacs. This bracing treatment suited him so well, that at the first rumour of an armistice being signed he could turn without misgivings to the thoughts of his private warfare.

This time it was to be regular warfare. He sent two friends to Lieut. D'Hubert, whose regiment was stationed only a few miles away. Those friends had asked no questions of their principal. "I owe him one, that pretty staff officer," he had said, grimly, and they went away quite contentedly on their mission. Lieut. D'Hubert had no difficulty in finding two friends equally discreet and devoted to their principal. "There's a crazy fellow to whom I must give a lesson," he had declared curtly; and they asked for no better reasons.

On these grounds an encounter with duelling-swords was arranged one early morning in a convenient field. At the third set-to Lieut. D'Hubert found himself lying on his back on the dewy grass with a hole in his side.* A serene sun rising over a landscape of meadows and woods hung on his left. A surgeon—not the flute player, but another—was bending over him, feeling around the wound.

"Narrow squeak. But it will be nothing," he pronounced.

Lieut. D'Hubert heard these words with pleasure. One of his seconds, sitting on the wet grass, and sustaining his head on his lap, said, "The fortune of war, *mon pauvre vieux*.* What will you have? You had better make it up like two good fellows. Do!"

"You don't know what you ask," murmured Lieut. D'Hubert, in a feeble voice. "However, if he . . ."

In another part of the meadow the seconds of Lieut. Feraud were urging him to go over and shake hands with his adversary.

"You have paid him off now—*que diable*.* It's the proper thing to do. This D'Hubert is a decent fellow."

"I know the decency of these generals' pets," muttered Lieut. Feraud through his teeth, and the sombre expression of his face discouraged further efforts at reconciliation. The seconds, bowing from a distance, took their men off the field. In the afternoon Lieut. D'Hubert, very popular as a good comrade uniting great bravery with a frank and equable temper, had many visitors. It was remarked that Lieut. Feraud did not, as is customary, show himself much abroad to receive the felicitations of his friends. They would not have failed him, because he, too, was liked for the exuberance of his southern nature and the simplicity of his character. In all the places where officers were in the habit of assembling at the end of the day the duel of the morning was talked over from every point of view. Though Lieut. D'Hubert had got worsted this time, his sword play was commended. No one could deny that it was very close, very scientific. It was even whispered that if he got touched it was because he wished to spare his adversary. But by many the vigour and dash of Lieut. Feraud's attack were pronounced irresistible.

The merits of the two officers as combatants were frankly discussed; but their attitude to each other after the duel was criticized lightly and with caution. It was irreconcilable, and that was to be regretted. But after all they knew best what the care of their honour dictated. It was not a matter for their comrades to pry into over-much. As to the origin of the quarrel, the general impression was that it dated from the time they were holding garrison in Strasbourg. The musical surgeon shook his head at that. It went much farther back, he thought.

"Why, of course! You must know the whole story," cried several voices, eager with curiosity. "What was it?"

He raised his eyes from his glass deliberately. "Even if I knew ever so well, you can't expect me to tell you, since both the principals choose to say nothing."

He got up and went out, leaving the sense of mystery behind him. He could not stay any longer, because the witching hour of flute-playing was drawing near.

After he had gone a very young officer observed solemnly, "Obviously, his lips are sealed!"

Nobody questioned the high correctness of that remark. Somehow it added to the impressiveness of the affair. Several older officers of both regiments, prompted by nothing but sheer kindness and love of harmony, proposed to form a Court of Honour,* to which the two young men would leave the task of their reconciliation. Unfortunately they began by approaching Lieut. Feraud, on the assumption that, having just scored heavily, he would be found placable and disposed to moderation.

The reasoning was sound enough. Nevertheless, the move turned out unfortunate. In that relaxation of moral fibre, which is brought about by the ease of soothed vanity, Lieut. Feraud had condescended in the secret of his heart to review the case, and even had come to doubt not the justice of his cause, but the absolute sagacity of his conduct. This being so, he was disinclined to talk about it. The suggestion of the regimental wise men put him in a difficult position. He was disgusted at it, and this disgust, by a paradoxical logic, reawakened his animosity against Lieut. D'Hubert. Was he to be pestered with this fellow for ever—the fellow who had an infernal knack of getting round people somehow? And yet it was difficult to refuse point blank that mediation sanctioned by the code of honour.

He met the difficulty by an attitude of grim reserve. He twisted his moustache and used vague words. His case was perfectly clear. He was not ashamed to state it before a proper Court of Honour, neither was he afraid to defend it on the ground. He did not see any reason to jump at the suggestion before ascertaining how his adversary was likely to take it.

Later in the day, his exasperation growing upon him, he was heard in a public place saying sardonically, "that it would be the very luckiest thing for Lieut. D'Hubert, because the next time of meeting he need not hope to get off with the mere trifle of three weeks in bed."

This boastful phrase might have been prompted by the most profound Machiavellism.* Southern natures often hide, under the outward impulsiveness of action and speech, a certain amount of astuteness.

Lieut. Feraud, mistrusting the justice of men, by no means desired a Court of Honour; and the above words, according so well with his temperament, had also the merit of serving his turn. Whether meant so or not, they found their way in less than four-and-twenty hours into Lieut. D'Hubert's bedroom. In consequence Lieut. D'Hubert, sitting propped up with pillows, received the overtures made to him next day by the statement that the affair was of a nature which could not bear discussion.

The pale face of the wounded officer, his weak voice which he had yet to use cautiously, and the courteous dignity of his tone had a great effect on his hearers. Reported outside all this did more for deepening the mystery than the vapourings of Lieut. Feraud. This last was greatly relieved at the issue. He began to enjoy the state of general wonder, and was pleased to add to it by assuming an attitude of fierce discretion.

The colonel of Lieut. D'Hubert's regiment was a grey-haired, weather-beaten warrior, who took a simple view of his responsibilities. "I can't," he said to himself, "let the best of my subalterns* get damaged like this for nothing. I must get to the bottom of this affair privately. He must speak out if the devil were in it. The colonel should be more than a father to these youngsters." And indeed he loved all his men with as much affection as a father of a large family can feel for every individual member of it. If human beings by an oversight of Providence came into the world as mere civilians, they were born again into a regiment as infants are born into a family, and it was that military birth alone which counted.

At the sight of Lieut. D'Hubert standing before him very bleached and hollow-eyed the heart of the old warrior felt a pang of genuine compassion. All his affection for the regiment—that body of men which he held in his hand to launch forward and draw back, who ministered to his pride and commanded all his thoughts—seemed centred for a moment on the person of the most promising subaltern. He cleared his throat in a threatening manner, and frowned terribly. "You must understand," he began, "that I don't care a rap for the life of a single man in the regiment. I would send the eight hundred and forty-three of you men and horses galloping into the pit of perdition with no more compunction than I would kill a fly!"

"Yes, Colonel. You would be riding at our head," said Lieut. D'Hubert with a wan smile.

The colonel, who felt the need of being very diplomatic, fairly roared at this. "I want you to know, Lieut. D'Hubert, that I could stand aside and see you all riding to Hades* if need be. I am a man to do even that if the good of the service and my duty to my country required it from me. But that's unthinkable, so don't you even hint at such a thing." He glared awfully, but his tone softened. "There's some milk yet about that moustache of yours, my boy. You don't know what a man like me is capable of. I would hide behind a haystack if . . . Don't grin at me, sir! How dare you? If this were not a private conversation I would . . . Look here! I am responsible for the proper expenditure of lives under my command for the glory of our country and the honour of the regiment. Do you understand that? Well, then, what the devil do you mean by letting yourself be spitted like this by that fellow of the 7th Hussars? It's simply disgraceful!"

Lieut. D'Hubert felt vexed beyond measure. His shoulders moved slightly. He made no other answer. He could not ignore his responsibility.

The colonel veiled his glance and lowered his voice still more. "It's deplorable!" he murmured. And again he changed his tone. "Come!" he went on, persuasively, but with that note of authority which dwells in the throat of a good leader of men, "this affair must be settled. I desire to be told plainly what it is all about. I demand, as your best friend, to know."

The compelling power of authority, the persuasive influence of kindness, affected powerfully a man just risen from a bed of sickness. Lieut. D'Hubert's hand, which grasped the knob of a stick, trembled slightly. But his northern temperament, sentimental yet cautious and clear-sighted, too, in its idealistic way, checked his impulse to make a clean breast of the whole deadly absurdity. According to the precept of transcendental wisdom, he turned his tongue seven times in his mouth before he spoke.* He made then only a speech of thanks.

The colonel listened, interested at first, then looked mystified. At last he frowned. "You hesitate?—*mille tonnerres!** Haven't I told you that I will condescend to argue with you—as a friend?"

"Yes, Colonel!" answered Lieut. D'Hubert, gently. "But I am afraid that after you have heard me out as a friend you will take action as my superior officer."

The attentive colonel snapped his jaws. "Well, what of that?" he said, frankly. "Is it so damnably disgraceful?"

"It is not," negatived Lieut. D'Hubert, in a faint but firm voice.

"Of course, I shall act for the good of the service. Nothing can prevent me doing that. What do you think I want to be told for?"

"I know it is not from idle curiosity," protested Lieut. D'Hubert. "I know you will act wisely. But what about the good fame of the regiment?"

"It cannot be affected by any youthful folly of a lieutenant," said the colonel, severely.

"No. It cannot be. But it can be by evil tongues. It will be said that a lieutenant of the 4th Hussars, afraid of meeting his adversary, is hiding behind his colonel. And that would be worse than hiding behind a haystack—for the good of the service. I cannot afford to do that, Colonel."

"Nobody would dare to say anything of the kind," began the colonel very fiercely, but ended the phrase on an uncertain note. The bravery of Lieut. D'Hubert was well known. But the colonel was well aware that the duelling courage, the single combat courage, is rightly or wrongly supposed to be courage of a special sort. And it was eminently necessary that an officer of his regiment should possess every kind of courage—and prove it, too. The colonel stuck out his lower lip, and looked far away with a peculiar glazed stare. This was the expression of his perplexity—an expression practically unknown to his regiment; for perplexity is a sentiment which is incompatible with the rank of colonel of cavalry. The colonel himself was overcome by the unpleasant novelty of the sensation. As he was not accustomed to think except on professional matters connected with the welfare of men and horses, and the proper use thereof on the field of glory, his intellectual efforts degenerated into mere mental repetitions of profane language. "*Mille tonnerres! . . . Sacré nom de nom . . .*"* he thought.

Lieut. D'Hubert coughed painfully, and added in a weary voice: "There will be plenty of evil tongues to say that I've been cowed. And I am sure you will not expect me to pass that over. I may find myself suddenly with a dozen duels on my hands instead of this one affair."

The direct simplicity of this argument came home to the colonel's understanding. He looked at his subordinate fixedly. "Sit down, Lieutenant!" he said, gruffly. "This is the very devil of a . . . Sit down!"

"*Mon Colonel,*" D'Hubert began again, "I am not afraid of evil tongues. There's a way of silencing them. But there's my peace of mind, too. I wouldn't be able to shake off the notion that I've ruined a brother officer. Whatever action you take, it is bound to go farther. The inquiry has been dropped—let it rest now. It would have been absolutely fatal to Feraud."

"Hey! What! Did he behave so badly?"

"Yes. It was pretty bad," muttered Lieut. D'Hubert. Being still very weak, he felt a disposition to cry.

As the other man did not belong to his own regiment the colonel had no difficulty in believing this. He began to pace up and down the room. He was a good chief, a man capable of discreet sympathy. But he was human in other ways, too, and this became apparent because he was not capable of artifice.

"The very devil, Lieutenant," he blurted out, in the innocence of his heart, "is that I have declared my intention to get to the bottom of this affair. And when a colonel says something . . . you see . . . ."

Lieut. D'Hubert broke in earnestly: "Let me entreat you, Colonel, to be satisfied with taking my word of honour that I was put into a damnable position where I had no option; I had no choice whatever, consistent with my dignity as a man and an officer. . . . After all, Colonel, this fact is the very bottom of this affair. Here you've got it. The rest is mere detail. . . ."

The colonel stopped short. The reputation of Lieut. D'Hubert for good sense and good temper weighed in the balance. A cool head, a warm heart, open as the day. Always correct in his behaviour. One had to trust him. The colonel repressed manfully an immense curiosity. "H'm! You affirm that as a man and an officer. . . . No option? Eh?"

"As an officer—an officer of the 4th Hussars, too," insisted Lieut. D'Hubert, "I had not. And that is the bottom of the affair, Colonel."

"Yes. But still I don't see why, to one's colonel. . . . A colonel is a father—*que diable!*"

Lieut. D'Hubert ought not to have been allowed out as yet. He was becoming aware of his physical insufficiency with humiliation and despair. But the morbid obstinacy of an invalid possessed him, and at the same time he felt with dismay his eyes filling with water. This trouble seemed too big to handle. A tear fell down the thin, pale cheek of Lieut. D'Hubert.

The colonel turned his back on him hastily. You could have heard a pin drop. "This is some silly woman story—is it not?"

Saying these words the chief spun round to seize the truth, which is not a beautiful shape living in a well,* but a shy bird best caught by stratagem. This was the last move of the colonel's diplomacy. He saw the truth shining unmistakably in the gesture of Lieut. D'Hubert raising his weak arms and his eyes to heaven in supreme protest.

"Not a woman affair—eh?" growled the colonel, staring hard. "I don't ask you who or where. All I want to know is whether there is a woman in it?"

Lieut. D'Hubert's arms dropped, and his weak voice was pathetically broken.

"Nothing of the kind, *mon Colonel.*"

"On your honour?" insisted the old warrior.

"On my honour."

"Very well," said the colonel, thoughtfully, and bit his lip. The arguments of Lieut. D'Hubert, helped by his liking for the man, had convinced him. On the other hand, it was highly improper that his intervention, of which he had made no secret, should produce no visible effect. He kept Lieut. D'Hubert a few minutes longer, and dismissed him kindly.

"Take a few days more in bed. Lieutenant. What the devil does the surgeon mean by reporting you fit for duty?"

On coming out of the colonel's quarters, Lieut. D'Hubert said nothing to the friend who was waiting outside to take him home. He said nothing to anybody. Lieut. D'Hubert made no confidences. But on the evening of that day the colonel, strolling under the elms growing near his quarters, in the company of his second in command, opened his lips.

"I've got to the bottom of this affair," he remarked.

The lieut.-colonel, a dry, brown chip of a man with short sidewhiskers, pricked up his ears at that without letting a sign of curiosity escape him.

"It's no trifle," added the colonel, oracularly. The other waited for a long while before he murmured:

"Indeed, sir!"

"No trifle," repeated the colonel, looking straight before him. "I've, however, forbidden D'Hubert either to send to or receive a challenge from Feraud for the next twelve months."

He had imagined this prohibition to save the prestige a colonel should have. The result of it was to give an official seal to the mystery surrounding this deadly quarrel. Lieut. D'Hubert repelled by an impassive silence all attempts to worm the truth out of him. Lieut. Feraud, secretly uneasy at first, regained his assurance as time went on. He disguised his ignorance of the meaning of the imposed truce by slight sardonic laughs, as though he were amused by what he intended to keep to himself. "But what will you do?" his chums used to ask him. He contented himself by replying "*Qui vivra verra*"* with a little truculent air. And everybody admired his discretion.

Before the end of the truce Lieut. D'Hubert got his troop. The promotion was well earned, but somehow no one seemed to expect the event. When Lieut. Feraud heard of it at a gathering of officers, he muttered through his teeth, "Is that so?" At once he unhooked his sabre from a peg near the door, buckled it on carefully, and left the company without another word. He walked home with measured steps, struck a light with his flint and steel, and lit his tallow candle. Then snatching an unlucky glass tumbler off the mantelpiece he dashed it violently on the floor.

Now that D'Hubert was an officer of superior rank there could be no question of a duel.* Neither of them could send or receive a challenge without rendering himself amenable to a court-martial. It was not to be thought of. Lieut. Feraud, who for many days now had experienced no real desire to meet Lieut. D'Hubert arms in hand, chafed again at the systematic injustice of fate. "Does he think he will escape me in that way?" he thought, indignantly. He saw in this promotion an intrigue, a conspiracy, a cowardly manoeuvre. That colonel knew what he was doing. He had hastened to recommend his favourite for a step. It was outrageous that a man should be able to avoid the consequences of his acts in such a dark and tortuous manner.

Of a happy-go-lucky disposition, of a temperament more pugnacious than military, Lieut. Feraud had been content to give and receive blows for sheer love of armed strife, and without much thought of advancement; but now an urgent desire to get on sprang up in his breast. This fighter by vocation resolved in his mind to seize showy occasions and to court the favourable opinion of his chiefs like a mere worldling. He knew he was as brave as any one, and never doubted his personal charm. Nevertheless, neither the bravery nor the charm seemed to work very swiftly. Lieut. Feraud's engaging, careless truculence of a *beau sabreur** underwent a change. He began to make bitter allusions to "clever fellows who stick at nothing to get on." The army was full of them, he would say; you had only to look round. But all the time he had in view one person only, his adversary, D'Hubert. Once he confided to an appreciative friend: "You see, I don't know how to fawn on the right sort of people. It isn't in my character."

He did not get his step till a week after Austerlitz.* The Light Cavalry of the Grand Army had its hands very full of interesting work for a little while. Directly the pressure of professional occupation had been eased Captain Feraud took measures to arrange a meeting without loss of time. "I know my bird," he observed, grimly. "If I don't look sharp he will take care to get himself promoted over the heads of a dozen better men than himself. He's got the knack for that sort of thing."

This duel was fought in Silesia. If not fought to a finish, it was, at any rate, fought to a standstill. The weapon was the cavalry sabre, and the skill, the science, the vigour, and the determination displayed by the adversaries compelled the admiration of the beholders.* It became the subject of talk on both shores of the Danube,* and as far as the garrisons of Gratz and Laybach.* They crossed blades seven times. Both had many cuts which bled profusely. Both refused to have the combat stopped, time after time, with what appeared the most deadly animosity. This appearance was caused on the part of Captain D'Hubert by a rational desire to be done once for all with this worry; on the part of Captain Feraud by a tremendous exaltation of his pugnacious instincts and the incitement of wounded vanity. At last, dishevelled, their shirts in rags, covered with gore and hardly able to stand, they were led away forcibly by their marvelling and horrified seconds. Later on, besieged by comrades avid of details, these gentlemen declared that they could not have allowed that sort of hacking to go on indefinitely. Asked whether the quarrel was settled this time, they gave it out as their conviction that it was a difference which could only be settled by one of the parties remaining lifeless on the ground. The sensation spread from army corps to army corps, and penetrated at last to the smallest detachments of the troops cantoned between the Rhine and the Save.* In the cafés in Vienna it was generally estimated, from details to hand, that the adversaries would be able to meet again in three weeks' time on the outside. Something really transcendent in the way of duelling was expected.

These expectations were brought to naught by the necessities of the service which separated the two officers. No official notice had been taken of their quarrel. It was now the property of the army, and not to be meddled with lightly. But the story of the duel, or rather their duelling propensities, must have stood somewhat in the way of their advancement, because they were still captains when they came together again during the war with Prussia. Detached north after Jena, with the army commanded by Marshal Bernadotte, Prince of Ponte Corvo, they entered Lübeck together.*

It was only after the occupation of that town that Captain Feraud found leisure to consider his future conduct in view of the fact that Captain D'Hubert had been given the position of third aide-de-camp to the marshal. He considered it a great part of a night, and in the morning summoned two sympathetic friends.

"I've been thinking it over calmly," he said, gazing at them with blood-shot, tired eyes. "I see that I must get rid of that intriguing personage. Here he's managed to sneak on to the personal staff of the marshal. It's a direct provocation to me. I can't tolerate a situation in which I am exposed any day to receive an order through him. And God knows what order, too! That sort of thing has happened once before—and that's once too often. He understands this perfectly, never fear. I can't tell you any more. Now you know what it is you have to do."*

This encounter took place outside the town of Lübeck, on very open ground, selected with special care in deference to the general sentiment of the cavalry division belonging to the army corps, that this time the two officers should meet on horseback. After all, this duel was a cavalry affair, and to persist in fighting on foot would look like a slight on one's own arm of the service. The seconds, startled by the unusual nature of the suggestion, hastened to refer to their principals. Captain Feraud jumped at it with alacrity. For some obscure reason, depending, no doubt, on his psychology, he imagined himself invincible on horseback. All alone within the four walls of his room he rubbed his hands and muttered triumphantly, "Aha! my pretty staff officer, I've got you now."

Captain D'Hubert on his side, after staring hard for a considerable time at his friends, shrugged his shoulders slightly. This affair had hopelessly and unreasonably complicated his existence for him. One absurdity more or less in the development did not matter—all absurdity was distasteful to him; but, urbane as ever, he produced a faintly ironical smile, and said in his calm voice, "It certainly will do away to some extent with the monotony of the thing."

When left alone, he sat down at a table and took his head into his hands. He had not spared himself of late and the marshal had been working all his aides-de-camp particularly hard. The last three weeks of campaigning in horrible weather had affected his health. When over-tired he suffered from a stitch in his wounded side, and that uncomfortable sensation always depressed him. "It's that brute's doing, too," he thought bitterly.

The day before he had received a letter from home, announcing that his only sister was going to be married. He reflected that from the time she was nineteen and he twenty-six, when he went away to garrison life in Strasbourg, he had had but two short glimpses of her. They had been great friends and confidants; and now she was going to be given away to a man whom he did not know—a very worthy fellow no doubt, but not half good enough for her. He would never see his old Léonie again. She had a capable little head, and plenty of tact; she would know how to manage the fellow, to be sure. He was easy in his mind about her happiness but he felt ousted from the first place in her thoughts which had been his ever since the girl could speak. A melancholy regret of the days of his childhood settled upon Captain D'Hubert, third aide-de-camp to the Prince of Ponte Corvo.

He threw aside the letter of congratulation he had begun to write as in duty bound, but without enthusiasm. He took a fresh piece of paper, and traced on it the words: "This is my last will and testament." Looking at these words he gave himself up to unpleasant reflection; a presentiment that he would never see the scenes of his childhood weighed down the equable spirits of Captain D'Hubert. He jumped up, pushing his chair back, yawned elaborately in sign that he didn't care anything for presentiments, and throwing himself on the bed went to sleep. During the night he shivered from time to time without waking up. In the morning he rode out of town between his two seconds, talking of indifferent things, and looking right and left with apparent detachment into the heavy morning mists shrouding the flat green fields bordered by hedges. He leaped a ditch, and saw the forms of many mounted men moving in the fog. "We are to fight before a gallery, it seems," he muttered to himself, bitterly.

His seconds were rather concerned at the state of the atmosphere, but presently a pale, sickly sun struggled out of the low vapours, and

Captain D'Hubert made out, in the distance, three horsemen riding
a little apart from the others. It was Captain Feraud and his seconds.
He drew his sabre, and assured himself that it was properly fastened
to his wrist. And now the seconds, who had been standing in close
group with the heads of their horses together, separated at an easy
canter, leaving a large, clear field between him and his adversary.
Captain D'Hubert looked at the pale sun, at the dismal fields, and the
imbecility of the impending fight filled him with desolation. From
a distant part of the field a stentorian voice shouted commands at
proper intervals: *Au pas—Au trot—Charrrgez!* . . .* Presentiments of
death don't come to a man for nothing, he thought at the very moment
he put spurs to his horse.

And therefore he was more than surprised when, at the very first
set-to, Captain Feraud laid himself open to a cut over the forehead,
which blinding him with blood, ended the combat almost before it
had fairly begun. It was impossible to go on. Captain D'Hubert, leaving his enemy swearing horribly and reeling in the saddle between his
two appalled friends, leaped the ditch again into the road and trotted
home with his two seconds, who seemed rather awestruck at the
speedy issue of that encounter. In the evening Captain D'Hubert finished the congratulatory letter on his sister's marriage.

He finished it late. It was a long letter. Captain D'Hubert gave
reins to his fancy. He told his sister that he would feel rather lonely
after this great change in her life; but then the day would come for
him, too, to get married. In fact, he was thinking already of the time
when there would be no one left to fight with in Europe and the epoch
of wars would be over. "I expect then," he wrote, "to be within meas-
urable distance of a marshal's baton, and you will be an experienced
married woman. You shall look out a wife for me. I will be, probably,
bald by then, and a little *blasé*.* I shall require a young girl, pretty of
course, and with a large fortune, which should help me to close my
glorious career in the splendour befitting my exalted rank." He ended
with the information that he had just given a lesson to a worrying,
quarrelsome fellow who imagined he had a grievance against him.
"But if you, in the depths of your province," he continued, "ever hear
it said that your brother is of a quarrelsome disposition, don't you
believe it on any account. There is no saying what gossip from the
army may reach your innocent ears. Whatever you hear you may rest
assured that your ever-loving brother is not a duellist." Then Captain

D'Hubert crumpled up the blank sheet of paper headed with the words "This is my last will and testament," and threw it in the fire with a great laugh at himself. He didn't care a snap for what that lunatic could do. He had suddenly acquired the conviction that his adversary was utterly powerless to affect his life in any sort of way; except, perhaps, in the way of putting a special excitement into the delightful, gay intervals between the campaigns.

From this on there were, however, to be no peaceful intervals in the career of Captain D'Hubert. He saw the fields of Eylau and Friedland,* marched and countermarched in the snow, in the mud, in the dust of Polish plains, picking up distinction and advancement on all the roads of North-eastern Europe. Meantime, Captain Feraud, despatched southwards with his regiment, made unsatisfactory war in Spain. It was only when the preparations for the Russian campaign* began that he was ordered north again. He left the country of mantillas and oranges without regret.

The first signs of a not unbecoming baldness added to the lofty aspect of Colonel D'Hubert's forehead. This feature was no longer white and smooth as in the days of his youth; the kindly open glance of his blue eyes had grown a little hard as if from much peering through the smoke of battles. The ebony crop on Colonel Feraud's head, coarse and crinkly like a cap of horsehair, showed many silver threads about the temples. A detestable warfare of ambushes and inglorious surprises had not improved his temper. The beak-like curve of his nose was unpleasantly set off by a deep fold on each side of his mouth. The round orbits of his eyes radiated wrinkles. More than ever he recalled an irritable and staring bird—something like a cross between a parrot and an owl. He was still extremely outspoken in his dislike of "intriguing fellows." He seized every opportunity to state that he did not pick up his rank in the ante-rooms of marshals. The unlucky persons, civil or military, who, with an intention of being pleasant, begged Colonel Feraud to tell them how he came by that very apparent scar on the forehead, were astonished to find themselves snubbed in various ways, some of which were simply rude and others mysteriously sardonic. Young officers were warned kindly by their more experienced comrades not to stare openly at the colonel's scar. But indeed an officer need have been very young in his profession not to have heard the legendary tale of that duel originating in a mysterious, unforgivable offence.

III

THE retreat from Moscow submerged all private feelings in a sea of disaster and misery.

Colonels without regiments, D'Hubert and Feraud carried the musket in the ranks of the so-called sacred battalion*—a battalion recruited from officers of all arms who had no longer any troops to lead.

In that battalion promoted colonels did duty as sergeants; the generals captained the companies; a marshal of France, Prince of the Empire,* commanded the whole. All had provided themselves with muskets picked up on the road, and with cartridges taken from the dead. In the general destruction of the bonds of discipline and duty holding together the companies, the battalions, the regiments, the brigades, and divisions of an armed host, this body of men put its pride in preserving some semblance of order and formation. The only stragglers were those who fell out to give up to the frost their exhausted souls. They plodded on, and their passage did not disturb the mortal silence of the plains, shining with the livid light of snows under a sky the colour of ashes. Whirlwinds ran along the fields, broke against the dark column, enveloped it in a turmoil of flying icicles, and subsided, disclosing it creeping on its tragic way without the swing and rhythm of the military pace. It struggled onwards, the men exchanging neither words nor looks; whole ranks marched touching elbow, day after day and never raising their eyes from the ground, as if lost in despairing reflections. In the dumb, black forests of pines the cracking of overloaded branches was the only sound they heard. Often from daybreak to dusk no one spoke in the whole column. It was like a *macabre* march* of struggling corpses towards a distant grave. Only an alarm of Cossacks* could restore to their eyes a semblance of martial resolution. The battalion faced about and deployed, or formed square under the endless fluttering of snowflakes. A cloud of horsemen with fur caps on their heads, levelled long lances, and yelled "Hurrah! Hurrah!" around their menacing immobility whence, with muffled detonations, hundreds of dark red flames darted through the air thick with falling snow. In a very few moments the horsemen would disappear, as if carried off yelling in the gale, and the sacred battalion standing still, alone in the blizzard, heard only the howling of the wind, whose blasts searched their very hearts. Then, with a cry or two of *Vive l'Empereur!* it would resume its march, leaving behind a few lifeless bodies lying huddled up, tiny black specks on the white immensity of the snows.*

Though often marching in the ranks, or skirmishing in the woods side by side, the two officers ignored each other; this not so much from inimical intention as from a very real indifference. All their store of moral energy was expended in resisting the terrific enmity of nature and the crushing sense of irretrievable disaster. To the last they counted among the most active, the least demoralized of the battalion; their vigorous vitality invested them both with the appearance of an heroic pair in the eyes of their comrades. And they never exchanged more than a casual word or two, except one day, when skirmishing in front of the battalion against a worrying attack of cavalry, they found themselves cut off in the woods* by a small party of Cossacks. A score of fur-capped, hairy horsemen rode to and fro, brandishing their lances in ominous silence; but the two officers had no mind to lay down their arms, and Colonel Feraud suddenly spoke up in a hoarse, growling voice, bringing his firelock to the shoulder. "You take the nearest brute, Colonel D'Hubert; I'll settle the next one. I am a better shot than you are."

Colonel D'Hubert nodded over his levelled musket. Their shoulders were pressed against the trunk of a large tree; on their front enormous snowdrifts protected them from a direct charge. Two carefully aimed shots rang out in the frosty air, two Cossacks reeled in their saddles. The rest, not thinking the game good enough, closed round their wounded comrades and galloped away out of range. The two officers managed to rejoin their battalion halted for the night. During that afternoon they had leaned upon each other more than once, and towards the end, Colonel D'Hubert, whose long legs gave him an advantage in walking through soft snow, peremptorily took the musket of Colonel Feraud from him and carried it on his shoulder, using his own as a staff.

On the outskirts of a village half buried in the snow an old wooden barn burned with a clear and an immense flame. The sacred battalion of skeletons, muffled in rags, crowded greedily the windward side, stretching hundreds of numbed, bony hands to the blaze. Nobody had noted their approach. Before entering the circle of light playing on the sunken, glassy-eyed, starved faces, Colonel D'Hubert spoke in his turn:

"Here's your musket, Colonel Feraud. I can walk better than you."

Colonel Feraud nodded, and pushed on towards the warmth of the fierce flames. Colonel D'Hubert was more deliberate, but not the less bent on getting a place in the front rank. Those they shouldered aside tried to greet with a faint cheer the reappearance of the two indomitable companions in activity and endurance. Those manly qualities had never perhaps received a higher tribute than this feeble acclamation.

This is the faithful record of speeches exchanged during the retreat from Moscow by Colonels Feraud and D'Hubert. Colonel Feraud's taciturnity was the outcome of concentrated rage. Short, hairy, black faced, with layers of grime and the thick sprouting of a wiry beard, a frost-bitten hand wrapped up in filthy rags carried in a sling, he accused fate of unparalleled perfidy towards the sublime Man of Destiny.* Colonel D'Hubert, his long moustaches pendent in icicles on each side of his cracked blue lips, his eyelids inflamed with the glare of snows, the principal part of his costume consisting of a sheep-skin coat looted with difficulty from the frozen corpse of a camp fol-lower found in an abandoned cart, took a more thoughtful view of events. His regularly handsome features, now reduced to mere bony lines and fleshless hollows, looked out of a woman's black velvet hood, over which was rammed forcibly a cocked hat picked up under the wheels of an empty army fourgon,* which must have contained at one time some general officer's luggage. The sheepskin coat being short for a man of his inches ended very high up, and the skin of his legs, blue with the cold, showed through the tatters of his nether garments. This under the circumstances provoked neither jeers nor pity. No one cared how the next man felt or looked. Colonel D'Hubert himself, hardened to exposure, suffered mainly in his self-respect from the lamentable indecency of his costume. A thoughtless person may think that with a whole host of inanimate bodies bestrewing the path of retreat there could not have been much difficulty in supplying the deficiency. But to loot a pair of breeches from a frozen corpse is not so easy as it may appear to a mere theorist. It requires time and labour. You must remain behind while your companions march on. Colonel D'Hubert had his scruples as to falling out.* Once he had stepped aside he could not be sure of ever rejoining his battalion;* and the ghastly intimacy of a wrestling match with the frozen dead opposing the unyielding rigidity of iron to your violence was repugnant to the delicacy of his feelings. Luckily, one day, grubbing in a mound of snow between the huts of a village in the hope of finding there a frozen potato or some vegetable garbage he could put between his long and shaky teeth, Colonel D'Hubert uncovered a couple of mats of the sort Russian peasants use to line the sides of their carts with. These, beaten free of frozen snow, bent about his elegant person and fastened solidly round his waist, made a bell-shaped nether garment, a sort of stiff petticoat, which rendered Colonel D'Hubert a perfectly decent, but a much more noticeable figure than before.

Thus accoutred, he continued to retreat, never doubting of his personal escape, but full of other misgivings. The early buoyancy of his belief in the future was destroyed. If the road of glory led through such unforeseen passages, he asked himself—for he was reflective—whether the guide was altogether trustworthy. It was a patriotic sadness, not unmingled with some personal concern, and quite unlike the unreasoning indignation against men and things nursed by Colonel Feraud. Recruiting his strength in a little German town for three weeks, Colonel D'Hubert was surprised to discover within himself a love of repose. His returning vigour was strangely pacific in its aspirations. He meditated silently upon this bizarre change of mood. No doubt many of his brother officers of field rank went through the same moral experience. But these were not the times to talk of it. In one of his letters home Colonel D'Hubert wrote, "All your plans, my dear Léonie, for marrying me to the charming girl you have discovered in your neighbourhood, seem farther off than ever. Peace is not yet. Europe wants another lesson. It will be a hard task for us, but it shall be done, because the Emperor is invincible."

Thus wrote Colonel D'Hubert from Pomerania* to his married sister Léonie, settled in the south of France. And so far the sentiments expressed would not have been disowned by Colonel Feraud, who wrote no letters to anybody, whose father had been in life an illiterate blacksmith, who had no sister or brother, and whom no one desired ardently to pair off for a life of peace with a charming young girl. But Colonel D'Hubert's letter contained also some philosophical generalities upon the uncertainty of all personal hopes, when bound up entirely with the prestigious fortune of one incomparably great it is true, yet still remaining but a man in his greatness. This view would have appeared rank heresy to Colonel Feraud. Some melancholy forebodings of a military kind, expressed cautiously, would have been pronounced as nothing short of high treason by Colonel

Feraud. But Léonie, the sister of Colonel D'Hubert, read them with profound satisfaction, and, folding the letter thoughtfully, remarked to herself that "Armand was likely to prove eventually a sensible fellow." Since her marriage into a Southern family she had become a convinced believer in the return of the legitimate king.* Hopeful and anxious she offered prayers night and morning, and burnt candles in churches for the safety and prosperity of her brother.

She had every reason to suppose that her prayers were heard. Colonel D'Hubert passed through Lutzen, Bautzen, and Leipsic* losing no limb, and acquiring additional reputation. Adapting his conduct to the needs of that desperate time, he had never voiced his misgivings. He concealed them under a cheerful courtesy of such pleasant character that people were inclined to ask themselves with wonder whether Colonel D'Hubert was aware of any disasters. Not only his manners, but even his glances remained untroubled. The steady amenity of his blue eyes disconcerted all grumblers, and made despair itself pause.

This bearing was remarked favourably by the Emperor himself; for Colonel D'Hubert, attached now to the Major-General's staff, came on several occasions under the imperial eye. But it exasperated the higher strung nature of Colonel Feraud. Passing through Magdeburg* on service, this last allowed himself, while seated gloomily at dinner with the *Commandant de Place*,* to say of his life-long adversary: "This man does not love the Emperor," and his words were received by the other guests in profound silence. Colonel Feraud, troubled in his conscience at the atrocity of the aspersion, felt the need to back it up by a good argument. "I ought to know him," he cried, adding some oaths. "One studies one's adversary. I have met him on the ground half a dozen times, as all the army knows. What more do you want? If that isn't opportunity enough for any fool to size up his man, may the devil take me if I can tell what is." And he looked around the table, obstinate and sombre.

Later on in Paris, while extremely busy reorganizing his regiment, Colonel Feraud learned that Colonel D'Hubert had been made a general. He glared at his informant incredulously, then folded his arms and turned away muttering, "Nothing surprises me on the part of that man."

And aloud he added, speaking over his shoulder, "You would oblige me greatly by telling General D'Hubert at the first opportunity that his advancement saves him for a time from a pretty hot encounter. I was only waiting for him to turn up here."

The other officer remonstrated.

"Could you think of it, Colonel Feraud, at this time, when every life should be consecrated to the glory and safety of France?"

But the strain of unhappiness caused by military reverses had spoiled Colonel Feraud's character. Like many other men, he was rendered wicked by misfortune.

"I cannot consider General D'Hubert's existence of any account either for the glory or safety of France," he snapped viciously. "You don't pretend, perhaps, to know him better than I do—I who have met him half a dozen times on the ground—do you?"

His interlocutor, a young man, was silenced. Colonel Feraud walked up and down the room.

"This is not the time to mince matters," he said. "I can't believe that that man ever loved the Emperor. He picked up his general's stars under the boots of Marshal Berthier.* Very well. I'll get mine in another fashion, and then we shall settle this business which has been dragging on too long."

General D'Hubert, informed indirectly of Colonel Feraud's attitude, made a gesture as if to put aside an importunate person. His thoughts were solicited by graver cares. He had had no time to go and see his family. His sister, whose royalist hopes were rising higher every day, though proud of her brother, regretted his recent advancement in a measure, because it put on him a prominent mark of the usurper's favour, which later on could have an adverse influence upon his career. He wrote to her that no one but an inveterate enemy could say he had got his promotion by favour. As to his career, he assured her that he looked no farther forward into the future than the next battlefield.

Beginning the campaign of France in this dogged spirit, General D'Hubert was wounded on the second day of the battle under Laon.* While being carried off the field he heard that Colonel Feraud, promoted this moment to general,* had been sent to replace him at the head of his brigade. He cursed his luck impulsively, not being able at the first glance to discern all the advantages of a nasty wound. And yet it was by this heroic method that Providence was shaping his future. Travelling slowly south to his sister's country home under the care of a trusty old servant, General D'Hubert was spared the humiliating contacts and the perplexities of conduct which assailed the men of Napoleonic empire at the moment of its downfall. Lying in his bed, with the windows of his room open wide to the sunshine of Provence,* he perceived the undisguised aspect of the blessing conveyed by that jagged fragment of a Prussian shell, which, killing his horse and ripping open his thigh, saved him from an active conflict with his conscience. After the last fourteen years spent sword in hand in the saddle, and with the sense of his duty done to the very end, General D'Hubert found resignation an easy virtue. His sister was delighted with his reasonableness. "I leave myself altogether in your hands, my dear Léonie," he had said to her.

He was still laid up when, the credit of his brother-in-law's family being exerted on his behalf, he received from the royal government not only the confirmation of his rank, but the assurance of being retained on the active list. To this was added an unlimited convalescent leave. The unfavourable opinion entertained of him in Bonapartist circles, though it rested on nothing more solid than the unsupported pronouncement of General Feraud, was directly responsible for General D'Hubert's retention on the active list. As to General Feraud, his rank was confirmed, too. It was more than he dared to expect; but Marshal Soult, then Minister of War to the restored king, was partial to officers who had served in Spain.* Only not even the marshal's protection could secure for him active employment. He remained irreconcilable, idle, and sinister. He sought in obscure restaurants the company of other half-pay officers who cherished dingy but glorious old tricolour cockades in their breast-pockets, and buttoned with the forbidden eagle buttons* their shabby uniforms, declaring themselves too poor to afford the expense of the prescribed change.

The triumphant return from Elba,* an historical fact as marvellous and incredible as the exploits of some mythological demi-god, found General D'Hubert still quite unable to sit a horse. Neither could he walk very well. These disabilities, which Madame Léonie accounted most lucky, helped to keep her brother out of all possible mischief. His frame of mind at that time, she noted with dismay, became very far from reasonable. This general officer, still menaced by the loss of a limb, was discovered one night in the stables of the chateau by a groom, who, seeing a light, raised an alarm of thieves. His crutch was lying half-buried in the straw of the litter, and the general was hopping on one leg in a loose box around a snorting horse he was trying to saddle. Such were the effects of imperial magic upon a calm temperament and a pondered mind. Beset in the light of stable lanterns, by the tears, entreaties, indignation, remonstrances and reproaches of his family, he got out of the difficult situation by fainting away there and then in the arms of his nearest relatives, and was carried off to bed. Before he got out of it again, the second reign of Napoleon, the Hundred Days* of feverish agitation and supreme effort, passed away like a terrifying dream. The tragic year 1815, begun in the trouble and unrest of consciences, was ending in vengeful proscriptions.

How General Feraud escaped the clutches of the Special Commission and the last offices of a firing squad* he never knew himself. It was partly due to the subordinate position he was assigned during the Hundred Days. The Emperor had never given him active command, but had kept him busy at the cavalry depot in Paris, mounting and despatching hastily drilled troopers into the field. Considering this task as unworthy of his abilities, he had discharged it with no offensively noticeable zeal; but for the greater part he was saved from the excesses of Royalist reaction by the interference of General D'Hubert.

This last, still on convalescent leave, but able now to travel, had been despatched by his sister to Paris to present himself to his legitimate sovereign. As no one in the capital could possibly know anything of the episode in the stable he was received there with distinction. Military to the very bottom of his soul, the prospect of rising in his profession consoled him from finding himself the butt of Bonapartist malevolence, which pursued him with a persistence he could not account for. All the rancour of that embittered and persecuted party pointed to him as the man who had never loved the Emperor—a sort of monster essentially worse than a mere betrayer.

General D'Hubert shrugged his shoulders without anger at this ferocious prejudice. Rejected by his old friends, and mistrusting profoundly the advances of Royalist society, the young and handsome general (he was barely forty) adopted a manner of cold, punctilious courtesy, which at the merest shadow of an intended slight passed easily into harsh haughtiness. Thus prepared, General D'Hubert went about his affairs in Paris feeling inwardly very happy with the peculiar uplifting happiness of a man very much in love. The charming girl looked out by his sister had come upon the scene, and had conquered him in the thorough manner in which a young girl by merely existing in his sight can make a man of forty her own. They were going to be married as soon as General D'Hubert had obtained his official nomination to a promised command.

One afternoon, sitting on the *terrasse* of the *Café Tortoni*,* General D'Hubert learned from the conversation of two strangers occupying a table near his own, that General Feraud, included in the batch of superior officers arrested after the second return of the king, was in danger of passing before the Special Commission. Living all his spare moments, as is frequently the case with expectant lovers, a day in advance of reality, and in a state of bestarred hallucination, it required nothing less than the name of his perpetual antagonist pronounced in a loud voice to call the youngest of Napoleon's generals away from the mental contemplation of his betrothed. He looked round. The strangers wore civilian clothes. Lean and weather-beaten, lolling back in their chairs, they scowled at people with moody and defiant abstraction from under their hats pulled low over their eyes. It was not difficult to recognize them for two of the compulsorily retired officers of the Old Guard. As from bravado or carelessness they chose to speak in loud tones, General D'Hubert, who saw no reason why he should change his seat, heard every word. They did not seem to be the personal friends of General Feraud. His name came up amongst others. Hearing it repeated, General D'Hubert's tender anticipations of a domestic future adorned with a woman's grace were traversed by the harsh regret of his warlike past, of that one long, intoxicating clash of arms, unique in the magnitude of its glory and disaster—the marvellous work and the special possession of his own generation. He felt an irrational tenderness towards his old adversary and appreciated emotionally the murderous absurdity their encounter had introduced into his life. It was like an additional pinch of spice in a hot dish. He remembered the flavour with sudden melancholy. He would never taste it again. It was all over. "I fancy it was being left lying in the garden that had exasperated him so against me from the first," he thought, indulgently.

The two strangers at the next table had fallen silent after the third mention of General Feraud's name. Presently the elder of the two, speaking again in a bitter tone, affirmed that General Feraud's account was settled. And why? Simply because he was not like some bigwigs who loved only themselves. The Royalists knew they could never make anything of him. He loved *The Other* too well.

The Other was the Man of St. Helena.* The two officers nodded and touched glasses before they drank to an impossible return. Then the same who had spoken before, remarked with a sardonic laugh, "His adversary showed more cleverness."

"What adversary?" asked the younger, as if puzzled.

"Don't you know? They were two hussars. At each promotion they fought a duel. Haven't you heard of the duel going on ever since 1801?"

The other had heard of the duel, of course. Now he understood the allusion. General Baron D'Hubert would be able now to enjoy his fat king's favour in peace.

"Much good may it do to him," mumbled the elder. "They were both brave men. I never saw this D'Hubert—a sort of intriguing dandy, I am told. But I can well believe what I've heard Feraud say of him—that he *never* loved the Emperor."

They rose and went away.

General D'Hubert experienced the horror of a somnambulist who wakes up from a complacent dream of activity to find himself walking on a quagmire. A profound disgust of the ground on which he was making his way overcame him. Even the image of the charming girl was swept from his view in the flood of moral distress. Everything he had ever been or hoped to be would taste of bitter ignominy unless he could manage to save General Feraud from the fate which threatened so many braves. Under the impulse of this almost morbid need to attend to the safety of his adversary, General D'Hubert worked so well with hands and feet (as the French saying* is), that in less than twenty-four hours he found means of obtaining an extraordinary private audience from the Minister of Police.

General Baron D'Hubert was shown in suddenly without preliminaries. In the dusk of the Minister's cabinet,* behind the forms of writing-desk, chairs, and tables, between two bunches of wax candles blazing in sconces, he beheld a figure in a gorgeous coat posturing before a tall mirror. The old *conventionnel* Fouché,* Senator of the Empire, traitor to every man, to every principle and motive of human conduct, Duke of Otranto, and the wily artizan of the second Restoration,* was trying the fit of a court suit in which his young and accomplished *fiancée** had declared her intention to have his portrait painted on porcelain. It was a caprice, a charming fancy which the first Minister of Police of the second Restoration was anxious to gratify. For that man, often compared in wiliness of conduct to a fox, but whose ethical side could be worthily symbolized by nothing less emphatic than a skunk, was as much possessed by his love as General D'Hubert himself.

Startled to be discovered thus by the blunder of a servant, he met this little vexation with the characteristic impudence which had served his turn so well in the endless intrigues of his self-seeking career. Without altering his attitude a hair's-breadth, one leg in a silk stocking advanced, his head twisted over his left shoulder, he called out calmly, "This way, General. Pray approach. Well? I am all attention."

While General D'Hubert, ill at ease as if one of his own little weaknesses had been exposed, presented his request as shortly as possible, the Duke of Otranto went on feeling the fit of his collar, settling the lapels before the glass, and buckling his back in an effort to behold the set of the gold embroidered coat-skirts behind. His still face, his attentive eyes, could not have expressed a more complete interest in those matters if he had been alone.

"Exclude from the operations of the Special Court a certain Feraud, Gabriel Florian, General of brigade of the promotion of 1814?" he repeated, in a slightly wondering tone, and then turned away from the glass. "Why exclude *him* precisely?"

"I am surprised that your Excellency, so competent in the evaluation of men of his time, should have thought worth while to have that name put down on the list."

"A rabid Bonapartist!"

"So is every grenadier and every trooper of the army,* as your Excellency well knows. And the individuality of General Feraud can have no more weight than that of any casual grenadier. He is a man of no mental grasp, of no capacity whatever. It is inconceivable that he should ever have any influence."

"He has a well-hung tongue,* though," interjected Fouché.

"Noisy, I admit, but not dangerous."

"I will not dispute with you. I know next to nothing of him. Hardly his name, in fact."

"And yet your Excellency has the presidency of the Commission charged by the king to point out those who were to be tried," said General D'Hubert, with an emphasis which did not miss the minister's ear.

"Yes, General," he said, walking away into the dark part of the vast room, and throwing himself into a deep arm-chair that swallowed him up, all but the soft gleam of gold embroideries and the pallid patch of the face—"yes, General. Take this chair there."

General D'Hubert sat down.

"Yes, General," continued the arch-master in the arts of intrigue and betrayals, whose duplicity, as if at times intolerable to his self-knowledge, found relief in bursts of cynical openness. "I did hurry on the formation of the proscribing Commission, and I took its presidency. And do you know why? Simply from fear that if I did not take it quickly into my hands my own name would head the list of the proscribed. Such are the times in which we live. But I am minister of the king yet, and I ask you plainly why I should take the name of this obscure Feraud off the list? You wonder how his name got there! Is it possible that you should know men so little? My dear General, at the very first sitting of the Commission names poured on us like rain off the roof of the Tuileries.* Names! We had our choice of thousands. How do you know that the name of this Feraud, whose life or death don't matter to France, does not keep out some other name?"

The voice out of the arm-chair stopped. Opposite General D'Hubert sat still, shadowy and silent. Only his sabre clinked slightly. The voice in the arm-chair began again. "And we must try to satisfy the exigencies of the Allied Sovereigns, too. The Prince de Talleyrand told me only yesterday that Nesselrode had informed him officially of His Majesty the Emperor Alexander's* dissatisfaction at the small number of examples the Government of the king intends to make—especially amongst military men. I tell you this confidentially."

"Upon my word!" broke out General D'Hubert, speaking through his teeth, "if your Excellency deigns to favour me with any more confidential information I don't know what I will do. It's enough to break one's sword over one's knee, and fling the pieces. . . ."

"What government you imagined yourself to be serving?"* interrupted the minister, sharply.

After a short pause the crestfallen voice of General D'Hubert answered, "The Government of France."

"That's paying your conscience off with mere words, General. The truth is that you are serving a government of returned exiles, of men who have been without country for twenty years. Of men also who

have just got over a very bad and humiliating fright. . . . Have no
illusions on that score."

The Duke of Otranto ceased. He had relieved himself, and had
attained his object of stripping some self-respect off that man who
had inconveniently discovered him posturing in a gold-embroidered
court costume before a mirror. But they were a hot-headed lot in the
army; it occurred to him that it would be inconvenient if a well-
disposed general officer, received in audience on the recommendation
of one of the Princes, were to do something rashly scandalous directly
after a private interview with the minister. In a changed tone he put
a question to the point: "Your relation—this Feraud?"

"No. No relation at all."

"Intimate friend?"

"Intimate . . . yes. There is between us an intimate connection of
a nature which makes it a point of honour with me to try . . ."

The minister rang a bell without waiting for the end of the phrase.
When the servant had gone out, after bringing in a pair of heavy silver
candelabra for the writing-desk, the Duke of Otranto rose, his breast
glistening all over with gold in the strong light, and taking a piece of
paper out of a drawer, held it in his hand ostentatiously while he said
with persuasive gentleness: "You must not speak of breaking your
sword across your knee, General. Perhaps you would never get
another. The Emperor will not return this time. . . . *Diable d'homme!**
There was just a moment, here in Paris, soon after Waterloo,* when
he frightened me. It looked as though he were ready to begin all over
again. Luckily one never does begin all over again, really. You must
not think of breaking your sword, General."

General D'Hubert, looking on the ground, moved slightly his
hand in a hopeless gesture of renunciation. The Minister of Police
turned his eyes away from him, and scanned deliberately the paper he
had been holding up all the time.

"There are only twenty general officers selected to be made an
example of. Twenty. A round number. And let's see, Feraud. . . . Ah,
he's there. Gabriel Florian. *Parfaitement.** That's your man. Well,
there will be only nineteen examples made now."

General D'Hubert stood up feeling as though he had gone through
an infectious illness. "I must beg your Excellency to keep my interference a profound secret. I attach the greatest importance to his never
learning . . ."

"Who is going to inform him, I should like to know?" said Fouché, raising his eyes curiously to General D'Hubert's tense, set face. "Take one of these pens, and run it through the name yourself. This is the only list in existence. If you are careful to take up enough ink no one will be able to tell what was the name struck out. But, *par exemple*,* I am not responsible for what Clarke* will do with him afterwards. If he persists in being rabid he will be ordered by the Minister of War to reside in some provincial town under the supervision of the police."

A few days later General D'Hubert was saying to his sister, after the first greetings had been got over: "Ah, my dear Léonie! it seemed to me I couldn't get away from Paris quick enough."

"Effect of love," she suggested, with a malicious smile.

"And horror," added General D'Hubert, with profound seriousness. "I have nearly died there of . . . of nausea."

His face was contracted with disgust. And as his sister looked at him attentively he continued, "I have had to see Fouché. I have had an audience. I have been in his cabinet. There remains with one, who had the misfortune to breathe the air of the same room with that man, a sense of diminished dignity, an uneasy feeling of being not so clean, after all, as one hoped one was. . . . But you can't understand."

She nodded quickly several times. She understood very well, on the contrary. She knew her brother thoroughly, and liked him as he was. Moreover, the scorn and loathing of mankind were the lot of the *Jacobin** Fouché, who, exploiting for his own advantage every weakness, every virtue, every generous illusion of mankind, made dupes of his whole generation, and died obscurely as Duke of Otranto.

"My dear Armand," she said, compassionately, "what could you want from that man?"

"Nothing less than a life," answered General D'Hubert. "And I've got it. It had to be done. But I feel yet as if I could never forgive the necessity to the man I had to save."

General Feraud, totally unable (as is the case with most of us) to comprehend what was happening to him, received the Minister of War's order to proceed at once to a small town of Central France with feelings whose natural expression consisted in a fierce rolling of the eye and savage grinding of the teeth. The passing away of the state of war, the only condition of society he had ever known, the horrible view of a world at peace, frightened him. He went away to his little town firmly convinced that this could not last. There he was informed of his retirement from the army, and that his pension (calculated on the scale of a colonel's rank) was made dependent on the correctness of his conduct, and on the good reports of the police. No longer in the army! He felt suddenly strange to the earth, like a disembodied spirit. It was impossible to exist. But at first he reacted from sheer incredulity. This could not be. He waited for thunder, earthquakes, natural cataclysms; but nothing happened. The leaden weight of an irremediable idleness descended upon General Feraud, who having no resources within himself sank into a state of awe-inspiring hebetude. He haunted the streets of the little town, gazing before him with lacklustre eyes, disregarding the hats raised on his passage; and people, nudging each other as he went by, whispered, "That's poor General Feraud. His heart is broken. Behold how he loved the Emperor."

The other living wreckage of Napoleonic tempest clustered round General Feraud with infinite respect. He, himself, imagined his soul to be crushed by grief. He suffered from quickly succeeding impulses to weep, to howl, to bite his fists till blood came, to spend days on his bed with his head thrust under the pillow; but these arose from sheer ennui, from the anguish of an immense, indescribable, inconceivable boredom. His mental inability to grasp the hopeless nature of his case as a whole saved him from suicide. He never even thought of it once. He thought of nothing. But his appetite abandoned him, and the difficulty he experienced to express the overwhelming nature of his feelings (the most furious swearing could do no justice to it) induced gradually a habit of silence—a sort of death to a southern temperament.

Great, therefore, was the sensation amongst the *anciens militaires**
frequenting a certain little café; full of flies when one stuffy afternoon "that poor General Feraud" let out suddenly a volley of formidable curses.

He had been sitting quietly in his own privileged corner looking through the Paris gazettes with just as much interest as a condemned man on the eve of execution could be expected to show in the news of the day. A cluster of martial, bronzed faces, amongst which there was one lacking an eye, and another the tip of a nose frost-bitten in Russia, surrounded him anxiously.

"What's the matter, General?"

General Feraud sat erect, holding the folded newspaper at arm's length in order to make out the small print better. He read to himself, over again, fragments of the intelligence which had caused, what may be called, his resurrection.

"We are informed that General D'Hubard, till now on sick leave in the south, is to be called to the command of the 5ᵗʰ Cavalry brigade in . . ."

He dropped the paper stonily. . . . "Called to the command!" . . . and suddenly gave his forehead a mighty slap. "I had almost forgotten him," he muttered in a conscience-stricken voice.

A deep-chested veteran shouted across the café, "Some new villainy of the Government, General?"

"The villainies of these scoundrels," thundered General Feraud, "are innumerable. One more one less!" He lowered his tone. "But I will set good order to one of them at least."

He looked all round the faces. "There's a pomaded, curled staff-officer, the darling of some of the marshals who sold their father for a handful of English gold. He will find out presently that I am alive yet," he declared in a dogmatic tone. "However, this is a private affair. An old affair of honour. Bah! Our honour does not matter. Here we are driven off with a split ear like a lot of cast troop horses—good only for a knacker's yard. But it would be like striking a blow for the Emperor. . . . Messieurs, I shall require the assistance of two of you."

Every man moved forward. General Feraud, deeply touched by this demonstration, called with visible emotion upon the one-eyed veteran cuirassier and the officer of the Chasseurs à Cheval* who had left the tip of his nose in Russia. He excused his choice to the others.

"A cavalry affair this—you know."

He was answered with a varied chorus of *"Parfaitement, mon Général. . . . C'est juste. . . . Parbleu, c'est connu. . . ."* Everybody was satisfied. The three left the café together, followed by cries of *"Bonne chance."**

Outside they linked arms, the general in the middle. The three rusty cocked hats worn *en bataille** with a sinister forward slant barred the narrow street nearly right across. The overheated little town of grey stones and red tiles was drowsing away its provincial afternoon under a blue sky. The loud blows of a cooper hooping a cask reverberated regularly between the houses. The general dragged his left foot a little in the shade of the walls.

"This damned winter of 1813* has got into my bones for good. Never mind. We must take pistols, that's all. A little lumbago. We must have pistols. He's game for my bag. My eyes are as keen as ever.

You should have seen me in Russia picking off the dodging Cossacks with a beastly old infantry musket. I have a natural gift for firearms."

In this strain General Feraud ran on, holding up his head, with owlish eyes and rapacious beak. A mere fighter all his life, a cavalry man, a *sabreur*,* he conceived war with the utmost simplicity, as, in the main, a massed lot of personal contests, a sort of gregarious duelling. And here he had in hand a war of his own. He revived. The shadow of peace passed away from him like the shadow of death. It was the marvellous resurrection of the named Feraud, Gabriel Florian, *engagé volontaire** of 1793, General of 1814, buried without ceremony by means of a service order signed by the War Minister of the Second Restoration.

IV

No man succeeds in everything he undertakes. In that sense we are all failures. The great point is not to fail in ordering and sustaining the effort of our life. In this matter vanity is what leads us astray. It hurries us into situations from which we must come out damaged; whereas pride is our safeguard, by the reserve it imposes on the choice of our endeavour as much as by the virtue of its sustaining power.

General D'Hubert was proud and reserved. He had not been damaged by his casual love affairs, successful or otherwise. In his war-scarred body his heart at forty remained unscratched. Entering with reserve into his sister's matrimonial plans, he had felt himself falling irremediably in love as one falls off a roof. He was too proud to be frightened. Indeed, the sensation was too delightful to be alarming.

The inexperience of a man of forty is a much more serious thing than the inexperience of a youth of twenty, for it is not helped out by the rashness of hot blood. The girl was mysterious, as young girls are by the mere effect of their guarded ingenuity;* and to him the mysteriousness of that young girl appeared exceptional and fascinating. But there was nothing mysterious about the arrangements of the match which Madame Léonie had promoted. There was nothing peculiar, either. It was a very appropriate match, commending itself extremely to the young lady's mother (the father was dead) and tolerable to the young lady's uncle—an old *émigré** lately returned from

Germany, and pervading, cane in hand, a lean ghost of the *ancien régime*,* the garden walks of the young lady's ancestral home.

General D'Hubert was not the man to be satisfied merely with the woman and the fortune—when it came to the point. His pride (and pride aims always at true success) would be satisfied with nothing short of love. But as true pride excludes vanity, he could not imagine any reason why this mysterious creature with deep and brilliant eyes of a violet colour should have any feeling for him warmer than indifference. The young lady (her name was Adèle) baffled every attempt at a clear understanding on that point. It is true that the attempts were clumsy and made timidly, because by then General D'Hubert had become acutely aware of the number of his years, of his wounds, of his many moral imperfections, of his secret unworthiness—and had incidentally learned by experience the meaning of the word funk. As far as he could make out she seemed to imply that, with an unbounded confidence in her mother's affection and sagacity, she felt no unsurmountable dislike for the person of General D'Hubert; and that this was quite sufficient for a well-brought-up young lady to begin married life upon. This view hurt and tormented the pride of General D'Hubert. And yet he asked himself, with a sort of sweet despair, what more could he expect? She had a quiet and luminous forehead. Her violet eyes laughed while the lines of her lips and chin remained composed in admirable gravity. All this was set off by such a glorious mass of fair hair, by a complexion so marvellous, by such a grace of expression, that General D'Hubert really never found the opportunity to examine with sufficient detachment the lofty exigencies of his pride. In fact, he became shy of that line of inquiry since it had led once or twice to a crisis of solitary passion in which it was borne upon him that he loved her enough to kill her rather than lose her. From such passages, not unknown to men of forty, he would come out broken, exhausted, remorseful, a little dismayed. He derived, however, considerable comfort from the quietist* practice of sitting now and then half the night by an open window and meditating upon the wonder of her existence, like a believer lost in the mystic contemplation of his faith.

It must not be supposed that all these variations of his inward state were made manifest to the world. General D'Hubert found no difficulty in appearing wreathed in smiles. Because, in fact, he was very happy. He followed the established rules of his condition, sending over flowers (from his sister's garden and hot-houses) early every morning, and a little later following himself to lunch with his intended, her mother, and her *émigré* uncle. The middle of the day was spent in strolling or sitting in the shade. A watchful deference, trembling on the verge of tenderness was the note of their intercourse on his side—with a playful turn of the phrase concealing the profound trouble of his whole being caused by her inaccessible nearness. Late in the afternoon General D'Hubert walked home between the fields of vines, sometimes intensely miserable, sometimes supremely happy, sometimes pensively sad; but always feeling a special intensity of existence, that elation common to artists, poets, and lovers—to men haunted by a great passion, a noble thought, or a new vision of plastic beauty.

The outward world at that time did not exist with any special distinctness for General D'Hubert. One evening, however, crossing a ridge from which he could see both houses, General D'Hubert became aware of two figures far down the road. The day had been divine. The festal decoration of the inflamed sky lent a gentle glow to the sober tints of the southern land. The grey rocks, the brown fields, the purple, undulating distances harmonized in luminous accord, exhaled already the scents of the evening. The two figures down the road presented themselves like two rigid and wooden silhouettes all black on the ribbon of white dust. General D'Hubert made out the long, straight, military *capotes** buttoned closely right up to the black stocks,* the cocked hats,* the lean, carven, brown countenances—old soldiers—*vieilles moustaches!** The taller of the two had a black patch over one eye; the other's hard, dry countenance presented some bizarre, disquieting peculiarity, which on nearer approach proved to be the absence of the tip of the nose. Lifting their hands with one movement to salute the slightly lame civilian walking with a thick stick, they inquired for the house where the General Baron D'Hubert lived, and what was the best way to get speech with him quietly.

"If you think this quiet enough," said General D'Hubert, looking round at the vine-fields, framed in purple lines, and dominated by the nest of grey and drab walls of a village clustering around the top of a conical hill, so that the blunt church tower seemed but the shape of a crowning rock—"if you think this spot quiet enough, you can speak to him at once. And I beg you, comrades, to speak openly, with perfect confidence."

They stepped back at this, and raised again their hands to their hats with marked ceremoniousness. Then the one with the chipped nose, speaking for both, remarked that the matter was confidential enough, and to be arranged discreetly. Their general quarters were established in that village over there, where the infernal clodhoppers—damn their false, Royalist hearts!—looked remarkably cross-eyed at three unassuming military men. For the present he should only ask for the name of General D'Hubert's friends.

"What friends?" said the astonished General D'Hubert, completely off the track. "I am staying with my brother-in-law over there."

"Well, he will do for one," said the chipped veteran.

"We're the friends of General Feraud," interjected the other, who had kept silent till then, only glowering with his one eye at the man who had *never* loved the Emperor. That was something to look at. For even the gold-laced Judases* who had sold him to the English, the marshals and princes, had loved him at some time or other. But this man had *never* loved the Emperor. General Feraud had said so distinctly.

General D'Hubert felt an inward blow in his chest. For an infinitesimal fraction of a second it was as if the spinning of the earth had become perceptible with an awful, slight rustle in the eternal stillness of space. But this noise of blood in his ears passed off at once. Involuntarily he murmured, "Feraud! I had forgotten his existence."

"He's existing at present, very uncomfortably, it is true, in the infamous inn of that nest of savages up there," said the one-eyed cuirassier, drily. "We arrived in your parts an hour ago on post horses. He's awaiting our return with impatience. There is hurry, you know. The General has broken the ministerial order to obtain from you the satisfaction he's entitled to by the laws of honour, and naturally he's anxious to have it all over before the *gendarmerie** gets on his scent."

The other elucidated the idea a little further. "Get back on the quiet—you understand? Phitt! No one the wiser. We have broken out, too. Your friend the king would be glad to cut off our scurvy pittances at the first chance. It's a risk. But honour before everything."

General D'Hubert had recovered his powers of speech. "So you come here like this along the road to invite me to a throat-cutting match with that—that . . ." A laughing sort of rage took possession of him. "Ha! ha! ha! ha!"

His fists on his hips, he roared without restraint, while they stood before him lank and straight, as though they had been shot up with a snap through a trap door in the ground. Only four-and-twenty months ago the masters of Europe, they had already the air of antique ghosts, they seemed less substantial in their faded coats than their own narrow shadows falling so black across the white road: the military and grotesque shadows of twenty years of war and conquests. They had an outlandish appearance of two imperturbable bonzes* of the religion of the sword. And General D'Hubert, also one of the ex-masters of Europe, laughed at these serious phantoms standing in his way.

Said one, indicating the laughing General with a jerk of the head: "A merry companion, that."

"There are some of us that haven't smiled from the day *The Other* went away," remarked his comrade.

A violent impulse to set upon and beat those unsubstantial wraiths to the ground frightened General D'Hubert. He ceased laughing suddenly. His desire now was to get rid of them, to get them away from his sight quickly before he lost control of himself. He wondered at the fury he felt rising in his breast. But he had no time to look into that peculiarity just then.

"I understand your wish to be done with me as quickly as possible. Don't let us waste time in empty ceremonies. Do you see that wood there at the foot of that slope? Yes, the wood of pines. Let us meet there to-morrow at sunrise. I will bring with me my sword or my pistols, or both if you like."

The seconds of General Feraud looked at each other.

"Pistols, General,"* said the cuirassier.

"So be it. Au revoir—to-morrow morning. Till then let me advise you to keep close if you don't want the *gendarmerie* making inquiries about you before it gets dark. Strangers are rare in this part of the country."

They saluted in silence. General D'Hubert, turning his back on their retreating forms, stood still in the middle of the road for a long time, biting his lower lip and looking on the ground. Then he began to walk straight before him, thus retracing his steps till he found himself before the park gate of his intended's house. Dusk had fallen. Motionless he stared through the bars at the front of the house, gleaming clear beyond the thickets and trees. Footsteps scrunched on the gravel, and presently a tall stooping shape emerged from the lateral alley following the inner side of the park wall.

Le Chevalier de Valmassigue, uncle of the adorable Adèle, ex-brigadier in the army of the Princes, bookbinder in Altona, afterwards shoemaker* (with a great reputation for elegance in the fit of ladies' shoes) in another small German town, wore silk stockings on his lean shanks, low shoes with silver buckles, a brocaded waistcoat. A long-skirted coat, *à la française,* * covered loosely his thin, bowed back. A small three-cornered hat rested on a lot of powdered hair, tied in a queue.

"*Monsieur le Chevalier,*"* called General D'Hubert, softly.

"What? You here again, *mon ami?** Have you forgotten something?"

"By heavens! that's just it. I have forgotten something. I am come to tell you of it. No—outside. Behind this wall. It's too ghastly a thing to be let in at all where she lives."

The Chevalier came out at once with that benevolent resignation some old people display towards the fugue of youth.* Older by a quarter of a century than General D'Hubert, he looked upon him in the secret of his heart as a rather troublesome youngster in love. He had heard his enigmatical words very well, but attached no undue importance to what a mere man of forty so hard hit was likely to do or say. The turn of mind of the generation of Frenchmen grown up during the years of his exile was almost unintelligible to him. Their sentiments appeared to him unduly violent, lacking fineness and measure, their language needlessly exaggerated. He joined calmly the General on the road, and they made a few steps in silence, the General trying to master his agitation, and get proper control of his voice.

"It is perfectly true; I forgot something. I forgot till half an hour ago that I had an urgent affair of honour on my hands. It's incredible, but it is so!"

All was still for a moment. Then in the profound evening silence of the countryside the clear, aged voice of the Chevalier was heard trembling slightly: "Monsieur! That's an indignity."

It was his first thought. The girl born during his exile, the posthumous daughter of his poor brother murdered by a band of Jacobins, had grown since his return very dear to his old heart, which had been starving on mere memories of affection for so many years. "It is an inconceivable thing, I say! A man settles such affairs before he thinks of asking for a young girl's hand. Why! If you had forgotten for ten days longer, you would have been married before your memory returned to you. In my time men did not forget such things—nor yet what is due to the feelings of an innocent young woman. If I did not respect them myself, I would qualify your conduct in a way which you would not like."

General D'Hubert relieved himself frankly by a groan. "Don't let that consideration prevent you. You run no risk of offending her mortally."

But the old man paid no attention to this lover's nonsense. It's doubtful whether he even heard. "What is it?" he asked. "What's the nature of . . . ?"

"Call it a youthful folly, *Monsieur le Chevalier*. An inconceivable, incredible result of . . ." He stopped short. "He will never believe the story," he thought. "He will only think I am taking him for a fool, and get offended." General D'Hubert spoke up again: "Yes, originating in youthful folly, it has become . . ."

The Chevalier interrupted: "Well, then it must be arranged."

"Arranged?"

"Yes, no matter at what cost to your *amour propre*.* You should have remembered you were engaged. You forgot that, too, I suppose. And then you go and forget your quarrel. It's the most hopeless exhibition of levity I ever heard of."

"Good heavens, Monsieur! You don't imagine I have been picking up this quarrel last time I was in Paris, or anything of the sort, do you?"

"Eh! What matters the precise date of your insane conduct," exclaimed the Chevalier, testily. "The principal thing is to arrange it."

Noticing General D'Hubert getting restive and trying to place a word, the old *émigré* raised his hand, and added with dignity, "I've been a soldier, too. I would never dare suggest a doubtful step to the man whose name my niece is to bear. I tell you that *entre galants hommes** an affair can always be arranged."

"But *saperlotte,** Monsieur le Chevalier*, it's fifteen or sixteen years ago. I was a lieutenant of hussars then."

The old Chevalier seemed confounded by the vehemently despairing tone of this information. "You were a lieutenant of hussars sixteen years ago," he mumbled in a dazed manner.

"Why, yes! You did not suppose I was made a general in my cradle like a royal prince."

In the deepening purple twilight of the fields spread with vine leaves, backed by a low band of sombre crimson in the west, the voice of the old ex-officer in the army of the Princes sounded collected, punctiliously civil.

"Do I dream? Is this a pleasantry? Or am I to understand that you have been hatching an affair of honour for sixteen years?"

"It has clung to me for that length of time. That is my precise meaning. The quarrel itself is not to be explained easily. We met on the ground several times during that time, of course."

"What manners! What horrible perversion of manliness! Nothing can account for such inhumanity but the sanguinary madness of the Revolution which has tainted a whole generation," mused the returned *émigré* in a low tone. "Who's your adversary?" he asked a little louder.

"My adversary? His name is Feraud."

Shadowy in his *tricorne** and old-fashioned clothes, like a bowed, thin ghost of the *ancien régime*, the Chevalier voiced a ghostly memory. "I can remember the feud about little Sophie Derval, between Monsieur de Brissac, Captain in the Bodyguards, and d'Anjorrant* (not the pock-marked one, the other—the Beau d'Anjorrant, as they called him). They met three times in eighteen months in a most gallant manner. It was the fault of that little Sophie, too, who *would* keep on playing . . ."

"This is nothing of the kind," interrupted General D'Hubert. He laughed a little sardonically. "Not at all so simple," he added. "Nor yet half so reasonable," he finished, inaudibly, between his teeth, and ground them with rage.

After this sound nothing troubled the silence for a long time, till the Chevalier asked, without animation: "What is he—this Feraud?"

"Lieutenant of hussars, too—I mean, he's a general. A Gascon. Son of a blacksmith, I believe."

"There! I thought so. That Bonaparte had a special predilection for the *canaille*.* I don't mean this for you, D'Hubert. You are one of us, though you have served this usurper, who . . ."

"Let's leave him out of this," broke in General D'Hubert.

The Chevalier shrugged his peaked shoulders. "Feraud of sorts. Offspring of a blacksmith and some village troll. See what comes of mixing yourself up with that sort of people."

"You have made shoes yourself, Chevalier."

"Yes. But I am not the son of a shoemaker. Neither are you, Monsieur D'Hubert. You and I have something that your Bonaparte's princes, dukes, and marshals have not, because there's no power on earth that could give it to them," retorted the *émigré*, with the rising animation of a man who has got hold of a hopeful argument. "Those people don't exist—all these Ferauds. Feraud! What is Feraud? A *va-nu-pieds** disguised into a general by a Corsican adventurer masquerading as an emperor. There is no earthly reason for a D'Hubert to *s'encanailler** by a duel with a person of that sort. You can make your excuses to him perfectly well. And if the *manant** takes into his head to decline them, you may simply refuse to meet him."

"You say I may do that?"

"I do. With the clearest conscience."

"*Monsieur le Chevalier!* To what do you think you have returned from your emigration?"

This was said in such a startling tone that the old man raised sharply his bowed head, glimmering silvery white under the points of the little *tricorne*. For a time he made no sound.

"God knows!" he said at last, pointing with a slow and grave gesture at a tall roadside cross mounted on a block of stone, and stretching its arms of forged iron all black against the darkening red band in the sky—"God knows! If it were not for this emblem, which I remember seeing on this spot as a child, I would wonder to what we who remained faithful to God and our king have returned. The very voices of the people have changed."

"Yes, it is a changed France," said General D'Hubert. He seemed to have regained his calm. His tone was slightly ironic. "Therefore I cannot take your advice. Besides, how is one to refuse to be bitten by a dog that means to bite? It's impracticable. Take my word for it—Feraud isn't a man to be stayed by apologies or refusals. But there are other ways. I could, for instance, send a messenger with a word to the brigadier of the *gendarmerie* in Senlac.* He and his two friends are liable to arrest on my simple order. It would make some talk in the army, both the organized and the disbanded—especially the disbanded. All *canaille!* All once upon a time the companions in arms of Armand D'Hubert. But what need a D'Hubert care what people that don't exist may think? Or, better still, I might get my brother-in-law to send for the mayor of the village and give him a hint. No more would be needed to get the three 'brigands' set upon with flails and pitchforks and hunted into some nice, deep, wet ditch—and nobody the wiser! It has been done only ten miles from here to three poor devils of the disbanded Red Lancers of the Guard* going to their homes. What says your conscience, *Chevalier?* Can a D'Hubert do that thing to three men who do not exist?"

A few stars had come out on the blue obscurity, clear as crystal, of the sky. The dry, thin voice of the Chevalier spoke harshly: "Why are you telling me all this?"

The General seized the withered old hand with a strong grip. "Because I owe you my fullest confidence. Who could tell Adèle but you? You understand why I dare not trust my brother-in-law nor yet my own sister. *Chevalier!* I have been so near doing these things that I tremble yet. You don't know how terrible this duel appears to me. And there's no escape from it."

He murmured after a pause, "It's a fatality,"* dropped the Chevalier's passive hand, and said in his ordinary conversational voice, "I shall have to go without seconds. If it is my lot to remain on the ground, you at least will know all that can be made known of this affair."

The shadowy ghost of the *ancien régime* seemed to have become more bowed during the conversation. "How am I to keep an indifferent face this evening before these two women?" he groaned. "General! I find it very difficult to forgive you."

General D'Hubert made no answer.

"Is your cause good, at least?"

"I am innocent."

This time he seized the Chevalier's ghostly arm above the elbow, and gave it a mighty squeeze. "I must kill him!" he hissed, and opening his hand strode away down the road.

The delicate attentions of his adoring sister had secured for the General perfect liberty of movement in the house where he was a guest. He had even his own entrance through a small door in one corner of the orangery. Thus he was not exposed that evening to the necessity of dissembling his agitation before the calm ignorance of the other inmates. He was glad of it. It seemed to him that if he had to open his lips he would break out into horrible and aimless imprecations, start breaking furniture, smashing china and glass. From the moment he opened the private door and while ascending the twenty-eight steps of a winding staircase, giving access to the corridor on which his room opened, he went through a horrible and humiliating scene in which an infuriated madman with blood-shot eyes and a foaming mouth played inconceivable havoc with everything inanimate that may be found in a well-appointed dining-room. When he opened the door of his apartment the fit was over, and his bodily fatigue was so great that he had to catch at the backs of the chairs while crossing the room to reach a low and broad divan on which he let himself fall heavily. His moral prostration was still greater. That brutality of feeling which he had known only when charging the enemy, sabre in hand, amazed this man of forty, who did not recognize in it the instinctive fury of his menaced passion.* But in his mental and bodily exhaustion this passion got cleared, distilled, refined into a sentiment of melancholy despair at having, perhaps, to die before he had taught this beautiful girl to love him.

That night, General D'Hubert stretched out on his back with his hands over his eyes, or lying on his breast with his face buried in a cushion, made the full pilgrimage of emotions. Nauseating disgust at the absurdity of the situation,* doubt of his own fitness to conduct his existence, and mistrust of his best sentiments (for what the devil did he want to go to Fouché for?)—he knew them all in turn. "I am an idiot, neither more nor less," he thought—"A sensitive idiot. Because I overheard two men talking in a café. . . . I am an idiot afraid of lies—whereas in life it is only truth that matters."

Several times he got up and, walking in his socks in order not to be heard by anybody downstairs, drank all the water he could find in the dark. And he tasted the torments of jealousy, too. She would marry somebody else. His very soul writhed. The tenacity of that Feraud, the awful persistence of that imbecile brute, came to him with the tremendous force of a relentless destiny. General D'Hubert trembled as he put down the empty water ewer. "He will have me," he thought. General D'Hubert was tasting every emotion that life has to give. He had in his dry mouth the faint sickly flavour of fear, not the excusable fear before a young girl's candid and amused glance, but the fear of death and the honourable man's fear of cowardice.

But if true courage consists in going out to meet an odious danger from which our body, soul, and heart recoil together, General D'Hubert had the opportunity to practise it for the first time in his life. He had charged exultingly at batteries and at infantry squares, and ridden with messages through a hail of bullets without thinking anything about it. His business now was to sneak out unheard, at break of day, to an obscure and revolting death. General D'Hubert never hesitated. He carried two pistols in a leather bag which he slung over his shoulder. Before he had crossed the garden his mouth was dry again. He picked two oranges. It was only after shutting the gate after him that he felt a slight faintness.

He staggered on, disregarding it, and after going a few yards regained the command of his legs. In the colourless and pellucid dawn the wood of pines detached its columns of trunks and its dark green canopy very clearly against the rocks of the grey hillside. He kept his eyes fixed on it steadily, and sucked at an orange as he walked. That temperamental good-humoured coolness in the face of danger which had made him an officer liked by his men and appreciated by his superiors was gradually asserting itself. It was like going into battle. Arriving at the edge of the wood he sat down on a boulder, holding the other orange in his hand, and reproached himself for coming so ridiculously early on the ground. Before very long, however, he heard the swishing of bushes, footsteps on the hard ground, and the sounds of a disjointed, loud conversation. A voice somewhere behind him said boastfully, "He's game for my bag."

He thought to himself, "Here they are. What's this about game? Are they talking of me?" And becoming aware of the other orange in his hand, he thought further, "These are very good oranges. Léonie's own tree. I may just as well eat this orange now instead of flinging it away."

Emerging from a wilderness of rocks and bushes, General Feraud and his seconds discovered General D'Hubert engaged in peeling the orange. They stood still, waiting till he looked up. Then the seconds raised their hats, while General Feraud, putting his hands behind his back, walked aside a little way.

"I am compelled to ask one of you, messieurs, to act for me. I have brought no friends. Will you?"

The one-eyed cuirassier said judicially, "That cannot be refused."

The other veteran remarked, "It's awkward all the same."

"Owing to the state of the people's minds in this part of the country there was no one I could trust safely with the object of your presence here," explained General D'Hubert, urbanely.

They saluted, looked round, and remarked both together:

"Poor ground."

"It's unfit."

"Why bother about ground, measurements, and so on? Let us simplify matters. Load the two pairs of pistols. I will take those of General Feraud, and let him take mine. Or, better still, let us take a mixed pair. One of each pair. Then let us go into the wood and shoot at sight, while you remain outside. We did not come here for ceremonies, but for war—war to the death. Any ground is good enough for that. If I fall, you must leave me where I lie and clear out. It wouldn't be healthy for you to be found hanging about here after that."

It appeared after a short parley that General Feraud was willing to accept these conditions. While the seconds were loading the pistols, he could be heard whistling, and was seen to rub his hands with perfect contentment. He flung off his coat briskly, and General D'Hubert took off his own and folded it carefully on a stone.

"Suppose you take your principal to the other side of the wood and let him enter exactly in ten minutes from now," suggested General D'Hubert, calmly, but feeling as if he were giving directions for his own execution. This, however, was his last moment of weakness. "Wait. Let us compare watches first."

He pulled out his own. The officer with the chipped nose went over to borrow the watch of General Feraud. They bent their heads over them for a time.

"That's it. At four minutes to six by yours. Seven to by mine."

It was the cuirassier who remained by the side of General D'Hubert, keeping his one eye fixed immovably on the white face of the watch he held in the palm of his hand. He opened his mouth, waiting for the beat of the last second long before he snapped out the word, "*Avancez.*"*

General D'Hubert moved on, passing from the glaring sunshine of the Provençal morning into the cool and aromatic shade of the pines. The ground was clear between the reddish trunks, whose multitude, leaning at slightly different angles, confused his eye at first. It was like going into battle. The commanding quality of confidence in himself woke up in his breast. He was all to his affair.* The problem was how to kill the adversary. Nothing short of that would free him from this imbecile nightmare. "It's no use wounding that brute," thought General D'Hubert. He was known as a resourceful officer. His comrades years ago used also to call him The Strategist. And it was a fact that he could think in the presence of the enemy. Whereas Feraud had been always a mere fighter—but a dead shot, unluckily.

"I must draw his fire* at the greatest possible range," said General D'Hubert to himself.

At that moment he saw something white moving far off between the trees—the shirt of his adversary. He stepped out at once between the trunks, exposing himself freely; then, quick as lightning, leaped back. It had been a risky move but it succeeded in its object. Almost simultaneously with the pop of a shot a small piece of bark chipped off by the bullet stung his ear painfully.

General Feraud, with one shot expended, was getting cautious. Peeping round the tree, General D'Hubert could not see him at all. This ignorance of the foe's whereabouts carried with it a sense of insecurity. General D'Hubert felt himself abominably exposed on his flank and rear. Again something white fluttered in his sight. Ha! The enemy was still on his front, then. He had feared a turning movement. But apparently General Feraud was not thinking of it. General D'Hubert saw him pass without special haste from one tree to another in the straight line of approach. With great firmness of mind General D'Hubert stayed his hand. Too far yet. He knew he was no marksman. His must be a waiting game—to kill.

Wishing to take advantage of the greater thickness of the trunk, he sank down to the ground. Extended at full length, head on to his enemy, he had his person completely protected. Exposing himself would not do now, because the other was too near by this time. A conviction that Feraud would presently do something rash was like balm to General D'Hubert's soul. But to keep his chin raised off the ground was irksome, and not much use either. He peeped round, exposing a fraction of his head with dread, but really with little risk. His enemy, as a matter of fact, did not expect to see anything of him so far down as that. General D'Hubert caught a fleeting view of General Feraud shifting trees again with deliberate caution. "He despises my shooting," he thought, displaying that insight into the mind of his antagonist which is of such great help in winning battles. He was confirmed in his tactics of immobility. "If I could only watch my rear as well as my front!" he thought anxiously, longing for the impossible.

It required some force of character* to lay his pistols down; but, on a sudden impulse, General D'Hubert did this very gently—one on each side of him. In the army he had been looked upon as a bit of a dandy because he used to shave and put on a clean shirt on the days of battle. As a matter of fact, he had always been very careful of his personal appearance. In a man of nearly forty, in love with a young and charming girl, this praiseworthy self-respect may run to such little weaknesses as, for instance, being provided with an elegant little leather folding-case containing a small ivory comb, and fitted with a piece of looking-glass on the outside. General D'Hubert, his hands being free, felt in his breeches' pockets for that implement of innocent vanity excusable in the possessor of long, silky moustaches. He drew it out, and then with the utmost coolness and promptitude turned himself over on his back. In this new attitude, his head a little raised, holding the little looking-glass just clear of his tree, he squinted into it with his left eye, while the right kept a direct watch on the rear of his position. Thus was proved Napoleon's saying, that "for a French soldier, the word impossible does not exist."* He had the right tree nearly filling the field of his little mirror.

"If he moves from behind it," he reflected with satisfaction, "I am bound to see his legs. But in any case he can't come upon me unawares."

And sure enough he saw the boots of General Feraud flash in and out, eclipsing for an instant everything else reflected in the little mirror. He shifted its position accordingly. But having to form his judgment of the change from that indirect view he did not realize that now his feet and a portion of his legs were in plain sight of General Feraud.

General Feraud had been getting gradually impressed by the amazing cleverness with which his enemy was keeping cover. He had spotted the right tree with bloodthirsty precision. He was absolutely certain of it. And yet he had not been able to glimpse as much as the tip of an ear. As he had been looking for it at the height of about five feet ten inches from the ground it was no great wonder—but it seemed very wonderful to General Feraud.

The first view of these feet and legs determined a rush of blood to his head. He literally staggered behind his tree, and had to steady himself against it with his hand. The other was lying on the ground, then! On the ground! Perfectly still, too! Exposed! What could it mean? . . . The notion that he had knocked over his adversary at the first shot entered then General Feraud's head. Once there it grew with every second of attentive gazing, overshadowing every other supposition—irresistible, triumphant, ferocious.

"What an ass I was to think I could have missed him," he muttered to himself. "He was exposed *en plein**—the fool!—for quite a couple of seconds."

General Feraud gazed at the motionless limbs, the last vestiges of surprise fading before an unbounded admiration of his own deadly skill with the pistol.

"Turned up his toes! By the god of war, that was a shot!" he exulted mentally. "Got it through the head, no doubt, just where I aimed, staggered behind that tree, rolled over on his back, and died."

And he stared! He stared, forgetting to move, almost awed, almost sorry. But for nothing in the world would he have had it undone. Such a shot!—such a shot! Rolled over on his back and died!

For it was this helpless position, lying on the back, that shouted its direct evidence at General Feraud! It never occurred to him that it might have been deliberately assumed by a living man. It was inconceivable. It was beyond the range of sane supposition. There was no possibility to guess the reason for it. And it must be said, too, that General D'Hubert's turned-up feet looked thoroughly dead. General Feraud expanded his lungs for a stentorian shout to his seconds, but, from what he felt to be an excessive scrupulousness, refrained for a while.

"I will just go and see first whether he breathes yet," he mumbled to himself, leaving carelessly the shelter of his tree. This move was immediately perceived by the resourceful General D'Hubert. He concluded it to be another shift, but when he lost the boots out of the field of the mirror he became uneasy. General Feraud had only stepped a little out of the line, but his adversary could not possibly have supposed him walking up with perfect unconcern. General D'Hubert, beginning to wonder at what had become of the other, was taken unawares so completely that the first warning of danger consisted in the long, early-morning shadow of his enemy falling aslant on his outstretched legs. He had not even heard a footfall on the soft ground between the trees!

It was too much even for his coolness. He jumped up thoughtlessly,* leaving the pistols on the ground. The irresistible instinct of an average man (unless totally paralysed by discomfiture) would have been to stoop for his weapons, exposing himself to the risk of being shot down in that position. Instinct, of course, is irreflective. It is its very definition. But it may be an inquiry worth pursuing whether in reflective mankind the mechanical promptings of instinct are not affected by the customary mode of thought. In his young days, Armand D'Hubert, the reflective, promising officer, had emitted the opinion that in warfare one should "never cast back on the lines of a mistake." This idea, defended and developed in many discussions, had settled into one of the stock notions of his brain, had become a part of his mental individuality. Whether it had gone so inconceivably deep as to affect the dictates of his instinct, or simply because, as he himself declared afterwards, he was "too scared to remember the confounded pistols," the fact is that General D'Hubert never attempted to stoop for them. Instead of going back on his mistake, he seized the rough trunk with both hands, and swung himself behind it with such impetuosity that, going right round in the very flash and report of the pistol-shot, he reappeared on the other side of the tree face to face with General Feraud. This last, completely unstrung by such a show of agility on the part of a dead man, was trembling yet. A very faint mist of smoke hung before his face which had an extraordinary aspect, as if the lower jaw had come unhinged.

"Not missed!" he croaked, hoarsely, from the depths of a dry throat.

This sinister sound loosened the spell that had fallen on General D'Hubert's senses. "Yes, missed—*à bout portant*,"* he heard himself saying, almost before he had recovered the full command of his faculties. The revulsion of feeling was accompanied by a gust of homicidal fury, resuming* in its violence the accumulated resentment of a lifetime. For years General D'Hubert had been exasperated and humiliated by an atrocious absurdity imposed upon him by this man's savage caprice. Besides, General D'Hubert had been in this last instance too unwilling to confront death for the reaction of his anguish not to take the shape of a desire to kill. "And I have my two shots to fire yet," he added, pitilessly.

General Feraud snapped-to his teeth, and his face assumed an irate, undaunted expression. "Go on!" he said, grimly.

These would have been his last words if General D'Hubert had been holding the pistols in his hands. But the pistols were lying on the ground at the foot of a pine. General D'Hubert had the second of leisure necessary to remember that he had dreaded death not as a man, but as a lover; not as a danger, but as a rival; not as a foe to life, but as an obstacle to marriage. And behold! there was the rival defeated!—utterly defeated, crushed, done for!

He picked up the weapons mechanically, and, instead of firing them into General Feraud's breast, he gave expression to the thoughts uppermost in his mind, "You will fight no more duels now."

His tone of leisurely, ineffable satisfaction was too much for General Feraud's stoicism. "Don't dawdle, then, damn you for a cold-blooded staff-coxcomb!" he roared out, suddenly, out of an impassive face held erect on a rigidly still body.

General D'Hubert uncocked the pistols carefully. This proceeding was observed with mixed feelings by the other general. "You missed me twice," the victor said, coolly, shifting both pistols to one hand; "the last time within a foot or so. By every rule of single combat your life belongs to me. That does not mean that I want to take it now."

"I have no use for your forbearance," muttered General Feraud, gloomily.

"Allow me to point out that this is no concern of mine," said General D'Hubert, whose every word was dictated by a consummate delicacy of feeling. In anger he could have killed that man, but in cold blood he recoiled from humiliating by a show of generosity this unreasonable being—a fellow-soldier of the *Grande Armée*,* a companion in the wonders and terrors of the great military epic. "You don't set up the pretension of dictating to me what I am to do with what's my own."

General Feraud looked startled, and the other continued, "You've forced me on a point of honour to keep my life at your disposal, as it were, for fifteen years. Very well. Now that the matter is decided to my advantage, I am going to do what I like with your life on the same principle. You shall keep it at my disposal as long as I choose. Neither more nor less. You are on your honour till I say the word."

"I am! But, *sacrebleu*! This is an absurd position* for a General of the Empire to be placed in!" cried General Feraud, in accents of profound and dismayed conviction. "It amounts to sitting all the rest of my life with a loaded pistol in a drawer waiting for your word. It's—it's idiotic; I shall be an object of—of—derision."

"Absurd?—idiotic? Do you think so?" queried General D'Hubert with sly gravity. "Perhaps. But I don't see how that can be helped. However, I am not likely to talk at large of this adventure. Nobody need ever know anything about it. Just as no one to this day, I believe, knows the origin of our quarrel. . . . Not a word more," he added, hastily. "I can't really discuss this question with a man who, as far as I am concerned, does not exist."

When the two duellists came out into the open, General Feraud walking a little behind, and rather with the air of walking in a trance, the two seconds hurried towards them, each from his station at the edge of the wood. General D'Hubert addressed them, speaking loud and distinctly, "Messieurs, I make it a point of declaring to you solemnly, in the presence of General Feraud, that our difference is at last settled for good. You may inform all the world of that fact."

"A reconciliation, after all!" they exclaimed together.

"Reconciliation? Not that exactly. It is something much more binding. Is it not so, General?"

General Feraud only lowered his head in sign of assent. The two veterans looked at each other. Later in the day, when they found themselves alone out of their moody friend's earshot, the cuirassier remarked suddenly, "Generally speaking, I can see with my one eye as far as most people; but this beats me. He won't say anything."

"In this affair of honour I understand there has been from first to last always something that no one in the army could quite make out," declared the chasseur with the imperfect nose. "In mystery it began, in mystery it went on, in mystery it is to end, apparently."

General D'Hubert walked home with long, hasty strides, by no means uplifted by a sense of triumph. He had conquered, yet it did not seem to him that he had gained very much by his conquest. The night before he had grudged the risk of his life which appeared to him magnificent, worthy of preservation as an opportunity to win a girl's love. He had known moments when, by a marvellous illusion, this love seemed to be already his, and his threatened life a still more magnificent opportunity of devotion. Now that his life was safe it had suddenly lost its special magnificence. It had acquired instead a specially alarming aspect as a snare for the exposure of unworthiness. As to the marvellous illusion of conquered love that had visited him for a moment in the agitated watches of the night, which might have been his last on earth, he comprehended now its true nature. It had been merely a paroxysm of delirious conceit. Thus to this man, sobered by the victorious issue of a duel, life appeared robbed of its charm, simply because it was no longer menaced.

Approaching the house from the back, through the orchard and the kitchen garden, he could not notice the agitation which reigned in front. He never met a single soul. Only while walking softly along the corridor, he became aware that the house was awake and more noisy than usual. Names of servants were being called out down below in a confused noise of coming and going. With some concern he noticed that the door of his own room stood ajar, though the shutters had not been opened yet. He had hoped that his early excursion would have passed unperceived. He expected to find some servant just gone in; but the sunshine filtering through the usual cracks enabled him to see lying on the low divan something bulky, which had the appearance of two women clasped in each other's arms. Tearful and desolate murmurs issued mysteriously from that appearance. General D'Hubert pulled open the nearest pair of shutters violently. One of the women then jumped up. It was his sister. She stood for a moment with her hair hanging down and her arms raised straight up above her head, and then flung herself with a stifled cry into his arms. He returned her embrace, trying at the same time to disengage himself from it. The other woman had not risen. She seemed, on the contrary, to cling closer to the divan, hiding her face in the cushions. Her hair was also loose; it was admirably fair. General D'Hubert recognized it with staggering emotion. Mademoiselle de Valmassigue! Adèle! In distress!

He became greatly alarmed, and got rid of his sister's hug definitely. Madame Léonie then extended her shapely bare arm out of her *peignoir*,* pointing dramatically at the divan. "This poor, terrified child has rushed here from home, on foot, two miles—running all the way."

"What on earth has happened?" asked General D'Hubert in a low, agitated voice.

But Madame Léonie was speaking loudly. "She rang the great bell at the gate and roused all the household—we were all asleep yet. You may imagine what a terrible shock. . . . Adèle, my dear child, sit up."

General D'Hubert's expression was not that of a man who "imagines" with facility. He did, however, fish out of the chaos of surmises the notion that his prospective mother-in-law had died suddenly, but only to dismiss it at once. He could not conceive the nature of the event or the catastrophe which would induce Mademoiselle de Valmassigue, living in a house full of servants, to bring the news over the fields herself, two miles, running all the way.

"But why are you in this room?" he whispered, full of awe.

"Of course, I ran up to see, and this child . . . I did not notice it . . . she followed me. It's that absurd Chevalier," went on Madame Léonie, looking towards the divan. . . . "Her hair is all come down. You may imagine she did not stop to call her maid to dress it before she started . . . Adèle, my dear, sit up. . . . He blurted it all out to her at half-past five in the morning. She woke up early and opened her shutters to breathe the fresh air, and saw him sitting collapsed on a garden bench at the end of the great alley. At that hour—you may imagine! And the evening before he had declared himself indisposed. She hurried on some clothes and flew down to him. One would be anxious for less. He loves her, but not very intelligently. He had been up all night, fully dressed, the poor old man, perfectly exhausted. He wasn't in a state to invent a plausible story. . . . What a confidant you chose there! My husband was furious. He said, 'We can't interfere now.' So we sat down to wait. It was awful. And this poor child running with her hair loose over here publicly! She has been seen by some people in the fields. She has roused the whole household, too. It's awkward for her. Luckily you are to be married next week. . . . Adèle, sit up. He has come home on his own legs. . . . We expected to see you coming on a stretcher, perhaps—what do I know? Go and see if the carriage is ready. I must take this child home at once. It isn't proper for her to stay here a minute longer."

General D'Hubert did not move. It was as though he had heard nothing. Madame Léonie changed her mind. "I will go and see myself," she cried. "I want also my cloak.—Adèle—" she began, but did not add "sit up." She went out saying, in a very loud and cheerful tone: "I leave the door open."

General D'Hubert made a movement towards the divan, but then Adèle sat up, and that checked him dead. He thought, "I haven't washed this morning. I must look like an old tramp. There's earth on the back of my coat and pine-needles in my hair." It occurred to him that the situation required a good deal of circumspection on his part.

"I am greatly concerned, mademoiselle," he began, vaguely, and abandoned that line. She was sitting up on the divan with her cheeks unusually pink and her hair, brilliantly fair, falling all over her shoulders—which was a very novel sight to the general. He walked away up the room, and looking out of the window for safety said, "I fear you must think I behaved like a madman," in accents of sincere despair. Then he spun round, and noticed that she had followed him with her eyes. They were not cast down on meeting his glance. And the expression of her face was novel to him also. It was, one might have said, reversed.* Those eyes looked at him with grave thoughtfulness, while the exquisite lines of her mouth seemed to suggest a restrained smile. This change made her transcendental beauty much less mysterious, much more accessible to a man's comprehension. An amazing ease of mind came to the general—and even some ease of manner. He walked down the room with as much pleasurable excitement as he would have found in walking up to a battery vomiting death, fire, and smoke; then stood looking down with smiling eyes at the girl whose marriage with him (next week) had been so carefully arranged by the wise, the good, the admirable Léonie.

"Ah! mademoiselle," he said, in a tone of courtly regret, "if only I could be certain that you did not come here this morning, two miles, running all the way, merely from affection for your mother!"

He waited for an answer imperturbable but inwardly elated. It came in a demure murmur, eyelashes lowered with fascinating effect. "You must not be *méchant** as well as mad."

And then General D'Hubert made an aggressive movement towards the divan which nothing could check. That piece of furniture was not exactly in the line of the open door. But Madame Léonie, coming back wrapped up in a light cloak and carrying a lace shawl on her arm for Adèle to hide her incriminating hair under, had a swift impression of her brother getting up from his knees.

"Come along, my dear child," she cried from the doorway.

The general, now himself again in the fullest sense, showed the readiness of a resourceful cavalry officer and the peremptoriness of a leader of men. "You don't expect her to walk to the carriage," he said, indignantly. "She isn't fit. I shall carry her downstairs."

This he did slowly, followed by his awed and respectful sister; but he rushed back like a whirlwind to wash off all the signs of the night of anguish and the morning of war, and to put on the festive garments of a conqueror before hurrying over to the other house. Had it not been for that, General D'Hubert felt capable of mounting a horse and pursuing his late adversary in order simply to embrace him from excess of happiness. "I owe it all to this stupid brute," he thought. "He has made plain in a morning what might have taken me years to find out—for I am a timid fool. No self-confidence whatever. Perfect coward. And the Chevalier! Delightful old man!" General D'Hubert longed to embrace him also.

The Chevalier was in bed. For several days he was very unwell. The men of the Empire and the post-revolution young ladies were too much for him. He got up the day before the wedding, and, being curious by nature, took his niece aside for a quiet talk. He advised her to find out from her husband the true story of the affair of honour, whose claim, so imperative and so persistent, had led her to within an ace of tragedy. "It is right that his wife should be told. And next month or so will be your time to learn from him anything you want to know, my dear child."

Later on, when the married couple came on a visit to the mother of the bride, Madame la Générale D'Hubert communicated to her beloved old uncle the true story she had obtained without any difficulty from her husband.

The Chevalier listened with deep attention to the end, took a pinch of snuff, flicked the grains of tobacco from the frilled front of his shirt, and asked, calmly, "And that's all it was?"

"Yes, uncle," replied Madame la Générale, opening her pretty eyes very wide. "Isn't it funny? *C'est insensé**—to think what men are capable of!"

"H'm!" commented the old *émigré*. "It depends what sort of men. That Bonaparte's soldiers were savages. It is *insensé*. As a wife, my dear, you must believe implicitly what your husband says."

But to Léonie's husband the Chevalier confided his true opinion. "If that's the tale the fellow made up for his wife, and during the honeymoon, too, you may depend on it that no one will ever know now the secret of this affair."

Considerably later still, General D'Hubert judged the time come, and the opportunity propitious to write a letter to General Feraud. This letter began by disclaiming all animosity. "I've never," wrote the General Baron D'Hubert, "wished for your death during all the time of our deplorable quarrel. Allow me," he continued, "to give you back in all form your forfeited life. It is proper that we two, who have been partners in so much military glory, should be friendly to each other publicly."

The same letter contained also an item of domestic information. It was in reference to this last that General Feraud answered from a little village on the banks of the Garonne,* in the following words:

"If one of your boy's names had been Napoleon—or Joseph—or even Joachim, I could congratulate you on the event with a better heart. As you have thought proper to give him the names of Charles Henri Armand, I am confirmed in my conviction that you *never* loved the Emperor. The thought of that sublime hero chained to a rock in the middle of a savage ocean makes life of so little value that I would receive with positive joy your instructions to blow my brains out. From suicide I consider myself in honour debarred. But I keep a loaded pistol in my drawer."

Madame la Générale D'Hubert lifted up her hands in despair after perusing that answer.

"You see? He *won't* be reconciled," said her husband. "He must never, by any chance, be allowed to guess where the money comes from. It wouldn't do. He couldn't bear it."

"You are a *brave homme*,*Armand," said Madame la Générale, appreciatively.

"My dear, I had the right to blow his brains out; but as I didn't, we can't let him starve. He has lost his pension and he is utterly incapable of doing anything in the world for himself. We must take care of him, secretly, to the end of his days. Don't I owe him the most ecstatic moment of my life? . . . Ha! ha! ha! Over the fields, two miles, running all the way! I couldn't believe my ears! . . . But for his stupid ferocity, it would have taken me years to find you out. It's extraordinary how in one way or another this man has managed to fasten himself on my deeper feelings."*

EXPLANATORY NOTES

THE END OF THE TETHER

'The End of the Tether' was composed between March and October 1902, and serialized in *Blackwood's Magazine* July to December 1902, to accompany 'Youth' and 'Heart of Darkness' in a single volume published by Blackwood in November 1902. The story was originally entitled 'The End of the Song' and partly arose out of discussions with Ford Madox Ford over the suicide of Ford's father-in-law, Dr William Martindale, in February 1902. Conrad wrote in a later Author's Note of 1917:

> 'The End of the Tether' is a story of sea-life in a rather special way; and the most intimate thing I can say of it is this: that having lived that life fully, amongst its men, its thoughts and sensations, I have found it possible, without the slightest misgiving, in all sincerity of heart and peace of conscience, to conceive the existence of Captain Whalley's personality and to relate the manner of his end. This statement acquires some force from the circumstance that the pages of that story—a fair half of the book—are also the product of experience. That experience belongs (like 'Youth's') to the time before I ever thought of putting pen to paper. As to its 'reality', that is for the readers to determine. One had to pick up one's facts here and there. More skill would have made them more real and the whole composition more interesting. But here we are approaching the veiled region of artistic values which it would be improper and indeed dangerous for me to enter. I have looked over the proofs, have corrected a misprint or two, have changed a word or two—and that's all. It is not very likely that I shall ever read 'The End of the Tether' again. No more need be said. It accords best with my feelings to part from Captain Whalley in affectionate silence.

Conrad drew upon his own maritime experiences in Singapore during visits between 1883 and 1888. Whalley was modelled on an amalgam of Captain Thomas Louttit, the master of the *Duke of Sutherland* just before Conrad joined the ship in 1878, Captain Henry Ellis, Master-Attendant in Singapore (Ellis being more obviously a model too for Ned Eliott), a Captain Robinson, old and blind and living in retirement with his daughter in Melbourne, and William Purdu, first mate over Conrad on the *Loch Etive* who fearlessly concealed his deafness (*The Mirror of the Sea*, 1906, Chapter 11).

   1 *THE END OF THE TETHER*: a commonplace phrase indicating the end of one's patience and resources, as of an animal at the limit of its chain but also here with nautical implications in terms of being at the end of a rope or measure. The tether is also arguably Whalley's tie to his daughter, Ivy, which finally has to be severed.

1 *Sofala*: after do-re-mi-fa, the fifth, fourth, and sixth notes on the diatonic musical scale. The ship travels regularly and monotonously from its home port of Singapore along the 800-mile trade route through the Strait of Malacca and up the west coast of the Malay Peninsula as far as lower Burma, and then back again. There is also reference in James Frazer's *The Golden Bough* (1890) to the kings of Sofala who would commit suicide if suffering physical disablement.

Captain Whalley did not look at it: Conrad cut two sentences in what remains of the manuscript in the Keating Collection, Beinecke Library, Yale, for giving too obvious a hint as to what was to follow: 'The stirring layer of sunshine that seemed to arise and float on the water had nothing to do with the dimness of his sight and the weariness of his mind. There was another cause for that.'

Serang: Malay boatswain in charge of East Indian deck crew, and of the anchors and rigging in a ship.

Malay: inhabitant of Malaysia and Indonesia.

helmsman: seaman steering ship at the helm (ship's wheel).

bridge: ship's raised control room from which its officers can direct operations and keep watch.

Low Cape to Malantan: trading points on the Sumatran coast en route out of Singapore and onwards to Malacca, Batu Beru, and Pangu, visited by Conrad in his time as first mate on the steamship *Vidar*, 1887–8 (on which see, for example, Maya Jasanoff, *The Dawn Watch*, William Collins, 2017, 120–35).

mangroves: shrubs that grow in sea water within coastal swamps.

2 *landfalls to a degree of the bearing*: ship's approaches to and arrivals on land, here precisely calculated and steered relative to a fixed degree point on the ship's compass.

huckster's round: a huckster was a door-to-door salesman, hawking his goods around on his regular visits to sell his wares. See 'A Smile of Fortune' (1912): 'These commercial interests—spoiling the finest life under the sun. Why must the sea be used for trade—and for war as well?'

Malacca: the strait of Malacca is a narrow stretch of water of nearly 600 miles (950 km) between the island of Sumatra and Peninsula Malaysia.

mat sails: boats (known as bedars) sailing on the east coast of Malaysia that carry one or two junk sails not made of cloth but of a matting material called tikal, also used for floor matting.

a retired young sailor: it is significant that in the manuscript Mr van Wyk was originally conceived of as a retired *old* sailor. It becomes dialectically important to Conrad that it should be a world-weary, rather cynical young man who, for all his defensive foreknowledge, is psychologically almost shattered by the fate of an old man who has remained trusting and innocent.

port of registry: the home port where the details of a ship are officially recorded, including name, number and tonnage.

Condor, a famous clipper: a fast sailing-vessel named after the large black bird of prey, a type of vulture.

3 *South Seas*: Pacific Ocean, south of the equator.

Bombay: populous city in west India, now also known as Mumbai.

a Whalley Island and a Condor Reef: the former fictional, the latter named after a ship sunk on its jagged rocks in 1860, off Cambodia.

General Directory: the *China Sea Directory* published in 1868 by the British Admiralty, the government department for the Royal Navy.

Isthmus of Suez: the Suez canal was opened in 1869, linking the Indian Ocean with the Mediterranean and allowing easy passage from Europe to Asia and the East.

he had lasted well, outlasting in the end: in the manuscript this was mainly governed by the verb 'survived', where here 'lasted' and 'outlasting' work together towards the eventual 'end of the tether'.

Gulf of Petchili: now the Gulf of Jili or Chihli, or Bohai Sea, east of mainland China.

Travancore and Deccan Banking Corporation: a version of the Oriental Bank in Singapore which crashed in 1884.

4 *A very pretty little barque, Fair Maid*: a small ship, named after the sailors' drinking song 'A-Roving'—'I'll go no more a-roving with you, fair maid'.

scuttled: deliberately sunk by making a hole in the ship.

chronometers: highly accurate navigational clocks also used to determine longitude.

morning watch: the watch or period of duty on board ship was usually in four-hour sections, morning watch being 04.00 to 08.00, and also referred to the group of men assigned that time.

5 *aft*: 'after', near the back or stern of the ship.

the Lord's Prayer: Matthew 6:9–13 ('Our Father which art in Heaven . . .').

companion-hatchway: a ladder through a covered opening cut in the deck to get to the quarters or cargo-hold below.

the trim: the adjustment of the sails.

carbon photographs: the carbon process developed in 1855, using gelatin rather than silver, to produce permanent black-and-white photographic prints.

the cuddy: small cabin or saloon under the poop deck at the rear of the vessel for the use of ship's officers.

plummet: feather-duster; French 'plumet', English more properly 'plumate'.

how fond of boat-sailing she used to be: in the manuscript there was a longer account of her practical prowess and bravery which Conrad cut for the serialization. He also cut a more detailed description of her way with flowers, a few lines after.

5 *his mate*: deck officer under the command of the captain or master.

6 *dog-watch*: one of two shorter periods on watch, 04.00–06.00 or 06.00–08.00 (when all but dogs are asleep).

roulades: musical flourishes elaborating a single phrase.

Hongkong: Hong Kong, island and port off the south of China, was a colony of the British Empire after 1842.

ensign: flag used as shroud, the Red Ensign being the standard of the British Merchant Service.

7 *freight*: shipment of goods as cargo.

a lee shore: where the wind blows into shore from the sea, preventing passage.

Shanghai: most populous city in China, with favourable port location.

8 *bath-chair*: chair on wheels to convey invalids.

buckle-to: apply oneself with determination, as in harnessing a horse.

gilt for the ginger-bread scrolls at stem and stern: gold-leaf or gold paint for the fancy carvings at both the forward and back parts of the ship.

9 *tonnage*: here the load of the cargo.

charters: hiring of ships.

by cable: telegram.

ballast: heavy material such as iron or stone placed at the bottom of the ship's hold to keep it stable.

ship-chandler's runner: the chandler was in charge of supplies and equipment for whom his runner acted as messenger.

poop: raised deck near the back of the ship.

10 *lazarette*: space between decks for storage.

11 *Consolidated Docks Company*: in Singapore.

tigers . . . of the New Waterworks: tigers often roaming free around the new reservoir. There were a number of new developments in the 1870s, amidst the old landscape.

portico: porch.

piles: vertical supportive stakes acting as foundations.

12 *preferred sailing merchant ships*: marking Whalley's age: 'And therein I think I can lay my finger upon the difference between the seamen of yesterday, who are still with us, and the seamen of to-morrow, already entered upon the possession of their inheritance. History repeats itself, but the special call of an art which has passed away is never reproduced. It is as utterly gone out of the world as the song of a destroyed wild bird. Nothing will awaken the same response of pleasurable emotion or conscientious endeavour. And the sailing of any vessel afloat is an art whose

fine form seems already receding from us on its way to the overshadowed Valley of Oblivion' (*The Mirror of the Sea*, Chapter 8).

HEI Company's service: Honourable East India Company.

coolies: now-derogatory name given by Europeans to unskilled, native hired labour around India and China.

accoutrements: dress and equipment.

Sikh trooper: a member of the Sikh religious sect, founded in the Punjab region of India, serving as a soldier in the British-Indian army.

13 *"Song of the Shirt"*: poem by Thomas Hood (1799–1845) in which a poor London seamstress sings of her harsh working conditions.

rattan-screens: stems of a climbing palm used for wicker furniture, partitions and (here) shelter against heat and light.

14 *skurry*: scurry, rush and race.

15 *out yonder*: the manuscript goes on to speak of Whalley's having thus to 'stay out in the world' to help his daughter a little more and a little longer.

berth: position (derived from allotted bunk onboard).

16 *Panama hat*: a light, white wide-brimmed hat of straw-like material to protect against the sun, originally made from leaves of jipijapa, a South American palm.

pipeclayed cork helmets: pith helmets whitened with kaolin clay which was used in making pipes.

17 *prau*: Indonesian name for swift, undecked boat propelled by sails and/or oars.

spars: masts.

18 *The log*: instrument for measuring speed and distance travelled by a ship, recorded in the logbook.

turn-out: carriage complete with passengers and horses.

19 *landau*: four-wheeled carriage first designed in Landau, Germany, for four passengers on two facing seats, with elevated front seat for the driver.

curved C-springs: suspension given by springs shaped at their end like the letter C.

imperial: small tuft of beard as worn by Emperor Napoleon III (1808–73).

His Excellency—: later refered to by Conrad as Sir Frederick, after Sir Frederick Aloysius Weld, appointed Governor of the Straits Settlements by the British East India Company in the 1880s.

equipage: carriage and horses, with attendants.

Archipelago: chain of islands of Indonesia and the Philippines between Asia and Australia.

20 *the Dido*: named after the Queen of Carthage tragically abandoned by her lover Aeneas in Virgil's epic poem, *The Aeneid*.

frigates: light, speedy naval-convoy escort vessels.

20 *patent slip*: dry dock for repairs.

graving basins: dry docks for cleaning, rust and barnacle removal, repainting, etc.

its wharves, its jetties: wharves are man-made on-shore landing places for ships; jetties are wooden structures extended from land over the sea, like a small pier for mooring.

sheer-legs: two tall poles like shears, used as an A-frame to hoist ships out of the water.

promontories: points of high land that jut out to sea.

quays: platforms, on parts of the coast made suitable for landing.

fire: great twenty-eight-day fire at Tanjong Pagar Dock in Singapore 1877.

21 *Master-Attendant*: based on Captain Henry Ellis who recommended Conrad for the captaincy of the *Otago* in 1888; he figures also in *Lord Jim* and *The Shadow Line*.

22 *Sir Frederick*: Sir Frederick Aloysius Weld (1823–91), an English-born New Zealand politician, serving as a cabinet minister and then colonial governor after his return to England, was made Governor of the Straits Settlements, Malacca, Penang and Singapore, from 1880 to 1887.

an alpaca jacket: of soft wool.

Ringdove: pigeon with black ring-shaped mark around the neck. The novelist William Faulkner gave his own boat this name in 1942, as a tribute to Conrad: compare the blind figure of Mahon in Faulkner's first published novel, *Soldier's Pay* (1926).

tending his hot irons: preoccupied with his own projects and opportunities—while, so to speak, the (blacksmith's) iron was still hot.

Gothic portal: opening that offers a grand entrance in the twelfth-century Gothic style, in St Andrew's Cathedral, Singapore.

rosace above the ogive: circular rose-window above the high-pointed (Gothic-style) arch above the door.

23 *lord in Bombay*: Viceroy of India.

French Cochin-China: French name for its colony, now southern part of Vietnam, Saigon being its largest city.

Sailors' Home: lodgings which feature also near the beginning of Conrad's *The Shadow Line*.

24 *Hamilton*: also figures in *The Shadow Line*, 'I have never seen any one so full of dignity for the station in life Providence had been pleased to place him in. I had been told that he regarded me as a rank outsider.'

neck and crop: completely and without ceremony, as of a rider spectacularly thrown over horse's neck and throat.

"if you had sent for me.": Conrad wrote David Meldrum, literary editor at Blackwood's, that the 'Eliott episode has a fundamental significance in so

far that it exhibits the first weakening of old Whalley's character before the assault of poverty. As you notice he says nothing of his position but goes off and takes advantage of the information. . . . But the episode is mainly the first sign of that fate we carry within us. A character like Whalley's cannot cease to be frank with impunity. . . . The pathos for me is in this that the concealment of his extremity is as it were forced upon him. Nevertheless it is weakness—it is deterioration' (*Collected Letters of Joseph Conrad*, vol. 2, 441). See also more generally Robert Hampson, *Conrad's Secrets* (Palgrave Macmillan, 2012).

25 *popinjays*: show-offs, like preening talkative parrots.

A syce: an Indian groom who looks after the horses.

a Burmah pony: a breed from the Shan state of Burma, known for its stamina especially in mountainous regions.

26 *as far north as Tenasserim*: an administrative region of Myanmar or Burma, its hills forming part of the long mountain chain in Southeast Asia.

27 *came out third*: as third mate.

the Manilla lottery: monthly government-led lottery in the Philippines of which Manila is the capital.

28 *German tramps*: tramp ships that picked up cargo from wherever they could, without fixed schedules or ports of call, as part of attempted German expansionism.

a beggar on horseback: proverb, 'set a beggar on horseback and he'll ride to the devil'; a person formerly poor becomes irresponsible and vain when made rich, and misuses his power.

29 *a stiver*: small Dutch coin of little value.

his traps: personal belongings.

30 *peristyle*: courtyard surrounded by a row of columns.

32 *sampans*: small rowing-boats.

pigtail: hairstyle, with long braid hanging from the back of the head and the rest shaven, customarily worn by Chinese men until the fall of the Qing dynasty in 1912.

obelisk: tapering stone pillar.

"Savee . . . John?": pidgin English for 'Do you understand?' where John is short for the generic name of John Chinaman, now offensive but not necessarily so at that time.

33 *Venus*: evening star.

a sailing-ship: a bird of the sea, whose swimming is like flying, as compared to the merely mechanical propulsion of a steamship in *The Mirror of the Sea*, Chapter 8: 'The taking of a modern steamship about the world (though one would not minimize its responsibilities) has not the same quality of intimacy with nature, which, after all, is an indispensable condition to the building up of an art. It is less personal and a more exact calling; less arduous, but also less gratifying in the lack of close communion between the artist and the medium of his art. It is, in short, less a matter of love. Its effects are measured exactly in time and space as no effect of an art can be.'

34 *evil*: the left hand being traditionally sinister, as opposed to the norm of being right-handed.

the bar of Batu Beru: sandbank or shoal off from the rock of this port of call.

Tuan: Malay for 'sir'.

awning: a canopy, covering of canvas or tarpaulin, protecting against rain or sun.

35 *Ya*: Malay for 'yes'.

binnacle: the case that holds the compass, near the ship's helm, with lamp for use at night.

37 *The alluvial coast*: soft shoreline of sand and mud resulting from erosion by sea and sediment deposits.

grinder tooth: molar tooth, at the back of the mouth.

saddle-backed summit: the upper surface curved like a saddle, in concave outline.

38 *lascar*: an East Indian sailor.

the bow: the front of the ship.

fathom: a measure of depth, 1 fathom being about 6 feet, 1.8 metres.

A leadsman: sailor who heaves over the lead sound-instrument at the end of a line in order to measure depth.

39 *telegraph*: an engine-order telegraph is a communications device used by the pilot on the bridge to order engineers in the engine room below to power the ship at a certain speed.

Jack: the second engineer, referred to as Massy's 'second'.

messed: ate their meals.

40 *in his cups*: drunk, intoxicated.

told off: appointed to.

41 *the shoal*: the shallow.

compass card: rotating card attached to the magnetic compass needle that gives the 32 bearing points and the 360 degrees of the circle.

42 *keel*: the main timber that runs the whole length of the underside of the ship.

not doubt, but the certitude: the word 'certitude' and its shaking by doubt into 'incertitude' are vital to the story from now until the end. In a general overview of Conrad's work in the *English Review* (December 1911–March 1912), Ford Madox Ford writes of the method of this particular tale, with 'whole long pages of description of land-fretted seas', as more than merely descriptive: 'All the while one has been on the ship, one has seemed to be so conscious of the ledges of rock below one that when the knife-thrust has come it has seemed for so long to be inevitable . . . And that is the great faculty of this author—that he can seem to make an end inevitable'—and not least so in the terrible effort to avoid it (*Conrad: The Critical Heritage*, 249). The mud and the rocks beneath the surface signal both the physical and psychological insecurity of Conrad 'with nothing but a thin plank in between us and the fathomless sea' (*Conrad: The Critical Heritage*, 241).

43 *"Ofiss"*: Office.

fire-ship: literal Malay translation for steamer.

sensitized plate: in early photographic processes, chemicals were applied to make the sheet that was to receive the image sensitive to degrees of light and shade.

his nativity: as in horoscopes, the astrological use of the person's birth date and star sign for purposes of prediction.

detecting: this is a favourite word for Conrad in this story, substituted for 'seeing' in the manuscript because so much depends here on what is both more and less than physical sight.

44 *astern*: backwards.

45 *survey*: regulatory inspection to check safety and security.

conning the ship: directing the steering of the vessel.

black on white: in black and white, explicitly spelt out.

47 *this deaf and dumb trick*: in the Yale manuscript Conrad had also included 'blind' but cut it to avoid over-explicitness.

"Starboard": right side.

the reach: straight and open stretch of water.

48 *the gangway*: ramp by which to leave the ship at harbour.

50 *Blue Anchor*: a shipping company taking direct routes from England to Australia.

52 *Pangu*: the next port of call after Batu Beru, see Florence Clemens, 'Joseph Conrad as a Geographer', *The Scientific Monthly*, 51.5 (Nov., 1940), 460–65.

the leeward cape: the high point of land on the side opposite to that from which the wind blows.

reef-infested region: area beset by craggy rocks just above or below the surface of the sea.

hulks: vessels deemed unseaworthy and stripped of their masts.

53 *high-pooped caravel*: a small, light sailing vessel with high raised deck.

hamlet: small village.

martello towers: small, round defensive turreted forts built along the English coast to defend against invasion by Napoleon.

54 *he had detected*: in the original *Blackwood's* serial version it was 'his ear had caught . . .' but 'detected' is related to both inference from the senses (by Whalley) and suspicion of secrecy (by Sterne).

55 *the offing*: more distant part of the sea in view.

   spurs: sharp rocks or mountain ridges.

56 *fish davit*: small crane on board ship for 'fishing' the anchor, to hoist it without damaging the hull.

57 *foredeck*: deck at the forward part of the ship.

58 *pilot-fish*: a small fish that according to sailors' legend led the large shark or whale to food.

   blindly: the whole sentence mimes the creative process of writers thinking through their words, their metaphors and similes, to make a discovery.

60 *stanchion*: fixed upright support of wood or iron.

63 *the struggle for life*: as in Charles Darwin's *The Origin of Species* (1859). Significantly, Conrad admired Alfred Russel Wallace's *The Malay Archipelago* (1869), an account of travels that led Wallace to his own independent discovery of the principle of evolution by natural selection. In a letter to Cunninghame Graham, 20 December 1897, Conrad speaks of existence as a machine that has 'evolved itself', 'made itself without thought, without conscience, without foresight, without eyes, without heart' (*Collected Letters of Joseph Conrad*, vol. 1, 425). In Conrad, wrote the novelist John Galsworthy, 'Nature is first, man second' (*Conrad: The Critical Heritage*, 205). In the bleakness of their post-Darwinian vision, the writer H. P. Lovecraft compared Conrad to Hardy, thinking Hardy overrated, while Conrad 'feels and expresses as few authors can the prodigious and inhuman tides of a blind, bland universe: at heart indifferent to mankind, but purposefully malignant if measured by the narrow and empirical standard of human teleology' (*Letters, Volume 2: Letters from New York*, edited by S. T. Joshi and D. E. Schultz, Night Shade, 2005, 127).

   secular: ancient.

64 *a small Rajah*: originally an Indian prince but here, less powerfully, a Malay chief.

   sarongs: long cloth garments wrapped around the body.

   chewing betel: the leaves of the betel palm and areca nut, forming a mild narcotic which stained the lips red.

   Kling: disparaging term for lower-caste Indian settler in Malaysia.

   his bearings: his right senses, but it is an apt metaphor here in relation to a ship's orientation.

65 *rattan*: climbing palm used for wickerwork and ropes.

   poll: head.

   stateroom: superior room on board ship for captain or officers.

66 *humbugging*: deceiving.

67 *nonplused*: unsure and at a loss.

    whirligig: anything that spins rapidly, such as a spinning top or a windmill.

68 *the port*: porthole, small circular window in side of ship.

70 *lumber*: miscellaneous gear.

    quartermasters: ship's officers responsible for steering equipment and storage.

    drawers: clothing covering the legs.

    streaming tail: pigtail.

    loafers: idlers avoiding work.

71 *Vanity of vanities*: Ecclesiates 12.8, 'all is vanity', pride in what is actually worthless.

    collier: coal miner or merchant.

    Hull: port city on the Humber Estuary, in East Riding of Yorkshire.

    sovereigns: British gold coins, originally worth 1 pound sterling (100 pence).

    grog-shop: low-class bar-room for sale and drinking of liquor.

    inferno: hell. Dante in his *Divine Comedy* (1320) placed gamblers in the seventh circle of hell.

73 *In the midst of life we are in death*: from 'The Order of the Burial of the Dead' in the Book of Common Prayer.

74 *Stations*: general order to man positions and duties.

    up stream: opposite position to that from which the current flows.

77 *cottage piano*: small upright piano.

78 *étagère*: a display cabinet.

    "Bismarck malade" colour: a shade of reddish-brown in French fashion.

79 *ungarnished forehead*: with receding hair.

81 *boys*: servants.

    chow: food.

82 *the last Acheen War*: the Dutch captured the province of Acheen in Sumatra in 1874 but the Achinese continued a guerrilla resistance through several later conflicts.

84 *a Balinini chief*: leader of the Balinini pirates from North-West Borneo.

    Tampasuk: district around river in North-West Borneo.

86 *characters on the wall*: as in the writing on the wall at Belshazzar's feast (Daniel 5).

87 *Bone of my bone, flesh of my flesh*: as Adam said of Eve, Genesis 2.23.

88 *life-buoys*: ring-shaped buoyancy floats designed to save from drowning those who have fallen in the water.

    cork fender: a bumper, here made of the soft bark of a cork oak, hung over the ship's side to protect it from the impact of collision or chafing against banks and wharfs.

88 *deck-lockers*: for storage.

91 *limpid*: clear, calm and open, transparent, as sometimes of water itself.

93 *Samson*: the great warrior who was betrayed by his wife Delilah, his strength lost in the cutting of his hair, and then his eyes gouged out by the Philistine enemy who set him to work as a slave grinding grain. When his hair began to grow again and his strength to return, he asked his captives to rest him against a temple pillar, and then, after praying to God for further strength, he tore down the temple, killing himself and all within it (Judges 16).

94 *floating yearly policy*: marine insurance to cover the shipment of his goods on any vessel between stated destinations.

    the remnant of sight: more specific than 'the little power' in the original version in *Blackwood's Magazine*.

    a fatal Yes or No: 'fatal' was characteristically inserted in the first edition, where in the *Blackwood's* serial it was simply 'Yes or No'. So many of Conrad's tiny minor revisions add to the felt insecurity and incertitude.

    with assurance: this phrase, a terrible hostage to fortune, was inserted after the serial publication.

95 *hesitating feet*: in the Blackwood's serialization it was less specifically 'hesitating walk'.

    as if the light were ebbing out of the world: 'The End of the Tether' was published in the same volume as 'Heart of Darkness', and it is characteristic of Conrad that Whalley's loss of sight and of light should be at once literal and symbolic.

    Titan: in Greek mythology the twelve Titans were the offspring of Uranus (heaven) and Gaea (earth), one of whom (Chronos) overthrew his own father. They took over the universe until their own eventual overthrow by Zeus and the Olympian gods, when they were hurled into the underworld (Tartarus) and imprisoned there.

96 *bulwarks*: protective, raised wooden fence-work along the ship's sides above deck-level.

    davits: small cranes on board ship for hoisting and lowering ship's smaller boat(s).

    muzzy: muddled and blurred, as with alcohol.

100 *belaying-pins*: pegs to which ropes can be secured.

     winches: rotating metal drums around which rope or chain is wound, to increase hauling power for loading and unloading cargo.

101 *bulkhead*: partition separating compartments and cabins below deck and making them watertight to prevent the danger of the sea filling all areas at once.

104 *soaker*: a drunkard, an alcoholic.

     taffrail: handrail that curves round the stern of the ship.

patent log: rotating apparatus trailing behind the ship to measure its speed through the water.

hull: the main body or shell of the ship.

on an even keel: keeping the keel (the central ridge on the underside of the vessel) level, not listing to either side.

105 *bullyrag*: intimidate, scold.

"Tell that to the marines!": an unlikely story! (as when trying to convince experienced seamen of some far-fetched fisherman's tale).

106 *But what expedient*: the word 'expedient' was added after the serial version, in another characteristic touch, offering only secondary means in relation to primal predicaments.

107 *Six bells*: 11.00 a.m.

bull's eye lantern: lamp with thick glass lens to concentrate the beam of light.

the stokehold fiddle: rail or grille fitted over the boiler-room hatch.

a deck-forge: for metal-working.

Capharnaum: meaning a disorderly collection, named after a ruined town, Capernaum, on the shore of the Sea of Galilee associated with Jesus Christ.

108 *eight bells*: 12.00 noon.

109 *as if he had never seen them before*: as earlier, with 'as if the light were ebbing out of the world', a wider and deeper extension of the meaning of Whalley's blindness and sense of darkness, contrasted with his earlier innocent faith in God and trust in humans.

All the days of his life he had prayed for daily bread, and not to be led into temptation: from the Lord's Prayer, Matthew 6.11, 13, and Psalms 23.6 ('Surely goodness and mercy shall follow me all the days of my life, and I shall dwell in the house of the Lord for ever').

Ada, Tuan: Malay for 'Here, present, sir.'

detected: in the serial version it was 'recognized'.

110 *steering-chains*: connecting the ship's steering wheel to the rudder behind.

113 *chain-guys*: lines of rope used for securing items on deck.

the masthead lamp flew over the bows: the light at the top of the mast thrown over the front part of the ship.

"Eight fathom": 48 feet, just under 15 metres. It is fifteen fathom in the serial version.

114 *stokers*: men who tend the furnace on a steamship, supplying fuel.

showed a good countenance: a calm, brave expression on his face.

The blocks: the pulleys from which the life-boats were lowered.

115 *the painter*: rope attached to the ship's bow for securing or towing.

115 *his own pockets*: so in *Lord Jim* Captain Brierly committed suicide by leaping overboard with four iron belaying-pins in his pockets. 'Put them in his
pockets to help him down, I suppose; but, Lord! what's four iron pins to
a powerful man like Captain Brierly. Maybe his confidence in himself was
just shook a bit at the last. That's the only sign of fluster he gave in his
whole life, I should think; but I am ready to answer for him, that once over
he did not try to swim a stroke, the same as he would have had pluck
enough to keep up all day long on the bare chance had he fallen overboard
accidentally' (Chapter 6).

116 *cant*: slope, angle.

one man's poison, another man's meat: the proverb more usually, 'one man's
meat is another man's poison'; meaning, what feels good, or a gain, for one
may be distasteful, injurious, or a loss, to another.

119 *"My sight is going"*: originally the tale seems to have ended with Whalley's
letter to his daughter. Conrad revised the typescript for *Blackwood's
Magazine* by adding the last two paragraphs of his daughter's reaction
which he claimed were true to the original conception in the destroyed
manuscript.

120 *she felt she had loved him, after all*: compare with the ironic ending to 'Heart
of Darkness' where Marlow falsely but protectively assures Kurtz's
beloved that his dying words were her name, spoken in love for her. In fact
they were 'The horror! The horror!'

AMY FOSTER

'Amy Foster' was composed in May and June 1901, entirely out of doors, while
Conrad was staying at Ford Madox Ford's Pent Farm, Postling, in Kent during
a three-week break in the final stages of Conrad's collaboration with Ford over
the novel, *Romance*. Ford said that he had given Conrad the basic story in his
account of an immigrant German in *The Cinque Ports* (1900):

> One of the most tragic stories that I remember to have heard was connected
> with a man who escaped the tender mercies of the ocean to undergo an
> almost more merciless buffeting ashore. He was one of the crew of a German
> merchant that was wrecked almost at the foot of the lighthouse. A moderate
> swimmer, he was carried by the current to some distance from the scene
> of the catastrophe. Here he touched the ground. He had nothing, no
> clothes, no food; he came ashore on a winter's night. In the morning he
> found himself in the Marsh near Romney. He knocked at doors, tried to
> make himself understood. The Marsh people thought him either a lunatic
> or a supernatural visitor. To lonely women in the Marsh cottages he
> seemed a fearful object. No doubt he was, poor wretch. They warned their
> menfolk of him, and whenever he was seen he was hounded away and ill-
> used. He got the name of Mad Jack. Knowing nothing of the country,
> nothing of the language, he could neither ask his way nor read the names

on the signposts, and even if he read them, they meant nothing to him. How long this lasted, I do not know; I remember hearing from the village people at the time that a dangerous person was in the neighbourhood. The fear of the folk was real enough. For a fortnight or so hardly one of them would open their doors after nightfall. The police at last got to hear of him, and, after a search of some days, he was found asleep in a pigsty. He had the remains of an old shirt hanging round his neck; and under one arm, an old shoe that he seemed to use as a larder; it contained two old crusts and the raw wing of a chicken. In all the time of his wandering he had not come more than nine miles from the place where he had come ashore.

(*The Cinque Ports*, Blackwood, 1900, 163)

Amy Foster herself was, according to Jessie Conrad in her memoir of her husband, *Joseph Conrad As I Knew Him* (Heinemann, 1926), based on the Conrads' servant-girl.

The story's working title was first 'The Husband', then 'The Castaway', 'Amy Forsett' or 'Amy Fossiter'. It was first published in the *Illustrated London News* (December 1901) before appearing as one of the four tales in *Typhoon and Other Stories*, 1903.

121   *Colebrook, on the shores of Eastbay*: a fictional name; the tale is set in the area between Postling and the fishing town of Dungeness on the coast of south-east Kent.

  the Ship Inn in Brenzett: the real village of Brenzett is 5 miles inland but here is moved to the sea coast, based (according to Cedric Watts) on the village of Dymchurch.

  a Martello tower: a small, round defensive fort built in Dymchurch during the early 1800s as part of the plan to defend against invasion by Napoleon; modelled on the sixteenth-century defence system, at Mortella (Myrtle) Point in Corsica. Throughout, the local detail and sense of the landscape (especially to a foreign eye) belong with Conrad's well-known account of the writer's role, in a famous preface of 1897: 'My task which I am trying to achieve is, by the power of the written word, to make you hear, to make you feel—it is, before all, to make you see.'

  Admiralty charts: produced by the Hydrographic Department of the Admiralty (in governmental command of the Royal Navy) since 1800, for safe navigation to harbour, including information on depth, hazards, sea-bed composition, tides, anchorage, and land and coastal features ("mud and shells").

  from choice: Kennedy's unnamed friend, the framing narrator to whom Kennedy tells the story that follows, positions the doctor as an educated figure, humane medical man and objective scientist, mediating between the narrow village community and the wider world beyond.

122   *chestnut*: horse, reddish-brain in colour.

Explanatory Notes

122 *And yet which of us is safe?*: casually spoken but at the heart of Conrad.

123 *well-to-do, apopletic grazier*: Amy's paternal grandfather, a wealthy man of terrible temper, reared and fattened cattle or sheep for market.

124 *stopping her ears, and did not prevent the crime*: an early warning, though there is no one to heed it, of the mixture of strength and weakness lodged in the girl's imagination, which Conrad will bring back at the end of the tale.

some German fellow: the Dutch physiologist, Jacob Moleschott (1822–93) of Heidelberg University, who was insistent on the physical and material basis of mind in his controversial sayings, 'the brain secretes thought as the liver secretes bile', and 'no thought without phosphorus' (where phosphorus was a nutrient said to be as essential for brain as it was for the development of bones: hence the wry recommendation by Mark Twain to eat fish).

the Ancients: the ancient peoples of Egypt, Greece, and Rome, and the belief in powerful forces and drives taking possession of human beings; related to the earlier reference to 'the Greek tragedy' of the relation of Amy Foster's father to his own father.

125 *a castaway*: Bertrand Russell wondered how much of the loneliness of the castaway emigrant 'Conrad had felt among the English and had suppressed by a stern effort of will' (*Autobiography* 1872–1914, Allen & Unwin 1967, 209). In her important article 'Conrad's Revisions to "Amy Foster"' (*Conradiana*, 20.2, Autumn, 1988, 181–93) Gail Fraser quotes from the more explicit manuscript draft (182; MS 24–5) held by the Beinecke Library, Yale University—the excised first thoughts appearing in brackets:

> Yes, he was a castaway, and the lot of the castaway is a hard one—as you (ought to kn) who have been wrecked yourself ought to know. No matter how sure we may be of kindness we feel *profoundly* our own strangeness (amongst the people) the strangeness of creatures thrown out (of the sea) suddenly by the sea upon the mercy (of people) of another race (of another people) perhaps whose tongue, thoughts manners are a (mystery) complete and momentous mystery. The faces (are) appear like masks, *all* the eyes are full of surprise and wonder. Your difference you feel creates a gulph—and there is no retreat. He must have experienced these sensations because (he did not know where he was) for him who knew nothing of the earth this was (for him) an undiscovered country.

The re-formulations show the increased sense of horror: 'thrown out of the sea . . . thrown out suddenly by the sea upon the mercy of people, of another people, of another race whose tongue, thoughts, manners . . . faces . . .' It is the sense of 'difference' that is powerful, not as in the relation between Amy's father and his own father the similarity of character.

a poor emigrant: Yanko Goorall, a Polish highlander from the mountains, was part of a wave of emigrants trying to escape Poland under Austrian rule, to make for America and the New World.

126 *put his trust in God*: in his revisions, Conrad is often at pains to emphasize Yanko's simple old Catholic faith, in contrast to the villagers' lack of true Christian spirit.

casement: hinged window frame.

127 *Elbe*: major German river that flows into the North Sea at Cuxhaven, northwest of Hamburg.

'tween deck: empty area between two other decks, usually main and lower, in the hull of a cargo ship.

battened down: secured by wooden or metal hatch-cover.

where people had to sleep . . . rocking all ways at once all the time: Gail Fraser notes how Conrad had here changed for serial publication the manuscript's simpler description 'where people lay . . . jumped all the time' ('Conrad's Revisions to "Amy Foster"', 186).

the iron track: by rail and train (later called 'steam machine'), but it is important to the feeling of estrangement throughout that the reported language feels as if it is sometimes in halting translation from a foreign tongue.

128 *Carmelite Convent*: the Carmelites, originally known as the Order of the Blessed Virgin Mary of Mount Carmel (the scene of Elijah's great contest with false prophets), are a Roman Catholic monastic order, the convent housing a community of nuns.

it was called Berlin: the capital of Germany, but again registered from the castaway's perspective.

steam-machine that went on the water: within this alien modern world, no longer travelling by train but by steamer, here a small boat powered by steam.

who made much noise: added, as Gail Fraser notes, in Conrad's revisions for serial publication to indicate something of the castaway's foreign idiom and tone ('Conrad's Revisions to "Amy Foster"', 186).

great house on the water: similarly, now a large steam ship which 'swims' the waters.

129 *the American Kaiser*: the President of the United States and its government, as in Kaiser (Caesar), emperor of the German Empire.

132 *(unaware he was being addressed as 'gracious lord' . . .)*: it is another crucial linguistic element in this tale that it should position itself, in translation, between two languages.

Carpathians: great mountain range of 1500 km (932 miles) through Central and Eastern Europe.

Hamburg emigrant ship Herzogin Sophia-Dorothea: the Duchess (Herzogin: German) Sophia-Dorothea, repudiated German wife of future King George I of England and mother of George II (1666–1726). Hamburg, the second largest city in Germany, was a naturally sheltered harbour.

Sclavonian peasantry: now Slavonia, region bordered by the rivers Danube, Drava and Sava, and part of the Austro-Hungarian Empire until 1918.

133 *amidships*: in the middle of the ship.

  spar: strong, thick pole used for masts.

134 *cobble*: more usually, coble: a fishing boat.

136 *Hindoo*: archaic spelling of Hindu, from the Indian sub-continent around
  the Indus river, here spoken in ignorance.

  Basque: one born in the Basque region, in an area of Spain and France
  bordering the Bay of Biscay around the western end of the Pyrenees.

  Goethe: Johann Wolfgang von Goethe (1749–832), German poet, playwright
  and novelist as well as scientist and statesman.

  Dante: Dante Alighieri (1265–1321), the great Italian poet who wrote *The
  Divine Comedy*.

  pallet: crude bed with straw mattress.

138 *Conceive you*: from the French injunction 'concevez-vous', meaning
  'Imagine, if you will'. Such occasional Gallicisms are evidence of French
  being Conrad's second language.

139 *He couldn't understand either why they were kept shut up most of the time.
  There was nothing to steal in them. Was it to keep people from praying too
  often?*: added at the manuscript stage and thus evidence of Gail Fraser's
  thesis: 'From manuscript to book version, therefore, Conrad's revisions
  reveal a consistent purpose. He concentrated chiefly on heightening the
  opposition between Yanko's perspective and Colebrook's point of view,
  and on defamiliarizing sights and sounds through imagery and language
  so that the reader experiences the young peasant's disorientation directly.
  As a result, in the most successful parts of the story—Yanko's voyage from
  his native village to the coast, for example—we are made intensely aware
  of the loneliness and alienation experienced by all foreigners' ('Conrad's
  Revisions to "Amy Foster" ', 192–3).

  scapulary: garment worn over the shoulders with opening for the head,
  like a vestment signifying religious devotion and often associated with
  a monastic order.

140 *slop-made pepper-and-salt suit on Sundays*: his Sunday best, as for going to
  church, is a rough ready-made suit with intermingled flecks of black and
  white.

  hussar's dolman: a dolman was a short, heavily braided military jacket, with
  a pelisse fur trimmed jacket thrown over it to protect the left shoulder,
  favoured by the elite light cavalry, originating in fifteenth-to-sixteenth-
  century Hungary.

  only the song of birds: in the original serialization in the *Illustrated London
  News*, it is 'only the heartless song of birds' (vol. 119, 28 December, 1901,
  1008).

  tap-room: public bar where the beer is served on tap, direct from the cask.

141 *He was called Yanko*: the first time the stranger's real name is disclosed,
  where Yanko is after the Polish, Janko.

like Goorall: goral is Polish for highlander, from the mountains of southern Poland.

143 '*walking out*' *together*: going for walks together as part of courting.

elevated: elated and intoxicated, high on alcohol.

Jack-in-the-box: from the toy in which a clownish or devil-like figure on a spring pops up when the lid is opened: here to do with Yanko, as an impish upstart coming out of nowhere as a person of strange, abrupt physical vitality; also the term for an untrustworthy swindler-type who substituted empty boxes for full ones.

144 *that dull nature*: dullness is often attributed to Amy Foster as well as the Colebrook community. Gail Fraser highlights a manuscript passage, cancelled before serial publication, on

> the common people of the earth and the sea shore the inarticulate who live beyond the pale, people of obscure minds of imperfect speech of slow eyes, whose complexity the heritage of mankind seems buried *deep out of sight* like a seed in hard ground waiting for the day, for the moment, for the fertilizing touch of a sunray or of a thunder shower, to pierce its shell of mud, to sprout to expand and grow and bear its own flower, tender or bizarre or ominous of terror and sorrow.
>
> ('Conrad's Revisions to "Amy Foster"', 191)

145 *he may have thought he was speaking in English*: this is where the story's sense of being conveyed in translation is at its most devastating. As an unsigned reviewer in the *Academy* put it, 9 May 1903, the misunderstanding is not trivial or chance as in so much sensational fiction of the time, but 'an absolute lack of understanding which reaches to the deeps of essential and inevitable tragedy. The simplicity of it ... Here is bare life ... bare to the nerve' (*Conrad: The Critical Heritage*, 154). The feverish delirium and unthinking reversion into the mother tongue befell Conrad himself on his honeymoon in 1896 and again in 1910 after the exhausting completion of his novel *Under Western Eyes* (see Introduction). In the breakdown of 1910 Conrad mirrored the situation of Razumov in *Under Western Eyes*, helplessly dependent on the woman Tekla in his smash-up—Conrad's own life becoming mixed up, in his mind, with the scenes of his novel, even to the point of conversing with his characters. This is consonant with the terrifying symbiosis of life and writing in Conrad's mind, back and forth across fictions over the years: 'I feel myself—strangely growing into a sort of outcast,' he wrote in a letter to his fellow-novelist John Galsworthy in 1903, 'A mental and moral outcast' (*Collected Letters of Joseph Conrad*, vol. 3, 54).

146 *called out terribly one word—some word*: always Conrad was concerned with the final barely speakable word, as with Kurtz's 'the horror' in 'Heart of Darkness'. As Conrad wrote in *Lord Jim*:

> Are not our lives too short for that full utterance which through all our stammerings is of course our only and abiding intention? I have given

up expecting those last words, whose ring, if they could only be pronounced, would shake both heaven and earth. There is never time to say our last word—the last word of our love, of our desire, faith, remorse, submissions, revolt. The heaven and the earth must not be shaken, I suppose—at least, not by us who know so many truths about either.

(*Lord Jim*, Edinburgh: Blackwood, 1900, Chapter 21)

So it is here in 'Amy Foster' with the final minimal cries of 'Water!', 'Gone!', 'Why?' and 'Merciful!'

146   *He was muddy*: ironically after all his cry for water, dying in a puddle. We are nothing, he wrote still more bleakly to Cunninghame Graham: 'Words fly away; and nothing remains . . . nothing remains—but a clot of mud, of cold mud, of dead mud cast into black space, rolling around an extinguished sun. Nothing. Neither thought, nor sound, nor soul. Nothing.' (*Collected Letters of Joseph Conrad*, vol. 2, 70).

147   *the other one*: in the manuscript it is the child's black eyes that makes the doctor think of the late Yanko as 'the other', unnamed again: 'I look after his ailments. And the other day I was looking at him lying on her knees, frightened but quiet with his black eyes (and I thought of the other) with that fluttered air of a bird in a snare. And I thought of the other, the father cast up mysteriously by the sea to perish in the depths of a most terrible despair' (Gail Fraser, 'Conrad's Revisions to "Amy Foster"', 190).

THE RETURN

'The Return' was painfully composed over five months in 1897. This was one of only two Conrad stories to suffer the 'distinction' (as Conrad himself wryly noted) of not being accepted for magazine publication in advance of its appearance in *Tales of Unrest* (1898). Conrad finished the story even as he was beginning 'Karain', a tale of gun-running, 'the only instance in my life when I made an attempt to write with both hands at once as it were'. He goes on, in his Author's Note to *Tales of Unrest*:

Indeed my innermost feeling, now, is that "The Return" is a left-handed production. Looking through that story lately I had the material impression of sitting under a large and expensive umbrella in the loud drumming of a heavy rain-shower. It was very distracting. In the general uproar one could hear every individual drop strike on the stout and distended silk. Mentally, the reading rendered me dumb for the remainder of the day, not exactly with astonishment but with a sort of dismal wonder. I don't want to talk disrespectfully of any pages of mine. Psychologically there were no doubt good reasons for my attempt; and it was worth while, if only to see of what excesses I was capable in that sort of virtuosity. In this connection I should like to confess my surprise on finding that notwithstanding all its apparatus of analysis the story consists for the most part of physical impressions;

impressions of sound and sight, railway station, streets, a trotting horse, reflections in mirrors and so on, rendered as if for their own sake and combined with a sublimated description of a desirable middle-class town-residence which somehow manages to produce a sinister effect. For the rest any kind word about "The Return" (and there have been such words said at different times) awakens in me the liveliest gratitude, for I know how much the writing of that fantasy has cost me in sheer toil, in temper, and in disillusion.

The story seems to have arisen out of a lunchtime meeting in February 1897 between Conrad and Henry James, and as Conrad's most Jamesian tale, certainly represents a major shift from exotic Malaysian sea-settings to the claustrophobic shock of sexual turmoil nearer home. Hence the physical impressionism alluded to in his Preface to the work. This is what Conrad called his 'London story' of 'the gospel of the beastly bourgeois' in a smart townhouse suddenly shaken to its very foundations (*Collected Letters of Joseph Conrad*, vol. 1, pp. 351, 393).

148 *inner circle train*: beginning with steam engines before developing electrification, the original Metropolitan District Railway line opened in December 1868 from South Kensington to Westminster as part of a plan for a below-ground 'inner circle' connecting London's main line termini; fully completed in 1884, it was later to become the Circle Line of the London Underground, including the City of London's financial centre and Oxford Circus in the West End.

third-class compartment: there were three classes of carriage, the third class being the least comfortable and well-lit.

fusillade: a series of shots.

woollen comforter: scarf.

149 *his club*: private gentlemen's club for social purposes.

did business or amused himself: in the manuscript lodged in The Henry W. and Albert A. Berg Collection of English and American Literature, The New York Public Library, Astor, Lenox and Tilden Foundations (hereafter cited as 'Berg'), there follows an account of the death of Hervey's father from whom he inherited a prosperous business which rather alleviates the so-called 'proper' sorrow of his loss: 'though he would have judged a beast anyone who would have proclaimed openly that sons are consoled in that way'. 'Openly' is a revision, sneaked into the text. His mother, it goes on, died five years later, mourned mainly by a lady companion who would now have to find a less easy place elsewhere: 'The one dying upstairs had been very easy to live with, and very kind, at times.' The son had spent 'a whole dismal week in the house' towards the end, yawning 'through two unsatisfactory meals a day'. The funeral and formal mourning period somewhat delayed his marriage.

grenadier: tall and erect, elite soldier (originally selected and trained to throw grenades).

149 *obelisk*: tapering stone pillar as monument or landmark.

a little more complex no doubt: Conrad drily added that 'a little' to the final version of his account of sexual appetite; it is not in the Berg manuscript.

150 *noble sentiments are cultivated . . . to conceal the pitiless materialism*: this sentence is not in the manuscript which speaks of 'a world ignobly virtuous and safe', adding a Henry-James-like version of cultivation as concealment. Here the first use of 'materialism' is introduced in the story: the idea of what is solidly material and/or economically materialistic is often emphasized in the revisions.

151 *frock-coat*: formal coat for well-to-do Victorian and Edwardian males, cut off just above the knee, here to do with his fashionable and expansive influence upon his crowd of followers.

Gothic tower: architectural style originating in the twelfth century and revived in the nineteenth century, emphasizing height.

They skimmed over the surface of life: a phrase replacing in the manuscript the initial statement 'They passed through life'. In 'Typhoon' (1902) Conrad writes of his sea captain sailing over the 'surface' of the oceans 'as some men go skimming over the years of existence to sink gently into a placid grave, ignorant of life to the last, without ever having been made to see all it may contain of perfidy, of violence, and of terror. There are on sea and land such men thus fortunate—or thus disdained by destiny or by the sea.' In what follows, in the indoor world of bourgeois artifice, mirrors are initially the means Conrad uses to suggest mere surface images, vanities, imitations, and appearances. But as an unsigned review in the *Daily Mail* indicated, 12 April 1898, the 'sheer force' of Conrad's 'psychological insight' made 'common things' be seen increasingly 'in an uncommon way' as the tale unfolded (*Conrad: The Critical Heritage*, 103). Hence the out-of-body external reflections and nightmarish kaleidoscopic fragmentations that follow.

ignoring the hidden stream, the stream restless and dark; the stream of life, profound and unfrozen: compare Matthew Arnold's poem, 'The Buried Life', and also his lines:

> Below the surface-stream, shallow and light,
> Of what we say we feel—below the stream,
> As light, of what we think we feel—there flows
> With noiseless current strong, obscure and deep,
> The central stream of what we feel indeed.

153 *the house had moved a little under his feet*: this sentence and the paragraph following are heavily worked on in the Berg manuscript (at first, for example, 'he felt the house move under his feet') always around the sense of sudden 'insecurity'. In *Under Western Eyes* (1911) when the protagonist is under questioning, 'It seemed to Razumov that the floor was moving slightly' (Part First, Chapter 2).

prevented him from hearing himself think: in the Berg manuscript it looks as if it was originally written as 'impossible to think' and then scrawled out. These reflexive motions of 'absolute blank' in mental shock—not hearing oneself think or, later, hearing oneself speak only as if from an inner distance—are always physically emphasized, especially in the revisions.

gaslights: lit by lamplighters, street gas lamps were prevalent in London from the early nineteenth century until the end of World War II.

154 *It penetrated him*: John Galsworthy spoke of Conrad as one of those few authors of courage who will ask of their characters: 'Are they persons really living—is it blood, or is it sawdust, in these veins?' Then Conrad would take his pin, said Galsworthy, 'searching for soft spots'. Oddly Galsworthy felt the characterization of Hervey was a failure; but here is Conrad exploring both blood and sawdust (*Conrad: The Critical Heritage*, 207).

his mental hold . . . to repeat it aloud: 'mental' is inserted in after-thought in the Berg manuscript and 'aloud' is squeezed in at the edge of the page.

the words. . . . the words . . . words: against the external background of glare and noise, with physical shock overwhelming the capacity for normal thought, this is the first point at which words are blurted out loud instead of being second-hand formulae: they emerge like messages of devastating force, as in the broken stammerings of *Lord Jim*. Conrad clearly wanted the repetition: in the manuscript 'the strange and appalling words' are 'short and appalling sentences'.

vibrated round him: compare Ottoline Morrell's unkind description of Conrad's own wife as

'a good and reposeful mattress for this hypersensitive, nerve-wracked man, who did not ask from his wife high intelligence, only an assuagement of life's vibrations' in *Ottoline: The Early Memoirs of Lady Ottoline Morrell*, ed. R. Gathorne-Hardy (London: Faber, 1963), 241.

157 *truth would be of no use to him*: the Berg manuscript continues: 'for truth helps no man; for truth is the road to humiliation; for truth does not uplift and console; for truth is sordid discouraging and cruel; a heaven-sent trial of anguish, pain and abasement which only lofty souls can face—and survive'. Conrad then goes on to speak of the common man's alternative: wearing the armour of 'hard falsehood'. The sentences about 'concealment' were added instead, after the manuscript stage of composition.

face it out: this is more like saving face, putting a brave social face on it by secondary dissemblance, than Captain MacWhirr's great primary utterance to the young mate, on ship in the eye of the storm of 'Typhoon': 'Keep her facing it. They may say what they like, but the heaviest seas run with the wind. Facing it—always facing it—that's the way to get through. You are a young sailor. Face it. That's enough for any man.'

158 *the Divorce Court*: established through the Matrimonial Causes Act, 1857.

158 *He realized that he had had a shock*: the shock and the realization of having
    it have a double effect, until Hervey's egotism, conventional morality and
    attempted dismissal of mere feeling can temporarily rescue him again
    from terrible insights.

159 *like the first man on the first day of evil*: this sense of the primal naked
    Adam, the 'simple human being', is in place of the secondary social life
    Hervey has been living—until the story ends with a sense of 'the last day'
    having come and gone.

    turn of the screw: the title of Henry James' horror novella which began to
    appear in *Collier's Weekly*, January 1898.

162 *the silence round him was absolute*: though silence can be a relief from the
    noise and chaos, this momentarily absolute silence, betokening the silence
    of some indifferent absolute in the universe itself, is the ultimate threat in
    Conrad. Human beings often shy away from or try to cover over its non-
    human force: 'An immense and imperturbable silence that swallows up
    without echo the murmur of regret and the cry of revolt' (*An Outcast of the
    Islands*, 1896, Part 5, Chapter 3).

163 *returned finally*: in the to-and-fro of realization coming and going, this
    matches the return of his wife and the title of the story.

164 *the normal silence*: as compared to the absolute silence, before his wife gives
    a look that is like a great, wordless cry.

165 *He was profoundly disappointed by what he had said*: in this now strange
    environment, this is the first of many instances of his words coming back
    upon him in momentary delay, or his hearing himself in the immediate
    aftermath, often in a hollow echo-like version of a mirror.

    like a clasp of eternal complicity: in the Berg manuscript this phrase is writ-
    ten over the less disturbing original: 'a sign of eternal association'.

166 *lost touch of the material world . . . a kind of empty universe*: in the Berg
    manuscript, as the walls of the house almost seem to come down, the
    material world becomes an 'intangible' universe before Conrad substitutes
    a much-favoured adjective in this story: 'empty'; also adding 'nothing but'
    before 'fury and anguish'.

167 *woman before his eyes*: in the Berg manuscript Conrad crosses out what
    follows: 'The awful and perfect peace was more false than a clamour of
    stoicism, more ignoble than a dishonest offer of secrecy'. It was often hard
    for Conrad to decide what was or was not too much in the writing of this
    extreme and anomalous situation.

168 *made love to you*: in the sense, initially, of 'pay amorous attention to'.

169 *"Nothing," she said*: an irony, the implications of which remain for the time
    in silence.

170 *The sound of that sentence*: more reflexive and complex in effect than the
    earlier scratched-out manuscript version, 'These words'.

He listened to himself with solemn emotion: another attempted self-reinforcement, in contrast with his more primary response, spoken out loud to himself in his initial shock: 'She's gone'. The novelist John Galsworthy considered the husband and the protagonist in *Lord Jim* to be egotistically stupid men 'with the brains and nerves of such', giving themselves away as stupid without being able to 'admit that they are' (*Conrad: The Critical Heritage*, 207).

171 *For some reason*: inserted in the Berg manuscript in place of simply 'He pulled out his watch . . .'.

174 *"Is this letter the worst of it?" . . . "The worst is my coming back" There followed a period of dead silence*: this is an instance of the sort of allusiveness in dialogue that resembles the style of Henry James, for example in his novella *The Beast in the Jungle* (1903):

> "It *would* be the worst," she finally let herself say. "I mean the thing I've never said."
>
> It hushed him a moment. "More monstrous than all the monstrosities we've named?"
>
> "More monstrous. Isn't that what you sufficiently express," she asked, "in calling it the worst?" (Chapter 4)

In the Berg manuscript this is followed by two heavily deleted speeches, discussed in the Introduction: the first is Hervey on her coming back: 'What made you?' he said, to which she makes a single word reply which seems to be 'Fear.' Conrad was always both attracted to and sceptical of the power of a final summarizing word. It is part of the complexity of this story that a simple explanation might be deleted, especially when later she says 'If I had believed you loved me . . . I would never have come back'. I am indebted to Julie Carlsen of the Henry W. and Albert A. Berg Collection of English and American Literature, New York Public Library, for help in deciphering the manuscript here.

175 *three exact replicas of his face*: again the ironic and satiric force of the mirror-images, as opposed to Hervey's attempt at more flattering self-reflections.

176 *He was ashamed of that unseemly posture*: an instance of the mirror image offering a bleak external truth. In the manuscript, it is first written as 'that exhibition of himself' and then crossed through.

Mrs Alvan Hervey: she is never given a name of her own.

177 *given with such readiness*: in the manuscript this crucial paragraph was carefully reformulated throughout, and this phrase is put in place of the originally more explicit formulation 'contrary to his expectation'.

conditions we had learned to think absolutely safe: it is central to Conrad in these selected stories that this absolute safety is itself impossible. In the 'Author's Note' to *A Personal Record* (1912), he writes: 'If in action we may admit with awe that the Impossible recedes before men's indomitable spirit, the Impossible in matters of analysis will always make a stand at some point or other.' There are instances, as in sea-faring, where the practical can subdue the sense of the Impossible, or where action can at least find out what is or is not momentarily possible in practice. But here inside the conscious uncertainty of this marriage, the Impossible seems more as it is in the world of imagination and analysis: a force never to be wholly dismissed, because always a returning threat; unaccountable in breaking orderly bounds and defying conventional explanation. 'Nothing could be foreseen, foretold—guarded against.' 'Impossible to know' becomes a tense refrain later on, a terror that seems related to the deeper silences and hidden secrets of the story.

179 *"Words!"*: the husband has already begun to stammer over the words, such as 'duty', that will not paper over the cracks. Hence cries and shrieks and wild laughter. 'Half the words we use have no meaning whatever,' wrote Conrad to Cunninghame Graham 14 January 1898, 'and of the other half each man understands each word after the fashion of his own folly and conceit. . . . As our peasants say: "Pray, brother, forgive me for the love of God". And we don't know what forgiveness is, nor what is love, or where God is' (*Collected Letters of Joseph Conrad*, vol. 2, 17).

181 *not without some wonder*: this paragraph on Hervey's realization of his own changes is itself heavily revised in the manuscript.

183 *He had missed the edge*: of such details (where in 'Typhoon' MacWhirr's sanity is saved by a box of matches remaining in its right place despite the rampaging storm), Ford Madox Ford offered an important interpretation:

> By all accounts Conrad was a very efficient master—but extravagantly nervous about details. All the several officers who once sailed with him have narrated the same thing to the writer. Conrad would indulge in extremely dangerous manœuvres, going about within knife-blades of deadly shores whilst his officers and crew shivered—but over very small details of the stowing of spars and the like he would go out of his mind and swear the ship to pieces. In the same way, in writing he would attack subjects almost impossible and go almost mad over a sentence.
> (*Joseph Conrad: A Personal Remembrance*, 111–12).

The drinking glass seemingly goes through the table, another instance of a loss of the reliable solidity of the world.

185 *unchanged*: Conrad first wrote simply 'and it was unchanged' and then inserted in the manuscript: 'and now he was shocked to see' that it was unchanged, a further deepening. So earlier: 'The violence of the short tumult within him had been such as could well have shattered all creation; and yet *nothing* was changed. He faced his wife in the familiar room in his own house. It had *not* fallen' (my italics).

186 *at last, recollecting himself, was frightened . . . the discovered unconsciousness of his actions affected him painfully . . . thoughts he had never had before*: all these phrases are honed in the manuscript, where 'recollecting himself' is inserted on second thought, as is 'discovered', and where initially it was

simply 'It made him think as he had never strongly before'—all the revisions increasing his sense of shock at the effect on himself.

187 *This woman . . . had returned to him . . . the secret of hearts alone shall return, forever unknown . . .*: in this repetition the title of the story becomes ever more powerful, right up until the stark three words in this story's final paragraph. In the Berg manuscript 'forever unknown' is another insertion, matching the increasing repetition of 'Impossible to know' and 'he would never know'. The phrase about 'the secret of hearts' itself returns two pages from the end.

188 *It was as if it hadn't been*: another of Conrad's deepening phrases inserted on further thought in the Berg manuscript.

190 *a material world*: Conrad inserted 'material' in the manuscript in juxtaposition with the 'immaterial' grace of love and faith.

he was coming back slowly to the world of senses: a revision in the manuscript of what was initially 'he was coming slowly to himself'.

191 *Arabesques*: ornamental design in Islamic art, here perhaps aesthetically transforming life's thorns into flowing flower-like lines.

192 *Nobody shall know!*: this now repeated phrase is part of the final movement whereby what was before the desired cover-up is now a further horror. It is related to the increasing disregard for material appearances as opposed to secret immaterial truths.

Why . . .: again a manuscript revision, where previously Conrad had simply stated it as a fact; so too he inserts into this sentence, 'like the last day of all' where previously it was 'the day that began presented itself like a day without a tomorrow'.

portière: curtain hung over a doorway.

as though the great night of the world: another neo-apocalyptic manuscript revision replacing 'as though the great darkness of the outside'.

193 *the flowing tide of a tenebrous sea*: the invasive darkness turns this London townhouse back into the deeps of a Conrad sea.

the return of idealized perfections: again the use of the story's title, though here ideals will not return. By the end of the paragraph 'Nothing came back', only silence.

194 *material serenity*: yet another revised insertion of 'material' in the manuscript.

whispering your confession over the edge of the world: the original manuscript formulation was 'To give her your thought, your belief, was like whispering over the sea' (Conrad having brought in the image of a sea of darkness engulfing the house).

den of coiners: hiding place for makers of counterfeit money.

house of ill-fame: a brothel.

195 *the hate . . .*: this long final clause is added with smaller handwriting in the manuscript.

196 *It was as though . . . his soul*: this is a manuscript revision of what was at
first: 'as though no sooner outside he had suddenly died—as though his
body had vanished out of the house together with his soul'.

 a door slammed heavily: at the end of Ibsen's play *A Doll's House* (1879), it
is the wife, Nora, who slams out of the patriarchal home, in a shock wave
that, it was said by New York theatre critic, James Gibbons Huneker,
reverberated around the world.

THE DUEL

'The Duel' was begun in Montpellier on a working holiday, in December 1906
or January 1907, and completed by April. It was described by Conrad as 'A
Military Tale', though reviewers thought it could as easily have been called 'An
Ironic Tale'. After initial difficulties in placing the story, it was first serialized in
The Pall Mall Magazine, January–May 1908, and in America as 'The Point of
Honor', in *The Forum*, New York, July–October 1908, where it was also pub-
lished as a separate volume.

 Conrad wrote a prefatory author's note in 1915 for *The Set of Six*,
originally published in 1908, in which 'The Duel' first appeared in book
form:

> It remains for me only now to mention The Duel, the longest story in the
> book. That story attained the dignity of publication all by itself in a small
> illustrated volume, under the title, "The Point of Honour." That was many
> years ago. It has been since reinstated in its proper place, which is the place
> it occupies in this volume, in all the subsequent editions of my work. Its
> pedigree is extremely simple. It springs from a ten-line paragraph in
> a small provincial paper published in the South of France. That paragraph,
> occasioned by a duel with a fatal ending between two well-known Parisian
> personalities, referred for some reason or other to the "well-known fact" of
> two officers in Napoleon's Grand Army having fought a series of duels in
> the midst of great wars and on some futile pretext. The pretext was never
> disclosed. I had therefore to invent it; and I think that, given the character
> of the two officers which I had to invent, too, I have made it sufficiently
> convincing by the mere force of its absurdity. The truth is that in my mind
> the story is nothing but a serious and even earnest attempt at a bit of his-
> torical fiction. I had heard in my boyhood a good deal of the great
> Napoleonic legend. I had a genuine feeling that I would find myself at
> home in it, and The Duel is the result of that feeling, or, if the reader pre-
> fers, of that presumption. Personally I have no qualms of conscience about
> this piece of work. The story might have been better told of course. All
> one's work might have been better done; but this is the sort of reflection
> a worker must put aside courageously if he doesn't mean every one of his
> conceptions to remain for ever a private vision, an evanescent reverie. How
> many of those visions have I seen vanish in my time! This one, however, has
> remained, a testimony, if you like, to my courage or a proof of my rashness.

What I care to remember best is the testimony of some French readers who volunteered the opinion that in those hundred pages or so I had managed to render "wonderfully" the spirit of the whole epoch. Exaggeration of kindness no doubt; but even so I hug it still to my breast, because in truth that is exactly what I was trying to capture in my small net: the Spirit of the Epoch—never purely militarist in the long clash of arms, youthful, almost childlike in its exaltation of sentiment—naively heroic in its faith.

The story was based on a legendary series of real-life duels between two French cavalry officers, Francois Fournier-Sarlovèze (1773–1827), an ardent duellist, and Antoine Dupont de l'Etang (1765–1838). Conrad read of it in Montpellier in 1906. There were many versions in French, German, and English: the earliest extended reports in English of the long, mysterious quarrel appeared in *Household Words*, 17 July 1858, and the American *Harper's New Monthly Magazine*, September 1858, both of which are selectively quoted below when comparison seems helpful.

197 *Napoleon I.*: Napoleon Bonaparte, born 1769 in Corsica, served in the French army in the 1790s in support of the French Revolution, engineering a coup in 1799 to become First Consul of the Republic, and crowning himself Emperor 1804. An outstanding general, he created a European Empire with famous victories in battle at Austerlitz 1805, over the Russians and Austrians; Jena and Auerstedt 1806, against the German kingdom of Prussia; and over the Russians again in the battle of Friedland 1807. Inside France from 1804 the Napoleonic Code became the rationally systematic basis of French civil law: hence Napoleon's symptomatic dislike of wanton duelling. Through the Napoleonic Wars (1803–15), Napoleon consolidated his hold over Europe with victory over the Austrians again at the battle of Wagram in 1809, followed by invasions of Spain and Russia—until military defeat by Prussian and Austrian forces at the battle of Leipzig (then, Leipsic) in 1813, and the subsequent capture of Paris, led to his enforced abdication in 1814 and exile to the island of Elba. He briefly recovered to become Emperor again in 1815, overcoming the restoration of the royal Bourbon dynasty in France, until defeated at the Battle of Waterloo in the same year. Exiled again, he died on the remote South Atlantic island of St Helena in 1821.

Conrad wrote to Edward Garnett, 21 August 1908, that he had originally thought to call the story 'The Masters of Europe' but 'rejected it as pretentious': the result was that all the early reviewers, he said, missed the 'Napoleonic feeling' by blindly following the mere tale (*Conrad: The Critical Heritage*, 220).

gild . . . lily: from Shakespeare, *King John* (4.2.11) on the king's plan for a second coronation.

officers of infantry of the line: commissioned officers in charge of combat troops, commanding the lines of foot-soldiers.

197 *Feraud and D'Hubert*: In Conrad's first version D'Hubert was called 'Durand'. There were many versions in French, German, and English: see *Conrad's "The Duel": Sources/Text*, eds J. H. Stape and J. G. Peters (Brill Rodopi 2015). One of the clearest and earliest English reports of the long, mysterious quarrel was published in the American *Harper's New Monthly Magazine* (September 1858), beginning thus:

> The late Paris duels have called up the subject of dueling anew; and among the most extraordinary affairs of that nature which inquiry has brought to light, is the story of a duel commencing in 1794 and ending only in 1813. . . . In 1794, then, there lived a Captain of hussars, Fournier by name, at Strasbourg, who was the most hot-headed and quarrelsome man in all that region. Again and again he had slain his man in duels, but no successes seemed to satiate his taste for this sort of murder. On one occasion he had wantonly provoked a young man, named Blumm—who was a great favourite among the good bourgeoisie of Strasbourg—and as wantonly had slain him. The whole town was full of excitement, and the whole town condemned Fournier as his murderer. Still, dueling was honorable; who should venture to punish the murderer, who was only [*sic*] duelist? It happened that, upon the night of the burial of poor Blumm, a great ball, long time announced, was given by the military commander of the place. Fournier was among the invited guests; but the general commanding, foreseeing what unpleasant *rencontres* [encounters] might grow out of his presence, gave orders to his aide-de-camp, Captain Dupont, to station himself at the door, and, citing the order of his general, to give *congé* [formal dismissal] to Fournier. Dupont accepted the commission.

There is also an account in the weekly magazine edited by Charles Dickens, *Household Words*, 17 July 1858:

> Soldiers of all ranks had ample opportunities of picking quarrels, whenever they wished it, and often when they did not wish it. In seventeen hundred and ninety-four a captain of hussars, named Fournier, indulged in this amusement to his heart's content. At a later period, his merit and his courage earned him the epaulettes of a general of division. His aggressive temper and his address with arms, rendered his name celebrated in the annals of the duel. He was invariably the victor in these unfortunate meetings; and Strasbourg had to reproach him for the loss of several of her sons on the most futile motives of quarrel, and especially for having killed, on very trifling grounds, a young man named Blume, generally beloved, the only support of a numerous family, whom he had challenged without any plausible reason, and slain without the slightest pity. The death of Blume was regarded as a public misfortune, and sympathised in by a public mourning. On the very day of Blume's funeral General Moreau gave a ball, to which were invited all the members of the high bourgeoisie. It was desirable to avoid the scandalous scenes which could not fail to take place between the fellow

townsmen, perhaps the relations of the unfortunate deceased, and the aggressor, who was styled his murderer. General Moreau, therefore, desired his aide-de-camp, Captain Dupont, afterwards the general who capitulated at Baylen, to prevent Captain Fournier from entering the ball-room.

hussars: elite light cavalry, illustrious for their reckless courage as horsemen and swordsmen, who adopted the colourful uniform of the Hungarian hussars in the fifteenth and sixteenth centuries.

Lieut.: abbreviation of Lieutenant

officier d'ordonnance: aide-de camp or adjutant, administrative assistant to a senior officer.

Strasbourg: city and port in north-eastern France, Alsace, on the Rhine.

interval of peace: the brief peace following upon the treaty of Amiens, 1802, ending hostilities between France and England and marking the end of the French Revolutionary Wars, before the commencement of the Napoleonic Wars, 1803–15.

198 *Alsatian costume*: in Alsace, women traditionally wore a large headdress or black cocked hat, large embroidered white blouse and black skirt with corselet and apron, and a stole over the shoulders.

200 *dolman*: Hussars wore a pelisse, a fur-edged braided jacket slung over one shoulder like a cape, and a dolman, a short, tight braided tunic under it.

salon: elegant reception room in a large house in which eminent and fashionable figures from the worlds of art, politics, and high society were received for the exchange of conversation and ideas.

maître-d'hôtel: literally, 'master of the household'; steward or butler.

202 *"C'est ça!"*: 'That's it; right!'

with astonishing indifference: in the corrected typescript in The Free Library of Philadelphia this succinct impression is given more extendedly: 'in evident good faith which astonished profoundly the other'.

203 *Gascon*: a native of Gascony, in the south-west of France, where traditionally inhabitants were supposed to be of a more passionate Latin temper compared to the more calm and rational north of D'Hubert.

sauerkraut-eating: fermented raw cabbage, the eating of which signifies a person of lower class.

204 *submit tamely to injustice*: in *Household Words*, the account goes:

> Dupont stationed himself in a corner of one of the antechambers, and immediately he caught sight of him accosted him abruptly.
> "What are you going to do here?"
> "Ah! That's you, Dupont? Good evening. Parbleu! [By Jove!] You see what I am doing; I am come to the ball."
> "Are you not ashamed to come to a ball the very day of the funeral of that poor unhappy fellow Blume? What will his friends and his relations say?"

"They may say what they please; it is all one to me. But, I should like to know, what business is that of yours?"

"It is everybody's business. Everybody is thinking and talking about it."

"Everybody is wrong then. I don't like people to poke their noses into my affairs. And now, if you please, let me pass."

"You shall not go into the ball-room."

"And, pray, why?"

"Because you must take yourself off instead. The General orders you to retire to your own apartments."

"Am I turned out of the house?"

"No; it is merely a precaution."

"Are you aware of the consequences of turning Fournier out of doors?"

"I do not want to hear any of your rhodomontades [boastful talk]. Just have the goodness to take yourself off."

"Listen!" said Fournier, in a fury. "I cannot have my revenge of the General, because he is my superior officer; but you are my equal; you have presumed to take your share in the insult, and you shall pay for the whole of it. We will fight!"

"Listen, in turn," replied Dupont. "I have long been out of patience with you; I am disgusted with your bullying ways; and I hope to give you a lesson, which you will long remember."

Fournier passed a sleepless night. He would have gone mad with vexation, had he not been consoled by the hope of killing Dupont.

Harper's has Fournier say, 'Ah! c'est ça! I can not fight the general, for his rank; you will, perhaps, have no objection?—you who commit impertinences at second-hand.'

205 *Picardy*: northern region of France, capital city Amiens. Again the greater rationality of the Northman is emphasized.

206 *perfectly absurd*: absurdity is a key term in this story from now onwards.

commented that assurance: from the French '*commenter*', but in English should be 'commented upon'. Conrad was more prone to Gallicisms in this story.

207 *"En garde, fichtre"*: 'On guard, damn you!'

break ground: 'give ground', but here as of a ship's anchor leaving the sea-bottom.

209 *fury*: in Greek mythology, the Furies or Erinyes were spirits of vengeance in female form.

210 *in the manner of a murderer*: added later, after the manuscript and the serialization versions, in *A Set of Six*.

fioritures: flourishes or embellishments in music.

214 *He intends to send you his seconds . . .*: *Household Words* has the first duel and its aftermath thus:

But the result of the combat was not what he expected, for Dupont gave him a frightful wound.

"You fence well," said Fournier, as he fell.

"Not badly, as you see."

"Yes; but now I know your game. You won't catch me another time as I will show when I am well again."

"You wish for another encounter?"

"Parbleu! [By Jove!] That's a matter of course."

Harper's says that Fournier 'even as he fell, claimed a new meeting'.

215 *sub-commisary of Intendance*: deputy administrator of supply corps.

kerseymere breeches, Hessian boots: fashionable clothing: knee-length trousers of fine woollen cloth with a fancy weave; decoratively tasselled light leather boots, originally worn by soldiers from Hesse, Germany.

transmigration of souls: the belief, most famously endorsed by Pythagoras (570–490 BCE), that the soul after the body's death passes into another form, human, animal, or plant.

216 *hole in his side*: *Household Words* describes the second duel:

In fact, after a few weeks' nursing, Fournier, for the second time, was face to face with his adversary. It was now his turn. He gave Dupont a home-thrust, with the comment:

"You see clearly you hold your hand too low to parry properly. After you have made your thrust, you gave me time to stick three inches of cold iron between your ribs."

"This is only the second act," cried Dupont. "We'll come to the catastrophe as soon as possible."

217 *mon pauvre vieux*: 'My poor old chap.'

que diable: 'What the devil.'

218 *Court of Honour*: tribunal convened to decide whether demands of honour between gentlemen had been settled or were grounds for duelling.

Machiavellism: manipulative cunning, after the Italian Renaissance diplomat and author of *The Prince* (1513), Niccolò Machiavelli (1469–1527).

219 *my subalterns*: officers of lower rank.

220 *Hades*: the underworld abode of the dead in Greek mythology.

turned his tongue seven times in his mouth before he spoke: from a French proverb meaning, 'Think before you speak, until you are really sure of what you want to say'.

mille tonnerres: literally, 'a thousand thunders', an interjection meaning 'by Jove!'

221 *Sacré nom de nom*: another mild oath, literally 'the holy name of a name', meaning 'Good God!' or 'For Heaven's sake!'

223 *truth . . . living in a well*: proverb from the ancient Greeks that truth lies in a well, hence hard to get to the bottom of.

224 *"Qui vivra verra"*: 'He who lives will see', as in 'Time will tell'.

224 *No question of a duel*: the Code of Honour forbade duels between different ranks.

225 *beau sabreur*: a good swordsman.

Austerlitz: otherwise known as the Battle of the Three Emperors, December 1805. It was Napoleon's greatest tactical victory, though his Grand (Imperial) Army of 53,000 men was outnumbered by the 89,000-strong coalition forces of Emperor Alexander I of Russia and Holy Roman Emperor Francis II. Feraud's promotion is a 'step' up the ladder.

the admiration of the beholders: the third duel, fought in Silesia (central Europe, now mainly Poland), is described in *Household Words*:

> Fournier would have liked to conclude the third act by the aid of the pistol, but Dupont claimed the military privilege which obliges officers to fight with their swords. Dupont was wise in maintaining his right, for Fournier's expertness as a pistol shot is still remembered with astonishment. He had accustomed his servant to hold between his fingers a piece of money, which he sent flying with a bullet at five-and-twenty paces distance. And frequently one of the hussars of his regiment, as he galloped past smoking his pipe was surprised to find it smashed between his lips . . . [The encounter] brought about no decisive result; they each received a trifling scratch. Then these two wise-heads, annoyed at so negative a result, agreed to recommence the struggle until one of the two should confess himself beaten, and should renounce all further resistance.

Danube: second-longest river in Europe, rising in the Black Forest in Germany and flowing into the Black Sea, nearly 3,000 km (over 1,800 miles) away.

Gratz and Laybach: Graz is a city in Austria, Laibach (now Ljubljana) the capital city of Slovenia, then both towns in the Austrian empire.

the Rhine and the Save: the Rhine, rising in Switzerland and flowing into the North Sea, is the longest river in Germany at 1230 km (765 miles); the Sava is a 990 km (615 mile) tributary of the Danube in the Western Balkans; the distance between the two rivers being nearly 2,000 km (1,240 miles).

226 *entered Lübeck together*: at the battle of Jena and Auerstedt in west Germany, October 1806, Napoleon virtually wiped out the Prussian army of King Frederick William III. Jean Bernadotte (1763–1844) was made prince of Pontecorvo in Naples by Napoleon after Austerlitz and then crown prince of Sweden in 1810, though later he turned against Napoleon to become King of Norway and Sweden. He led the Napoleonic forces into Lübeck, a port in northern Germany, late in 1806.

what you have to do: at some point, according to the accounts in *Household Words* and *Harpers*, the two drew up a bizarre formal convention—*Harper's* offering the clearest translation:

1ˢᵗ. As often as MM. Dupont and Fournier find themselves within thirty leagues of each other, they shall meet half-way between, for a duel with swords.

2d. If either of the combatants finds himself restrained by the exigences of the service, the other shall make the entire journey, in order to effect a meeting.

3d. No excuse, except such as may grow out of the exigences of military duty, shall be admissible.

The convention was executed in good faith; on every occasion on which it was possible for the two hot-heads to meet, they met, and fought desperately. . . .

Sometimes the promotion of one or the other, by destroying their military equality, interfered with the prosecution of their agreeable engagements.

Household Words has it: 'Whenever the two madmen were able to meet, they fought, and the most extraordinary correspondence, in the second person, too, the most familiar form of French speech, was exchanged between them. . . . "DEAR FRIEND, I shall be passing through Strasbourg at noon, on the 5ᵗʰ of November next. You will find me at the Hôtel des Postes: we will have a fight."'

228 *Au pas—Au trot—Charrrgez!*: 'At walking pace—At a trot—Forward charrrge!'

blasé: 'unconcerned, unimpressed, world-weary'.

229 *Eylau and Friedland*: the Battle of Eylau was a blood-bath fought (like the duels) to no conclusion between the Napoleonic army and the Imperial Russian Army, 7–8 February 1807. It was followed on 14 June by the Battle of Friedland where the French routed the Russians who then sued for peace. Napoleon entered upon a winter campaign in what had been Poland to inflict further damage on the Russians.

unsatisfactory war in Spain . . . the Russian campaign: Napoleon became overstretched in the Peninsular Wars (1807–14) against Spain, Portugal, and England, whilst also conducting the disastrous Russian campaign, in which the Grand Army took Moscow in 1812 only to find it deserted and set ablaze. As a result of the Russian scorch-and-burn policy of destroying crops and livestock, Napoleon was forced to retreat that winter in search of food and supplies, losing over 70,000 men.

230 *sacred battalion*: the Sacred Band of Thebes in the fourth century BCE was a troop of select soldiers, comprising pairs of male lovers, that defeated the Spartans. The term was used for Napoleon's most resolute rear-guard forces, loyal still on his return from Elba in 1815.

marshal of France, Prince of the Empire: Michel Ney (1769–1815) led the remnants of the Grand Army in the retreat from Moscow.

macabre march: grim and deathly, the dance of the macabre was of skeletons escorting the living to their graves, to the strains of a lively waltz.

230 *Cossacks*: originating in the steppes of eastern Europe, these fierce military communities of horsemen and infantry were employed by the Russians in martial action. They were admired by Napoleon himself.

231 *the white immensity of the snows*: from 'Often from daybreak . . .', this was a passage singled out for praise by the poet Edward Thomas in a review in *Bookman*, October 1908, for its pace and movement, weight and colour (*Conrad: The Critical Heritage*, 226). Conrad inserted the poignant word 'sacred' before 'battalion' in the first serial publication in *The Pall Mall Magazine*, in revision of the manuscript where the battalion is also described, more simply, as 'listening to the wind searching their very hearts'. In the first serialization the paragraph had ended, 'it would resume its march, leaving behind a few lifeless bodies lying huddled up, tiny dark specks on the white ground'; in the manuscript it had originally been 'it would resume its march, leaving behind a few dark bodies lying prostrate and a few stains of frozen blood on the white ground'.

cut off in the woods: this moment of their fighting together, in near-silence, rather than clamorously fighting each other, might have led to a fundamental realignment of their relationship. But it is only temporary. Edward Garnett in the *Nation*, 22 August 1908, writes of 'Mr. Conrad's serene impartiality, his mordant humour, his special faculty of depicting the change and movement of life, flowing on even while it arrests us with some sharply stamped aspect, then gliding away to form anew some strangely significant episode' (*Conrad: The Critical Heritage*, 223).

232 *Man of Destiny*: name given to Napoleon, cited by Walter Scott in his *Life of Napoleon* (1827) and in George Bernard Shaw's play of that name (1895).

fourgon: coach or wagon.

had his scruples as to falling out: the manuscript in The Free Library of Philadelphia then speaks of those scruples arising 'from a point of honour and also a little from dread'.

could not be sure of ever rejoining his battalion: the manuscript adds yet another awkward consideration, 'And it imposes a physical effort too from which his starved body shrank'.

233 *Pomerania*: region on southern shore of the Baltic sea, split between Germany and Poland.

234 *return of the legitimate king*: Louis XVIII (1755–1824), grandson of Louis XV, returned from a twenty-three-year exile to be made king of France on the restoration of the Bourbon dynasty from 1814 until the end of his life, save for the Hundred Days of Napoleon's own return to rule in 1815, following his escape from Elba.

Lutzen, Bautzen and Leipsic: towns in Saxony, eastern German. The battles of Lutzen and Bautzen (May 1813) saw Napoleon resist and push back the Russian and Prussian coalition forces. The 'Battle of the Nations' at Leipzig in October 1813 resulted in heavy defeat for a weakened

Napoleonic army and the coalition's recapture of Germany, prior to invading France.

Magdeburg: eastern German town on the river Elbe held by the French.

Commandant de Place: commander of the town garrison.

235 *Marshal Berthier*: Louis-Alexander Berthier (1753–1815), Minister of War and Napoleon's chief of staff.

campaign of France . . . under Laon: the Battle of Laon (a fortress town situated on a rocky height above the Picardy plain) in March 1814 saw the Prussians defeat Napoleon in his campaign to defend Paris.

promoted . . . to general: in the source as described in *Household Words*, it is Fournier who is the first of the two to obtain promotion to general:

> MY DEAR DUPONT, I am informed that the Emperor has done justice to your merits by promoting you to the rank of General of Brigade. Accept my sincere congratulations on an advancement which is no more than the natural consequence of your knowledge and your courage. For myself, there is a double motive for rejoicing at your nomination. In the first place, the satisfaction given by a circumstance so flattering to your future prospects; and secondly, the permission which it gives us of having a turn together at the first opportunity.

236 *Provence*: region in the warmth of south-eastern France on the Mediterranean.

Marshal Soult . . . Spain: Jean-de-Dieu Soult (1769–1851) was one of Napoleon's foremost generals in the disastrous struggles of the Peninsular War in Spain and Portugal where again Napoleon overstretched his resources, fighting on too many fronts. After Napoleon's abdication, Soult declared himself a Royalist and became Minister of War between November 1814 and March 1815. On Napoleon's return from Elba, he went back to being a Bonapartist.

tricolour cockades . . . eagle buttons: the tricolour, the red, white, and blue of the French flag during the Revolution, here worn as a rosette; the eagle was the symbol of Napoleon in imitation of the legions of the ancient Roman empire.

Elba: island in the Mediterranean off the coast of Italy where the defeated Napoleon was exiled from May 1814 until his escape back to France in March 1815.

237 *the Hundred Days*: the period of Napoleon's return to power between his escape from Elba and his final defeat at the hands of Wellington at Waterloo, June 1815.

Special Commission . . . firing squad: following the return to power of Louis XVIII, a 'White Terror' involved vengeance upon hundreds of people associated with the Revolution and Napoleon in Royalist reaction.

238 *terrasse of the Café Tortoni*: the terrace of a fashionable café in Paris.

239 *The Other was the Man of St Helena*: Napoleon, confined to the remote and tiny South Atlantic island, 16 × 8 kilometres, until his death in 1821.

French saying: 'faire tant des pieds et des mains', meaning, 'to pull out all the stops'.

cabinet: study or office.

conventionnel Fouché: Joseph Fouché (1759–1820), Member of the National Convention, the Parliament of the French Revolution from 1792 to 1795, made Duke of Otranto by Napoleon in 1809, served as Minister of Police under both Napoleon and Louis XVIII.

the second Restoration: the first Restoration of the Bourbon dynasty through Louis XVIII was in 1814, the second in 1815 after the Hundred Days, following Napoleon's escape from Elba. The clergyman diplomat, Talleyrand, was the architect of both the first and, with Fouché, the second Restoration.

fiancée: the widower Fouché in 1815 married Ernestine de Castellane-Majastres (1788–1850), thirty years his junior, later the author of memoirs of the empress Josephine and the Napoleonic court.

240 *every grenadier and every trooper of the army*: grenadiers were originally specialist soldiers who threw heavy hand grenades but later the term covered an elite of strong combatants who took the lead in assaults: on horseback, they were known as heavy cavalry; troopers were soldiers of lower rank in the cavalry.

well-hung tongue: 'avoir une langue bien perdue', meaning 'to have a loose tongue, to be very talkative'.

241 *Tuileries*: royal palace in Paris, built in 1564, burned by the revolutionary Paris Commune in 1871.

Allied Sovereigns . . . Talleyrand . . . Nesselrode . . . Emperor Alexander's: the Allied Sovereigns in the coalitions against Napoleon were Francis II (1768–1835) the last Holy Roman Emperor who as Francis I was also the first Emperor of Austria, King Frederick William III of Prussia (1770–1840), George IV of England (1762–1830), and Emperor Alexander I of Russia (1777–1825). Charles-Maurice de Talleyrand-Périgord (1754–1838) was another diplomat-politician who deserted Napoleon after serving as his foreign minister, becoming foreign minister to Louis XVIII. Karl Nesselrode (1780–1862) was a Russian diplomat and foreign minister.

What government you imagined yourself to be serving?: 'had' needs to be inserted: 'What government had you imagined . . .'

242 *Diable d'homme!*: 'the very devil of a fellow!'

Waterloo: Belgium town where Napoleon suffered his final defeat by British and Prussian forces under the Duke of Wellington, June 1815.

Parfaitement: 'exactly so'.

243 *par exemple*: 'for example'.

Clarke: Henri Jacques Guillaume Clarke (1765–1818) served as a Minister of War under Napoleon and under Louis XVIII who made him Marshal of France in 1816.

Jacobin: the most extreme political club in the French Revolution which, under Robespierre, established the Reign of Terror with its massacres and public executions. In his youth Fouché was a prominent member, in violent opposition to the royalists and aristocrats, supporting the execution of Louis XVI in 1793. By 1816, for all that he had turned Royalist, he was proscribed as a regicide, and died in exile in Trieste.

244   *anciens militaires*: old soldiers, veterans.

245   *Cuirassier à Cheval*: soldier mounted on horse, wearing a 'cuirass', armour covering chest and back; light cavalry (literally 'hunters on horseback') in the Imperial Guard escorting Napoleon.

     Parfaitement . . . C'est juste . . . Parbleu, c'est connu . . . Bonne chance: 'Exactly so . . . That's right . . . By Jove, that's well known . . . Good luck'.

     en bataille: literally 'in battle', here 'carelessly, at an angle'.

     winter of 1813: on retreat from Moscow.

246   *a sabreur*: a swashbuckler.

     engagé volontaire: a volunteer and not merely a conscript.

     ingenuity: in the French sense of 'innocence'.

     émigré: political emigrant, like many aristocrats who had fled revolutionary France to avoid the guillotine by exile abroad.

247   *ancien régime*: the old political and social system of France under the monarchy before the French Revolution.

     quietist: as of religious believers, originating in late seventeenth century France and Spain, practising passive contemplation, stillness, and abnegation of will before God.

248   *capotes*: great-coats.

     black stocks: neckcloths.

     cocked hats: hats with opposite brims turned up to give two or three points, associated with the military during the French Revolution.

     vieilles moustaches!: literally 'old moustaches', meaning 'aged veteran soldiers with many years of service'.

249   *Judases*: Judas Iscariot was the disciple who betrayed Jesus for thirty pieces of silver.

     gendarmerie: soldiers involved in the duties of police.

250   *bonzes*: Buddhist monks and teachers, especially in China and Japan.

     "Pistols, General": in the *Household Words* version of the original source, the account of the proposed final duel goes:

> Dupont, the more reasonable of the two, now and then thought of the absurdity of a quarrel, which still went on after so many struggles, and

asked himself whether he should not be doing right in killing Fournier, to make an end of the matter. Besides that, he was going to get married. One morning he called on Fournier. "Are you come to fix a day for a match?" inquired the latter, on seeing him enter. "Perhaps I am; but first of all, let us talk a little. Listen to this; I intend to get married; and before I enter the serious state of matrimony, I should like to have done with you."

"Oh! oh!"

"Our quarrel has now lasted for nineteen years. I do not wish to continue a style of life which my wife might consider not exactly comfortable; and therefore, in virtue of the fourth article of our treaty [that the present treaty being entered into in good faith, its conditions may be modified with, the consent of the parties], I am come to propose a change in the mode of combat, and so to have a final meeting, the result of which shall be decisive. We will fight with pistols."

"You don't think of such a thing!" cried Fournier, in astonishment.

"I know that that is your strong point; but, to equal the chances, we will do this, if you like. One of my friends has, at Neuilly, an inclosure planted with trees, and completely surrounded with walls; there are two doors to it, one at each end. On a day, and at an hour to be agreed upon, we will go to the inclosure separately, armed with our two holster-pistols ready loaded, to take a single shot with each. We will try which can find the other, and whoever catches sight of the other, shall fire."

"That's a droll idea."

251 *Le Chevalier de Valmassigue . . . the army of the Princes, bookbinder in Altona, afterwards shoemaker*: Chevalier is the French aristocratic equivalent of 'knight', Valmassigue being the place associated with the uncle. The army of the Princes was a counter-revolutionary force formed by French aristocrats, mainly as émigrés, in 1792. Altona is in north-west Germany, near Hamburg. Dickens's prisoner in the Bastille in *A Tale of Two Cities* (1859), Dr Manette, may be remembered here as also becoming a shoemaker.

à la française: 'in the French style or manner'.

"*Monsieur le Chevalier*": 'Sir Knight'.

mon ami: 'my friend'.

fugue of youth: from the French 'la fougue de la jeunesse', meaning, 'the hot-headed spirit of youth'.

252 *amour propre*: 'pride'.

entre galants hommes: 'between gentlemen'.

saperlotte: mild interjection, 'Good gracious!'

253 *tricorne*: the three-cornered version of the cocked hat.

Sophie Derval . . . de Brissac . . . d'Anjorrant: these appear to be Conrad's inventions, rather than historic persons.

canaille: 'the mob'.

254 *va-nu-pieds*: 'a tramp' (literally, 'going about bare-footed').

s'encanailler: 'to make himself part of the rabble'.

manant: 'churl'.

Senlac: invented town name.

255 *Red Lancers of the Guard*: 2nd Regiment of the Light Horse Lancers of Napoleon's Imperial Guard, formed as an elite cavalry, dressed in scarlet uniform, after Holland was taken by France in 1810.

"*It's a fatality*": in the Library of Philadelphia manuscript: 'It's revolting'. The change to a sense of a whole life destroyed, without actual death by duel, fits well with the 'gust of homicidal fury' D'Hubert feels later in the final duel, in 'the accumulated resentment of a lifetime'.

256 *amazed this man of forty . . . his menaced passion*: the Library of Philadelphia manuscript has 'awarded' for 'amazed' and 'his thwarted or his menaced passion'; then has a further sentence: 'It was the revolt of jeopardised desire.'

the absurdity of the situation: the manuscript has it further developed: 'dread of fate that could play such a vile trick on a man, awe at the remote consequences of an apparently insignificant and ridiculous event in his past which could by no means be suppressed'.

258 "*Avancez*": 'Forward!'

He was all to his affair: from the French 'Il était tout à son affaire', meaning 'He was totally concentrated on what he was about'.

259 *I must draw his fire*: the source narrative as rendered in *Household Words* goes finally:

> As soon as they were inside the inclosure, the two antagonists sought after each other cautiously, halting to listen at every step. They advanced slowly, with their cocked pistols in their hands, eye on the watch, and ear all attention. At the turn of an alley they perceived each other; by a rapid motion they threw themselves behind the trunks of a couple of trees; in this position they remained for a considerable time, when Dupont resolved to act. At first he gently waved the tail of his coat just outside the tree which protected him; he then protruded half the thickness of the fleshy part of his arm, drawing it back again instantly. It was lucky for him that he did so; for, immediately afterwards, a bullet sent a large piece of bark flying. Fournier had lost a shot.
>
> In the course of a few minutes, Dupont recommenced the same manoeuvre on the opposite side of the tree-trunk, and he embellished his original idea by showing the tip of his pistol-barrel, as if he in turn were watching for an opportunity to fire. Holding his hat in his right hand, he displayed it as far as the rim. In a twinkling, the hat was blown away; fortunately, there was no head inside it. Fournier, therefore, had wasted his second bullet. Dupont then sallied from his fortress, and

marched up to his adversary, who awaited him in the attitude of a brave man for whom there is no further hope. When Dupont was within a couple of paces of his enemy, he said: "I can kill you, if I like; it is my right and my privilege; but I cannot fire at a human creature in cold blood. I spare your life."

"As you please."

"I spare it to-day, you understand clearly; but I remain the master of my own property, of which I allow you the provisional enjoyment. But if ever you give me any trouble, if ever you try to pick a quarrel with me, I shall take the liberty of reminding you that I am the lawful owner of a couple of bullets specially destined to be lodged in your skull; and we will resume the affair exactly at the point where I think proper to leave it to-day."

So ended a duel which began in seventeen hundred and ninety-four, and only finished in eighteen hundred and thirteen.

259 *force of character*: in the manuscript, less deeply, 'fortitude'. Ironically it requires the counter-intuitive laying down of his arms in order for him to be safer.

260 *impossible does not exist*: from Napoleon's letter 9 July 1813, to General Jean Le Marois, the governor of Magdeburg, seeking ammunition and supplies: ' "That is impossible," you write to me. That is not French.'

en plein: 'in full'.

261 *thoughtlessly*: in the manuscript, 'instinctively'; but the sentences following ('The irresistible instinct of the average man . . . Instinct, of course, is irreflective') require a different and less conventional word at the head.

262 *à bout portant*: at point-blank range.

resuming: from French 'résumer', to 'sum up'.

263 *Grande Armée*: Napoleon's great imperial army formed in 1804 comprised 600,000 troops in 6 corps, including Austrian and Polish contingents.

sacrebleu! This is an absurd position: 'damn it', in a final turn of absurdity back upon Feraud.

265 *peignoir*: woman's light dressing gown.

266 *reversed*: not just the gaze but everything is finally turned round at this point.

267 *méchant*: 'nasty, unkind'.

268 *C'est incensé*: 'it is mad'.

Garonne: river in south-west France.

269 *brave homme*: 'courageous fellow'.

fasten himself on my deeper feelings: the final paragraph goes as follows in The Free Library of Philadelphia manuscript:

"My dear what else could I do? I ought to have blown his brains out—strictly speaking. I didn't. How can I let him starve? They've deprived him of his pension for 'breach of military discipline' when he broke bounds to fight his last duel with me. He's utterly incapable of doing anything in the word—except fight. Moreover he's doubled up with rheumatisms. I can't let him starve. And after all I am under infinite obligation—you know why. He put our married life on the only proper basis as it were. All the same it's funny how in one way or another this man has managed to fasten himself on my life."

The Oxford World's Classics Website

www.worldsclassics.co.uk

- Browse the full range of Oxford World's Classics online

- Sign up for our monthly e-alert to receive information on new titles

- Read extracts from the Introductions

- Listen to our editors and translators talk about the world's greatest literature with our Oxford World's Classics audio guides

- Join the conversation, follow us on Twitter at OWC_Oxford

- Teachers and lecturers can order inspection copies quickly and simply via our website

www.worldsclassics.co.uk

American Literature

British and Irish Literature

Children's Literature

Classics and Ancient Literature

Colonial Literature

Eastern Literature

European Literature

Gothic Literature

History

Medieval Literature

Oxford English Drama

Philosophy

Poetry

Politics

Religion

The Oxford Shakespeare

A complete list of Oxford World's Classics, including Authors in Context, Oxford English Drama, and the Oxford Shakespeare, is available in the UK from the Marketing Services Department, Oxford University Press, Great Clarendon Street, Oxford OX2 6DP, or visit the website at www.oup.com/uk/worldsclassics.

In the USA, visit www.oup.com/us/owc for a complete title list.

Oxford World's Classics are available from all good bookshops. In case of difficulty, customers in the UK should contact Oxford University Press Bookshop, 116 High Street, Oxford OX1 4BR.

A SELECTION OF   **OXFORD WORLD'S CLASSICS**

JOHN BUCHAN	**Greenmantle**
	Huntingtower
	The Thirty-Nine Steps
JOSEPH CONRAD	**Chance**
	Heart of Darkness and Other Tales
	Lord Jim
	Nostromo
	An Outcast of the Islands
	The Secret Agent
	Typhoon and Other Tales
	Under Western Eyes
ARTHUR CONAN DOYLE	**The Adventures of Sherlock Holmes**
	The Case-Book of Sherlock Holmes
	The Hound of the Baskervilles
	The Lost World
	The Memoirs of Sherlock Holmes
	Sherlock Holmes: Selected Stories
	A Study in Scarlet
FORD MADOX FORD	**The Good Soldier**
JOHN GALSWORTHY	**The Forsyte Saga**
JEROME K. JEROME	**Three Men in a Boat**
JAMES JOYCE	**A Portrait of the Artist as a Young Man**
	Dubliners
	Occasional, Critical, and Political Writing
	Ulysses
RUDYARD KIPLING	**Captains Courageous**
	The Complete Stalky & Co
	The Jungle Books
	Just So Stories
	Kim
	The Man Who Would Be King

A SELECTION OF   **OXFORD WORLD'S CLASSICS**

RUDYARD KIPLING	Plain Tales from the Hills
	War Stories and Poems
D. H. LAWRENCE	The Rainbow
	Sons and Lovers
	Women in Love
WYNDHAM LEWIS	Tarr
KATHERINE MANSFIELD	Selected Stories
ROBERT FALCON SCOTT	Journals
ROBERT TRESSELL	The Ragged Trousered Philanthropists
VIRGINIA WOOLF	Between the Acts
	Flush
	Jacob's Room
	Mrs Dalloway
	The Mark on the Wall and Other Short Fiction
	Night and Day
	Orlando: A Biography
	A Room of One's Own and Three Guineas
	To the Lighthouse
	The Voyage Out
	The Waves
	The Years
W. B. YEATS	The Major Works

	Late Victorian Gothic Tales
	Literature and Science in the
	Nineteenth Century
JANE AUSTEN	Emma
	Mansfield Park
	Persuasion
	Pride and Prejudice
	Selected Letters
	Sense and Sensibility
MRS BEETON	Book of Household Management
MARY ELIZABETH BRADDON	Lady Audley's Secret
ANNE BRONTË	The Tenant of Wildfell Hall
CHARLOTTE BRONTË	Jane Eyre
	Shirley
	Villette
EMILY BRONTË	Wuthering Heights
ROBERT BROWNING	The Major Works
JOHN CLARE	The Major Works
SAMUEL TAYLOR COLERIDGE	The Major Works
WILKIE COLLINS	The Moonstone
	No Name
	The Woman in White
CHARLES DARWIN	The Origin of Species
THOMAS DE QUINCEY	The Confessions of an English
	Opium-Eater
	On Murder
CHARLES DICKENS	The Adventures of Oliver Twist
	Barnaby Rudge
	Bleak House
	David Copperfield
	Great Expectations
	Nicholas Nickleby

A SELECTION OF   OXFORD WORLD'S CLASSICS

CHARLES DICKENS   The Old Curiosity Shop
                       Our Mutual Friend
                       The Pickwick Papers

GEORGE DU MAURIER   Trilby

MARIA EDGEWORTH   Castle Rackrent

GEORGE ELIOT   Daniel Deronda
                       The Lifted Veil and Brother Jacob
                       Middlemarch
                       The Mill on the Floss
                       Silas Marner

EDWARD FITZGERALD   The Rubáiyát of Omar Khayyám

ELIZABETH GASKELL   Cranford
                       The Life of Charlotte Brontë
                       Mary Barton
                       North and South
                       Wives and Daughters

GEORGE GISSING   New Grub Street
                       The Nether World
                       The Odd Women

EDMUND GOSSE   Father and Son

THOMAS HARDY   Far from the Madding Crowd
                       Jude the Obscure
                       The Mayor of Casterbridge
                       The Return of the Native
                       Tess of the d'Urbervilles
                       The Woodlanders

JAMES HOGG   The Private Memoirs and Confessions
                         of a Justified Sinner

JOHN KEATS   The Major Works
                       Selected Letters

CHARLES MATURIN   Melmoth the Wanderer

HENRY MAYHEW   London Labour and the London Poor

A SELECTION OF   **OXFORD WORLD'S CLASSICS**

WILLIAM MORRIS   News from Nowhere

JOHN RUSKIN   Praeterita
                        Selected Writings

WALTER SCOTT   Ivanhoe
                        Rob Roy
                        Waverley

MARY SHELLEY   Frankenstein
                        The Last Man

ROBERT LOUIS STEVENSON Strange Case of Dr Jekyll and Mr Hyde
                           and Other Tales
                        Treasure Island

BRAM STOKER   Dracula

W. M. THACKERAY   Vanity Fair

FRANCES TROLLOPE   Domestic Manners of the Americans

OSCAR WILDE   The Importance of Being Earnest
                           and Other Plays
                        The Major Works
                        The Picture of Dorian Gray

ELLEN WOOD   East Lynne

DOROTHY WORDSWORTH   The Grasmere and Alfoxden Journals

WILLIAM WORDSWORTH   The Major Works

WORDSWORTH and   Lyrical Ballads
COLERIDGE

A SELECTION OF   OXFORD WORLD'S CLASSICS

ANTON CHEKHOV   About Love and Other Stories
                     Early Stories
                     Five Plays
                     The Princess and Other Stories
                     The Russian Master and Other Stories
                     The Steppe and Other Stories
                     Twelve Plays
                     Ward Number Six and Other Stories

FYODOR DOSTOEVSKY   Crime and Punishment
                     Devils
                     A Gentle Creature and Other Stories
                     The Idiot
                     The Karamazov Brothers
                     Memoirs from the House of the Dead
                     Notes from the Underground and
                         The Gambler

NIKOLAI GOGOL   Dead Souls
                     Plays and Petersburg Tales

MIKHAIL LERMONTOV   A Hero of Our Time

ALEXANDER PUSHKIN   Boris Godunov
                     Eugene Onegin
                     The Queen of Spades and Other Stories

LEO TOLSTOY   Anna Karenina
                     The Kreutzer Sonata and Other Stories
                     The Raid and Other Stories
                     Resurrection
                     War and Peace

IVAN TURGENEV   Fathers and Sons
                     First Love and Other Stories
                     A Month in the Country

A SELECTION OF   **OXFORD WORLD'S CLASSICS**

HANS CHRISTIAN ANDERSEN	**Fairy Tales**
J. M. BARRIE	**Peter Pan in Kensington Gardens and Peter and Wendy**
L. FRANK BAUM	**The Wonderful Wizard of Oz**
FRANCES HODGSON BURNETT	**The Secret Garden**
LEWIS CARROLL	**Alice's Adventures in Wonderland and Through the Looking-Glass**
CARLO COLLODI	**The Adventures of Pinocchio**
KENNETH GRAHAME	**The Wind in the Willows**
ANTHONY HOPE	**The Prisoner of Zenda**
THOMAS HUGHES	**Tom Brown's Schooldays**
CHARLES PERRAULT	**The Complete Fairy Tales**
ANNA SEWELL	**Black Beauty**
ROBERT LOUIS STEVENSON	**Kidnapped** **Treasure Island**

ANTHONY TROLLOPE

The American Senator
An Autobiography
Barchester Towers
Can You Forgive Her?
Cousin Henry
Doctor Thorne
The Duke's Children
The Eustace Diamonds
Framley Parsonage
He Knew He Was Right
Lady Anna
The Last Chronicle of Barset
Orley Farm
Phineas Finn
Phineas Redux
The Prime Minister
Rachel Ray
The Small House at Allington
The Warden
The Way We Live Now

Travel Writing 1700–1830

Women's Writing 1778–1838

FRANCES BURNEY   Cecilia
                         Evelina

ROBERT BURNS   Selected Poems and Songs

JOHN CLELAND   Memoirs of a Woman of Pleasure

DANIEL DEFOE   A Journal of the Plague Year
                         Moll Flanders
                         Robinson Crusoe

HENRY FIELDING   Jonathan Wild
                         Joseph Andrews and Shamela
                         Tom Jones

WILLIAM GODWIN   Caleb Williams

OLIVER GOLDSMITH   The Vicar of Wakefield

SAMUEL JOHNSON   The History of Rasselas

ANN RADCLIFFE   The Italian
                         The Mysteries of Udolpho

SAMUEL RICHARDSON   Pamela

TOBIAS SMOLLETT   The Adventures of Roderick Random
                         The Expedition of Humphry Clinker

LAURENCE STERNE   The Life and Opinions of Tristram
                             Shandy, Gentleman
                         A Sentimental Journey

JONATHAN SWIFT   Gulliver's Travels
                         A Tale of a Tub and Other Works

HORACE WALPOLE   The Castle of Otranto

MARY WOLLSTONECRAFT   Mary and The Wrongs of Woman